THREE TIMES LOSER....

Akash Verma is a management graduate and currently works with a media company.

In his fourteen-year-old professional career, he has worked in the FMCG and entertainment sector. His work has taken him to many parts across the country and he finds this experience very relevant while giving shape to his stories. This is his first attempt at writing a full-fledged fiction novel.

Akash is currently based out of Gurgaon, India. You can catch him watching movies or reading anything under the sun when he is not working.

Also by the same author

It Happened that night

THREE TIMES LOSER....

LOVE NEVER DIES

Akash Verma

Srishti
PUBLISHERS & DISTRIBUTORS

Srishti Publishers & Distributors
N-16, C. R. Park
New Delhi 110 019
editorial@srishtipublishers.com

First published by
Srishti Publishers & Distributors in 2011

10 9 8 7 6 5 4

All characters in this book are fictitious, and any resemblance to real persons, living or dead, is coincidental.

Printed and bound in India

Love cannot save you from your own fate.

Jim Morrison

Musician, Songwriter and Poet

Acknowledgements

I would like to thank the following people, places and things for being an inspiration behind Three Times Loser. The list is random and does not have any specific order:

1. My blue BSA SLR cycle in school that ran over hundreds of kilometers.
2. St. Peter's College, Agra.
3. St. Patrick's College, Agra.
4. Agra : Kamlanagar, Paliwal Park, Bye Pass, Sikandra.
5. The Chinese Van that once existed opposite Anjana theatre: Should be in some local junkyard by now.
6. Our road trips from Agra to Delhi: Nirula's – yes; Chanakya-yes; Gaffar Market- yes; GB Road – no.
7. Agra Fort Railway Station.
8. Late Mr. PB Sinha: My Math teacher.
9. Lucknow University Campus.
10. Pub No. 55- yes it existed; and it still does in the memory of my friends.
11. Spicy Bite, Ritz, Ravindralaya, River Gomti, Ganna Sansthan: all of them exist; in Lucknow.
12. Red Alert – the Lucknow University rock band.
13. Bonnie Scott Whisky, MMB Whisky, MMB Gin – Brands you wouldn't have heard of; but we used to drink; in abundance.
14. All the Lucknow university hostels: They still seem like home.
15. Jalvayu Towers, Sector 21, Noida – where I rented an apartment for the first time.
16. My first office trip to Goa. Goa has always been wonderful since then.
17. Recording Studios – a lot of them, across companies and cities.
18. Fireball, 32nd Milestone, Gurgaon; ISBT, New Delhi.
19. Dehradun and Mussoorie: Places where I can settle down any day; if I am not burdened with the task of earning a living.

20. My friends: from my school in Agra, college in Lucknow and from the radio industry in Delhi.
21. Anoop Singh Bartwal and Jagdish Chandra Tiwari, our dear friends, who left us a tad earlier. I wish you guys were still there in this world.
22. Srishti Publishers and Jayant Da for their unflinching support and faith in my writing.
23. Dhanjit for the cover design and Siddharth Pabbi for helping me with the final edit.

The list is endless but I would rather stop here, to start the story. I hope it is good enough for you to read; and to remember.

PART 1: MEGHA

26th June, 2011: Gurgaon, India

The intercom shrieked through the pervading silence of the fourteenth floor's plush apartment at the Beverly Plaza, Gurgaon. Megha cursed once, before waking up to its fifth shrill beep and staggered sleepily towards the living room, to pick up the god damn invention of modern science.

'Who the hell can it be at this hour?' she muttered half asleep.

'Madam, courier!' the hoarse female voice of the lady guard at the main gate spoke, before she could even open her mouth.

'Send him in!' Mehga said coarsely and banged the receiver down.

The damage was done and her precious one hour afternoon siesta had gone for a toss. She entered the washroom and threw some cold water on her face; and waited for a few seconds before wiping it with a towel. She looked into the mirror at her thirty three year old face that was groggy with sleep. She came out and glanced at the watch in the living room; it was already three in the afternoon, just an hour was left for her six year old daughter Sneha to come back from her school. She entered the bedroom and lazed on the bed once again, desperately wanting to squeeze in the last few moments of tranquility before the courier guy bugged her. The door bell rang.

She took the brown envelope from the courier boy and signed on the receipt.

'*Bhaiyya,* can't you guys come in at a slightly more convenient time than this?' she said angrily. The courier guy who would be in his mid thirties returned a sheepish smile, as if deriving a perverse pleasure from screwing up her afternoon. She shook her head in disgust and shut the main door of her apartment.

'Another forty five minutes and Sneha would be here! I should get going with her lunch,' she mumbled while getting into the kitchen. She looked at the mini calendar stuck behind a magnet on the refrigerator. It was Friday; Sneha's "Maggi Day" and she wouldn't settle for anything lesser than that, as soon as she would enter the house. The thought of her daughter calmed her a bit and she smiled while putting in four large stacks of noodles into water and then placing the bowl inside the microwave. The dish was ready in five minutes and clutching the bowl with the oven glove in one hand and a glass of mango shake in another, she landed both of them adeptly on the dining table. She switched on the air conditioner in the living room and was taking the glove off when she glanced at the brown envelope on the table. It was addressed to her. She found the arrival of this unexpected envelope bearing her name a bit strange as she picked it up curiously, trying to size up what was inside. The envelope did not bear any mention of the sender. It was her name that was written with black ink, and the neat handwriting looked strangely familiar. Megha's eyes traversed along her name and address, trying to decode the mystery about this unexpected packet. There was something odd in the manner her name was written as she observed it closely. There were two dots inside the alphabet "a" to make it resemble a human face, the smiling face of a girl to be precise. It was him; had to be only him. He always wrote her name in that manner, in all of those countless notes, letters and greeting cards. Megha almost stopped breathing for a few seconds.

Dear Megha

I am sure that this letter from me after so many years would completely take you by surprise. It's been a long time, almost twenty three years! It seems like a century to me. I am aware that you are now settled, with a daughter. Sneha! What class does she go to?

I have very fond memories of the time that we spent together in Agra and they have always stayed with me. Agra, what a place it was and what a time we had along with Samir and Happy! It's hard to forget our days at school, cycling through the lanes of Paliwal Park, the picnic at Sikandra, the mindless fun at SK Gupta coaching classes and sitting idle and chatting for hours at the Chinese Van opposite Anjana theatre. I can go on and on about this but I would rather stop, as it seems like invading into your life after a hiatus; and forcing you to glance at the past long gone by.

I stay in this peaceful yet picturesque hill station called Mussoorie now. I teach music in this beautiful town. The reason of writing this letter to you is that I have something in my possession that is very precious and belongs to you as much as me. It has been with me for many years Megha but now I can't keep it with me anymore. I want you to come and take it from me before it's too late.

I will wait for you on 28th June at Dehradun airport. Mussoorie is about two hours away from the airport and I would recommend that you be in Dehradun by 4PM so that we can get into the town by the evening. Take care and see you Megha.

Yours

Alok
House Number 403
Off Mall Road
Near Government School
Mussoorie.

Megha looked up; as the tears that had settled around the curvature of her eyes like thin beads, ran like an over flown stream over her cheeks.

'Why have you come back into my life after so many years Alok? What's there between us that I should come all the way to see you? What is it that you have and want to return?' Her heart cried for answers as she succumbed on the dining chair and stared at the letter that lay in front of her. She dived back into time.

Akash Verma # 5

September 1988: Agra, India

Oye…Alok… Oye. Happy Singh's vocal cords hurt as he cried his name for the third time in the narrow Q block lane of Kamlanagar.

He shook his head in disgust as he mouthed some expletives to himself when the side door of Alok's ground floor HIG apartment creaked open; and the front tyre of his BSA SLR cycle showed its face like a celebrity.

Alok emerged from the door and raced on his cycle towards a waiting Happy.

'What's the matter Surd? Why are you creating such a ruckus?' Alok said, as he cycled ahead without even waiting for poor Happy.

Happy followed him on his Hero Racer bicycle, 'where were you last evening Alok? I came twice to your house to see you! If you had other plans, you should have told me,' he complained.

'I was at Samir's house, Surd! Picking up some notes,' Alok replied as he paddled his cycle briskly.

'Oh really! You were studying and you want me to believe this?' Happy cried from behind.

'Ok Surd ok, I went out for an evening show, but really it was completely unplanned,' Alok said.

'What happened?' Happy asked.

'I went to take notes from Samir but Mandakini seduced me en-route; and so I had to force Samir to come for the movie as well. You tell me Surd what could I do?' Alok said as if he were helpless.

'So you guys watched Dance Dance, the new Mithun movie and that too without me you bastards,' Happy screamed as if he would murder Alok then and there.

'I will watch it once again with you Surd, relax!' Alok said calmly. Happy shook his head in disbelief as he looked at the traitor.

They met Samir close to the Kamlanagar water tank waiting for them. He joined them as they cycled together. Samir looked visibly quiet.

'Are you planning to go for the play rehearsals today in the evening?'

Alok asked Samir who chose not to reply.

'Can you answer my question Samir?' he repeated his question again.

'You have unnecessarily pushed me into this Alok. I do not want to participate in theatre or for that matter any cultural activity. Why do you always manage to push me into something that I do not want to do?' he kept cycling without looking at him.

Alok smiled, 'Oh come on Samir, I never push you,' he tapped his shoulder.

'Bullshit Alok. There's nothing happening at the rehearsals; and till now that jerk Chacko hasn't assigned any roles to a few of us,' he complained.

'All he has been doing is asking us to go through the stupid Macbeth again and again,' Samir cried out again.

Chacko was the School Cultural Teacher.

'Relax man, it will happen soon. I am joining you for the rehearsals today,' Alok said.

'Fuck your rehearsals Alok; do you know how close the boards are? They are only six months away and what are we doing? Bloody acting in a play when all I need to do is study hard for the boards; achieve something, have a good career and do something for myself as well as my mother. I am a *pucca chutiya*,' Samir seemed to be completely pissed with himself.

Samir Dixit was the only son of a businessman father and a mother who taught in a local government school. The couple had held on to each other for fourteen odd years but then decided to seek a divorce due to irreconcilable differences; Samir was only ten year old then. The divorce had left an aftertaste of insecurity and bitterness within Samir and that usually came to display at times like these. The three boys cycled quietly till they reached Bypass Road.

'Did you meet uncle yesterday?' Alok asked. Samir nodded.

'What happened?'

'Nothing much, same old stuff. How are your studies going? What do you want to do after ISC? What tuitions are you taking? Why don't you study for IIT? Same old crap. Frankly speaking, we have nothing to talk about whenever we meet up,' Samir said.

He took a pause, 'I don't think he understands me at all. Does he even know that I have freaking no interest in engineering? So, after he asked me all those moronic questions, I just got up and came back. Why do people need to get married, man?' he looked at Alok disgustedly.

'I can give you one good reason. They get a license to fuck,' Happy, who had kept quiet for a while chuckled as he raced ahead of them.

'Shut up you surdy ass,' Alok cried out.

The trio crossed Vijaynagar at 8 AM.

'Do we get to see your girlfriend today?' Happy teased Alok.

'There is no *girl friend shirlfriend* Happy, are you crazy?' Alok retorted.

'Oh yeah Alok! As if we don't know that you miss a heartbeat every time you see her. It's written all over your face buddy,' Happy gestured.

'Listen man, Megha is cute, that's it. There are so many other girls in St. Marks whom I find cute,' Alok said maintaining his calm as his heart fluttered with the excitement of encountering her again.

'Ok, as you say. So, with your permission; I am going to have a go at her starting today. Don't you think, I have a fair chance now that I am clean shaven and cute?' Happy said and grazed his hand through his neatly cropped straight hair.

Alok looked at him in mock anger, 'Sardar, you are fucked.'

'Look at the bastard now; a mere mention of her name and *hero ki fati*,' Happy looked overjoyed with himself.

'But why don't you talk to her Alok? It's been over two months that you have been after her and all that you have done till now is bloody stealing odd glances whenever you see her. What makes you think that she even likes you?' Samir broke his silence.

'I know man, I can make out from the vibe that I get. And look who's talking here Samir? It seems as if you have been awarded with a PhD in dating girls?' Alok mocked as both Samir and Happy fell silent with the revelation.

'But seriously Alok, you need to do something real fast. Forget us, as we are friends; but what will Megha think about a boy, who doesn't have enough balls to do something for the girl he likes?' Samir said.

'Moreover, these cute chicks are gifted with a short term attention span and especially these St. Mark's chicks,' Happy added like an expert.

'Trust me guys, nothing will happen. Everything has a time and I do things my own way,' Alok said calmly.

'*Sala chutiya*,' Happy muttered.

Megha looked really cute sitting consciously on the ladies Hero cycle when Alok saw her in the Paliwal Park. Her fair skin glowed under the morning light and the pink 'n' white combination of the uniform that she wore made her look attractive to the core.

'She is so sexy man!' Happy remarked as they passed by her in the park.

Alok looked towards his left to steal a glance at Megha who rode on her cycle. Alok felt as if she smiled. Megha's tall frame made her look like a grownup, though she was still in the final year of the school and her face was a unique blend of beauty, sensuousness and maturity.

'How many more days will you fantasize about her before you actually say something? Don't you think it's high time to speak up?' Samir said as they parked their cycles in the stand at St. Thomas College, their Alma Meter.

Alok pretended as if he hadn't heard him, 'Let's go guys. It's assembly time.' They walked hurriedly towards the main school building which lay before them majestically.

Akash Verma # 9

SK Gupta, their Mathematics teacher entered the class of 12 B at 8.45 AM. He was in his late fifties and gifted with a healthy frame that turned even healthier at the paunch. He was dark in complexion and his lips were endowed with a red outline which housed a *paan* inside for all of twenty four hours of the day. Happy had once remarked, 'how would Gupta be making love with a *paan* in his mouth? Can you imagine the red betel juice getting into your partner's mouth while he would be smooching?' Happy had guffawed.

He offloaded a bundle of books and papers carelessly on the table and glanced at the class that looked at him with apprehension and fear. SK Gupta was going to announce the monthly arithmetic test results today, and a list of boys in that class of fifty six knew beforehand that they were surely flunking.

'The average of your section has come down miserably this month,' he roared without exchanging any pleasantries.

A few faces in the class changed colors as they moved from looking distraught to pathetic.

'There are twenty of you in this class who have flunked the tests. What are you guys up to? Are you going to flunk the damn ISC as well and spoil the results of our prestigious school? I am warning you, that I am certainly going to throw a few of you out of this school much before that,' he let out a serious warning

'I have thirty years of experience in teaching Maths and have yet to see something like this in my career,' he roared again at his hapless victims. The excitement in his voice fuelled the betel juice in his open mouth to fly out and land on the front row desks and some of it over his dark chin. He paused for a few seconds perhaps rehearsing his next move.

'How many times should I tell you that Math is not History or Geography that you can cram at the very last moment and pass? You need to understand it from here,' he pointed towards his head.

'If you don't understand it, ask for help and come to me for tuitions. I am always there for you to turn you into math experts,' he openly canvassed for bribery.

Everyone knew that taking tuitions from him would at least guarantee freedom from monthly tests and term examinations. Approximately thirty percent of the class took tuitions from him and were the privileged few who were insured against Gupta's wrath. The balance seventy percent just prayed to the almighty during his class to emerge safe from Gupta's vicious attacks.

'Vikas, can you go and fetch my cane from the teacher's room?' Gupta asked the thin bespectacled boy sitting in the front row. Vikas had started taking tuitions from Gupta the day he had set his foot in class twelve.

A cold chill ran through the entire class as they saw Vikas entering the class with the thin brown colored two and a half feet oiled monster. Alok looked at Happy sitting next to him with an 'I care a fuck for all this' look on his face. Samir sat quietly in the third row with a face that displayed traces of fear and meekness. Alok looked at the monster swinging wildly in Gupta's hand and knew that it was coming for him.

SK Gupta started calling out the roll numbers one after the other and granted them either relief or pain. Alok waited for his turn.

'Alok Mathur!' Twenty eight out of hundred,' Gupta literally screamed and looked at Alok who approached him with his right palm stretched out much before the monster could rest on it. Gupta was merciless with the right palm. The left one met with a similar treatment thereafter. Alok winced in pain as he returned to his seat. Happy was busy rubbing his hands vigorously on his grey polyester trousers while mouthing expletives. '*Behenchod, chutiya saala*, let my time come and I will shove this cane up his black ass. All that he wants from us is to spread our legs and go to him for tuitions. I am not relenting to his bloody wishes, let me see what he can do?' he squealed.

Gupta who looked breathless after inflicting forty blows on the boys, heard Happy's discontented voice. 'You Harpreet! Is there some problem over there? Why don't you get up from your seat?' he howled.

'You are gone Surd,' Alok couldn't stop himself.

'Alok! You also get up, and both of you just get the hell out of this class and snigger to your hearts content outside,' he said as he pointed his thick dark finger towards the class door. They came out of their row and started walking towards the door when Samir turned around to give them a huge grin. Unluckily for him, he could not stop himself from laughing.

'Who dared to laugh in my class?' Gupta yelled. Vikas his flunky looked in Samir's direction certifying who the culprit was.

'Samir! Was that you? You get out with them as well!' he shouted.

'Are we going to flunk in these boards?' Samir looked quizzically at Alok. The three of them sat on a raised cement plank about ten meters away from the edge, on the roof of St. Thomas Junior wing.

'What time does the play rehearsal start?' Alok ignored Samir's remark.

'What the bloody hell Alok! You are worried about the stupid god-damn annual day play rehearsal while I am shitting bricks about my future here,' Samir cribbed loudly.

'Why can't you stop wailing like an orphan for once Samir? Who is stopping you from studying and scoring brilliantly in boards? Are we?' Alok looked at Happy to buy some support.

Harpreet Singh alias Happy was a pure Sikh, born into a business family. He was the youngest among the three brothers who assisted his father in the two wheeler garage that they had at *Hari-Parwat*, one of the major cross-roads in Agra. He had long, overflowing hair till the year 1984 that brought about a major change in the psyche of the Sikh community in India. Following the attacks on the community due to the murder of the then lady Prime-Minister Indira Gandhi by her Sikh bodyguards, millions of them resorted to various ways to protect and guard their identities. Many of them moved to other safer places than Delhi and North India; while some of them tried to conceal their identity by resorting to shaving off their beard and long hair. Happy's entire family vanished to Amritsar for three months till the time the riots subsided in North India. And when they returned; all the three brothers and their father looked different. They had short hair and clean shaven fair faces. Happy's friends could not recognize him at first.

'I have a license to flirt around with all the girls now; and not just the Sikh chicks,' Happy would joke around.

'We have to teach a proper lesson to this Gupta,' he said looking at the girls playing basketball in the ground on the other side of the wall that belonged to St. Mark's. The junior wing roof was one privileged place from where one could get a balcony view of the girl's college. What better way to celebrate *punishment*?

⋺ *Three Times Loser....* # 12 # ⋲

"Hello baby?" Happy waved stupidly at the girls playing basketball about hundred meters away.

Luckily they did not notice them.

Alok pulled his hand away, 'Have you gone nuts Surd? If they complain about us we'll be expelled.'

'Megha is taking Math tuitions from SK Gupta,' Samir said plainly.

'What are you saying brother, how do you know?' Happy exclaimed.

"My dad lives in the same locality as Gupta and I saw her exiting his house the other day,' Samir replied.

'I think she is in the 3PM batch,' he added. They were silent for a while.

'What were you saying about flunking a while back?' Alok looked at Samir.

'I simply said that we are going to flunk Maths and some other subjects for sure, if we keep going the way we are now,' he said stressing on each spoken word.

'So, why don't we go for Math tuitions guys? If we do that, I think we can at least be better prepared for the boards, otherwise you are right, we may bloody flunk,' Alok said as if making a wise analysis.

'And where do you recommend that we go for these tuitions?' Happy posed innocently.

Alok spoke with mock seriousness, 'We have many options though, but going to SK Gupta isn't too bad either. I think going to him will certainly insure us against terminal examinations and hopefully the boards as well.'

Happy jumped off the plank and stood in front of them like an enraged Sumo wrestler, 'Bloody fucker do we look like *chutiyas* to you? Let's go to Gupta?' he made a convoluted face and mocked him, 'Just because your sweetheart is taking tuitions from him does not mean that we dump our brains in the well and follow you there like idiots. I am not taking tuitions from that spineless pimp.'

Samir kept silent, but his expressions were in agreement with Happy Singh.

The actor in Alok waited for a few minutes and then spoke, 'Okay fine, if you guys don't want to go, it's up to you. I have made up my mind and I am going for tuitions to him starting today. I do not want to flunk and neither do I want to take this daily humiliation dose from Gupta.'

'If that's your decision then you may go alone; but we won't go for sure. Do you think we will be a part of your romantic shit Alok?' Happy replied with equal force and looked at Samir who seemed to have softened his stand.

'Samir what's your decision? Do you want to pass the school exams and the boards or stand here with this Surd every day?' Alok asked.

Samir looked as if he was already weighing the options; standing out and flunking versus staying in and passing, 'Can't we look at some other teacher?' he said weakly.

'What's wrong with Gupta, Samir? And just because Megha goes there we won't? What's the logic here? This Surd has gone mad,' Alok said.

'Ok, as long as it helps,' he relented as he looked at the grumbling Surd.

—

It was two in the afternoon when Alok entered his two bedroom HIG flat. Sandhya, his mother was giving finishing touches to the *aloo – gobhi* in the kitchen.

'How was your day Alok?' she asked staring at the pressure cooker on the gas stove.

'Ok, just another ordinary day mom. It's getting tougher by the day,' Alok replied stressing on the word 'tougher'.

Sandhya gazed at him, 'why what happened? It is studies getting tougher by the day *nah*? I have been telling you for so long to get more serious about them, but all that interests you these days is that English *naach gana.*'

'I have been studying mom. What makes you think otherwise?' he said while flinging his school neck-tie on the bed.

Sandhya turned off the gas stove and came out of the kitchen. Alok was taking the shoes off in his room.

'Who do you think I am? I am your mother Alok who has turned you into this eighteen year old man. I am aware that how much you have been studying these days.'

Alok looked up in mock anger, 'Mom I have been studying, what's wrong with you? Every night; for so many god-damn hours?'

'Huh, do these friends of yours give you any time to study?' she said pointing at scores of posters of pop-stars staring at them from the walls in his room. A fair punk with earrings called Joy Michael and an obnoxious looking dwarf called Mince looked at them intently.

'Mom! Please. You always tend to mix up the issues. But frankly, some subjects are really flying some feet above my head. I am finding it tough to study on my own,' he said eyeing his innocent mother.

'So what do you want to do about it?' she asked.

'I was thinking if I could take up Maths tuitions. SK Gupta our Maths professor is an excellent teacher and studying with him would mean covering the ISC syllabus along with the quarterly exams syllabus,' he said while laying the trap.

'How much will it cost?' Sandhya asked tentatively.

'700 bucks,' Alok replied.

'It's too expensive Alok, how will we afford this?' Sandhya said exasperatedly.

'Ok, no issues Mom. If it's tough, fine. I will try to manage Maths myself. But these concepts I tell you are so complicated and difficult mom. Anyways,' he heaved an artificial sigh and got up to walk out of the room.

Sandhya followed her son, 'Is it really that tough Alok? Can't you take help from your friends?'

Alok sat down on one of the dining chair and cupped his face in between his palms.

'It is Mom, but do not bother much. How much can friends help? They themselves do not understand it and the intelligent ones would not want to share it with anyone,' he said and looked at his mother from the corner of his eyes.

'Then how will you manage it all by yourself Alok? Maths is such a critical subject! Can't the tuition cost a little less?' she asked hopefully.

'It's not your vegetable seller mom whom you are haggling with,' he said.

Sandhya seemed to be convinced, 'Hmm... I understand. When do you want to join?'

'I would not like to waste even a day,' Alok said with urgency as if he was aiming for a hundred percentile in the subject.

'Fine, I have been saving some money over last few months...*chalo* it will help you,' she said and kept her right hand on Alok's head.

Alok found both of them half perched on their bicycles as he took a left into the Professors Colony. Happy was ogling at one of the school girls being ferried home on a scooter by her father while Samir was staring at the road.

'I wasn't expecting both of you here,' he said slowing down his cycle.

'You take us for a ride all the time *aur hum saale gadhe ban jaate hain.* Let's go now, that bastards wallet is waiting for our hard earned cash,' Happy said as he pedaled the cycle. Samir and Alok followed him.

They parked their bicycles and walked in the two storey mud colored bungalow of SK Gupta. The afternoon batch was scheduled to start at 3PM and only a couple of students had arrived till now. They were busy comparing notes and talking with each other when the trio crossed them and rang the doorbell. A middle aged man wearing a white dhoti and a vest came out.

'Yes, what can I do for you?' he seemed to be in a hurry.

'Umm…we are from St. Thomas College, wanted to meet Mr. Gupta for tuitions,' Samir said while the other two looked around.

'Oh so you are from *sahib's* school! You guys wait here and I will be back in a moment,' he said and disappeared inside.

'So, what batch should we join? Is 4'O clock fine with everyone,' Happy asked and winked at Samir.

Alok jumped in, 'No way…4 is too late. I want to take the 3PM batch so that we have ample time for everything after that. Let's take the first batch guys.'

'Hmm…ample time for everything....bloody first rate liar,' Happy mocked.

Samir smiled at Alok who shook his head in frustration.

'Do we look like complete idiots to you? Two donkeys dressed like human beings?' Happy chided Alok again.

'Surdy, you are free to go back and fail. No need to take this class at all,' Alok said plainly.

Happy shook his head, 'That's going to happen any which way. SK Gupta or no SK Gupta, I am flunking.'

'Can I tell you something Surdy?' Alok said.

Happy looked at him intently like a moron.

'The problem with you is two; one that you don't have brains and despite knowing it, you do not want to take good advice,' Alok said and looked at Samir.

Happy tapped Alok's shoulder from behind, 'While you just have one, you have brains but you don't have balls. For 2 months you have been after Megha with zero result,' Happy said and flexed his eyebrows like a joker.

'That we will see Surd, let the time come,' Alok was about to say more but the man had reappeared.

'*Sahib* is calling you inside,' he said and pointed his finger towards a room.

'So, what brings you here, the three jewels of St. Thomas College?' Gupta said half reclining on his sofa.

He was wearing the same off white shirt with red betel specs splattered all over it and the trousers had been replaced by a white pajama.

'Sir, we are finding Math a bit tough to understand, and were wondering if you could help us with the tuitions?' Alok said.

'Oh! So you guys have finally realized that Maths is not History that can be crammed at the last moment, but needs to be understood from here,' he said pointing towards his head.

'Yes sir, we understand and need your able assistance to help us pass the board exams,' Alok said theatrically like a defeated warrior begging for help.

'Hmm…what batch do you guys want to join?' Gupta got up as he straightened his starched white pajama and fiddled with his tool.

'3 PM sir, and it would be great if we could start from today,' he said while handing over seven crisp hundred rupee notes to Gupta.

'He wasn't wearing underwear beneath his ridiculous pajamas. Did you notice? How could one go in front of the students like this?' Happy said as they left the room after depositing the fee.

'How do you notice all these strange things Happy?' Samir hushed as they came out of the house.

'Didn't you see his tool dangling left, right and centre in front of your eyes, bloody ridiculously cheap,' Happy gushed.

'If you have finished discussing Gupta's anatomy can we start with the math tuitions please?' Alok said and looked at the two of them.

They walked into a room that Gupta had converted into a small classroom where he conducted the tuitions. The classroom was bursting with wooden desks, each one of them facing two chairs. They were laid in three rows with little breathing space between each column, through which a human body could slither with difficulty. Gupta had already entered the class and was about to write something on the blackboard when the three of them entered and stood at the exit door facing his white pajama covered black ass.

Alok's eyes searched for Megha among the twenty five odd students of the batch. She sat in the third row towards extreme right.

'Why don't the three of you sit where ever you find a place?' Gupta saw them and gestured.

Some heads turned back, hers didn't. The place next to her was empty and Alok rushed to occupy that space. He hurriedly kept the books on the table and sat on the chair next to her. She gently looked towards her left and their eyes met. She looked completely surprised to find him there of all places; which she quickly hid under a demure smile.

Alok looked towards his left, Happy was sitting on the last row alone; and Samir had settled next to a curly haired guy with a distinct pencil moustache. Alok looked at him for a moment and then moved his gaze towards Gupta who had turned around after drawing a right angled triangle on the blackboard.

'So, does the class remember Pythagoras theorem that we did yesterday?' he said and looked at the students.

A few of them murmured with their confirmation while the rest sat silent.

'So, what is the theorem? Can anyone give me an answer?' Gupta asked. Vikas, the first ranker from St.Thomas and Gupta's pet raised his hand immediately. Gupta nodded in affirmation.

'Sir, the square of the hypotenuse in a right angled triangle is equal to the sum of the squares of the other two sides,' he said with a smile on his face and a possible hard on in his pants for the brilliance that he just displayed. Happy looked at Vikas as if he was chanting *Vedas* in Sanskrit.

'Correct, so if the other two sides of the right angle are eight and six centimeter each what will the hypotenuse or the third side be?' Gupta asked while playing with a half broken piece of chalk in his hand.

He looked at Happy, 'why don't you take a shot at it Harpreet?'

Harpreet, the poor Surd, had only taken three shots in his life; a shot with a cricket bat, a liquor shot and a daily shot with his tool in the bathroom.

Happy had no god damn clue about the answer and looked at Gupta as if he was some form of extra terrestrial life.

'Well...I don't know sir, I don't seem to remember,' he fumbled with words.

Gupta made a disgusted face, 'Why will you? What do you do in the class? That's why you fail every exam and come here begging for help. Sit down and pay attention from today, this 'don't know' will not work here.'

Happy sat down and looked at Alok angrily; holding him completely responsible for this wrongdoing against him.

'Megha, can you tell us the answer? We studied this yesterday,' Gupta asked.

Alok looked at her face which was changing colors in fraction of seconds. She stood up and her face had turned red by now.

'Umm...did you say eight and six centimeters sir?' she spoke with difficulty.

'Yes...and we don't have all the time here. It's so bloody easy!' Gupta spoke like an interrogation officer.

Alok felt like getting up and breaking Gupta's face as he scribbled on the blank paper of Megha's notebook kept on her table. Megha looked down sensing some movement near her body. Alok had written down and encircled the number ten on the notebook.

'Ten centimeter sir...ten,' she blurted out.

Gupta was silent for full thirty seconds, 'how did you arrive at ten? Can you explain?'

There was a pin drop silence in the class, only the eyes moved. Megha started sinking again.

'Sir A square plus B square is equal to C square, hence square of the first side measuring eight is sixty four and square of the second side measuring six centimeter is thirty six. The total comes to hundred centimeter and square root of hundred is ten centimeters,' Alok rallied through the answer in one breath.

Happy looked at Alok in awe as if he was the reincarnation of mathematics wizard Pythagoras himself.

'Are you Megha or do I have Idiot written on my face?' Gupta said coldly.

'Sorry sir...I thought the question was meant for the entire class,' Alok made a sorry face. Gupta gave him one long hard stare and then loosened up. Perhaps he was reminded of the crisp twenty one notes of hundred rupees that had greased his palm thirty minutes earlier.

'I am letting you off now as today is your first day here, but you need to pay hundred percent attention in the class or else you are going to have it from me. Life will be miserable my friend,' he said sternly and turned towards the blackboard.

Both Alok and Megha took their seats as Gupta got immersed in the world of Pythagoras with the class.

Thank You: Megha scribbled on her notebook on which he had written down the answer.

It's ok. What happened? You turned red like a carrot: Alok wrote as he turned the notepad towards him.

I get really nervous when someone asks me a question: Megha wrote.

Old thing. Happens all the time in school as well: Megha wrote.

I thought you were going to faint! : Alok wrote.

It wasn't that bad, you are stretching it now: Megha wrote.

Anyways, why did you answer on my behalf? : Megha wrote.

I would have broken some bones if you would have fainted and fallen on me: Alok wrote.

Alok smiled and Megha rolled her eyes.

So, are you Alok? : Megha wrote.

As if you didn't know Megha: Alok wrote.

Why would I? : Megha wrote.

All the girls from St. Marks know who I am: Alok wrote.

Oh my God! And why do they know you? What's the big deal about you? : Megha wrote.

I don't know. Ask them: Alok wrote.

Hmm…I've heard that you are very cool in all extra- curricular activities: Megha wrote.

Ask the ones who think that I am cool: Alok wrote.

So, are you participating in the St. Thomas Annual Day? : Megha wrote.

I am. Acting in a play and we are doing a song: Alok wrote.

So how do you know my name?: Megha wrote

JLT: Alok wrote.

Megha looked at Alok and smiled.

I am coming to your Annual Day with our big 'all girls' gang: Megha wrote

Great! I will see you there: Alok wrote.

Gupta had ended the lecture and students rushed out of the class. Samir and Happy were waiting at the exit door.

'Bastard! How did you know the answer? When did you study bloody Pythagoras?' Happy said loudly like a wife who had caught her husband cheating on her.

'I did not Surd! I just flicked through the book for half an hour before coming here…when will I study? Eighteen hours in a day, I am with you guys,' Alok put his arm around Happy's shoulders as they walked towards their parked cycles.

'Alok, swear on me. I hope you are not cheating us and studying through the night while I am following you in the drama rehearsals playing some insignificant role,' Samir howled from behind.

'What Samir? I swear man,' Alok gestured.

Megha had hopped on to her cycle and grinned at Alok as she left. He smiled back.

'What happened? Did you guys talk? And why were you giving answers on her behalf?' Happy shot him with a flurry of questions.

'Nothing happened my friend; nothing,' Alok said and pulled his cycle back. The same curly haired guy with pencil thin moustache was standing next to his cycle and passed him a dirty look. Alok stared back at him and then drove away.

'Who's that creep? And why was he giving me those looks?' Alok asked as they cycled.

'He is Ashutosh from St. Anthony's. He is the son of her father's best friend. He was sitting next to me in Gupta's class,' Samir replied.

'Is that his claim to fame in life?' Alok said.

'It's possessiveness my friend and he would have seen you guys talking in the class. He wants to be the first one to claim her,' Happy said.

'Is she a vacant railway birth or stray cattle?' Alok said.

They laughed all the way back.

Three Times Loser.... # 22

Alok entered his house late in the evening with a Playboy tucked under his loose cotton shirt. The foreign magazine was a part of the rich repository of Happy Singh that he very proudly flaunted amongst the entire starved ilk of St. Thomas. Happy rendered his services to an extremely select group, obviously in exchange of equally beneficial barters. Alok was a part of this exclusive clique; hence the prized issue with Brooke Shields exposing every part of her anatomy was touching his groin beneath the shirt.

Alok's father a middle aged, bespectacled man was on his first whisky when he saw his son entering the house.

'So, how did it go?' he said.

'What?' Alok said loosening up.

'Wasn't it your first day at tuition today? Do you think it's really going to help?' he said taking a sip.

'Papa, I can't do it on my own and need someone's help. I will flunk otherwise.'

'Why don't you sit down Alok? Do you think you will score a ninety percent plus if you take this tuition?' he taunted.

'I don't know about ninety; but I will definitely pass. Perhaps a first class.'

'What will you do with that, won't even guarantee admission in one of the better colleges in Delhi. How about engineering?'

'I don't want to do engineering Papa, we have discussed this earlier.'

'Then what do you wish to do Alok, if not engineering? What is plain graduation going to fetch you? Nothing beyond a clerical job! I am not a rich businessman who can take care of you all through your life,' he said getting all worked up.

'I am going to retire in the next five years and what's going to happen then? So, if you do not want to score marks and don't want to become an engineer, then why are we paying so much for your tuitions? Sandhya why don't you come here and listen to your son's words of wisdom,' he looked towards the kitchen and shouted.

'I don't know that Papa, but during three years of graduation, I will decide what to do next,' he said with his arms folded and leaning against the wall.

Meanwhile Sandhya had entered the drawing room and had parked herself on the sofa. She had her hands soiled after kneading the dough;

hence she tried to keep a safe distance between both.

'Alok, you have to tell us today what's in your mind? Do you know how much he has pestered me over that tuition money?' she said looking at his father.

'And you sit down first,' she told Alok and pointed at the chair.

'I am fine mother, I have a faint stomachache,' he replied. The thought of exposing Brook Shields during that discussion worried him.

'Well, I do not want to be an engineer but I do want to be a graduate and this tuition can help me become both,' he added, swiftly wanting to shift the focus away from his posture.

'So what do you want to do Alok? Sing like those foreigners pasted all over in your room? I am telling you Sandhya, we have been too lenient with this boy,' his father was ending his second peg of whisky by now.

'It's not me but it's been you Prakash! You have hardly spent any time towards his upbringing. How much attention can I pay to a growing boy amidst of all this domestic work? Have you even tried to bother about his studies ever; what's he doing, who are his friends etc. etc.?'

'But I have always been so busy Sandhya, what could I have possibly done? You are there in the house for all twenty four hours in a day, couldn't you have paid attention?' Prakash argued feebly.

Mom changed her stance, 'just look at your neighbor Mr. Chawla? He also works as hard as you do but takes so much of interest in Amit's studies, and its not surprising at all that the boy gets ninety two percent in tenth and then in twelfth pre-boards he has scored a whopping ninety four percent.'

The discussion seemed to have moved away from Alok and this turf actually didn't need his participation.

He looked sideways towards the nearest exit and ambled towards it, 'I need to go and visit the washroom urgently. I will be back in a while,' he said leaving behind his parents embroiled in the freshly surfaced discord.

The trio entered Gupta's tuition class at five minutes to three. Megha had not arrived yet and Happy was insisting Alok to sit with him.

'Happy, let Samir sit with you today as he feels left out,' he tried to cajole a visibly upset Surd.

'Samir, my ass! You have forgotten your friends Alok and the only thing that interests you these days is that chick Megha,' Happy tried the age old melodramatic filmy route.

'Ok, calm down Surd I will sit next to you guys today,' Alok said pointing towards a couple of empty chairs.

Happy having calmed down settled on the chair with Alok by his side. Megha entered the class with SK Gupta and looked around for an empty chair. Ashu glanced at her hoping that she would oblige him by sitting by his side; but by then she had spotted Alok and raced forward to sit next to him. Ashu winced on his seat while Happy's eyes played ping-pong as they jumped on the faces of Megha and Alok.

Gupta started the discourse.

'So, let us revise the Pythagoras Theorem once more before we move to Calculus, another great topic,' Gupta said as he made a right angled triangle on the board.

'So, if the hypotenuse is ten centimeters and one of the sides is six centimeters what is the size of the third side? Guys this is the same principle as yesterday; just twisted differently. Let me see that how many amongst you have actually grasped it?' he said and looked fleetingly towards the twenty five odd students.

A few of them had had confident smiles playing on their lips with a 'come hither' expression while the others squirmed. Happy was desperately trying to avoid an eye-contact with Gupta.

'Ok Harpreet; you tell us the answer. I am sure you would have revised yesterday's notes,' Gupta seemed to have found his guinea pig.

Happy Singh's revision since yesterday had been two issues of a Playboy and Penthouse along with thirty minutes of non-stop triple X fun on his VCR that went by the name of 'Sexy Kitten'. Poor Pythagoras unfortunately featured nowhere.

Happy got up sheepishly looking at Gupta and could only mutter, 'Sir...Umm...Umm.'

'Do you know the answer or not?' Gupta said.

Happy looked at Alok who was desperately trying to turn into a ventriloquist and through the movement of his lips decoded the number eight for him which was the correct answer. Unfortunately Happy could not figure it out at all.

'Like a fool you are looking here and there and thinking that the answer will drop down from the ceiling? Will Pythagoras come down from the heavens and give you the answer? I don't know how idiots like you have reached twelfth standard? How will you guys pass?' Gupta roared and walked towards the board.

He turned back after taking a couple of steps, 'Bloody duffers! Sometimes I feel that it is I who is an idiot by admitting guys like you in my quality tuition classes, bloody spoiling my name and reputation. Now sit down and don't keep standing like a buffoon. Ok, you stand up, what's your name? Oh yes, Megha you tell us the answer.'

The sudden challenge stunned Megha. Alok who looked at her face from the corner of his eye could see a disaster happening again. Face turning red, a choked throat and a body gripped with fear.

'So, what's the answer madam? Two sides ten and six centimeters each so what's the third?' Gupta spoke chewing the words.

Megha's brain was processing fast and had decoded the answer, but the paralyzed body fought hard not to give it away. It was at that moment when Alok gripped her hand under the table. Like a flush of oxygen entering her sinking body, like a nicotine recharge; Megha started coming back.

'Eight, eight sir,' Megha could hear herself speaking. The face came back to its original pinkish color and the tremble in her body recouped.

She looked at Alok who quickly freed her from his grip and returned to his earlier posture.

'Good answer Megha! Why can't duffers like you learn, if she can?' Gupta said as he looked at Happy.

Happy, who sat next to Alok was a witness to their first sexual encounter and that interested him more than Gupta's snide ones. He looked at them agape and Gupta's comment fell on his deaf ears.

How dare you hold my hand? : She wrote.

Megha, you were almost gone: He wrote.

Fuck it! How could you do that in front of everyone? : She wrote.

No one saw it I swear. I thought some comfort will help: He wrote.

Fuck your comfort. What if Gupta had seen? : She wrote.

That isn't fair Megha. I helped you and you are abusing me rather than saying thank you: He wrote.

Don't give me the Bollywood line the hero speaks, after sleeping with a rain drenched heroine? : She wrote.

What line? : He wrote.

I did it only for your benefit otherwise the cold would have been fatal: She wrote.

Ha Ha: He wrote.

But really, it did help you. You got your confidence back. Didn't you? : He wrote.

I would have slapped you if it hadn't Alok: She wrote.

Why? : He wrote.

I don't even know you well. How can you hold my hand? : She wrote.

He did not reply for some time and looked engrossed in the lecture.

But anyways, thank you: She wrote.

I won't be around everytime; you get one of those heart attacks: He wrote.

She smiled and they kept silent for a few minutes.

Why is Gupta so rude? : She wrote.

That's because we are the only people he can be rude with: He wrote.

Why? : She wrote.

He is a henpecked husband, atleast that's what everyone says and he is so scared of the school princi: He wrote.

But what does he achieve by pulling us down? That's not learning I would say, that's plain ridicule: She wrote.

Ridicule is the tribute paid to the genius by the mediocre: He wrote.

Wow, that's a great line. Who said that? : She wrote.

Me: He wrote.

Liar: She wrote.

Oscar Wilde. Now don't ask me who he was? : He wrote.

She looked at him with mock anger as Alok chuckled with his head lowered down on the desk. As soon as the class ended and Megha had left, Happy fired at him with words that seemed like bullets, 'Samir this guy held her hand in the fucking class!' he said pointing at Alok as if he had murdered someone in broad daylight.

Alok replied while picking up his bag, 'Nothing big happened here Samir, I was just comforting the poor girl. She was completely psyched out.'

'Bastard! This friend of yours was also psyched out when that mother fucker asked me the same question. Why the hell didn't you hold my hand then?' Happy said rolling his pupils around in the additionally dilated eyes.

'Once a Surd will always be a Surd; lets go Samir we are getting late for the rehearsals,' Alok said pulling Samir along.

'I am not leaving you Alok until I know the truth. How the fuck did you reach to holding hands with her? What's happening behind our backs?' Happy said as he desperately tried to catch up with them.

'We are getting late for the rehearsals Happy, and there is no corny story hidden underneath. And after that we are meeting at the Chinese Van around 6.30. Will you come?' he asked a confused looking Happy as he got onto his BSA cycle.

'If need be, Happy Singh will rise from his grave to unearth this secret, bastard.'

The dramatics and song practice happened on the semi-circular stage located at the end of the football field in St. Thomas School. On the school Annual Day the stage was adorned with colorful curtains on the side and the top; along with paper confetti that was stuck on the stage walls and thrown across the floor to make it look like a rather tacky imitation of the Proscenium Theatre. But, not today when Alok and Samir raced their bicycles through the barren football ground and parked it near the stage, the walls were desolate. They could see some students from senior wing who were gathered around a dark skinned creature with thick moustaches and curly hair as they listened to him with rapt attention. The creature was their English and dramatics teacher; John Chacko.

Chacko was a Kerala born Malyalee in his early forties. A man of moderate nature and wisdom, he would pass off as an obscure entity in a boy's school if it was not the accent in which he spoke the Victorian language.

'So, how will you *bayz* get through *yeem bee yay* and *yii yii t* when you can't even remember these simple lines from Macbeth?' Chacko said.

'MBA and IIT,' Alok said softly in Samir's ears as they converged close to the group from behind.

'So *fiinally* the lead *aktor* is yere! *Thaank Gawd*! *Vere* have you been?

Zimbly disappeared?' he said.

'Sir, actually my bike got punctured yesterday after the tuitions, so couldn't make it,' Alok said scratching his head.

'Is *thaat* a good enough *excuze*? *Yevery* where there are so many *otos*, you could have taken one' he said.

'Sorry sir, I will try to be punctual from today. I will take an auto if a similar situation arises,' Alok said smiling.

'You *kollage bayz* find this *vary* funny? I am also a *bissi* man but I *simbly* take out time for plays. Tomorrow when you *bayz* will get *bissi* in *yearning meney*, you will not get *anii* time for *aall* this. Now *jumb* off the stage and let's start the *plaay* practice,' he said and signaled them to move away.

Both Alok and Samir turned back and walked away laughing out loudly.

Is this a dagger which I see before me, the handle towards my hand?
Come, let me clutch thee! I have thee not, and yet I see thee still
Art thou not, fatal vision, sensible

Alok delivered this soliloquy like a seasoned actor as Samir looked intently at his friend enacting the role of King Macbeth, The Thane of Cawdor, who is stuck in between his desire to become the King of Scotland and the feeling of guilt enveloping him for committing the murder.

'*Vaary* good ! Keep looking out of thaat *yimaginary vindow* as you say those lines,' Chacko said. Alok nodded and the play continued.

'*Naw, naat at aal* ! You are looking too young to be King *Dunkan Saamir*,' Chacko said and came up on the stage. Samir was playing the role of King Duncan the old king of Scotland who was murdered by his faithful lieutenant Macbeth.

'Sir, I think he will be fine with make-up,' Alok butted in.

'No Alok , the *awdience* will *zimbly* laugh at us, *Dunkan* did not look like a *yang kollage* kid. He was a *maature yold maan*,' Chacko said focusing his gaze on Samir.

Samir was perplexed and did not know whether to open his mouth or keep silent. Like always he went for the second option.

'But all of us will look like college students sir, I am sure an artificial beard will balance the look,' Alok made an attempt.

'It's not about a *zimble* beard, Alok! It's about the *bawdy*, the *lookk*, *Saamir* does not fit the role. Why don't you take up the role of the soldier guarding *Dunkan Saamir*? I think that should be fine. This *baay* Suresh looks good for the king's role, let him do that. Come on *bayz* let's start, I have to go to the *chaarch*,' Chacko said pronouncing his verdict and breaking poor Samir's heart in return.

Samir dragged his feet towards the wing and passed on a disgusted look to Alok on his way out. Alok sighed and could merely shake his head. The rehearsal ended after about an hour.

'Ok *bayz*, I will see you tomorrow. You can have your *pope song* practice now,' Chacko said and walked out after smiling at the boys.

'What did the Malyalee do after landing in USA?' Alok asked Samir who waited in the wings with a frowning face. Samir looked in no mood to participate.

'He changed his name from Karunakaran to Kevin Curren,' Alok said with a serious face hoping that the joke would evoke a laugh.

After having failed he paused momentarily before wrapping his arm around Samir's shoulder. Samir did not say anything and looked away. He spoke after a minute, 'why don't you get done with your song practice? I am waiting for you here, as always.'

The chosen group for the song had assembled on one side of the stage where Mr. Wilson had placed his synthesizer. He was also from Kerala but did not boast of a rock-star accent like Chacko. Slender looking and soft spoken; Wilson was the school music teacher and manager of the school choir. Alok walked slowly towards the group and took his position in the centre of the front row as the key vocalist. Samir waited in the wings.

No dark sarcasm in the classroom
Teachers leave them kids alone
Hey! Teachers leave them kids alone
All in all it's just another brick in the wall

Soon the group that had some overlap of students from the just rehearsed Shakespearean tragedy was singing the chorus of the Pink Floyd cult anthem for students across the globe 'Another Brick in the Wall'. St. Thomas had recently graduated to pop music a few months back. After having moved away from '*Lord God You Are My Glory*' to '*Another brick in the wall*' was quite a transition for the one hundred and fifty year old missionary school. The reason for this switch was primarily the arrival of Mr. Wilson, who had done a short stint with some school in *Dubaih(Dubai)* where he stayed with his *Andy(Aunty)* who sang *pope* songs in one of the five star hotels. So, when Mr. Wilson came to St. Thomas from the *Gelf (Gulf)* he carried along with himself a baggage of modern pop songs which the students loved, hearing and singing, as they were doing today.

After three quick rehearsals Mr. Wilson asked the group to pack up for the day. Samir was waiting for Alok near the bicycles and moved ahead before Alok could speak. Alok raced from behind to catch up with him.

'Hey, what's wrong, *zimbly* rushing ahead?' he joked.

Samir maintained silence for a few minutes and took a right into the Paliwal Park instead of taking a left that took them to the Anjana Theatre.

'Aren't we going to the Chinese Van Samir? Happy said that he would be waiting,' he shouted at Samir who had raced ahead.

Samir did not respond and kept cycling. Alok had to pedal briskly to catch up with him.

'Hey, where do you think are you going Samir?' an irritated Alok said holding him by the hand. Samir pulled his hand away unwillingly.

'Nowhere Alok; I am going home. What am I doing the whole day except following you and Happy and wasting my time? What if I fail? I am not as rich as Happy and not talented like you. Let me for once think about myself Alok, let me think once about my future rather than just whiling away my time with you guys.'

'Hey, listen Samir, listen,' Alok turned sideways and forced Samir to apply brakes.

'Why are you so cheesed off? Is this to do with that role reversal?' he asked looking into Samir's eyes.

'Yes, partly. Right from the start I was not convinced of spending my time acting in that stupid play, and now to top it, I am a fucking guard who stands with his weapons looking at the bloody king sleep. My character does not have one single line to speak. So, everyday, that Chacko wants me to come for the rehearsal and stand for two hours like a jerk without speaking anything,' tears had welled up in Samir's eyes.

'But someone's got to play that part man,' Alok said.

'Yeah, you can say that Alok because you are playing the lead.'

'So, what's your point Samir? You don't like being in the play or you don't like doing that role?'

'That role,' Samir said.

'So why didn't you say so to Chacko?' Alok said

'What could I have said? He clearly said what he wanted me to do.'

'Why couldn't you tell him that you could do Banquo's role or his son's part if you looked young enough for Duncan's part?' Alok said.

'Mmm…I don't know he could have said that himself if he wanted it.'

'And how is he supposed to know about your interest in those roles Samir?'

Samir stood silent on that narrow road that meandered through the Paliwal Park that had a small artificial lake on one side while an uneven and not very well kept garden spread over a couple of hectares on the other. The lake also offered a ride in the self pedal boats and one lonely couple was about to end their joyride and steer the boat towards the bank. An odd car and two wheelers passed them at regular intervals, as they stood there staring at each other that evening which had started clawing its feet into the night.

'I don't know,' Samir said.

'Only if you could open your mouth Samir, when it's really required, a lot of things may change,' Alok said.

'Like what?' Samir asked.

'Like you would have got a better role and we would not be fighting here but digging into hot *kebabs* at the Van,' Alok said.

'So, are you coming or do you want to cry more about your role, on your flunking exams in future and about your dad?' Alok asked.

'No need to drag my family in this Alok,' Samir said; suddenly looking agitated.

'Look at you Samir and see how that mouth opened? Do that more often and see how it works for you.'

'Now are you coming or both of us ditch that Surd? But let's not forget that he will screw us for this,' Alok said.

'No, let's go to the Van,' Samir said.

'I felt so much like a loser Alok, when Chacko just swapped roles,' Samir said on their way to the Van.

'You are never a loser until you quit trying. You for god's sake; you have not even started trying, Samir,' Alok said.

'Hmm...,' Samir replied.

'And a winner never stops trying,' Alok said.

'That sounds like a good line. Who said that,' Samir offered a weak smile

'It's who else but me Samir!' Alok replied with a straight face.

'Cheers..,' Happy said holding a Rosy Pelican beer bottle in his hand.

The three boys were seated on half damaged cane stools placed behind the Chinese Van. The Chinese van; as it was called by the city's youth, served everything from Bread Omelets to Chicken Sweet Corn Soup; from Vegetable Pakoras to Chicken Manchurian. The van was completely immobile sitting quietly on the pavement opposite Anjana Theatre, sinking its deflated tyres in the ground, displaying its illegal love for that land.

Alok passed the bottle to Samir after taking a sip.

'No...I am not having this!' he said moving his sight away from the bottle.

'What's there in the beer man? We are not asking you to do brown sugar,' Happy laughed.

'Have a sip Samir, there's nothing in it. Just try it man! What did I tell you on the way...a winner never stops trying,' Alok said as he winked at Happy.

'*Oye* take it, take it Samir, we will drop you home if you get drunk. Drink beer to screw fear,' Happy guffawed.

'Huh... scoundrels,' Samir said and while taking a sip he made a face and twisted his mouth.

'Bastards, seriously I have no idea that why do I hang out with friends like you!' Samir said shaking his head in disbelief.

'But I am very surprised about one thing' Happy looked at them mysteriously.

'What?' Samir asked.

'What could a girl like Megha like in a bastard like him,' Happy said pointing towards Alok and jumping with excitement on the cane stool.

Akash Verma # 33

The afternoon sun was burning the football field of St. Thomas school with its strong gaze. The lunch break was in progress and few students of class 12 B had huddled together to form a small semi-circle; in a corner under the shade that was absolved of the scorching sun. Happy Singh was at the centre of this circle.

'So, who all are in for a 'fucking' trip to Delhi this Friday?' he said stressing on the F word.

A curly haired and fair looking Rajan along with his fat friend called Sunny nodded in affirmation. They were the elite members of the secret porn society that Happy ran.

Happy turned towards Alok who stood in one corner eyeing the eagles circling the football ground, and ready to pounce on the open tiffin boxes of the junior section kids running around the ground in the blistering heat.

'Are you coming along Alok?' Happy said trying to size up his friend's intentions.

'Dad won't allow, Surd. He looks damn pissed with me over tuitions,' Alok said wryly.

'What about the leather jacket that you wanted to buy for the Annual Day? You can only get that kind of imported stuff from Gaffar Market,' Happy dangled the bait.

'True, but can't help it. Dad won't allow. You guys buy it for me, I will try and arrange for the dough,' he said making a helpless face.

'Will you let me go on a date with Megha if you can't make it yourself smart ass?' Happy asked rolling his eyes.

'Surd, stop being stupid, trust me you don't have to try hard, it comes naturally to you.'

'What happened? *Fati mere lal,'* Happy said and rapped Alok on his shoulder.

'If you want that jacket, buy it for yourself in Delhi, we are not doing it for you,' Happy said raising both his hands in defiance.

'Shut up Happy, but how will I go? Gotta think of a plan.'

'Do whatever; but be there to park your ass in my car sharp at 10 AM on Saturday.'

'What do you want to do in Delhi?' Alok said

'Beer on the highway, shopping at Gaffar, movie in Chanakya, dinner at Nirula's and a fuck at GB road,' Happy spoke like a commander while Rajan and Sunny stared at him like lost soldiers.

'Happy what's wrong with you? I am not doing this GB road thing. GB road is a brothel man, I have heard about that. And from the confidence you showcase, it seems that you have already visited this place earlier,' Alok looked at Happy in disbelief.

'He went there along with his Delhi cousin, that Vinni,' Rajan said.

'What an experience man! I didn't tell you and Samir because I knew you guys would get scandalized. You guys are still not that experienced, you know,' Happy mocked.

'Fuck you and your experience. I am not going for it.'

'Ok, ok, I won't push you into anything. Just come and experience the Delhi fun, dip your dick in GB road only if you want to,' Happy laughed away.

'When do we get back?' Sunny asked.

'Sunday early morning,' Happy said

'By the way who is Alok's chick? Don't have a clue about her,' Rajan said.

Before Alok could open his mouth; Happy snapped back, 'None of your concern, moron, just pack your ass for Delhi.'

The school bell rang signaling end of the afternoon break. The band of boys walked back to their class as the afternoon sunlight started to recede in the opposite direction.

Alok entered the class at 3PM sharp and saw Megha sitting alone.

'Hi,' he said.

'Hi,' she replied smiling at him.

'Where's your bodyguard today?' he said while taking out his books from the bag.

She rolled her eyes, 'Who? Oh Ashu? Please don't ask, he takes this friendship thing between our families very seriously and tries to be overprotective towards me because of that,' she said.

'Overprotective? My foot! Anybody who talks to you seems like a villain to him. I think he is besotted by you,' Alok said.

'What rubbish! I don't think so. I have zero feelings for him. He's a nice friend to have around and nothing else. He is unwell today I guess,' she said.

'Thank God,' Alok said.

'For what?' she said.

Alok shook his head and grinned as Gupta started with the Math class again.

I won't be coming in this Saturday: he scribbled in her notebook as the class was halfway.

Why? What happened to you: she turned the notebook towards her and wrote.

Off to Delhi with friends: He wrote.

What for? : She wrote.

Buy some stuff and have some fun with friends: He wrote.

What fun? : She wrote and looked at him quizzically.

Movie at Chanakya and thereon to Nirula's: He wrote. He completely skipped GB road though.

You are lucky. Ok, have fun in Delhi: She wrote.

I hope you are coming for our annual day: He wrote.

No I think I will go to Delhi. There seems to be more fun in Delhi than Agra: She wrote.

He smiled at her. The class ended.

Happy Singh's white Maruti zipped away from the Q block in Kamlanagar carrying the four boys at ten in the morning on Saturday.

Happy was whistling as he drove while Sunny was trying to fit in some incoherent lyrics in his complete out of sync melody. Rajan was chewing a gum on the backseat while Alok stared at the multi-storied buildings and single storied houses that flocked the bypass road.

'So, what story did you give to uncle, *oye* Alok?' Happy said looking at him.

'I thought about a lot of them but by the end nothing seemed to be working out,' Alok said looking out of the window.

'So, then what did you finally say?' Happy asked looking ahead.

'I told him that your uncle died yesterday because of a massive heart attack in Delhi and you have to represent the family at his *Uthavani* as your father is away to Ludhiana. Being a close friend I can't leave you alone in this sad moment, hence to lend you emotional support I will have to accompany you to Delhi, along with these two jerks parked on the seat behind. Dad couldn't say no,' Alok said and looked at Happy who looked visibly impressed.

'*Oye* Surd look ahead, the road is not here in the car, it's out there,' Alok said pointing towards the road.

Happy shook his head and looked back at Sunny and Rajan as he chuckled, 'We are all bastards.'

Happy stopped the car at an English wine shop after they had crossed Sikandra, Emperor Akbar's tomb.

'Why are we stopping?' Rajan asked drowsily.

'Why does an airplane stop at the airport?' Happy asked turning his head towards Rajan.

Before Rajan could figure out the answer; Happy answered, 'To refuel,' and jumped out of the car.

'Here you go friends,' Happy said while dangling two large polythene bags that housed four bottles each of chilled Kingfisher beer. Sunny grabbed the bags and tucked them in the middle of the back seat.

'Surd, don't tell me that you will drink while driving?' Alok chipped.

'No, I will drive while drinking. Drink beer and fuck fear,' Happy said and chuckled. Rajan and Sunny joined the merriment as Happy raced the car on the highway.

'One hundred and forty nine more to go,' Alok said looking at the milestone.

'I am feeling hungry guys,' Sunny said taking a sip from the beer bottle and handing it to Happy.

'Let's finish the beers first, and then talk about food. There are still three more to go,' Happy said taking a huge swig.

'Surd, don't fucking get drunk on the highway. We will all die,' Alok said dryly.

'Don't worry brother. I am just fine. We will have food near Palwal at that famous *Bittu ka Dhaba.* He makes awesome *kadhai paneer* and *butter chicken.* I tell you guys its better than a lay,' Happy said.

'I really want to have some good food after this beer,' Sunny said with a slur, already fantasizing about the *kadhai paneer and chicken.*

'Surd, don't you think you have been hiding too many things from Samir and me? Alok said staring at the highway.

Happy understood, '*Oye* nothing *yaar*, I knew you guys would find all this a bit too much that's why. I want to enjoy life up to the hilt man. Who knows what will happen tomorrow?'

'What will happen tomorrow? From two beers everyday you will graduate to four, Surd,' Alok said.

'Do you know how uncertain is tomorrow, Alok? I have seen this fear and uncertainty about tomorrow from close quarters. Do you remember 1984?'

'*Oye,* my entire family kept hopping from one relative's house to the other for three months in Amritsar. I have seen those times. This bloody fear that had crippled not just my family but our entire community, I just can't forget it. I want to live for today and not worry about tomorrow Alok. Who has seen tomorrow anyways?' he said taking another sip.

'Let's eat Happy, these guys seem to have passed out,' Alok said looking at a half asleep Sunny and Rajan on the back seat.

'I understand Happy but I think you need to slow down, you seem to be in a real hurry,' Alok said.

The somber expressions on his face quickly changed, 'I don't belong to your ilk man, one who believes in friendships, love, dating and all that. I am more a wham bam, thank you mam kind of a guy. Lives life king-size,' he chuckled.

'Fuck you, Surd and that isn't right. Fun, trivial lies, trips to Delhi, dating girls etc. is all right but paid sex and all of that at our age is criminal. These two guys in the car told me all about your visits to that joint with that demented cousin of yours. You can't hide behind some life philosophy of yours and forget about your career and life.'

'Ok man ok, no more lectures! No more fucking around; after today,' Happy said.

'You don't seem to get it Happy and I am not going to this whorehouse with you guys,' he said as he pointed towards a blue tin board on the highway.

Happy nodded as he read it aloud, 'Speed thrills but kills.'

Gaffar Market the imported hub of the city had spread its tentacles, in the heart of West Delhi, in Karolbagh. From electronic goods to apparels and from porn magazines to food joints, jostled for space in this unplanned market predominantly run by refugees from West Punjab, still trying to find their feet in the bustling capital. The smuggled goods market flourished with élan and was a cherished jaunt of young and the old who nurtured a secret desire of aping the distant western world, both in thought and deed.

The quartet began their adventure in the overpopulated and crowded bylanes of Gaffar Market around 3PM. Shops stuffed with imported goods were screaming for attention, their owners busy handling hordes of customers and currency. Four of them walked around swiftly scanning shops, looking for what each one of them wanted. Alok scouted for a leather jacket to be worn on the annual day, Rajan a pair of Nike shoes, Sunny a Sony walkman while Happy hunted for the latest issues of Playboy. Happy was the luckiest.

An arrayy of imported magazines was laid down on one of the pavements. To an amateur eye it would look like a collection of "good housekeeping" and "fashion" magazines but to a connoisseur like Happy that was a sure-shot stairway to kingdom of sex. He came straightaway to the point:

'Do you have the latest ones?' Happy asked to a t-shirt clad bony man.

'What do you want?' he asked knowing well that the four teenagers would have zilch interest in housekeeping and fashion.

'The latest issues of Playboy, Penthouse and People magazine; do you have the Samantha Fox issue as well?' Happy asked greedily. Samantha Fox, a western pop-star was the current sexual fantasy of Indian youth, solely responsible for at least a million jerk-offs in the country each day.

'Yeah, I have it but it will cost a bit more; that one is in high demand,' the vendor said like the pop-stars unofficial pimp.

'How much will it cost man? Don't you know me? I am your regular customer,' Happy said infusing familiarity.

'Everyone's a regular customer here. Anyways 500 bucks for 3!' he said and looked around.

'Are you crazy? 500 bucks for 3? Are you selling gold here? Take

250, it's just that I am getting late or else I would have gone to Old Delhi,' Happy said. Old Delhi book market was another jaunt of pornography for the sex famished youth.

'Try your luck then,' he paused, 'Ok final. It won't be lower than 400!'

'350 and it's a deal man, here goes your dough,' Happy said as he forcibly thrust the currency in the man's palm.

'*Sardarji tussi vadde harami ho,*' the man grinned as he disappeared inside an electronic shop behind the pavement. He reappeared in five minutes carrying a black polythene bag and handed it to Happy. Happy gazed inside and displayed his full set of thirty two to the man. The quartet then set out to accomplish their remaining mission which was much easier; buying clothes and electronics.

'*Touch me, touch me I want to feel your body,*' Happy hummed the Samantha Fox hit single like a Punjabi Bhangra blissfully as he unlocked the car.

The evening had set in and the boys decided to gorge on the latest fad in Delhi, *Chholey Bhature* and hot chocolate fudge at Nirula's in Chanakya Puri. Nirula's was a product of the snacking opportunity that an intelligent Delhi entrepreneur had sensed; and launched a series of mid and small size eateries all across Delhi, that served everything from *dosa* and *chhole bhature* to *mutton seekh kakabs* and *butter chicken*. The experiment was a knockout and the fast food chain had become a craze amongst the youth in the capital. For outsiders, like this quartet from Agra it was an experience that was impossible to ignore. After the sumptuous feast they walked towards Chanakya theatre, a stone's throw away from the restaurant and one of the few theatres in Delhi that screened Hollywood movies. Chanakya always attracted a very chic crowd that included the hottest Delhi chicks and that precisely was the reason why it was a key destination in the boy's Delhi itinerary today.

'Wow! What babes' man! Just look at the legs of the one in black skirt,' Happy ogled.

'Shut up Surd, speak softly. We have a reputation to protect,' Alok hushed. Rajan and Sunny were dazzled with the bevy of beauties around them who looked stunning.

'*Oye,* just look at that girl in the yellow top Alok! Just look at the way she is exposing her assets,' Happy said staring at a near perfect bodied slender girl in a small group; completely unaware of the physical anxiety that her mini top was causing to the male libido around.

'Let's buy the tickets Happy, lets go,' Alok almost dragged Happy by the arm.

'I am not going anywhere! Just look at her man,' Happy said with raw sexual excitement in his voice.

Alok signaled Rajan to buy the tickets and pushed Happy towards the Chanakya entrance, Sunny followed them, looking around like a lost lamb.

'Is this your first visit to Chanakya?' Alok asked Happy as they entered the theatre lobby.

'Oh yes man and I think I have been a real loser, never to have come here earlier,' Happy said turning back; trying to catch the last few glimpses of the girl in the yellow top.

'Anyways, there's always a next time. The problem with me is, that most of the times that I have been hanging around are with losers like them, or my cousin Vinny,' he said pointing at Rajan and Sunny.

'But from now on, this is the place that is going to be the first on my list.'

'What movie are we watching?' he asked Alok disinterestedly.

'Top Gun, the latest Tom Cruise movie,' Alok said, as they climbed the stairs to the balcony.

'How many nude scenes does the damn movie has?' he asked instantly and then started to whistle as they entered the dark movie hall.

'Now we are ta'king,' Happy said loudly as he saw Tom Cruise undressing Kelly McGill halfway through the movie. He had shown hardly any interest in the high testerone action thriller until now.

'Shhh....just shut up Happy and keep watching,' Alok muttered sitting next to him.

'Are they going to go all the way brother...how long is this scene?'

'How the fuck do I know Happy? I am also watching it for the first time,' Alok hushed.

'Oh, ok. I hope this goes on forever, the girl is too hot.'

'Just shut up Happy and let everyone watch,' Alok said.

'Hey mister, do you mind settling down on your seat, your head is obstructing my way,' the guy sitting behind Happy, muttered from his seat.

'*Oye,* are you here to watch Happy's head or the movie?' Happy replied without looking back.

'Fuck! These idiots I tell you!' the guy said to the girl sitting next to him.

Happy turned back to look at him, 'These idiots, will fuck you here, asshole.'

'Leave it na Ashish, what's the point?' his girlfriend said .

'She's smarter than the idiot sitting next to her,' Happy laughed and reclined on the chair. The love making scene from the movie had meanwhile faded off and the bedsheets had given way to an intense air battle between F-14's.

'What an idiot? Didn't even let me watch the movie,' Happy said gulping down whisky from a pink plastic glass.

'You really hunt for trouble wherever you go. Why can't you shut up for a change?' Alok said picking up a piece of dry Chilly Chicken.

'*Oye,* what did I do man? I was talking to you guys, why did that idiot need to jump in?' Happy said looking at Sunny and Rajan who were busy untangling Hakka noodles from their plastic forks.

They had settled in one of the many Chinese restaurants bang opposite Chanakya theatre after the movie. The eateries were lined in one row and each one of them had made seating arrangements by placing some plastic chairs and tables for their customers.

'This is better food than our Chinese Van. What do you say?' Happy looked at Alok who nodded.

'If you guys are done; let's leave,' Alok said sipping whisky.

'Done? The night is still young and we are not done,' Happy laughed.

'Why? What do you want to do now?'

'Two more of these, and then GB road beckons us!' Happy said raising his plastic glass.

'I am not going Happy and I think you guys shouldn't go as well. I have heard that this place is risky.'

'After whisky nothing is risky,' Happy guffawed.

'Fuck you man, I am not going,' Alok repeated.

'*Oye* ok Alok, you just come with us. We won't push you to do anything. You watch us while we make out. Ok?' Happy chided.

It was ten when their car took a right from the Gandhi Statue on SP Marg in South Delhi.

'*Oye,* what's that statue?' Happy asked.

'That's Gandhi Happy, leading the countrymen to Dandi when the British had taxed Indian salt. Haven't you read about it?' Alok said sitting on the front seat.

'I am also someone like Gandhi then.'

The rest looked at him with disbelief; liquor was taking its toll.

'I am leading you to GB road that's why. *Chalo GB Road,*' Happy's loud laughter crackled on the streets of the posh SP Road.

GB road, the famous flesh capital of the country was situated in the heart of Old Delhi and looked alive and breathing at midnight. Scores of young and old men, local and outbound travelers paraded in front of the shut hardware shops; embedded in the ground floors of hundred year old looking buildings. Alok who was standing with the gang at a cigarette shop after having their car parked on one side of the road, found this sight quite amusing.

'Are these guys daft? Walking around at 12 in the night and hunting for women? Where do they expect to find them?' Alok said looking at Happy who had an angel-like expression on his face.

'Just look up Alok, just look towards the heaven,' Happy said.

Alok's eyes traveled upwards and met about a hundred eyes looking in their direction.

'Oh my god,' Alok said as he witnessed for the first time a full blown cinemascope version of paid prostitution.

The first floor displayed a picture perfect of India's cultural diversity. It had everyone; from a Bengali lass to a mid 30's Bihari woman, from an Assamese teenager to a Malyalee standing on the cusp of her retirement. Women, women and more women in all shapes and sizes were dressed in loud colored sarees, salwar suits while some of the daring ones in jeans and colored tops. Layers of blaring lipstick covered their lips and mascara on their eyes absolved them of their true skin color. Their eyes that beckoned with a "come hither" look had got the entire man-kind present at that unearthly hour into frenzy. Alok was finding this ever amusing while the remaining three were panting like dogs in heat.

'So, what do you want to do now?' Alok asked Happy whose eyes were fixed on the floor above. How he wished that like spiderman he could cling to that first floor balcony with his web shooters?

'I just want to be up there,' Happy said pointing his finger to the balcony.

'So, what are you boys looking for?' a turtle colored T-shirt clad man asked, standing next to them at the shop.

'Boy's? Who's a boy here mister?' Happy snapped turning around.

'Ok sir. Men, men! I take my words back. So, what are the men looking for? Looking out for some good fun?' the man smiled.

'Of course, this is not a temple and we are not here to pray. What can you get us?' Happy asked like a professional shopper.

'I can get you the best ones in GB road. You have to trust me on this one.'

'How much?' Rajan asked twitching his thumb and the first finger.

'How many girls are you looking for?' the man asked looking at Alok.

'Not for me man. It's for them,' Alok shrugged and pointed towards the other three.

'The best ones will cost 500 each. You guys are looking for one or two?' the man asked.

'500 bucks is too much for one. Be reasonable *Oye*,' Happy said.

'It's almost midnight guys and the most of the good ones are already booked. Please hurry up or else we will be left with nothing.'

'*Oye* please understand man. Ok, at-least give us some student discount,' Happy chuckled.

'Ok, you guys are incorrigible. How many girls do you need?' he said shaking his head.

'Can't there be just one girl; for all three of us?' Happy asked sheepishly.

'No smart ass, 500 bucks isn't enough for three cocks. Do you think I am from Agra mental asylum?'

'No, you have not come from there but we have,' Happy argued with a wide grin.

'Oh my lord, who do I have here? These crazy lunatics?' the man said holding his forehead.

'Ok,1000 bucks for three,' he said after a minute.

'700 bucks and we are done,' Happy replied as he clasped the man's palm forcefully into his.

'Ok fine, follow me, but not more than an hour. Ok?' the man said.

'An hour for the three of us, that's too less,' Rajan retorted .

'That's enough for Julie mister. One look at her naked body; and you will discharge on the spot,' the man replied and signaled the boys to follow him.

'I am waiting here. You guys finish your hourly shift and come back,' Alok said.

'*Oye* come yaar. Atleast watch the fun if you don't want to be a part of it,' Happy said as he dragged Alok by his arm.

The pimp led them through a narrow rickety staircase to the coveted first floor courtyard of GB road. They walked through a plethora of prostitutes who made lewd gestures at the boys who walked amidst them in a trance. A couple of them tried to pinch Sunny's chubby cheeks while one of the more adventurous ones tried flicking his ass. They walked through them like first time models on the ramp; with a bunch of over exuberant spectators cheering from the galleries. The male convoy stopped in front of a closed door.

The pimp stepped forward and knocked on the closed wooden door. The boys waited in silence. The door opened with a crackle and a twenty something buxom woman stepped out.

'Are you out of your mind Hari? You have got four customers at this hour? Am I a human being or a machine?' she said angrily knotting her hair and looking at the pimp.

'Don't worry Julie darling, these are young boys out to have fun. They won't take much time,' the pimp winked at her.

'*Oye* who do you think is a young boy here?' Happy who was busy checking out the girl's curves snapped as if his masculinity was being questioned.

Hari the pimp tapped his shoulder that just meant one thing: Just shut the fuck up or your night is ruined. Happy understood the signal and immediately weathered down.

'They might tip you as well Julie, so don't you bother. Ok?'

'Tip? But this wasn't supposed to be a part of the deal?' Rajan asked.

'Do you guys want to get laid or not? Can't you make out that she is throwing so much of a tantrum and is not willing to entertain any more customers at this hour?' Hari muttered into his ear. Julie pretended as if she was not interested in being a part of their conversation.

'Ok it's fine, we will do something. But let's not waste any more time,' Happy said rubbing his palms together in anticipation. Alok looked disinterestedly towards the buzzing corridor.

'Tell them that it won't go beyond an hour Hari, and send these boys inside,' she spoke in a masterly voice as she disappeared behind that wooden door.

'So, should we start? I am going first,' Happy turned around and declared.

'Not so soon my friend. I need the money first,' Hari said as he opened up his palm.

'One more thing guys, she needs some time to warm up,' Hari said as he counted the currency that Happy had placed on his palm.

'What's about this warm up man? I am raring to go,' Happy said all worked up.

'Don't worry guys; you'll enjoy the warm up before the real action. You must witness how Julie dances; with and without clothes. I am telling you that it's better than the real thing,' Hari proclaimed while keeping the money in his shirt pocket.

'Ok, let's see your warm up session then. But only for sometime Hari before the real action begins,' Happy said forcefully. Hari nodded and turned back.

'I will wait downstairs, you guys have fun,' Hari said as he walked out of the door.

The quartet entered the dimlit blue room with calculated steps and looked around. The room had a large sized old wooden bed on one side that occupied most of the space; and a small bedside table that had a postcard picture of a girl who wore a pink *lehanga* and carried a fake smile plastered on her makeup laden face. Alok looked at it closely and it was indeed Julie a few years younger. On the other side of the bed, kept carelessly was a dirty forty watt Panasonic two- in- one waiting to open its mouth.

'Where is that Julie gone?' Happy said with concern. With these four grown-ups and some amount of furniture inside, the room already looked crowded.

'Relax, boys and settle down. Do you want to drink something?' Julie entered the room from behind a curtain that hid a door. She had changed her appearance from a salwar suit into a shining blue night gown that was exposing her breasts to the fullest. The black bra strap intentionally creeped out of her gown and enhanced her sex appeal.

'No, we are fine. Anyways who has come here to sit?' Happy said and caught her by the hand.

The other three looked a bit surprised by his daring demeanor.

'Hey, just relax and be patient. Everything will happen in time. Let's get into the mood,' she said sexily and pushed the boys onto the bed. As they sat on it half reclined she had switched on the two in one.

Mere dil gaaye ja Zoo Zoo Zoobie Zoobie Zoobie the latest bollywood blockbuster blared in the room as Julie took the centrestage and started gyrating to the beats of the song. The quartet looked at her mesmerized as her dance steps reminded them more of Kama sutra than Mandakini the heroine on whom this song was picturised. They seemed to love every second of it except Alok who after initial excitement was finding it all moronic and lewd.

The situation was now turning into an uncontrollable one for Happy. Unable to suppress his emotions any further he jumped on to the floor and held the girl by her waist and started following her dance steps. It was a funny sight as Happy's dancing prowess was none to boast of and to top it he was trying to match his awkward steps with the rehearsed movements of the prostitute. Rajan and Sunny who were feeling left behind, jumped into the party after a bit of cajoling by Happy. The other three danced away to glory with the prostitute as Alok reclined on the bed feeling sleepy. In a while Julie took off her gown and danced in the middle of the room with fully exposed breasts and a pair of jeans that she was wearing underneath the gown. The boys had their tongues touching the ground. A bit hesitant initially, soon their manhood demanded justice and they started fondling with the prostitute in open, groping her at the right places and she like an adept salesman replied with pleasurable moans as their hands touched her naked flesh. As the scene inside got heavy, Alok got up and as if in a spell, started walking towards the door. Julie tried to stop him and pull him back into the orgy. Alok stared at her coldly as he shook his head in a denial and freed his arm from hers to walk out of the room

'Isn't he interested in doing it?' she asked Happy who was getting ready to gobble her right breast.

Happy raised his head to mutter, 'He is an idiot in love. What to do?'

Alok would have been alone in the open for not less than five minutes before Sunny and Rajan emerged out of the door.

'Where's Happy?' Alok turned around.

'He is inside, the bastard is insisting on taking the first shot,' Rajan said adjusting his trouser.

'I tell you man, this Julie is really fucking hot. We are in for a good time now,' Sunny chuckled.

'Anyway, how long will this stupidity take?' Alok asked.

'You need to ask that Surd. After him it is just the two of us,' Sunny said looking at Rajan.

'So, that means it won't take much time,' Alok smiled as he looked at them.

'Bastard,' both of them made a face.

As the three of them waited outside Julie's room, they witnessed a bit of commotion in the first floor alley. The doors were flung open and men hiding behind them rushed outside and started fleeing in different directions. The boys were wondering about what had happened when they saw a familiar face piercing through the crowd and approaching hastily in their direction. It was Hari's.

'Let's get the fuck out of here. Fast,' he was out of breath as he spoke.

'Why? What happened? We are not done yet,' Sunny said.

'It's a surprise police raid. The cops haven't been paid their commission last month so that's the result. Where's that sardarji?'

'He is inside but what about us? We had a deal and there are still two shots pending,' Rajan said desperately.

Hari looked at him as if he were a moron, 'You guys truly belong to Agra. If the cops get hold of you, they will give you innumerable shots on your thick backsides. Just get your friend out fast.'

'There's no point in arguing guys, I think he is right. Let's get Happy out of that room fast,' Alok said.

Rajan walked towards the door looking shattered as if his world had fallen apart as he knocked on the door. He banged the door twice but still there wasn't any movement.

'I can hear his grunts and nothing else,' Rajan whispered.

Alok raced towards the door and banged on it, 'Happy, fucking police is here man! Get out fast before they put us behind the bars.'

It worked, and a minute later Happy was on the door holding on to his falling trousers.

'*Oye* what happened Alok? You guys are hell bent on cutting my fun short. What a babe man, I tell you,' Happy said with a look as if he was being denied an entry into heaven.

Suddenly they heard loud footsteps coming up from the stairs accompanied by sound of police whistles.

'They are here guys, you boys should be getting out of here fast,' Hari said pulling both Alok and Happy by their arms. Rajan and Sunny followed them helplessly looking sad if someone close in the family had just died.

Their funeral march continued for a few moments until Hari guided them down through another fleet of stairs that ran from the other end of the passage. In a couple of minutes they were all standing in front of the locked up doors of a paints and furnishing shop on the ground floor.

'So, can we have our balance money? The deal isn't complete yet,' Happy asked the pimp.

'Who saved your ass from the cops? I think you should be paying me a tip over the 700 bucks that you guys had paid up,' Hari the pimp replied.

'So, are you implying that we aren't getting our money back?' Happy said sounding pissed.

'Yes. In our trade once the money changes hands, it never comes back,' Hari said sternly.

Happy wanted to resist but Alok's gentle press on the shoulder calmed him.

'It's ok Happy. Let's go back,' he said as they retreated. Hari turned around to walk back into his world.

It was close to 2 PM when their Maruti crossed Faridabad. Sunny and Rajan had collapsed due to exhaustion, frustration (no sex) and intoxication on the back seat of the car. Happy was unusually quiet.

'What's wrong with you Happy? Tired? Should I drive?' Alok volunteered.

'No, I am doing fine,' he said and looked into Alok's eyes, 'am I on a completely wrong track brother?'

'Nah! You are a priest Surd! They are going to give you a wild card entry in the Vatican for the noble life you lead,' Alok replied with a straight face.

'Do they have good looking women there? If yes then I am game brother,' he chuckled as Alok looked at him in mock disgust.

'Thinking about Megha? Right? ' Happy broke the silence after half an hour. Alok did not reply.

'Tell me one thing frankly brother, do you love her or do you lust for her?' he asked like an intellectual.

'If only you had some brains in your head instead of this truckload of shit Happy,' Alok said and punched him lightly on the jaw.

Happy looked at Alok in confusion for a second and then burst into a song, '*Julie, Aa Aa Aa I love you*,' he sang loudly as his hoarse voice filled up the silent Delhi- Agra Highway.

Three Times Loser.... # 50

The annual day celebration at St. Thomas is a grand affair. The buzz for the festival starts building up about a month before the D day, and precipitates after a few weeks of the annual day, only once the school gets tired of talking about it. Today was the day of reckoning. A privileged few would get that life-time opportunity to showcase their straps from the elevated platform of a well lit stage to a world that was built of a) their fellow deprived students who would be cheering for them from the aisles and cursing their luck for not being up there b) their parents who till today had only thought that their son was good for nothing c) their teachers who would get a once-in- a year orgasm from the marvel that they had created out of an uncouth bunch and most of all d) St. Marks girls – one big chance to caste an impression on the girl that each one of them secretly dreamt of.

The lady teachers from the primary wing were helping out Mr. Chacko and his Macbeth gang to transform these under eighteen year old Indian kids into Shakespearean Royal Englishmen. Talcum powder, mascara and fake make-up had a huge role to play in this. After three layers of make-up on his face, Alok couldn't take it anymore.

'Isn't this enough madam? Who is going to object if Macbeth was just this much "white"?' he said pointing towards his face.

'No Alok, you still look dark. This isn't our Macbeth,' Miss Mathur the class sixth teacher muttered without paying attention. Macbeth's fake moustache was hanging between her teeth and she was deeply engrossed in applying the fourth layer of powder cum moisturizer paste on his face. Alok frowned and allowed her hand to torture him for a few more minutes.

'Yes! Now I think we are done,' she said happily while sticking the beard on his chin with some gum.

'Mr. Chacko! Why don't you come here and take a look at your Macbeth?' she shouted for the ring leader who was in the neighboring room.

'*Waw, this guy loogs zimbly the charakter. Good work madam. Is your andy coming for the function?'* Chacko said as he walked towards them.

Miss Mathur was unmarried and stayed with her aunt in Agra. She nodded while cleaning her hands with a towel.

'So *now that you are raady what are the other bayz up to? Let me go and get these laazy bayz up to speed, its olready 6 'o clok,'* Chacko said and hurried to the other room.

Alok checked out his bearded English nobleman look in the mirror and made a face. He was wearing a loose skirt that was stitched at the bottom to make it look like a nobleman's robe, a pair of gladiator sandals with leather beads that ran up to his ankle and a brass necklace that circled around his neck.

'What have they turned me into? I look like one of those clowns from Apollo circus with a beard,' he muttered to himself.

'Are you ready for the final act Lord Macbeth? Just look at me, my Lord?' Alok heard a familiar voice from behind.

'Is this you? Oh my god Samir! Look at you! 'Alok said staring at a coal colored figure that vaguely resembled a human, with hair that oozed with oil, eyes smeared with kohl and holding a wooden pointed object that dimly resembled a spear.

'Fuck Samir! How can a white King Duncan's night watchman be a black African?' he asked.

'It's fucking Chacko's interpretation of Macbeth. I bet he would ever let go of a play where someone doesn't look darker than him,' Samir chuckled.

'I don't believe this Samir, you are bloody laughing it off here and I thought you would be ready to break down on my shoulders again. A black African night watchman who looks like a jerk and does not even get to open his mouth for once in the entire play,' Alok took a jibe.

'Who says that this faithful soldier won't open his mouth,' Samir smirked.

'Why? Has Chacko taken a pity on you and given you some lines to speak at last? What are they; "Help" or the "The King just got murdered",' Alok said while adjusting his beard.

'You, along with the world are going to witness today Lord Macbeth that what happens when this insignificant soldier opens his mouth. Do you remember your sermon that day at Paliwal Park O Lord?' Samir said as he looked into his eyes mysteriously.

Is *this a dagger which I see before me,*
The handle toward my hand? Come, let me clutch thee.
I have thee not, and yet I see thee still.
Art thou not, fatal vision, sensible

To feeling as to sight? Or art thou but
A dagger of the mind, a false creation,
Proceeding from the heat-oppressed brain?
I see thee yet, in form as palpable......

Alok mouthed the famous Macbeth soliloquy with élan and exited out of the stage towards King Duncan's chamber, with a dagger in hand. The lights went off and the stage background changed to a chamber in Macbeth's palace where King Duncan lay asleep on the bed, being guarded by two soldiers at the door, one of whom was Samir. The soldiers were supposed to be intoxicated and sleeping when Macbeth enters the king's chamber, murders him and sneaks out while the guards remain sleeping. Well that was supposed to be the real scene where all Samir had to do was act like an intoxicated sleeping soldier. Alok, as Macbeth, entered the chamber and in a dramatic manner murdered the king in cold blood with a dagger. The king died in the sleep, letting out just one loud whimper. Looking visibly shaken; the murderer Macbeth walked out of the chamber towards the exit when his eyes met Samir's, the guard who slept there. The sleeping guard winked at him.

The lights went off again and the background changed to another room where Lady Macbeth is waiting for her husband who has gone to commit the gruesome act of murder. Macbeth returns to his wife feeling like shit for the deceit that he has committed towards the king. Macbeth's wife consoles him saying that King Duncan's murder was imperative for him to become the king. She tells him that now that the king is dead they will have to cover up this murder and put the blame on someone else. To do this, she also plants the blood stained dagger in the hands of the sleeping guards so that they appear like convicts who had murdered the king.

Soon Duncan's sons and other noblemen arrive and they walk towards the king's chamber to wake him up as they need to restart their journey. As per the original Shakespearean tragedy, Macbeth enters the chamber first and to disguise this murder kills the two sleeping guards so that no one else gets to talk to them. He then comes out horrified and proclaims to everybody around that it is the guards who had treacherously murdered the king as their clothes were stained with blood and they were in the possession of dagger with which the king was murdered. He tries to conceal his sin by announcing further that he murdered the soldiers in a fit of rage. But this is what happened on St. Thomas stage…

Alok alias Macbeth enters the king's chamber leaving others behind. He finds the king dead and the guards sleeping with blood stained clothes and the dagger lying close to them. All that Alok had to do was take out his fake sword and kill the soldiers who had to die without offering any resistance. As Alok raised his sword one of the soldiers suddenly opened his eyes and got up to sit on the floor. This black soldier was Samir.

'What are you going to do my lord?' Samir alias the sleeping guard said with folded hands.

Alok was taken aback at this sudden emergence of dialogue from his mouth; a dialogue which was never there in the script.

'I have served the king and thee for such a long time and this is the reward that I get?' Samir said in his self invented Shakespearean lingo.

Alok's throat went dry and with his hand held high and sword hanging in the air he looked around. Chacko who was standing in the aisle, looked at them with a face that had lost all blood. It looked as if he would get a heart attack and collapse there. Other actors in the play standing behind Chacko looked completely blown away. The other guard on stage looked at Macbeth and his partner like a zombie.

Alok glanced at the crowd that was scattered in front of the stage, a mix of families, parents, grandparents, teachers, kids and yes he could trace the section where St. Marks Girls sat. He tried to figure out if Megha was there, but couldn't. He turned his eyes towards Samir who looked at him with the same pleading expression.

'Tell me O lord is this that I deserve? Please tell me, please tell me…' Samir kept repeating his impromptu plea. Chacko had perhaps wet his pants in the aisle. Alok looked at the crowd again who had no clue that this wasn't a part of the script. For them it was a dramatic highpoint and they looked completely engrossed in the play.

'Tell me O lord is this what I deserve?'Samir repeated painfully.

Alok moved forward and muttered, 'Chacko and the principal will tell you later what you deserve; if you don't fucking die right now.'

As Alok spoke this, he let the sword fall down and hit the soldier alias Samir artificially. Samir let out an overtly dramatic *bollywood* cry that lasted for a good sixty seconds before succumbing on the floor. Alok staggered out of the stage choked with the anxiety that this impromptu drama had created. The act ended with a thunderous applause from the captivated audience.

'O my *gawd*, I can't believe what this *baay* has done?' Chacko was screaming at Samir who stood quietly in one corner of the room.

'I am *simbly* going to ask the principal to *restikate* this *fallow tomorro* for sure. Who the hell gave you the permission to say those *blaady* lines?' Chacko lashed out again.

'I did,' Alok said as he entered the room.

Samir looked completely surprised while Chacko became wilder.

'How the hell can you give permission when it is me who is *kontrolling* this *plaay*?' Chacko rolled his eyes in anger.

'Sorry sir, but just before the play started; I thought that this scene looked very dry and hence asked Samir to say these lines to make it more dramatic. Did you notice that how much did the crowd clap after the scene got over?' Alok said adding excitement to his words.

'Both of you are *blaady* mad *baays*? You idiots, these were not the original lines from the play? Don't you get this?' Chacko screamed again.

'Sir, tell me one thing, who the hell from the audience would ever get to know this? They all thought it was very much a part of the play. But I admit, I made a mistake of not having informed this to you earlier,' Alok said with a long face that Samir knew had FAKE written all over it.

'God save both of you if the principal asks me even once about this tomorrow,' Chacko yelled as he left the room after giving both of them a sinister look. Alok heaved a sigh of relief.

'You really saved my ass today Alok. Thanks,' Samir raced towards Alok and hugged him

'All that is fine but you really blew my head off with your on stage histrionics Samir! Fuck, I was stunned for a few moments. Why did you do what you did there on stage?' Alok asked in mock anger, running his finger through the hair.

'I wanted to see what this shy, unsure and scared boy could do once he opened his mouth. Thanks Alok for making me realize that the other side of every fear is freedom,' Samir said.

'Hey, that's well said. Who has said this?' Alok quipped.

'Who else but me Alok!' Samir replied as they laughed in unison.

Teachers leave those kids alone
All in all it's just another brick in the wall

The Pink Floyd cult was towards its end and the group singing it was lost in the music with Alok leading the pack. As he sang into the microphone, wearing his new leather jacket, he thought of himself as a rockstar. Besides him, there was atleast one girl in the crowd who agreed with him. Megha had liked Alok right from the time she had seen him cycling through the narrow lanes of Paliwal Park with his friends. He was different, fun-loving yet sensitive, playful yet mature, intelligent, seemed to have a mind of his own and to top it, she found him damn cute.

'I think I am falling in love with this guy on stage,' Megha said to herself and looked admiringly at the guy in the black jacket who bowed in front of the audience after finishing the song.

'He is damn cute *na*..,' Vandana her friend muttered in Megha's ear.

Megha nodded.

'Does he have a girlfriend? Looks quite hot though,' Vanita, her other friend said looking at Megha.

'How do I know girls? Why don't you go and ask him?' Megha said, irritated.

Both of them looked at each other and made a face.

'Why don't we talk to him? Maybe one of us could get lucky? What say Megha?' Vanita said.

'Please do that if you wish to do so. I am not going anywhere,' Megha said without moving her gaze from the stage.

'Now this is not done Megha, you have to come with us. We are just going to say hi to him and compliment him on his performance, 'Vandana said and pulled her by the hand.

'And who knows? Maybe he likes one of us!' Vanita said and winked.

'OOOOH…' Vandana said dreamily.

'You guys are so impossible,' Megha made a disgusted face as she dragged her feet behind them towards the backstage.

Alok was walking down the stairs along with Samir and Happy when he bumped into the three girls.

'Hey! Hi there! Where have you been Megha? I thought that you have ditched me after making all those promises of coming here,' Alok smiled.

'Wow, so you guys know each other?' Vanita said rolling her eyes.

'And there were some promises as well of meeting today, right Megha? And you never gave us a hint about all this,' Vandana mocked.

'Oh…well, we go for the same coaching class and that's how we know each other. That's it,' Megha said sheepishly.

'Should I tell them the truth?' Happy muttered in Samir's ear with an eye on Vanita and Vandana.

'Shut Up. Don't be stupid,' Samir shot back.

'Hope you guys enjoyed our annual function,' Alok said, trying to steer away the conversation and causing more stress to Megha.

'Of course we did and you were awesome. Am I right Megha?' Vanita teased her again.

Megha ran her fingers through the hair nervously, 'Yeah, I liked it. Good fun.' She had left her hair untied over a loose hanging pink sweatshirt and a pair of blue jeans.

"Do you guys want to have a Double Seven in the canteen?' Alok asked.

'Will it be open at this hour? It's almost eight,' Vanita said.

'*Oye* of course it will be. Today is the annual day and the canteen is open till ten,' Happy said looking all excited.

They started walking towards the canteen that was on the other end of the school near the parking lot. Happy and Samir walked with the girls while Alok and Megha walked a few feet behind.

'Why haven't you been coming to the coaching for last few days? Haven't seen you there since you went to Delhi,' Megha said.

'What to do ya? The practice sessions for the play and the song used to start immediately after the school got over. I was reaching home everyday around eight,' Alok said.

'Can I tell you something?' Megha said and looked at Alok. She looked stunning in the early winter moonlight, her pink outfit, long falling hair and deep brown eyes. Alok couldn't move his mesmerized gaze from her face.

'You were simply mindblowing today and I really mean it,' she said.

'Oh yes, and I am completely aware about that,' Alok said plainly.

'And how is that?' Megha looked surprised.

'Why don't you take a look at the faces of your Alok- struck friends?' Alok chuckled.

'Bull shit Alok! Hmphh!' Megha raced ahead to walk with her friends leaving Alok behind.

'Can I drop you home Megha?' Alok said as the group came out of the canteen.

Happy looked at Samir with raised eyebrows while Vandana and Vanita smiled at each other. Megha looked a bit uncomfortable.

'It's fine Alok! Vanita can drop me in her car; I think her parents should be here any moment,' Megha said and looked at Vanita who had a question mark on her face.

'Oh come on Megha, how can a poor car fit so many of you? I'll drop you home. Just wait for a second here and let me get my cycle,' Alok said and walked towards the cyclestand.

'Come on; let's go!' Alok said as he stopped his BSA SLR next to Megha.

'Where should I sit on this? These drop handle bars allow no space for anyone to sit in the front while you do not have a carrier at the back,' Megha asked sheepishly.

'Sit in front; and no worries; I will be able to drive using the upper side of the handle bars. Come on, sit,' he said as he moved his hands gently from the handle allowing Megha to squeeze in.

'Are you comfortable?' he asked her.

She nodded silently.

'Okay guys, I will catch you later,' Alok said and paddled the vehicle.

Happy looked agape at Alok's bicycle as it trudged towards the St. Thomas main gate, '*Oye* we will follow you Alok,' he shouted from behind as he winked at Samir who was bidding goodbye to her friends.

The Wazirpura road looked deserted at this hour with a couple of scooters and an odd motorcycle whizzing past Alok's BSA SLR at uneven intervals. Both of them were silent and Megha could hear Alok's soft breath over her ears. Megha's body quivered once, as she felt his breath over her skin.

'Your school looks really dead,' Alok broke the silence as he looked at the St. Marks building enveloped in darkness.

'Who would you find here at this hour? The girls would be in the hostel block and teachers in their quarters,' Megha replied. Alok nodded.

He took a right into the Paliwal Park which looked barren. About twenty percent of the street lights seemed to be in working condition and attempted hard to pierce through the maze created by the darkness.

'So, why did you offer me this uncomfortable ride when I could have gone in Vanita's car?' Megha tilted her eyes and asked.

'Because I wanted you to see this,' he muttered close to her ears and stopped the cycle in front of the Paliwal Lake.

She got down from the bicycle gently to see the lake submerged in the darkness. The pedal boats lay huddled together on one side. Despite the darkness, lake looked beautiful under the moonlight, its surface reflecting the falling rays and creating a surreal effect. They walked towards a wooden plank that hosted a staircase used for leading people towards the barrage of boats. They sat on the staircase; on two stairs, one above the other.

'It's beautiful, isn't it?' she exclaimed as she looked at Alok who stared at her intently. He nodded and came down one step to sit next to her. A tingling sensation whizzed past her body.

'Do you know that it's quite possible that one of the stars that you see in the sky, may actually not exist at this moment?' he said looking at the sky.

'How is that possible when I can see them right now, with my own eye?' she replied looking upwards.

'Some of these stars are so far away in the galaxy that for their light to reach the earth it may take over a hundred or a million years,' he paused, 'so what you see now may actually be the light emitted from a star a million years back and so between today and that time, the star might have already gone bust,' Alok said and made a wheezing sound.

Megha stared at him with eyes filled with admiration, 'I think I have fallen for you. I love you,' she said softly.

'I think me too,' Alok said and leaned forward.

Their lips touched each other softly. Megha held Alok by the shoulder and pulled him closer. Alok held her by the waist and put his palm beneath her long falling hair and kissed her with deep passion. One kiss led to the other and their first physical brush lasted for a while under that moonlit night at Paliwal Park.

⋽ *Akash Verma # 59 #* ⋶

'Are you fine?' Alok asked Megha as they cycled out of the park and entered Civil Lines where she lived.

'Yeah,' she replied with a smile soaked in shyness.

'You can drop me here,' she said asking Alok to halt his bicycle a couple of blocks away from her house.

'I can drop you home,' Alok said.

'No. Dad would be waiting for me at home and to see his daughter coming back at 10PM on a bicycle wouldn't be the best of the sights,' she said as she got down.

'Your wish is my command! ' Alok shrugged.

'Are you going to come for the classes from tomorrow? There is hardly any time left for the boards?' she asked.

'Sure, I will. See you,' Alok smiled as he turned back his bicycle.

'Bye,' she grinned and walked towards her house.

He took a deep left from Megha's alley into another road that would lead him to the bye-pass. Alok had to break hard to avoid crashing into a group of four bicycles that thronged the road like a barricade.

'Fuck,' he muttered to himself and looked up to see Ashutosh standing there with three other boys. He looked completely pissed while the others tried hard to look tough and mean.

'Hey, be careful guys! You could have knocked me down with this circus that you are trying at this hour,' Alok almost screamed as he stopped his bike.

'I will knock you down this very moment Alok if you don't keep your hands away from Megha,' Ashu said coldly.

'If I tell this poor guy of what these hands were up to an hour back, I think he will murder me,' Alok muttered.

'What's your problem if she wants to be friendly with me?' he asked.

'It's not her who is trying bastard; it's you who is trying hard to get close. Don't you try and fool me Alok! I have been observing you from the day that you joined Gupta's class and the way you were trying to get overfriendly with her after your stupid annual function got over today, I was watching all that,' Ashu roared.

'Let me give you a small advice Ashu,' he paused, 'only if you could have spent some more time in being lesser stupid than this, Megha would have liked you more.'

'He is talking too much. Should we give him a taste of our medicine?' One of the boys with betel stained teeth said. He looked like a creature straight out from a third grade bollywood movie.

'Alok, are you leaving Gupta's classes or not? I do not want to see you anywhere near Megha,' Ashu said.

'Are you going to ask me to leave this town next?' Alok said with a grin on his face.

'If you don't get it now Alok, we will make sure that you do get what I am trying to tell you before you leave this place,' Ashu was beginning to get very agitated.

'No I don't get it, and stop this bollywood movie right here because I am not going to pay for it any further,' Alok said and put his foot on the pedal gesturing to move.

One of the other cronies with Ashu held the handle of his bicycle and attempted to stop him from moving.

'Don't you guys have anything better to do in life than hanging out with a loser like him,' Alok said and pushed the guy.

'Enough Alok, you have had it now,' Ashu said and held Alok by his jacket collar.

'Hey, watch it before you do anything to my jacket,' Alok said as he punched Ashu in the stomach.

He went down on his knees with a howl. The betel stained guy held Alok by the neck and started tightening his grip. Alok pushed him in the front and slapped him hard on the face. He lost his balance and fell on one of the parked cycles. The other two guys appeared from behind and held both his arms. Ashu was up on his feet and quickly came forward to punch Alok on the face. It hit him hard and his nose started bleeding instantly. Alok collected his senses in a moment and kicked Ashu in the groin. Ashu collapsed on the ground with a whimper. The same duo got into the act again and caught Alok from both sides .The betel stained guy lunged forward in their direction. He slapped Alok and pushed him behind. On seeing Alok being held captive by his allies, Ashu gathered enough courage to land a series of punches on his face and stomach.

'Why are you behaving like a pussy Ashu?' Alok said panting but still holding a grin.

'Why don't you fight with me like a man and stop acting like a wimp?' he said again.

Ashu cupped Alok's face between his palms and pressed his cheeks with his fingers.

'There will be enough occasions for that but first you try and get out of here on your two legs,' he said seething with anger.

'*Oye,* what's going on here? Is that you Alok?' they heard Happy Singh's voice in the background.

'Yes it's me Surd, trying to teach these cowards a little lesson,' Alok said.

'*Oye* sure, I would gladly help you in this one,' Happy said and jumped right into the action scene. Samir looked at them from a distance.

Happy caught the two of them holding Alok and pushed them hard. They tumbled on the bicycles lying on the ground.

'Four versus one is not good guys. Let's fight now,' Happy gestured at them.

Ashu looked at them with resentment and signaled his companions to stop the fight.

'It's okay Happy, I don't want cops getting into this; the patrolling time has already started. Hope you have got the message Alok,' Ashu said.

'I have a piece of advice for you Ashu, completely free!' Alok said as he inched closer to him.

'Learn to fight your own battles and definitely without these monkeys,' he said and looked at the other three who huddled behind him.

Happy gestured them to get lost as the three of them turned back towards their bicycles. Ashu did not move an inch from his place and kept staring at them.

'So, where did you disappear with your girl, bastard? We went looking for you guys all over the town. Am I right Samir?' Happy asked excitedly.

'Nowhere, I just dropped her home; and during the ride we stopped for a few minutes at the lake,' Alok said padding his nose with the handkerchief

'Hmm…our man thinks that we are some imbecile kids from mental asylum who can be taken time and again for a ride,' Happy exclaimed.

'And what did you do at the lake? Did any action happen?' he asked after a few minutes.

'No Surd. What action do you expect to happen at the lake? It's not your GB road where action happens every moment of the day,' Alok replied.

'I know that you are hiding something, but anyways what did that bloody idiot want from you? Happy asked.

'Who? Ashu? Nothing Surd, that guy is a gone case. The only thing that I feel for him is just plain symapthy,' Alok said.

'Why do you feel symapthy for him *oye*? They were all set to bash you up today?' Happy asked.

'If he thinks that he can get a girl like Megha; then Kelly Mcgillis is definitely not out of your league Surd,' Alok chuckled.

Happy had a puzzled look on his face, 'Who the hell is she? Is she some new hot girl in St. Marks?'

'The Top Gun Heroine Happy,' Samir quipped.

'Oh! I missed that hot scene in the movie because of that idiot!" Happy reminisced about the Chanakya tryst.

The trio's run up to boards was nowhere close to their true intentions. Books remained as distant to them as they had been during the entire year that had whizzed past. Samir's fervent pleas of studying for longer hours fell on the deaf ears of Alok and Happy. Alok had been busy with the new found love in his life while Happy had turned into a privileged member of Chanakya and GB road. He had visited Delhi nearly six times over last couple of months.

'Where are you off to? Alok's mother asked raising her eyebrows.

'Why did you ask?'Alok replied without looking up as he tied his shoelaces.

'Because every Saturday now is a special study leave that the school has handed out to the students for putting in extra effort,' she said coming out of the kitchen.

'So, what do you think am I doing Mom?' Alok said looking up.

'I don't know Alok, you tell me? I really don't see books coming out of your eyes and ears these days. Shouldn't it be like that a couple of months before your boards?' she said pulling open the door of the Allwyn refrigerator in the passage.

'I am off for a joint study session along with Samir and Happy. Where do you think am I going?'Alok looked at her innocently as if she was blocking his entry into the holy ISKCON temple at Vrindavan.

'Happy and studies?? Huh? I think the last time that he touched his books was in kindergarten,' she said, annoyed, as she carried a bowl of milk from refrigerator into the kitchen.

'Mom, you can't speak about my friends like that and don't you worry, we will all do well in the boards,' he said while getting up. Sandhya kept the bowl of milk on the stove and heaved out a sigh as she saw him leaving the house.

Happy's white Maruti entered the gates of Sikandra, Emperor Akbar's tomb post the afternoon. Samir sat next to Happy in front looking somber while Megha and Alok were engaged in a lover's tiff on the rear seat.

'We could have gone to a nice restaurant instead of coming to this godforsaken lonely tomb,' Megha muttered.

'This is a lovely open place Megha and I get suffocated sitting in those dingy restaurants in town. Imagine you can't even talk freely there!' Alok raised his hands and looked around for support.

'Yes brother, I agree. They are so clamped for space. Reminds me of our college canteen,' Happy said and looked behind.

'You don't have eyes behind your head Happy... better watch out,' Alok said. Megha made a face and looked out of the window.

'So here we go friends,' Happy said as he brought the car to a halt in the monuments parking lot.

The trio along with Megha walked towards the entrance.

The deep red stone laden pathway glistened under the rays of the overcast sun. Groups of monkeys (black faced *langurs)* crowded the way looking for a generous give away of fruits or bread from the hands of a few tourists who walked towards the monument. Happy started teasing an elderly looking baboon with his handkerchief posing it as a food item. The baboon looked interested at first, but on finding out that it was a ploy by another animal made a grunting sound and bared his sharp canines at Happy. The Surd retreaded immediately.

'*Oye,* what's this guy up to *yaar*? It would have bitten me' Happy said animatedly.

'The animal is telling you to mind your own fucking business Surd,' Alok said.

Happy let out a sheepish smile.

'Why don't we go that way?' Alok pointed in a direction away from the tomb.

'Why? Now that you wanted to explore this place let's go and check out this place fully. Why don't we hire a guide as well?' Megha mocked.

Alok glanced at her and pulled her by the hand, 'Let's go!'

Happy changed his track and turned to follow them when Samir held his arm.

'What?' Happy looked at him.

Samir looked at him and gestured him to leave them alone. Happy didn't look very pleased but had to give in and followed Samir in the other direction.

'Akbar had started building this place while he was alive,' Alok said.

Megha did not reply and continued walking.

'Finally his son Jahangir completed it after Akbar died and put him to rest here. I think his other family members are also buried here, his daughters I guess,' Alok said.

They had reached a series of semicircular domes lined up closely towards the end of the boundary. Alok turned around to see Happy and Samir entering the tomb.

'Was this the only place to come out on a date Alok? A tomb for god's sake! It's a place of mourning and not love,' Megha exclaimed angrily.

'Restaurant is also a place for food, eating! How can that be the perfect place for a date?' Alok quipped.

Megha couldn't resist a feeble smile.

'Atleast that's a better place than this secluded monument where there's not a soul in the vicinity except these monkeys,' she said.

'Can you kiss in a restaurant the way you can do here?' Alok said and pulled Megha inside one of the domes and kissed her on the lips. For a moment Megha looked dazed and tried to pull herself back, but Alok had held her hand tightly and she could feel her body melt under the touch of his lips on her skin.

'The weather is turning out to be good these winters,' Megha said covering her arms with a peach colored shawl.

'So now the weather looks good, huh? And a while back, all you were doing is complaining about this whole place,' Alok said as he dusted the mud on the slab and sat next to her.

'If it's got to do with the kisses, you should have told me. I would have kissed you in the car itself to avoid all that nasty chatter,' he smiled.

'What nonsense? You are shameless,' she smiled and looked the other way.

'Where are your friends? I don't see them around,' she said.

'Happy would be ogling at the tourists and trying to catch a glimpse of someone's cleavage,' Alok replied.

'Samir is quite reserved, isn't he?'

'What are you saying? Once that guy opens his mouth he can turn the world around, do you know what did he do on the Annual day?'

'No! What?' Megha looked at Alok quizzically.

Alok dived right back into that day and recounted the entire anecdote that left Megha rolling on the hard stone slab with laughter.

'Ha ha ha… I am sure that Chacko would have been *zimbly* hysterical that night,' she said.

'Just that he didn't have a heart attack. Samir would have been behind bars by now,' Alok said

'You have two good friends,' she said.

'I am two times lucky.'

'And a great girlfriend,' she said.

'Yeah three times lucky okay! I want it no more.'

'This is our eighteenth date today over last two months, after your annual function,' she said.

'You count? Strange.'

'Hmmm.... I never forget these little things,' she said.

'Ok, so let's always remember today as well. Let us leave a symbol here somewhere that reminds us that we were here together on this day; and everytime that we are here in future it would remind us about the old times,' she said excitedly looking at him.

'No! That's straight out of a Hindi movie. I think the next thing that you would want us to do is write our names on the wall?' Alok jumped.

'*Arrayy*... no baby, why would I spoil this monument? Do you have something disposable on you?' she asked.

'Currency? Will a ten rupee note do?' Alok mocked.

'No! Do you have a handkerchief?' she said sounding irritated.

Alok pulled out a white handkerchief from his pocket and handed it to her.

'Hmmm... that looks quite plain, we will have to make it recognizable or else it would be difficult to identify,' she said.

She thought for a few seconds and then a bright smile flashed on her face.

'Can you pass me my handbag please?' she said and pointed towards her brown leather bag.

She rummaged around the purse and took out a chocolate brown Lakme lipstick.

'Is our symbol going to be a lipstick? No!!' Alok shrieked.

Megha chose not to answer him but opened it up to apply it gently on her lips, a couple of times over .Then she turned towards Alok and inched forward.

'Are we smooching with your lipstick on? I don't think I will like it,' Alok said.

She looked at him in the eyes and slowly brought the handkerchief closer to her face to kiss it and leave an exact replica of her smoldering chocolate lips. She found Alok staring at her almost open-mouthed.

'Now, let's find a place for this souvenir,' she said and pulled Alok by his arm.

They walked a few steps when Megha sighted a barren well on the left.

'What's that? Looks like it hasn't been used for ages,' she said looking inside the well.

She turned towards Alok who was trying to peek inside, 'Will you tie this up on the iron rod please?'

She handed over the handkerchief to him. A cylindrical iron rod ran above the well that would have been used for lowering buckets inside the well to bring water up from the depth.

'Wouldn't someone untie this?' he said walking towards the other side.

'No, people won't mess around with it. They would mistake it for a cloth tied here by a devotee for fulfillment of a wish. No one will touch it in this country,' she said.

Alok reached the other-side of the well and stretched his arms to tie the handkerchief around the iron rod. He glanced at her standing on the other side. She looked radiant standing under the sun; her palm cupped her eyes to prevent sunlight falling into them, the hair fluttered in the blowing cool breeze while the expression on her face was serene, peaceful, an everlasting memory that would always stay with him.

'*Oye,* can we stop for a double seven? I am thirsty.'

'No Happy, we have wasted the whole of today, let's get some hours of studies at least,' Samir said.

Alok looked at Megha who shook her head in negative.

'I think we should be going Happy...,' by the time Alok said this, Happy had already stalled the car opposite Satkar restaurant.

'How much time will it take guys? Why would you want a man to die of thirst?' Happy said and gestured them to hop out of the vehicle.

Samir shook his head and got out with an equally reluctant Megha. Alok followed them.

'*Oye* wait *oye* Samir! Let me lock the car first,' Happy said.

Alok and Megha walked together in the dimly lit air-conditioned restaurant where before anyone else; their nostrils met up with the entrapped smell of Punjabi flavors. It took some moments for Alok's eyes to adjust to the new surroundings and the first sight that greeted him were the faces of Mrs. Chawla and Mrs. Arora, his mom's close friends.

'What are you doing here Alok?' Mrs. Chawla asked as if he had entered a sacred place where mortals were denied entry.

'And, who is she??' Mrs. Arora asked authoritatively as if she had caught Alok with her own daughter.

Both the Punjabi ladies were followed by a handful of other 40+ year old Punjabi women dressed in salwar suits and printed sarees who looked at both of them as if they had accosted two runaway serial killers.

Alok turned around to see both Happy and Samir entering the restaurant.

'She is Happy's sister, Happy my friend *auntijee*,' Alok smirked and pointed at Happy whose eyes became as big as a football.

'We are here for a coffee after a long study session aunty. Now if you can please excuse us?' Alok said and smiled politely at them once again.

The aunty brigade gave the group enough space to squeeze ahead from one side. Both Alok and Megha inched slowly amidst a dozen prying eyes of stern looking aunties fixed on their faces. The group of women left the restaurant dejected like an empty handed army platoon post a terrorist raid.

'What were so many of them doing here?' Megha said, her face complexion coming back to normal.

'Kitty party, good my mother was not here today.'

'Why the fuck did you lie?' Happy looked offended as he sipped the cola from a straw.

'Our Surd is worried that Megha is her sister from now!' Alok chuckled as Happy looked bugged.

'It's already three, are we meeting at the coaching?' Megha asked.

'I am bunking today,' Alok said.

'Me too,' Happy joined in unison.

'I think we should go guys, when will we study?' Samir said getting all worked up. Megha agreed with him.

'Who's stopping you brother? You carry on,' Alok said and winked at Happy.

'Yeah, do that Samir,' Happy said as they got out of the restaurant.

'We will see you at the Chinese Van in the evening, Ok?' Alok said as they got inside Happy's car.

'Yeah, I will take a cycle rickshaw from here. See you and thanks for the lovely time,' Megha smiled.

'Me too; and I hope we go there the next time soon' Alok shouted back from the car.

The car took a sharp left turn to enter Kamlanagar from the bye-pass.

'So, brother Samir, off to Gupta's class now?' Happy chuckled and looked at Alok.

'Fuck you Surd! I am not going either,' Samir muttered angrily.

Three Times Loser.... # 70

'I am surely flunking boards this year,' Samir said thoughtfully sitting on the plastic stool in front of the Chinese Van.

'Why?' Alok looked at him profoundly with one strand of noodle hanging in between his lips and a bowl of Talumein chicken soup in his hands.

'Don't you know the answer? What have we done the entire day today except chaperoning you and your sweetheart at Sikandra?' Samir snapped back.

Happy turned his face away from the sleazy poster of a South Indian film that had a dusky woman covering her naked breasts with her palms, towards his two friends at the Chinese Van.

'Do you regret it?' Alok's expression didn't change as he gulped down another potion.

'Of course I do,' Samir said.

'Then why didn't you study rather than coming with us?' Alok asked smacking his lips.

'Because…because ummm because you guys wanted so!' Samir stammered to complete the sentence.

'If only you could listen to your heart more, than listening to others,' Alok said and got up to wash his hands from the plastic tap at the rear of the Van.

'I should not and I am really a sucker for listening to you two, my best friends,' Samir said.

'Don't get into your emotional guilt trip again Samir, I am not going that way,' Alok said wiping his face.

Happy a witness to this ping pong of words for a while now jumped in, 'Relax brother relax, Samir you go and study my friend, who stops you?' he asked trying to calm him down.

'No, I am a fool here…an absolute ass,' Samir said.

'Who is a fool here?' Megha chirped as she took one of the stools and sat next to Samir.

'Ask our man,' Alok said.

'How was the class anyway?' Alok asked.

'What do you expect? Today he pulled up Apurva and ridiculed her so much that she started crying.'

'This guy is a jackass and we know that. Anyways, care to eat something?' Alok asked.

Megha shook her head.

'I am leaving guys,' Samir got up suddenly.

'Where are you going brother? We are all leaving in some time,' Happy said and looked at Alok for affirmation.

'I am not staying...you guys can stay; till whenever,' Samir said.

'Good, atleast you are listening to your heart for once,' Alok said.

'Fuck you,' Samir said and drove away on his bike.

'What happened to him?' Megha said looking amused.

'Unlike the women, our man gets his periods once a day,' Happy guffawed.

'You guys are so mean!' Megha said as she made a face and they got into an intense discussion about Samir's inability to stand up to a situation.

'I have got to be going now, need to study,' Megha said after fifteen minutes. Before the boys could make an offer to drop her back, she had hopped off on to a cycle rickshaw that raced away on the MG Road.

'I guess we should leave now as well,' Alok said a few minutes after Megha had left. Happy nodded.

Alok took out his wallet and walked towards the Van counter to pay the tab.

'Hi Alok!' a familiar voice sprang from behind.

Both Happy and Alok turned around to find Ashu standing under the streetlight.

'So, what brings you here today? Are you looking for another round of fight?' Alok asked while handing a fifty rupee note to the waiter cum Van cashier.

Happy had an alarmed look on his face like a fighter sizing up his opponent when he enters the ring.

Ashu inched closer towards Alok, 'Can we talk for a few moments in privacy?' he said and looked at Happy.

'Why? What is it that you want to talk about?' Alok said as he pushed the wallet back into the pocket.

'Please. Alok it's important,' he said.

'Ok, but Happy stays with me. We don't hide anything between us.'

'Alok, I love Megha,' Ashu broke the silence after a few minutes.

'So?' Alok said nonchalantly looking at him.

'I mean I have loved her all my life, I guess as soon as I gained consciousness.'

'So?' Alok maintained the same tone and expression.

'If you love her Ashu that's really not my problem, is it?' Alok said.

'We are not bothered about your one sided juvenile love story man,' Happy said. Alok signaled Happy to shut his trap up.

'Do you love her Alok?' Ashu said.

'Even if I do or do not, how does that bother you?' Alok said.

'It does Alok, it does. Because before you showed up all was going fine between us. Yes, she didn't love me, but still there was a chance that it could have happened and things would have gone the way our families wanted,' Ashu said.

Silence fell between them for a few minutes.

'I know that you guys are family friends but what has that got to do with you and Megha?' Alok broke the silence.

'We were supposed to fall in love and get married Alok before you walked in and tossed away my dreams along with my dad's,' Ashu said.

'How is that?' Alok asked alarmingly.

'Megha's dad and my father have been friends for over thirty years. Megha's dad runs a generators business and like it happens with a lot of businesses, he suffered a huge financial crisis about eight years back. It was my dad who had helped him that time to clear most of his market debts and since then he has been helping him financially.'

'So, what does this have to do with you and Megha or for that matter me and Megha going around?'

'My family dotes on Megha and especially my father. Don't you know what happens in traditional families in north India?'

Alok looked at Happy who made a disinterested face.

'No, I don't,' he said.

'They look at Megha as their future daughter in law and this is an unsaid understanding between the two families. No one says it upfront but everyone understands.'

'I don't think that Megha has an inkling of whatever you are saying here,' Alok said.

'She knows that her dad is indebted to our family but maybe she can't see the real picture, more-so now from the time that you have walked into the scene, she doesn't seem to see beyond you,' Ashu said with a pained expression.

'Just because your dad is helping them out with money, it doesn't mean that she has to force herself to marry you. All of us right now are so young, hardly out of school and you are thinking about marriage and all that. It's just so filmy man.'

'I know it's too early but here in Agra and especially our community people do get married pretty early. The tradition forces them to,' Ashu said and looked at the queue that had lined up to buy the 9PM tickets in Anjana theatre.

'I don't want to understand all this, but what if Megha does not marry you? What happens then,' Alok asked after a while.

'I don't know, perhaps our family relationships will snap, her brother who wants to study medicine abroad may have to fund his trip on his own without my dad's financial assistance. Who knows?'

'Isn't this fucking blackmail? Why do you need to look at a relationship from a profit and loss lens?'

'Your family is lending them money because they want Megha to be your goddamn wife and if she does not, then that help stops. What's this Ashu? Doesn't this make you sick? You are trying to buy a relationship and not earn it.'

'As far as I am concerned,' Ashu paused, 'I have loved just one woman till now and she is Megha, seriously, with a hand on my heart; and if this financial equation between our families was bringing her closer to me, I had no regrets frankly.'

'And I was the only thorn in your path that led you to Megha,' Alok said.

'Yeah, and I tried to pluck that away through force but couldn't succeed,' Ashu said and looked at the hardened face of Happy.

'So why did you decide to tell me all this?'

'To make you realize the seriousness of the situation and implication of what you guys are getting into.'

'Are you trying to scare me emotionally?'

'That isn't my intention at all.'

'What if I tell you, I don't care?'

'You won't, if you care for Megha,' he said and looked into Alok's eyes.

Ashu left the two of them sitting on the plastic stools in front of the theatre.

'What gas was this ass-hole giving brother? Shit! ' Happy said as they got up.

'I think we should help Samir, he really wants to do well in boards!' Alok said lost in a thought.

'Don't we all? What do you have to say about Ashu? Sentimental idiot, felt like slapping him,' Happy said.

'Let it be Happy, he has his own demons to fight and we have ours,' Alok said as he got up from the stool.

'I think we should better start preparing for the boards Surd. There's hardly any time left now,' Alok said walking towards the cycle.

'What happened to you suddenly? Whose spirit has entered your body? Is it Resnick or Halliday?' Happy guffawed.

'I am off to my Delhi rendezvous this weekend. Do you want to join the fun?' Happy asked.

'No Happy, I should get back to studies. I don't think all this would be helping anyone and especially Samir.'

'So, you mean no more outings, beers, picnics etc.?'

'No.'

'No more meeting up with Megha as well?' Happy quipped.

'Nope,' Alok said.

'And why would you undergo such an ordeal? Does it have to do anything with that idiot Ashu?'

Alok shook his head in denial.

'Don't talk to Megha about this,' Alok said.

'Why?' Happy asked raising his eyebrows.

'Don't!' Alok said firmly.

Happy shook his head as he watched Alok getting on to his bike and racing away.

None of them saw Alok since that day. He had stopped attending college about a week before their four week preparatory holidays started in school. He had stopped coming to Gupta's classes as well, the only place where Megha could meet him. Megha checked with Samir and Happy but they seemed clueless. She tried to reach him through the telephone but it was always Alok's father who picked up the phone. After a series of blank calls, one day she gathered enough courage to ask for him:

'Hello…Er... Hello,' she said.

Silence.

'Hello,' she said again.

'Who is this?' an angry voice asked.

'Can I speak to Alok please?' she asked.

'Who is this?' the angry voice said.

'I am Megha uncle...is Alok around?' she asked hesitatingly.

'No. He is not at home,' the angry voice said.

'Can you please ask him to call me once he is back?' she requested.

'Why?' the angry voice asked.

Megha put the receiver down.

'Where the hell is that Alok?' Happy said gulping down the Double Seven cola.

'Hell only knows,' Samir sighed.

'Why is he behaving like this? Not even talking to me?' Megha said looking at the busy MG road and seated cross-legged on the plastic stool at the Chinese Van.

'Bastard has never done something like this. I have been to his house so many times but he is never around. I am sure he is there inside but doesn't want to meet us. Don't know why?' Happy said and took another sip.

'How are your studies going Surd? You have stopped attending coaching as well,' Samir said.

'I don't feel like going, especially when Alok isn't around,' Happy said.

'I hate him for doing this to me and I don't care if he doesn't want to meet me,' Megha almost shouted as she got up suddenly.

'Hey wait! Where are you going?' Samir reacted.

'Tell your friend that I am gone from his life, forever,' she turned around to say and walked away.

It was the first day of boards at St. Thomas and the air was filled with anticipation, nervousness and excitement of the D day finally arriving. Soon after the morning assembly the classes of tenth and twelfth dispersed and started moving to their allocated classrooms for writing the papers. Happy and Samir looked around for Alok but he was nowhere to be seen.

'Where the fuck is he? Can't locate him,' Happy said looking around at scores of students walking hurriedly towards the classes with a wooden writing board and a stationery box in their hands.

'Let it be Surd, let's go. I think we missed him, we'll catch up with him later,' Samir said as he pulled Happy by his arm.

Happy moved his gaze away reluctantly and both of them walked towards the class.

The quadrangular examination hall was slightly dark despite the six entry doors being laid ajar by the teachers. The morning sunlight in the month of March seeped in the hall after meandering through the wide expanse of the school courtyard and fell on the bunch of students sitting in neatly laid rows.The authorities had taken adequate measures to ensure that there was safe distance between students and they were not tempted to look into their neighbor's answer-sheet. Happy was in the tenth row fidgeting with his stationery box and pleading with Vishal sitting in front to give him a full-on display of his answer sheet once the need arose. He occasionally glanced at the fourth row corner seat that was empty till now and belonged to Alok. Samir sat diagonally opposite to him in the eighth row with his eyes shut.

'Last minute prayers,' Happy muttered to himself.

'Any plans for keeping Gupta's reputation alive, or screwing it up by flunking Surd?' Alok appeared from behind and gently hit Happy at the back of his head.

'What the fuck man? Where the hell have you been?' Happy said excitedly and looked up. The high decibel voice of Happy prompted others to look back along with Samir.

'Where were you for all these days?' Samir almost screamed.

'I was around only…shhhh lets talk after the exam gets over and best of luck guys,' Alok said with a finger on his lips and a smile on his face as he glided through the rows and descended on his chair.

They kept looking at him till the time the examination papers landed on their table.

'It was not as tough as we had expected,' Alok said devouring the *bun samosa.*

'Yeah, thank God, I should score above 80,' Samir said looking relaxed.

'I will pass as well, thanks to Vishal,' Happy said gulping down a cola sip and bringing his hands in an animated *namaskar* pose.

'But bugger, where the hell did you disappear for all these days?' Happy said raising his eyebrows.

'I was around Happy, here only, wanted to give you people an opportunity to pass the exams, otherwise all of us would have flunked,' Alok winked and took another bite.

'Bastard, there is no need to lie. I know you enough by now. I am sure that there is something else behind all this,' Happy said and they went quite for a while.

'Has that Ashu episode got to do something with all this?' Happy asked.

'What's all this, I know nothing about it,' Samir said.

Happy narrated the whole incident verbatim to him.

'So, you have decided to move on just because that idiot is after her?' Samir rebuked.

'There's nothing like that man and I was never into something very serious with her. I liked her and she liked me, we went around for a while and that was fun,' Alok said.

'But I thought you loved her,' Samir said.

Alok kept quiet.

'So now that some jerk came up to you and gave you his sob story, which may be a complete hogwash; you've decided to part ways with her and to top it you stop meeting your best friends,' Samir said.

'If we would have continued like this Samir, forget others but you definitely would have flunked,' Alok said.

'So you behaved like a big fucking hero by doing all this, couldn't you have done something better?' Samir asked.

'Whatever,' Alok replied. Samir shook his head in disbelief.

'What about Megha? Why didn't you meet or talk to her? Is it because of Ashu's same stupid story?' Samir asked.

'It's not a story, it's the truth Samir and I know it,' Alok said.

'So, where goes all your *gyaan* about you are never a loser until you quit trying,' Samir said trying to ape him.

'Now that you are quitting without trying aren't you a loser yourself?' Samir said and got up. Happy got up as well.

Alok followed and walked in between them. He wrapped his arms around their shoulders tightly.

'Not too bad, being a loser for the first time. Quite unlike you two,' he chuckled.

'Bastard,' Happy muttered.

He looked at both of them intently, 'Promise me that you will never tell her about the Ashu incident.' They looked into his eyes and couldn't refuse.

It was the last day of the board examinations at St. Thomas College. The boys were waiting for the clock to strike one and as the school bell tolled, groups of students ran out in the courtyard in frenzy, jumping and screaming with joy. The trio walked out of their classroom chatting excitedly about their plans for the ensuing holidays.

'I am going to be in Delhi for a while now. Oye *balle balle*,' Happy said happily and did a small jig.

'Yeah, GB road is going to be your permanent abode for all these days,' Samir said.

'Surd you will die fucker, don't do all this!' Alok said.

'*Oye*, no more restrictions till the holidays are over. I suggest you guys join me as well, my uncle has a huge bungalow in Patel Nagar,' Happy continued his blabber.

'Guys, I am going to Lucknow,' Alok said as they climbed on their bikes.

'For how many days would you be gone brother?' Happy said carelessly.

'Don't know, perhaps a long time, Dad is getting transferred,' Alok said.

'What the fuck? When did that happen?' Samir said and braked.

'Umm…just now…I mean a few days back,' Alok muttered.

Happy left his bike and it fell on the ground with a thud. He walked up to Alok's bike and held it by the handle.

'Now, this is taking it too far brother! First you disappear and don't tell us where you are; and then you reappear out of the blue to tell us that your family is moving out of Agra? I mean are we your friends or not?' he cried.

'Can't help it Happy, can I?' Alok asked.

'No, you can't but surely you could have told us about it earlier,' Samir said.

'So when are you leaving for Lucknow?' Happy said.

'Tomorrow,' Alok muttered.

'Fuck you,' Happy said and walked off.

They cycled in silence towards the school gate.

Megha stood there with her hands folded on the chest and looking beautiful in the St. Marks school dress. She had large almond shaped brown eyes that in the normal course flashed sparks of mischief, but they lay sad and dried up today. Her long flowing hair that felt like the spring breeze when they fell on his skin were pulled back and hung in silence. The pink lips that danced with a smile whenever he made a wise-crack were colorless and dry.

Alok slowed down his cycle and stopped it next to her.

'Hi,' he said.

'Hi,' she murmured with a dead pan expression.

'How did the exams go?' he asked.

'Good. What about you?' she asked.

'Fine,' he said.

'Where were you Alok?' she asked and a tiny stream of water trickled down from her left eye.

Alok turned back to look at Happy and Samir. A morbid looking Happy and Samir glanced back and cycled ahead, leaving both of them alone at the school gate.

'I was around. Just getting back to studies all this while,' he said.

'You didn't even bother to tell me or just call me up once? Just like that? Don't you think that I care?' she said and another stream of tears traversed on her pink cheek.

'Do you love me?' she said. Alok didn't reply.

'So you don't. But you said that you did the other day,' she said.

'We are hardly out of school Megha; it's really very early for us to think about all this,' he said.

'Hmmm…who is asking you to marry me Alok?' she waited.

He remained quiet for a few minutes and then spoke.

'I am moving to Lucknow, my dad is getting transferred there.'

Megha's face turned white and the tiny streams of water turned wilder and thicker.

'What about us Alok?' she sobbed.

'We will stay in touch, we'll be friends. I would be visiting Agra often.'

'What about us?' she asked again. He kept silent, didn't speak.

After a few minutes she pulled out her handkerchief and wiped her face. She looked at him with red eyes that waited for an answer that never came.

She turned around and walked back in the other direction. Alok's eyes kept following the girl he had loved, and let go, till the time they turned moist and blurred his vision.

Alok rested his chin on the lowermost iron bar of the third class window in the Awadh Assam Express. It was late in the night and the train inhabitants waited for the machine to pull away from the station and run towards their destination as soon as possible. Sandhya was busy laying the blue bed-sheet on the lower berth while his father adjusted their four large VIP suitcases under the seats.

'Can't you help us?' he asked Alok; looking irritated.

'Yeah, tell me what needs to be done?' Alok said with his eye on the drab suitcases and his heart god knows where.

'Forget it Alok,' his father said and got back to his task furiously.

'Your friends are here!' his mother said looking out of the window.

He craned his neck and caught a glimpse of Happy, Samir and Megha on the platform.

He jumped from his seat and came out of the train.

'Why are you going brother? It would all be so dull without you. I will miss you,' Happy said as he hugged him.

'Sorry about yesterday Alok, but I was really psyched out with you going away,' Samir said as he hugged him as well.

'I am not too far from Agra guys and we are friends. Distances won't be a hurdle, if we don't want them to be,' he said.

'I hope you will be here at least once a month,' Happy said.

Alok nodded.

'Aren't your parents complaining? This is late,' Alok said looking at Megha.

Her eyes had gone redder and her face paler than yesterday.

'Don't bother,' she said and looked at Happy and Samir. They excused themselves and dispersed with the pretext of drinking water.

'When are you coming back Alok?' she asked.

'Don't know,' he said.

'What do you mean Alok? Was all of this a joke or some kind of your boy gang fun?' she asked raising her voice. It got immersed within a million other voices on the platform.

'No,' he said.

'Then?' she asked.

'I love you Alok and here you are going away without saying anything. What do I do?' her tear glands started breathing again.

The engine whistled and the train got enveloped in a flurry of frantic activities on the platform.

'I need to go, the train is moving now,' Alok said desperately trying not to look at her.

'You need to give me an answer,' she said firmly. Happy and Samir closed on to them from a distance.

'I am sorry for all this Megha but I can't keep the promises I made to you,' Alok said and turned his face towards the train that had started trudging.

'What about our love?' she shouted.

'It was the best thing to have happened; but I was a loser I guess,' he turned around and shouted back.

Alok clasped the iron bar of the third floor compartment and pulled his body on to the staircase to look back at the platform.

He could see wide stretched palms of Happy and Samir, waving with morose facial expressions. But his eyes searched for Megha.

She had moved forward and walked swiftly alongside the moving train, 'Will you come back?' she shouted.

He was too numb to react. He just raised his hand to wipe away the tears that crowded his face to look at her for the last time. Megha's beautiful face, anguished, panicked, sad and longing for him. He stared at her in silence till his eyes lost the view of her face.

It was the last time that they saw each other.

PART 2: MANDIRA

27th June, 2011: New Delhi, India

'You suck man. Why can't we ever stick to our deadlines Srini?' Mandira Dutta raised her hands in exasperation and looked at the poor 25 year old something Brand Manager.

'Mandira, we got this brief on the business plan presentation at 10PM, a day before! Don't you think that the deadline is a bit too tight?' Srini attempted to retort.

'Don't give me that bull Srini! Aren't you supposed to deal with such deadlines all your life? Don't forget that you belong to an A rated Indian B School!' Mandira asked raising her tired eyebrows.

'Yeah, but this is a Business Plan for the next year and not some regular presentation that the marketing factory in The Uni- Cola Company churns out each day,' Srini replied.

'I would recommend that you better spend this time in wrapping up this presentation, rather than arguing with me. I need it in an hour; and I don't have all the time in this world.'

'I will get this done by tomorrow morning Mandira,' Srini fumbled.

'Not tomorrow morning but tonight, in an hour sir,' she mocked at him,' I need to go through this piece completely before presenting it to Arvind and his boss tomorrow. Don't you know it?'

'I will try my best Mandira,' he said as he picked up his laptop from her desk.

'You know what Srini, that's precisely the difference between an Indian versus an American B School passout. You guys out here are just plain lazy,' Mandira said irritatingly.

Srini nodded nervously in affirmation not fully comprehending what her boss had just muttered.

'So, get going and don't waste your time here Srini, please!' she said hurriedly.

The wave of raw sarcasm and insult overwhelmed him as he hurried towards the exit.

'Ok, I will try and finish this as soon as possible,' he said as he grabbed the handle of the glass door.

'One hour,' Mandira announced and lit up a cigarette as she saw Srini exiting out of the door.

Mandira squashed the butt of her ninth cigarette of the day in the ashtray below and looked at the table-clock. It was close to 9PM and the presentation was far from over. She had to go through it in detail, rehearse it and put in her personal notes. It had to be perfect, no less and no more. Anything that Mandira did; needed to be perfect. No tolerance for screw-ups at all.

She shut her laptop and put it inside her designer laptop bag that had a barechested Jim Morrison on it, and exited her cabin.

'Srini, next one hour and it needs to be in my inbox,' she said tapping the wall of his work station on her way out of the office.

Srini nodded nervously again in affirmation, 'Ok Mandira.'

'Hope the presentation is good this time or else you have another night-out in waiting,' she said while walking away from the hapless brand manager.

She unlocked the door and turned on the knob to enter her plush three bed-room apartment in New Friends Colony. The house was enveloped in complete darkness before Mandira switched on the electricity in the living room to bring it alive. There was a gentle knock at the door.

'Keep it on the table next to the door; and come slightly early in the morning,' she shouted.

Raghu, her driver kept the laptop bag on the table and walked out of the door. She followed him to lock the door, and while walking back, glanced at the table that had a few envelopes kept on it. She picked them up as she walked into the kitchen and opened the door of her microwave. It had some pasta and baked vegetables.

'Good, this Kalpana babe is picking up fast,' she muttered to herself.

Kalpana was her new cooking maid and under Mandira's strict surveillance had graduated from cooking mutter-paneer to a healthy diet of macaroni and pasta.

She opted for a quick shower before settling down with the presentation and entered the washroom. Comfortably clad in a Ed Hardy loose T-Shirt and track pants she looked at herself in the mirror, while applying the Vitamin C boosted Body Shop moisturizer on her face. She looked good, despite being 38, despite being the mother of an eight- year- old and despite being divorced at 34. The color of her hair was still black apart from an odd strand of white. The skin still flawless, radiant and smooth despite a super hectic schedule coupled with domestic and international travel. In one word she was still sexy enough.

She picked up the hairbrush and pulled her shoulder length hair back, to leave them open.

After coming back from the US, she had joined The UniCola Company as a management trainee to become the Marketing Director in a short span of nine years. Not bad at all; considering that TUCC (The Uni- Cola Company) was the global beverage leader and anybody would give his or her right arm to work there, considering that the male female ratio in the company was 4:1 and considering that within Indian companies, a majority of women still managed functions like human resources, administration, IT etc.

Mandira knew that she was a potent combination of toughness, aggressiveness and cockiness, a lethal cocktail. If anything needs to get fixed, just get Mandira and she'll get it done- Arvind her boss and the Indian CEO of TUCC always said in meetings. It always made others in the room squirm with jealously and Mandira even more determined, confident and forceful. She didn't care about this side of her's, in-fact, she loved it. Men within the company felt intimidated and women never dared to cross her path making her professional ride smooth till now.

She walked out of the bedroom and picked up her cell-phone to dial Srini's number.

'Mandira, I am just sending it...sending it,' he fumbled nervously.

'Ten minutes Srini... Ok...and no more,' she said and disconnected. She threw the Blackberry carelessly on the couch and picked up the television remote. She flicked through the channels to freeze on 'The American Idol' and descended on her lounge cum massage chair. As she stretched her hand sideways to keep the remote, it caressed the envelopes that she had kept on the couch. With her eyes on the television she glanced through them. Blackberry bills, electricity bills, American Express card bills and a courier addressed to her. She sized up the envelope and tore it from one side to take the letter out. Still not fully attentive, she read the first line.

Dear M, it read, and Mandira's heart palpitated. It was him, it could only be him. No one else called her by that name.

Dear M

Did I surprise you with this letter? It has been eighteen long years since the time I saw you last at the Airport in Lucknow. I know that now you have a flourishing career in TUCC, the global soft drink giant as the Marketing Director of the world's top brand. Wow! That's what you always wanted, to be at the top, wherever you are, wherever you go. I thought Samarth was a good guy from whatever I had heard of him but I guess you took the right decision. You have always taken the right decisions M. Always.

How is Ankit doing? I am aware that he's at Scindia in Gwalior. It's a great place to be when you are growing up. It turns you into a man. I am sure he would grow up to be as rocking as you are, M.

Do you remember 'Leaving on a jet plane', the song? The last song that we sang together in that auditorium, just before you left for US, in my concert. It still gives me goose-bumps.

I stay in this peaceful yet picturesque hill station called Mussoorie now. I teach music in this beautiful town. The reason of writing this letter to you is that I have something in my possession that belongs to you. It has been with me for last so many years M, but now I can't keep it with me anymore. I want you to come and take it from me before it's too late.

I will wait for you on 28th June at the Dehradun airport. Mussoorie is about two hours away from the airport and I would recommend that you be in Dehradun by 4PM so that we can get into the town by the evening. Take care and see you M.

Yours

Alok
House Number 403
Off Mall Road
Near Government School
Mussoorie.

Mandira read the letter twice and then folded it to keep it inside the envelope. The Blackberry beeped. It was Srini.

'Sent it Mandira, please have a look. I am waiting in the office for a feedback,' the text said.

She read the message and kept the phone aside and rushed inside her bedroom. She pulled out the old suitcase from the loft and placed it on the bed. It was light, as it only carried her old photographs and letters from her dad while she was away in US. She rummaged through a lot of them; Ankit's first birthday, the day that he was born, the first time he walked, the snaps of her engagement with Samarth and the last photograph that they had clicked together before her divorce, when they went to Bangkok for a vacation. It had Samarth pulling her towards him while she tried desperately to hold on to the last piece of pizza that she wanted to eat. She loved pizza, more than men; and sometimes it made a better choice.

Mandira loved Samarth till the time he lost his track. She would have pardoned him if he had multiple relationships with women. She would have given him a chance. Happens! In our fast paced metro lives it happens! But those relationships were not with women; Samarth had multiple men in his life!

She caught him red handed making out with a male colleague one day in their own house and she asked him to leave the place and her life. He pleaded with her to take him back but she gave him alimony in return. The grant was the same house that was on her name and where she had caught him cheating on her, Mandira gave it away along with enough cash. He went richer by some million bucks and she went back home with Ankit. The two of them dealt with their lives in their own unique way.

She was searching hard, looking at the stack of photographs till it came. She held the photograph in her hand. Stuck sideways with him they looked inseparable. M and Alok were singing on the mike together, 'I am leaving on a jet plane.' They sang close, inebriated, inseparable.

The memory rushed back like a blizzard.

Akash Verma # 89

September 1989: Lucknow, India

'How does one gets to the Astronomy Department?' Alok asked the *gutka* chewing guard relaxing in the cemented booth at the entrance of Lucknow University gate.

The guard didn't look happy to be bothered and looked at him irritatingly as if he had asked him his wife's cup size. For a few moments he kept looking at Alok's face and then pointed his finger towards the sky.

'But where is that?' Alok asked again.

The guard spitted red *gutka* juice on one side and opened his mouth with great difficulty.

'Go straight and then take a right till you hit the oldest looking building, and that is the Physics and Astronomy department in the University,' he said and slouched on the chair again.

It was his first day at college after four months of their arrival in Lucknow. He liked Lucknow; it was bigger, cleaner and better behaved. But he missed his friends all the time and Megha the most. The board results were out in a couple of months and Alok did brilliantly and so did Samir. Happy had just managed to scrape through, all thanks to Vishal. Both Samir and Megha had taken admissions in St John's College. And so did Ashu. Happy Singh had managed a seat in Agra College, a haven for housing the discarded bad elements of the town. Every student who wanted to enter the student politics or be a local hooligan had to be in Agra College. Megha kept inquiring about him from Samir every now and then, asking questions, without getting any answers.

He entered the dilapidated building scrutinizing the environment. One could easily identify the first year students amongst the lot. They looked tentative and took smaller steps versus the experienced ones from the university who were accustomed to the almameter and marched confidently alone, and in groups to their destinations.

'Could you direct me to the Astronomy department please?' Alok asked a short, studious looking guy who was engrossed in the notice board as if it displayed a Playboy centre-spread. The guy took a few seconds to react, 'Are you asking me?'

'Yeah, could you direct me to the Astronomy department?' Alok asked again.

'First year?' he asked.

'Yeah,' Alok said looking around.

'Day scholar?' he asked again.

Alok nodded.

'Come. Let's walk; I am also looking for Astronomy department. Harish Chandra Tiwari and you?' he said stretching out his hand at a baffled looking Alok.

'Alok Mathur,' he said as he shook it.

'Which school did you go to?' he asked.

'I am not from Lucknow, we have just got transferred here from Agra,' Alok replied.

'Oh, that sounds familiar! Even I don't belong here, I am from Dehradun as well,' he said. Harish had a mischievous face with a perpetual smile.

The rickety staircase took them to the third floor where they entered a small room that could take not more than twenty students.

'This is small, Astronomy does not seem to be popular here,' Alok said as he settled down.

'Who would want to study Astronomy? People come here either to relax or use this as a parking bay while they prepare for engineering or MBA,' he said.

'Which of these two reasons are you here for?' he asked Alok.

'None, I am here for none,' Alok said looking around.

'Then why have you opted for this? There aren't going to be girls here either,' he asked.

'No choice! Didn't like Chemistry, and thought I would get to learn something new atleast,' Alok said.

'So, what do you like?' Harish asked.

'Music,' Alok said. Harish seemed a bit surprised with this answer.

The head of the faculty Dr. P.M Saxena took the first sermon of their college life that ended in ninety minutes.

'All that this guy crapped for two hours is how Astronomy is the mother of all sciences, bloody self righteous prick,' Harish said, aggravated.

'Leave it boss! He gets an audience like us just once a year, and that also a handful of students, what else do you expect from the poor guy?' Alok said and rested his back on the pale yellow pillar on the groundfloor. They were sitting on the staircase of the astronomy department at the ground –floor. The next class was about to start in a couple of hours.

'Hey, you the one with those fancy shoes,' a hoarse voice sprang from behind. A group of fresher's sitting next to them turned back to stand up meekly.

'I am talking to you idiot!' the voice came closer and Alok felt someone grip him tightly by the shoulder.

They turned around to find a motley group of students staring at them. A couple of them looked similar to their ilk, but a majority of them complete ruffians; dressed in a *kurta* and jeans or a *kurta* with pajamas, they chewed *gutka* furiously; with the tip of their lips colored red as it engaged in a continuous foreplay with *panmasala.*

'Don't you know how do you behave with the seniors? Get up!' the leader of the pack, a heavy built guy with thick moustaches barked.

Harish got Alok to get up by staring at him hard enough.

'Don't you guys know how to greet seniors?' the leader roared again.

'Good morning sir,' a chorus of voices sprang out from scared throats.

'You there! Don't you have a tongue that can speak?' the leader asked Alok.

'Good morning sir,' Alok said.

'Hmm…what's your name and what course?' he asked.

'Alok…Astronomy,' he said.

'Bastard is here to become an astronaut…he wants to go to the moon,' he laughed to look at the fresher's who smiled nervously.

'And why are you wearing these fashionable shoes? Are you here to study or is this a fashion show?' he asked coming closer to Alok and stepping on to his ankle height Nike.

Alok pulled his foot back quietly.

'What's wrong with these shoes sir?' he asked.

'Are you asking me a question? Are you asking Vinay Shukla a question?' he hissed.

'Do you even know who Vinay *Dada* is?' one of his side-kicks commented excitedly.

'Is he your elder brother because that's what *Dada* means?' Alok said plainly.

'Bloody asshole, don't try to act smart with us. *Gaand me danda daal denge*,' Vinay said.

The fresher's faces surrounding them had started turning pale.

'Give me your shoes,' Vinay roared.

Alok quietly removed his shoes and placed it in front of them.

'Give me your handkerchief,' Vinay commanded.

Alok took it out from the back-pocket of his jeans and handed it over to him.

Vinay used his handkerchief to pick up the shoes by its laces. He gestured his gang to wait there while he walked towards the bushes on the side. A multitude of eyes followed him while a few of them looked at Alok whose face had minimal expressions. Vinay, reaching closer to the bushes placed the shoes in front of him on the ground. He turned around to give a cold stare to everyone around and then he unzipped himself. He was peeing in Alok's Nike's in front of the entire crowd. The girls who stood there sighed and turned their faces away. The men looked at Vinay in disbelief. After unloading himself inside the shoes; he picked up Alok's shoes with his handkerchief and held them by the laces as he walked back. The crowd was speechless. Vinay placed the shoes in front of him on the ground.

'Now, wear them,' he commanded.

The environment went standstill; forget the fresher's but even his own gang did not utter a word. Harish looked completely shaken as if in a trance.

'Since you seem to like them so much sir; I give them to you, in charity,' Alok said looking into his eyes. Vinay was taken aback by this unexpected answer. The students standing around them glanced at each other, a couple of them smiled. Alok took off his socks, threw them on the ground and turned around to walk away.

'Are you trying to mock us hero? Make fun of us? Just wait there,' Vinay snapped and lunged forward.

Suddenly a tall, curly haired guy blocked his path and came in between him and a walking Alok.

'*Arrayy* hang on Vinay bhai, not on the first day! Not today' he said while holding on to Vinay by the waist.

'No Baba, this fresher has insulted me in front of everyone, I can't let him go. Just leave me and I will teach this bastard a lesson,' he shouted with a pent up anger and struggled to break free from Baba's grip.

'No Vinay, not at all! The elections are just around the corner and what sort of an impression are we creating in front of these fresher's? Just think about it?' he said passionately as he held on to the burly Vinay.

'Baba's right Vinay bhai, let him go. We'll sort this guy out sometime later,' one of his side-kicks said.

Vinay struggled with his grip for a few moments and eventually gave away to the wishes of Baba and his gang.

He stared at Alok, 'I am leaving today; but we'll meet soon and you will regret that day fucker. Be very watchful, the countdown starts today,' he said as they left.

'Didn't you feel scared?' Harish asked after they had left.

'Of whom? That guy?' Alok said.

Harish shook his head in affirmation.

'No way Harish! He was a weakling. Ask him to do that alone without his gang and he would be shitting bricks. But I lost my shoes and that is the sad part,' he said.

'You can't walk barefoot for the entire day! Let's go to Mahangar closeby and buy something for you to wear,' Harish offered.

'Yeah I guess so,' Alok replied.

'You can get a pair of *Kolhapuris* from my room as well,' someone spoke from behind.

They turned around to find the same guy who had mediated in the altercation called "Baba" standing there and talking to them. He inched closer and slapped Alok by the shoulder.

'That was brave by the way! No fresher messes up easily with seniors in this University. But now that you have; there is a reputation to protect,' he said smiling.

'I will do that; but first I need to protect my reputation of not being a beggar. I need a pair of shoes or something to wear urgently,' Alok said pointing at his bare feet.

'Oh yes, let's go to my room and I shall help you resurrect that at least,' he said as they chuckled.

'What's your name?' Harish asked.

'Sarvesh Singh,' he replied.

'But everyone calls me Baba, don't know why.' he said and guffawed.

'Do they fit you?' Baba said sipping tap water from an old looking Bisleri bottle in Room No. 55 at Tilak Hostel. The room was big enough to have space for two single beds a study desk and a chair alongwith a huge assortment of empty beer and cheap whisky bottles.

'Yeah, they are fine, should we get going now? The next class is at 2PM,' Alok asked as he tried Baba's Kolhapuris.

'This place looks more like a pub than a hostel room Baba,' he spoke again.

'Your hostel room number is 55. Let's call it Pub 55 Baba, you can get in any time that you like but you can't get out of here, how is that?' Alok chuckled.

'Let's have a drink before we leave,' Baba said pulling out a bottle of gin from under the bed.

'It's not even 12 and I am not too much into hard stuff,' Alok said looking at his watch.

'Now that you have inaugurated Pub 55, you get the first peg. For *Shubh Mahurat* sake!' Baba said pressing his shoulder.

'Ok sir, let's do that for good luck,' Alok said. Harish looked bewildered.

'Cheers to our first drink in Pub 55!' Baba said and did a little awkward jig after crinkling glasses with Alok .

Alok took a swig and then settled down on the chair. Harish sat next to Baba on the bed.

'So, do you like Lucknow?' he asked. Alok shook his head in a yes. Baba looked at Harish who reciprocated Alok's gesture and then he made another drink for himself.

'The university is quite unlike the peaceful town. In three words: Aggressive, Uncouth and Violent. The politics is slowly turning this place from bad to worse. Most of the student community here is from the eastern belt of UP who have landed up here to do everything except studies. From politics to bloody *goondagardi,* from a dagger to an AK 47, you can find everything right here,' Baba said.

'That guy Vinay who had a scrap with you a while ago, will be running for the general secretary post this year,' he added.

'So, what's his agenda in becoming the general secretary?' Harish asked innocently.

'Entering state politics, the key to enter the refuge of money, power and fame,' Baba replied.

'All four mainstream parties are active in the state and right here in the university. Lok Satta, Bharitaya Samaj Party, Jan Samaj and Lok Dal,' he added with an "I know it all" look on his face.

Lok Satta was the traditional housekeeper of Indian politics, a one hundred and fifty year old party run under a dynastic rule, Bharatiya Samaj Party was the right wing traditional Hindu outfit that had re-entered the Indian political arena through a recently discovered disputable issue of constructing the Ram Temple over a mosque in Ayodhya, Jan Samaj was essentially a UP fronted party for socially backward classes and minority communities that thrived in a state that housed them in the largest numbers in the country and lastly Lok Dal the quintessential national opposition with a group of leaders with mixed agenda and vested interests.

'And why does Vinay and team look up to you?' Alok's voice slurred a bit.

'Gaja Raj Gope, he is a distant relative and running for the President's post in the elections; also from Gonda, they fear him,' Baba said.

'Gope, well that's a strange sounding surname! So, do you support him?' Alok asked.

'Nick name! It's been given to him by his followers. I support him as a family yes, but not for the party,' Baba said.

'He is a BSP candidate, the Hindu right wing,' he said thoughtfully.

'Hmmm...do we have an English music band in here?' Alok asked as he polished off the last sip.

'As in a *Raak Band?*' Baba pronounced the word in the typical eastern Uttar Pradesh lingo.

'Yeah,' Alok said plainly looking at his twisted face.

'They practice in the Commerce Hall after five. I am not sure what do they do except for beating drums, swaying their heads like mad men and singing in English that goes over our heads,' Baba said standing in front of the Commerce Block.

'But they do get a lot of girls when they perform at the end of our college festivals. *Saali loundiyan marti hain in sab pe(Bloody girls out here can die for them)*,' Baba added and winked as they took rapid steps towards the hall.

Alok could hear the rhythmic movement of the drum beats that started getting stronger as he inched forward. He raced ahead with charged steps, the effect of the alcohol vanishing with every advancing footstep, the heart pounding with excitement and as he entered the hall through the iron shutter, he could hear it loud and clear. Road House Blues blared at him on the face; much stronger, more rehearsed, raw energy of what he heard made him forget the choreographed orchestra of St. Thomas in a jiffy. He wanted to be a part of it there and then.

They stopped when they saw a group of three men entering the hall. The first one, a tall lanky fellow with hair falling on the forehead, golden brown skin, athletic and a face flushed with excitement. He was followed by the other two, a curly haired *neta* looking fella looking curious gazing around and the third one, a shorter scrawny looking guy who looked startled as if he had just seen some Playboy bunnies on the ramp.

'Were you guys practicing?' Alok asked nervously as he approached closer.

'No, flying kites,' the dark skinned drummer replied carelessly.

Alok sniggered.

'Let's go sandy? I don't have much time today,' the lead guitarist shouted adjusting the tuning key.

'*Saale chinky tere paas kabhi practice ka time hota hai*?' Sandy replied and rolled the stick to fall gently on the cymbal.

'Chinky is newly married, can't you see sandy? He has so much to do after getting back home,' the thin guy on the keyboards muttered looking engrossed on the machine.

'Yeah, and we *chutiyas* have nothing to do except drinking

daaru,' the bony guy with thick moustaches on the Bass guitar shouted.

'Should we do Stairway to Heaven now?' Sandy shouted. The chinky nodded. He appeared to be an inhabitant from a North Eastern state or Nepal. Alok along with Baba and Harish had settled in close to where the band practiced. Alok looked at them with admiration that seemed to be crawling out of his eyes. Baba looked indifferent while Harish still appeared startled enough.

'Let's go Thoku,' Sandy said and looked at the Bass guitarist, as he hit the pedal on the Bass drum and rolled the stick on the cymbal to ignite the magic. The *chinky* who was being chided a while back took the composition in his hand, as he effortlessly immersed in the melody on the strings of his guitar. They moved through the song in complete harmony and Alok had goose bumps as he heard the band live; so close bursting with rare energy. He was in a daze by the time they finished the song and couldn't stop his hands from coming together and clapping.

'Awesome,' he exclaimed.

Thoku the guy on the Bass glanced at him with a '*you don't have to tell us that we are the superstars*' look. The rest of the gang did not even bother to do that and went on with their practice oblivious of the outsider's presence.

'Should we leave now Bubul Da?' Sandy on the drums asked the keyboard player who seemed to be fiddling with the keys even after their session had ended. Sandy looked like the guy incharge of the band. Bubul gave him a comforting nod.

Bubul raised his eyebrows which pushed the creases on his forehead, 'Where is this Khanna? He has been missing since last three sessions.'

'Would be lying in between the two legs of some chick,' Thoku said carelessly.

'All that Khanna does; is to land up at the practice two days before the concert and that's it,' he said complainingly.

'And don't you recall the last gig at MB Club; he was so drunk that he could barely sing? I had to camouflage all of it under the guitar along with supporting vocals from you guys,' *Chinky* said packing his guitar in the case.

'Guys it's fine, I will call him up tonight,' Sandy said as he hushed them up realizing that strangers were being privy to their grubby little secrets.

'Can I practice with you guys sometime?' Alok asked hesitatingly.

'Who are you?' Thoku asked in a blunted tone.

'Umm…Alok Mathur,' he replied.

'What do you do?' Chinky asked picking up the guitar case and slinging it across his shoulder.

'I sing. I am a vocalist,' Alok said confidently. Baba and Harish looked at his face.

'No, we don't need a vocalist, we do have one,' Sandy said dismantling his drum kit.

'Maybe you can try me as well, I love your entire play list, I know all of them,' he said.

'No! Thanks, but not now buddy. We will come back to you if we need one in future,' Sandy replied coldly and got back to his task. The *Chinky* left and the others got absorbed in packing their kits leaving the three of them unwanted.

'Let's go,' Alok said and turned back slowly. Baba and Harish followed him

'I can really do a good job with them,' Alok said thoughtfully

'Can you really sing in English? Like those guys there?' Baba asked looking circumspect and glanced at Harish who walked with him. Alok nodded.

They came out of the Commerce Block where the *Chinky* was trying to kick start his Yezdi.

'What's your name buddy?' Alok yelled. The *Chinky* looked back at Alok and hesitated to reply for a couple of seconds.

'*Chhotu*,' he said.

'See you soon friend,' Alok said and walked ahead with the other too.

'What kind of names do these guys have? *Thoku, Chhotu, Bubul, Sandy*? What were their parents thinking while naming these kids?' Harish said.

'They are nicknames Harish, not the real ones given by their parents,' Alok said and smiled.

'*Arrayy Bhaiyya,* but it's still hard to believe that you can sing all these *raak* songs,' Baba added as they walked towards the University gate.

The first six months passed like a flash at the Lucknow University. With every passing day their bond became thicker and the friend circle wider. They were now found more in college canteens rather than the classrooms and their extra study sessions took place in Pub No.55 a.k.a Baba's hostel room and movie theatres of Lucknow. The phone calls to Samir had dwindled completely over last four months till today when he received a letter from him embraced within a white envelope. It read:

Dear Alok,

Hope you are doing well and it seems that you have forgotten us completely. Not even a trunk-call and not even a letter. How are your studies at the University? Made new friends? Must have! *Yaar,* there's a bad news Alok! Happy Singh died! The Surd, I am told, committed suicide. I know you would get shocked after hearing this, brother, but even I did not have the faintest of the idea.

Alok choked and it seemed that his throbbing heart would tear his chest and burst out. He stretched his eyes to prevent tears from gushing out but they did, like a flood blurring out his view. He wanted to read further:

I think something unnatural happened. No one is spelling out the truth and everyone is trying to keep it under the wraps, especially Happy's family. They are saying that he was facing some family trauma and it was the reason behind the suicide. I don't believe this; we all know Happy and what kind of an insensitive bugger he was. Wasn't he? He would blow away that family trauma with his fart. There is also a rumor that has been going around; that he was infected with an incurable disease. I think it's called AIDS and it is spread through monkeys. I don't know much about this and the monkeys, but I am told that you get it from careless sex with bad women. I am not sure but I am told that Happy had a lot of sex with whores. Happy's family hid it from the world for over a month and it was only exposed later after the news got out. As it is after you had left we hardly met. We went to different colleges and knowing Happy he would have rarely gone to attend classes. The last time that we had met was at the Chinese Van. Our Van! Remember? We talked a lot about us as we revisited our old times.

I see Megha sometimes in the college corridors, but now she has stopped asking about you. I guess she has got tired of just asking questions and getting no answers. I have caught her smiling more often; guess she is getting back to normalcy. We sat at the Van the last time for an hour before he died. I was eating soup and Happy was drinking a beer and eating chowmein. I clearly recall what he said when we were parting ways. '*Oye,* Samir the next time we meet here, it has to be with Alok.' The Surd had guffawed then in his trademark stupid style. I miss him and I am sure that you would do that more than me. He was always closer to you than I was.

Alok, finally I have started to open my mouth more often. Though I had got a call from a good engineering college in Nagpur, I have decided to pursue English Literature from St. Stephen's in Delhi. There were huge arguments with parents but in the end I managed to persuade them. It's my life after all. I would be leaving shortly; perhaps by the time that you would be reading this letter. I will be in touch and will send you my new college address. I owe this to you Alok and you know that my friend.

Do write to me, I will look forward to your letter. Whenever you are there in Agra do try and visit Happy's house, the Chinese Van, St.Thomas School, Sikandra and all our other hangouts. The Surd would feel better.

Your friend
Samir

Alok folded the letter neatly and put it inside the envelope when the water from his eyes fell on the white paper and formed a transparent lump that receded within seconds. He felt an unbearable pain in the head, the veins around it had started throbbing at a ridiculous pace. Fresh tears appeared and coupled with nervous sweat on his body; they broke free. He could hardly put his head on the mattress and howl before blacking out on the bed.

Alok opened his eyes to the worried looking face of his mother and Dr. Mishra; their recently acquired family neighborhood physician who looked at him intently.

'What happened *beta*? You seemed to have lost your consciousness; I had become so worried,'

Sandhya said lovingly, stroking his hair.

'I don't know Mom, I thought that I had overslept,' Alok replied softly unsure of telling her about Happy's suicide.

'Even I thought so, and after a couple of hours when you did not get up inspite of trying hard, is when I called up Mishrajee,' she said.

'What happened to you Alok? Very stressed? Too much to study?' the doctor asked.

'No, nothing like that. I don't know what happened?' he said while getting up.

'We need to be careful *Bhabiji*, this generation of today; they really do not pay heed to their health and then pay a price later. I think Alok is stressed and he needs to completely relax for a couple of days. I have also written a couple of medicines that he should take regularly,' the doctor said getting up.

'Where is Mathur *Sahab*?' he asked.

'He has gone on an official tour to Allahabad,' she said. The doctor nodded and looked affectionately at Alok before leaving. Sandhya heaved a sigh of relief and shut the door.

'I am leaving *Ma*,' Alok said surfacing out of the washroom door.

'What's wrong with you Alok? Didn't you hear what the doctor said?' Sandhya said as she organized Alok's bed.

'I don't feel like sitting inside *Ma*. It's suffocating and I want to get out,' he said and walked towards the main door.

'*Beta*, your father isn't going to be here tonight and it's already seven. Don't you think you should relax rather than roaming out?' she asked.

'I will go and get the medicines, will be back soon. This is nothing *Ma* just some freaked out chance,' Alok said walking out as Sandhya looked at him.

He was at Pub No.55 in twenty minutes. A handful of muffled voices greeted him as he knocked on the wooden door of Baba's room.

'The door is open, come right in,' Baba's bass heavy voice boomed from inside.

'*Arrayy Alok bhai*,' Baba looked delighted to see the new visitor. There were three others besides him sprawled on the bed and engaged in a common vocation, drinking. He got up to hug Alok and offered him the only chair in the room to sit. Over the last few months in Lucknow, Alok had discovered two standard practices that Lucknowites loved to follow a) a penchant for hugging each other and shaking hands whenever they met, even if it was for the tenth time in a day b) addressing each other with respect even if they had met to kill each other; the mother and father expletives were preceded with a much formal *aapki maa ki xxx* rather than an informal abuse practiced everywhere else in the country *teri maa ki*.

By then a glass filled with whisky had already landed in front of him. The other three in the room looked at Alok with awe due to the unwanted attention that Baba had showered on the stranger. It did not take long for Baba to sense that that Alok was not his normal self.

'Let's step out for a while, I need to buy some *Gutka,'* Baba said getting up and signaling Alok to come along. He did not look at the other three.

They came down from the staircase and walked on the narrow road linking the hostel with the university. It had turned pitch dark and an odd streetlight flickered on that road to cause an occasional flash in the patches of darkness. They walked silently for a few minutes.

'What happened *bhai*? All well?' he asked. Alok did not reply and they ended up walking for a few more minutes to reach the dried up fountain near the library. The place was dimly lit and an odd student would pass from there before heading in a different direction.

'Let's sit here for a while.' Baba gestured as they sat down on the thick cemented boundary of the fountain.

'Happy Singh died, the Surd committed suicide,' he blurted out and looked on the other side to hide his tears.

'Who was Happy?' Baba replied after a few minutes as he emptied a *gutka* packet in his mouth.

Alok turned his gaze towards Baba and started talking about Happy Singh, his mad, moody, daring, emotional and horny friend whom he loved so much. Their story and anecdotes would have gone for the entire night if Baba had not opened his mouth to spit out the *gutka* and disturbed the flow of Alok's conversation. Alok realized that he was overdoing it, hence recoiled and succumbed back into silence.

They kept quiet for a few moments as Baba got rid of the *Gutka* leftovers by spitting it out 3-4 times.

'Why do you eat this damn thing? It's not good.' Alok said trying to change the conversation. Baba did not seem to hear him.

'Kick! *Bhai*! Kick' he replied after a moment.

'Life is constant; only our body perishes but the soul never dies. The soul is like a train moving continuously from one station to the other. The train stops at a station signaling the end of a journey but then starts after a while towards a new journey. Similarly when one dies, the soul just takes a break to start a new journey with new relationships, acquaintances, friends, enemies. Like a train that starts again from a new destination with new passengers,' Baba said intently.

'But not all passengers get down at a station; you do have a lot of people who continue their journey to different stations and some even till the last destination,' Alok asked.

'Hmm…nice. Well, I would equate this with our *Karma*. When the soul starts a new journey, what remains from the past is the *Karma* that can either be good or bad. So, these people who continue their journey with the train or the soul is akin to our *Karma* and it takes a few lifetimes or a few stations to get rid of our bad *Karma*. It's best if we only have only good *Karma* riding with us on our never ending journey, making it more enjoyable,' he added.

'That was solid Baba, what a cool philosophical thought,' Alok said feeling a bit lighter.

'A few centuries old Egyptian and Buddhist theories, I just made them sound a little simpler, he said with a broad and confident smile.

'That's why across religions and philosophies one thought that is common, is about good *Karma*, I guess one should ultimately work in accumulating that,' he added.

'Yeah… I guess you are right. Baba, you speak so well why don't you write?' Alok asked.

'I will start writing only after you start singing *raak music*, Alok Bhai,' Baba guffawed.

They looked at each other and shook hands warmly.

'*Chal pub mein daaru peete hain*!' Baba said and pulled Alok by the shoulder as they walked towards the hostel.

He stood in front of the thick iron gates of Ravindralaya, near the Lucknow Railway Station. In about ten minutes he could see them hopping out of a black and yellow colored pig shaped metal carcass popularly called "*Suaar*" in local student lingo and a "Tempo" by others.

'Has the entry started?' Baba said as he walked towards Alok .

Ravindralaya to a Lucknowite was akin to what a Prithvi Theatre meant to a Mumbaikar or the Siri-fort auditorium to an average Delhiite. It was a centre for pure artistry, display and admiration of pure talent; from theatre to poetry and from an Urdu *mushaira* to a rock show. The auditorium had also housed Bollywood superstar Jagtap Bachchan's poetry recital of his father's work while today it was hosting the cultural festival of the single largest club of the University, fondly called Baileys. The day-long festival had students competing in various cultural events, and this was supposed to end with a ninety minute performance by the only professional rock band of Lucknow, Red Scorpion.

Baba glanced coldly at the student's guarding the entry as they let them pass without offering any resistance or asking for the mandatory tickets, but for a warm greeting. One amongst the numerous advantages of being the long distant cousin of a feared university presidential candidate, Gaja Raj Gope.

'What are we doing here Alok bhai? We could have had a good time in the University Canteen instead of coming here,' Baba complained as they walked towards the main hall. The auditorium looked crowded with students, mostly males. While some of them were having animated discussions in groups and a few rehearsing for their act that was scheduled to start in some time; a large section of them were busy ogling at any female anatomy that walked by.

'This place looks quite different though from regular university environment, much relaxed,' Harish said while absorbing the surroundings. Baba shook his head disapprovingly as they entered the dark hall inside the auditorium.

The festival started soon thereafter; with the solo vocal competition where a handful of finalists came up on the stage and showcased that why Kishore Kumar and Mohd. Rafi would never get erased from the memories of Indians. The time flew as the audience got mesmerized with talented singers, actors and orators displaying their skills unabashedly on the eighty feet wide wooden stage.

'That's it, now let us go man!' Baba said and got up after the winners were announced and the festival was officially over.

'C'mon Baba now is the time for the rock show to start! What do you think I am here for?' Alok said pulling him by the hand.

'Are you crazy, I am not going to sit here and clap with hundreds of these other fools? Something that I don't understand, a bloody *raak show*,' he said irritatingly.

'It's music Baba and you will like it after a while, even if it is in English, I assure you,' Alok insisted.

'No way guys; we are leaving,' Baba said as he walked out of the hall in a huff. Alok and Harish raced behind him.

'Hey, hang on Baba,' Alok yelled as he overheard a loud conversation that was happening next to the exit door, in the green room. It was Sandy shouting animatedly at some people in the room whose faces were not visible to Alok from that angle. He inched closer towards them tip-toed.

'Now what are we supposed to do? Play without this idiot?' Chhotu asked exasperatedly.

'Don't ask me, ask this asshole!' Sandy said pointing towards a guy in black leather jacket sprawled like a corpse on the only couch in the room. Alok sneaked behind the door of the green room quietly.

'Can we pull this off ourselves? Chhotu can you and Sandy chip in with some vocals?' Bubul asked unearthing his keyboard out of the case.

'Yeah, and then we can be the first rock band in the history to pull off a two hour concert without a lead vocalist,' Thoku said annoyingly lighting his cigarette.

'Can we wake this guy up?' Chhotu asked.

'Try' Sandy said.

Alok looked at them trying to bring that collapsed body to senses, but it was of no use. It kept glued on to the couch and let out an occasional whimper as they tried to wake him up.

'That's Khanna, their lead singer from third year and completely wasted,' Baba hushed from behind. Alok turned around to see Baba and Harish lining up behind him. He turned his face slowly towards the band and came out from the hiding.

'Can I try guys?' the voice reached them like a bullet itching to stick to its target as they turned their faces towards the door.

'Oh God! Not you again! Why don't you get it boss?' Sandy said as he shook his head. None of the others even bothered to react.

'I mean, I can try. And let me tell you guys; that we are in a terrible fix here. This is a paid fucking show and not some complimentary crap that you can manage,' he paused, 'You have close to a thousand students outside who are here to see you sing and not do some stuff with the guitar and drums. Am I making some sense here guys?' Alok asked firmly.

'If we don't give them some good entertaining stuff guys, the crowd's going to create a riot here, and your equity with the people out there is taking a serious beating,' he added pointing a finger towards the hall.

He could see that he had their complete attention, 'So here is the deal, you give me a chance to practice with you for about half an hour and see if we can pull this off. If we can, you are resurrected and if we can't then your situation can't get better than what it is right now,' he said chewing each word.

'Hmmm...I guess you have a point! Can we try him guys?' Sandy said after a minute with his eye on the others.

'What will our man say? After all he got us the show,' Thoku said looking at an inebriated Khanna.

'Is he in a fucking position to say anything?' Sandy asked annoyingly.

'I think we should give this guy a chance or else we go solo,' the elderly looking Bubul said. Sandy nodded and gestured at Alok who joined them excitedly leaving a bewildered looking Baba and Harish behind.

'So, what are we doing?' Alok asked.

'What do you know?' Sandy asked.

'Floyd?' Alok said and looked at them.

'Hmmm...by the time I go and set up my kit on the stage, why don't you guys do a quick rehearsal, Chotu?' Sandy looked at the Chinky who started strumming his guitar.

Alok caught up with the rhythm and started humming one of his favorite songs from the Pink Floyd stable. Bubul accompanied them on the keyboard and soon they went up-tempo and got into the groove. To the audience of Baba and Harish, it seemed that they were enjoying. The tracks kept changing from 'Time' to 'Roadhouse Blues' and from

'Holiday' to 'Heaven', it was all cover versions of popular rock music and Alok had virtually thrived on it over last few years.

'How is it going?' Sandy asked entering the green room. They were just ending 'Every Breath You Take'.

'Sounds nice,' he paused and looked at Alok.

'He can do the job, I like him,' Chhotu said unloading his guitar on the table.

'Yeah, importantly his rhythm is good considering that this is his first time with us,' Bubul said flirting with the keyboard.

'I think he can pull it off with us today. But don't turn adventurous, remember that we are backing you up and the moment you feel a bit lost, just shut up. We will pick it up from there,' Thoku said gulping down water from the bottle.

'Guys, time for us to go, just fifteen minutes to start,' Sandy sounded them.

'And here is our magic potion!' Bubul said as he put a full bottle of Bonnie Scott whisky on the table.

Sandy wrapped his arms around Alok's shoulder, 'This is only to feed your nervousness and calm your stage-fright but not to get high, like our man here,' Sandy said looking at Khanna who still lied listless.

'Let's go guys, it's time,' Sandy said after a couple of drinks and they walked through the wings on to the main stage engulfed in darkness.

Alok switched on the mike and squinted through the darkness in the auditorium. They were hundreds of them, boys and girls, excited adolescence, muffled voices and all of them anticipating entertainment. It was then that the realization dawned and fear in his heart crept in. They call it stagefright, standing in front of a crowd with a hope to stand up to their expectations. A bead of warm sweat ran through his forehead but in a few seconds the alcohol in the blood ran fast enough to overcome his fear and normalize his pounding heart. All this happened within a few seconds before the lights went up and the stage exploded!!

The first four riffs from Chhotu's guitar set his pulse racing as Alok dived no holds barred into 'Deep Purple's Smoke on the water'. The crowd that was used to Khanna was circumspect with the new vocalist but three songs into the show, they started liking him. The ones, who didn't, succumbed to the brute force.

'*Yaar*, this guy is not as good as Khanna! He looks raw,' one said to another.

'The guy who's on the stage is our *bhai,*' Baba muttered threateningly, 'if you want to stay, you stay or fuck off.' They looked back and surrenderd.

As Alok's confidence soared, their performance got better with every passing song. The audience was getting into frenzy, especially the girls. The climax was approaching and the band was on a high from the electric music and their on-stage chemistry that had undergone a huge surge over last ninety minutes. The energy had become infectious with the guitarists running around the stage, falling on their feet, leaping in the air while the drummer throwing sticks into the crowd after an upbeat solo. For Alok, the experience was first-of-its-kind and he had no idea about what he did on stage, but gauging the audience reaction, he thought that they rocked. They all came together as the final song got over and bowed down before a blown away crowd that yearned for more; and then the curtains came down.

Alok looked at Sandy and hugged him tightly till he spoke.

'You were very good man, especially for someone who was up here for the very first time,' Sandy said while getting out of the embrace. Alok turned around and before he could realize, an unknown intruder flung herself over his body and almost squeezed him.

'You were awesome dude,' she said with a slurring voice. It took a couple of seconds for Alok to appreciate what had happened. He focused his gaze on the stranger. A chiseled dusky face, flawless complexion, silky hair with large almond shaped eyes that appeared a bit drunk. To sum up in a word she was hot.

'Whoa, that was sudden! Hi!' Alok said in a shaky voice.

'Mandy? Is that you? We have been looking for you all over,' a kurta and jeans clad girl said while climbing up the stairs of the stage. A bespectacled guy who looked like a moron followed her.

She took her drowsy eyes away from Alok and turned her face towards the kurta girl.

'Yeah, was around Suvee, just came up to shake hands with this awesome singer,' she said as she stretched out her hand and looked into his eyes.

'Hey, I am Mandira,' she said.

'Alok, he said .

The kurta clad girl and that dumb looking guy stood behind her.

'My friends, Suveesha and Rohit,' she said signaling at them.

Alok raised his hand in a symbolic Hi and smiled.

'What year?' she asked.

'2nd year, Astronomy,' he said

'Interesting! Univ?' she asked.

He nodded.

'I will see you soon. Gotta go now! But you were awesome tonight,' she said and disappeared like a breeze with her friends. By the time Alok could regain his composure after the sudden impact, a score of students were hustling their way up on the stage being led by Baba.

'*Bhai tum toh saale chha gaye (*Brother you rocked in the damn show)!' Baba hugged Alok and lifted him up in the air.

'*Poore Raakstar Behenchod. Bhai kasam se saare saaman kamar hila-hila key paagal ho gaye (*You were like a full on rockstar and all the women in the auditorium went mad dancing to your music),' he said gleefully.

'You guys in the crowd gave us all the support as well. Thank you,' Alok said appreciatively to the crowd that had gathered around him. They had an awed look on their faces as they stood at some distance from him except for Baba and Harish who had broken into the inner circle.

'This calls for a celebration in Pub 55, should we go brother?' Baba looked at Alok in anticipation. Alok gestured positively and smiled.

'See you guys soon,' Alok turned towards the rest of the band.

'Are you coming for the practice on Monday?' Sandy asked.

'Umm...me! Two days later! What about him?' Alok asked pointing towards the green room and referring to Khanna.

Sandy glanced at the other members, 'We have decided that for taking the band to the next level we need a better and more dedicated vocalist. We think that you can do the job better,' he paused, 'regarding Khanna, don't bother, we will handle him. I think if our quality goes up, we automatically get more and more shows, 'he smiled.

'So, are you game? Sandy asked.

'Only a fool wouldn't be. Of course man,' Alok said blissfully and shook his hand. The other members of the band hugged him in turns and then they parted.

'Yes!' Alok pumped his fist in the air and turned around to join Baba and Harish.

'*If you wanna get down, down on the ground Cocaine*,' Baba hummed the melody in an Eric Clapton meets Kishore Kumar manner. Alok smiled and looked around at about a dozen of them who were packed like sardines in Pub No. 55. He was on his third while Baba had raced ahead by a couple, Harish was ready to collapse.

'*You won't like, you won't like, you won't like, Cocaine*,' Baba raised his pitch again, quite like his growing enthusiasm towards *raak music.*

'It's *she don't lie, she don't, she don't lie,* Baba and not what you are singing,' Alok said tilting his head.

'*Arrayy,* it's the same thing brother. But the way you performed today, fucking the crowd became your fan. I am sure that from tomorrow you will be the new star of the university. Guys will envy you and girls will bloody fall at your feet, I am telling you,' he said in a slurring voice.

'Is it? I don't think so Baba, people loved the music and not the person.'

'What brother, are you crazy? Everyone loves the guy on stage and especially if he is doing something that's alien to all of them, like your *raak music*,' he said and took another sip. The others in the room blindly followed their basic instinct without taking any interest in the on-going conversation between the two; they kept emptying their whisky glasses.

Harish by now had dozed off on the bed. Baba wallowed towards the open window to open his mouth and let out a thin stream of *Gutka* through its open bars and started murdering rock music again in his semi drunken stupor.

Alok shut his eyes and as his head rested on the chair, Megha floated back into the memory, looking ethereal and smiling at him.

The three of them entered the campus together the next morning. Baba and Harish looked visibly excited to be with their friend who had created euphoria in Ravindralaya last evening. Alok looked nonchalant as they navigated their way through the law and physics departments to reach Maths Block. As they walked, Alok could sense a few curious glances, a girl nudging her friend, a couple of unknown faces acknowledging them and exchanging pleasantries. Yes; he was being noticed after yesterday.

'What time is your class?' Baba asked resting himself on the entrance staircase.

'In about an hour,' Alok replied planting himself next to him.

'*Arrayy* my uncle got wild last night when I reached home at 2 AM,' Harish said.

'Why? What happened?' Alok asked casually.

'He gave me a bloody solid lecture on what I was doing with my life and all of that. However, all I wanted to do at that time was just crash down on my bed,' Harish said shaking his head.

'So you should have told him that,' Alok said.

'Alok *bhai* you *na*? He would have then carried it on till the morning and if he would have called my dad once, the old man would have taken the first train to Lucknow from Dehradun,' he said looking agitated.

'Is your dad paranoid about you?' Alok asked.

'Aren't all our dads? Isn't yours?' he asked.

'Yeah, maybe,' Alok replied.

'Hey, what's that, who are these guys?' Harish asked and got up to catch a better view.

'Oh! Them? The campaigning for yearly elections would have started. Is it 8th today?' Baba asked

'Na katta, na bandook, na goli aur na tope,
Ab charo taraf hai ek hee naam, gope, gope, gope, gope.'
(Neither a pistol or a gun, nor a bullet or a cannon
Just one name will resound in all directions and that is Gope, Gope, Gope, Gope)

The shouting of frantic slogans reverberated in the atmosphere.

'These are *Bhaiyya's* men. I am sure he is going for filing the nomination; let's go and meet him,' Baba got up and shook Alok by the shoulder.

'Let it be Baba, I am not interested in meeting these politicians. Why don't you go and come back?' Alok said disinterestedly.

'Alok bhai come na? *Jungle mein rahna hai to sher ko sahna hai (If one has to stay in the jungle one needs to befriend the lion)*, one should know these important people,' he said and pulled Alok by the hand. Alok got up unwillingly and dragged his steps behind Baba as they walked towards the frenzied mob.

'*Paon lagoon dudda*,' Baba gestured to touch the feet of a burly and heavily bearded man who definitely didn't look like a student.

'*Arrayy Baba! Kahan ho Bhaiyya?* Haven't seen you around for long? *Hain na Kailash?*' Gope looked at his sidekick who first nodded and then opened his mouth to let out a thick flush of betel juice.

'*Bhaiyya company change kar liyen hain aaj kal. Englis bolne walon ke saath baithak chlatee hain gope Bhaiyya aajkal pachpan number kamre main*!' (*He has changed his company these days and is found with people who speak in English in his room No. 55*),'he said with a sarcasm laden smile.

News traveled fast, really fast in the corridors of Lucknow University, Alok thought.

'Nothing like that *Bhaiyya;* just a bit busy these days,' Baba said sheepishly and then whispered something in Gope's ears. Alok could see his fleshy face glow with excitement as his eyes lit up when he looked in Alok's direction. Baba raised his hand and signaled Alok to come closer.

'*Bhaiyya,* meet Alok, a very close friend of mine and a good student. *Kaam ka aadmi hai Bhaiyya*,' Baba said patronizingly.

'Hmm…good to meet you Alok; Baba was praising you, let's keep meeting. Baba, get him along when you come to our hostel the next time,' Gope said as he shook hands with Alok.

'Abki baari, jo sabpe bhaari,
Woh hain Bhaiyya Akhil Tiwari.'
(This time the one who would edge out everyone
Is our brother Akhil Tiwari)

The chants of a different breed suddenly resonated from close quarters.

'*Bhaiyya lagta hai kee kutta aa raha hai*?' (*Brother, it seems that the dog is coming here*) Kailash whispered in Gope's ears.

'Let him come while you ask our people to pick up the tempo,' Gope said.

Kailash looked at their group and as if his eyes spoke; but the chanting within them grew manifolds within minutes.

They could see the Tiwari group converging fast on them. Leading them was a tall, moustached guy clad in kurta pajama who was being followed by about a hundred odd students. The dwindling distance between them was inversely proportional to their rising decibels.

'Hamara neta kaisa ho
Akhil Tiwar jaisa ho.'

Tiwari's group launched into bursting a new slogan as they merged within the Gope's troupe like one herd of cattle amalgamating into another, touching and sniffing each other and then walking into opposite directions. The two leaders looked into each other's eyes like warriors. Gope looked sullen while Tiwari looked at him incisively. Following Tiwari was a known and hardened face, Vinay, who walked past them looking into Alok's eyes. The decibel of their voices dipped nadir as soon as their show of one upman ship was over.

'So, what were you whispering in his god damn ear?' Alok asked Baba after they had left.

Baba looked at him and gave out a peal of laughter. Alok prodded him again.

'I told him that you are going to be extremely popular among local students, especially girls who are interested in these *Firangi* tastes, like your *raak* music and all,' he spoke.

'So?' Alok asked.

'So, I told him that you can be a big help in the up-coming elections.'

'Are you crazy Baba? How can I out of all people be of help to Gope?'

'Girls! They are the toughest to get, be it life or student elections.'

'And how can I help him get those girls?'

'You can accompany us when we do class to class canvassing.'

'Me? Accompanying Gope, for a political election? Have some heart Baba!'

'Why not? If you are able to help him in some manner, trust me *Bhaiyya* will return that assistance manifold.'

'I don't want that Baba, and most of all I don't want to be a part of any political gibberish.'

'You don't have to be a part of it; politics here becomes a part of you. You wouldn't even come to know of it.'

'I don't want to and I will not be a part. That's for sure,' Alok said firmly looking ahead as Baba smiled.

'I think she is waving at you,' Harish said looking towards the Maths Block

'Do you know her?' Harish asked in surprise as if the dusky girl with a flawless complexion standing near the stairs was Madhuri Dixit.

'Yeah, Mandira. I met her last night, but what is she doing here?' Alok asked and walked towards her. Baba and Harish followed him like two lambs.

'Hi!' A beaming Mandira greeted Alok.

'Hey, what are you doing here of all places?' Alok asked.

'Suvee had some work near IT college and I had a couple of hours with me. So, thought of saying hi to you,' she said smilingly.

'What if I was not there?' Alok asked.

'I took a chance. So what's the big deal?' she said.

'Hmmm...*Chai*?' he asked.

'I am not much of a tea drinker but if you insist I can give you company,' she smirked.

'Fine. Let's go then,' Alok said and pointed towards his two friends.

'Meet Baba, sorry Sarvesh and Harish,' he introduced them. Mandira smiled and said Hi.

'We have a class Alok, we will catch up with you later,' Harish said. Alok nodded.

They walked towards the Science canteen a couple of blocks away through the narrow lane that traveled through the Chemistry and Biology block.

'Is this called a lover's lane here?' she asked.

'Yeah,' he said.

'I am sure that there would be more students here, than in the classes at this hour,' she said as they glanced at a host of couples who formed their own personal spaces in the corridor and seemed to be discussing everything but books. Alok chuckled as they entered the cool confines of the Science canteen, which looked like a thousand-year- old structure.

'I hope this damn thing doesn't fall off on our heads,' Mandira said sitting on the wooden bench.

'It won't, don't worry, atleast it hasn't from the time that I took admission here,' Alok said as he signaled at an equally ancient *Magru,* the part time cook cum waiter in the canteen.

'So what college do you go to?' Alok asked.

'Awadh, 2nd Year, English Honors and History,' she said. Awadh or AGDC (Awadh Girls Degree College) was the premier girl's college of Lucknow, and very fondly talked about for the beauty of girls who studied there.

'And you Astronomy, right?'

'Yeah, so you do remember yesterday,' he smiled.

'Oh yes I am sorry if I came on a bit strongly last evening. I had a bit too much to drink,' she said apologetically.

'Don't even mention, you managed,' he said.

'Born and brought up here?' he asked.

'Yeah, born here but did my schooling from Delhi, Modern School, had to come back here after my mom expired,' she said.

'Oh I am sorry,' he said.

'It's fine, dad has always been away since he is in the administrative services. But off-late he has been posted here for last five years. Since he stayed alone here along with my grandmother, I decided to do my graduation from Lucknow instead of Delhi. This gives me some time with them.' Alok nodded gently.

'And what about you? From Lucknow?' she asked.

'No, we moved here from Agra last year. I did my schooling there.'

'And this passion for music? You seem to enjoy it completely.'

'Yeah, I guess that's one passion I have. What about you?'

'I just like listening to it and no more. Any girlfriend?'

'There used to be one; but not anymore.'

Why?' she asked.

'JLT,' he winked.

Alok took a sip of the hot tea from the cheap canteen glass. A group of students entered through the low arch entrance of the Science canteen mouthing choicest Hindi expletives and some nonsensical blabber about elections that drew Alok's attention. He immediately recognized a couple of them as they sat on the bench a few rows away, Khanna and Vinay. They sat next to each other facing Alok while Mandira had her back towards them.

'So are you guys only into cover versions or do you have some original compositions as well?' she asked.

'I think it's too early for Lucknow to handle that. From what I could sense over my stay here is that rock music is just mushrooming out here and what people seem to have heard; is only hit international stuff. So better for artists like us to give them what they like versus giving them what we like,' he said.

'You have a point,' she looked convinced.

'I have a class now,' Alok said.

'And I need to go, Suvee would be free by now,' she said.

Alok kept a five rupee coin on the table and they got up from the bench to move out. He saw Khanna nudging Vinay by his elbow as they walked towards the canteen door.

'Hey there,' Khanna greeted Mandira in his gruffy voice. He still sounded drunk.

'Hi,' Mandira did not look pleased enough to see him.

'How have you been?' he added.

Mandira didn't reply but let go of a phony smile that screamed "Why don't you mind your own fucking business?'

'So, rock star? I believe you somehow managed my band last night?' Khanna mocked. Vinay sat there with a dumb face trying to come up to pace with the Victorian language being exchanged.

'Managed, he was very good on the contrary,' Mandira jumped into the dialogue.

Khanna looked at her with disgust.

'If only I was there, I would have shown the crowd what good really means,' he spat venom.

'If only you were not so pissed drunk, you could have been there,' Alok said looking into his eyes.

Khanna was filled with rage as he tried to get up and kickstart an altercation but Vinay pulled him back by his hand.

'*Electsun ka time hai Khanna Bhaiyya. Take it eejee,*' he whispered.

Alok waited for a couple of seconds and then left the canteen with Mandira.

'You really gave it back to him,' she said trying to match his rapid steps.

'Do you know him?' he asked ignoring her question.

'Yeah, I have met him a couple of times with common friends. He looks like a lech, quite a creepy kind of guy' she said annoyingly.

'He is hurt, dealing with a punctured ego. I hope the poor chap can take it,' he said.

'Means?' a perplexed looking Mandira asked. Alok simply smiled back at her.

'Rickshaw,' Mandira called out for a cycle rickshaw at the University gate.

The rickshaw puller stopped for her and Mandira got onto it.

'Why don't you come home tomorrow, I am planning a small get together.' she fixed her gaze on Alok and asked.

'Ok. Can I bring in a couple of friends?' he replied. She thought for a minute and then nodded.

'14 Kalidas Marg at 8PM. See you,' she said.

Alok stood there for a few minutes looking at the rickshaw meandering through the heavy flow of traffic on the University road and then disappearing into it.

'*Bhai*, why have you got us here of all places? You could have gone alone,' Harish said adjusting his jeans as they stood in front of Mandira's bungalow. The gate was lit up brightly with two tubelights that perched up on both sides of the entrance like sentinels. There was a small picket on the left hand side and piercing eyes of a *khaki* clad policeman rummaged through their person.

'You will like it man! There would be good looking girls around. Wouldn't you like meeting them? Alok said.

'Who doesn't? But this place is not for us. Looks too hi-fi,' Baba said.

'Is Mandira in?' Alok asked the guard without paying heed to a fidgety Baba and Harish.

'Who are you?' the guard asked as if he was replying to some vagabonds seeking an entry into a five star hotel.

'Why? Am I asking you for an entry into your house?' Alok said irritatingly. The guard got the message and immediately fine-tuned his demeanor.

'Sir, who should I say is here?' he asked.

'Tell her it's Alok,' he said curtly. The guard picked up the intercom and after getting a go-ahead from inside, he promptly let them in through the gate.

The cemented pathway led them to a huge pastel colored bungalow, slightly old but regal enough to intimidate them. They climbed the three steps of the staircase to land in an empty gallery that had five pieces of cane furniture placed on the left hand corner. Alok looked around hoping to find someone and then attempted to glance through the iron mesh on the wooden entry door. The attempt was futile as he heaved a sigh and walked towards the door bell. Before he could ring the bell, Mandira popped out of the door.

'Hi there,' she said not looking her natural radiant self. Alok reciprocated and so did a slightly hesitant looking Harish and Baba.

'Good, that you guys are not too late. We have just started,' Mandira said and signaled them to follow her.

'Yeah. You don't look your normal self, are you feeling ok?' Alok asked.

'Don't bother, I am fine,' she said without looking back.

After passing through a couple of rooms that showed enough signs of opulence she led them through a wide staircase to the terrace of the bungalow that overlooked the posh Kalidas Marg. The terrace was amply lit and about fifteen to twenty odd youngsters were scattered in small groups and engrossed in private conversations. There were two waiters scurrying around with individual trays of liquor and snacks in their hands, attempting to pay heed to every ensuing demand. They walked up to one of the groups and Alok could recognize only two faces amongst them, Suveesha and dumb faced Rohit. The group lit up as soon as they saw Alok. Some privileges of being a rock singer of the only rock band in the Hindi heartland. Alok could feel the prying eyes of people from the neighboring groups falling on him. The world was really small and so it seemed to him at that moment.

'So, how have you been?' Suvee asked.

'Good, and you?' he asked while shaking hands with Rohit. He introduced Baba and Harish to them who still looked uncomfortable.

'So, when do we get to see you on stage next?' she asked flirtingly.

Alok pointed his first finger towards the sky, 'Only he knows.'

'We really liked you that day and all of us had a great time,' she said and other faces in the crowd advocated her feelings.

'Thank you,' he replied and looked at Mandira who seemed to be engrossed somewhere.

'What is wrong with you?' he hushed in her ears. She shook her head in negative faking a smile.

'Oh hullo there, how have you guys been?' a deep baritone reverberated in the atmosphere. Alok turned around to see a bespectacled man in early fifties walking towards them.

'Hello Uncle, how have you been?' Rohit was the first one to respond. It took a minute for Alok to realize that he was Mandira's dad; she had borrowed his height and most of all a big and hearty smile. He stepped back to give him space to stand.

'Wouldn't you introduce me to your friends Mandira?' he asked her. She started introducing them one by one and in the end stopped at Alok and his gang.

'Papa, this is Alok and his friends, Harish and what's your real name Baba?' she asked scratching her head.

'Sarvesh...err, Sarvesh Singh,' Baba replied sheepishly.

'Haven't seen them before, yeah?' he asked looking at Mandira.

'*Arrayy,* didn't I tell you over dinner yesterday, the same musician whom I met at the concert a couple of days back?' she said trying to remind him.

'Oh yes, I am telling you young man she seems to be completely impressed with you and let me tell you a little secret. My daughter is really hard to impress,' he said and winked at Alok. Suvee chuckled, Mandira blushed and Alok looked embarrassed. Baba and Harish looked at each other and smiled.

'So, what do you study young man?' he asked while picking up a glass of whisky from the waiter's tray.

'Astronomy sir, 2nd year and now going into third,' Alok said.

'Interesting. Where?' he added.

'Lucknow University sir,' he said.

'Ohh…so how is the university Alok? Has the agitation slowed down?' he asked taking a sip.

'You mean Mandal sir?' Alok asked. He nodded.

'Well, it never came to a point when things went out of proportion sir. I don't think it created much of an effect,' Alok said looking at Baba.

'There were a few agitations by a group of students but they either died down their own natural death or were stubbed down forcibly,' Baba said.

'Stubbed down; by whom?' Madira's father questioned rolling a salted peanut in his mouth.

'Sir, I think you would know this being an IAS officer, don't you?' Baba asked as her dad smiled mysteriously.

'Who did that?' Mandira asked.

'It's the state and university political nexus, who else? Don't we know that the current state government that is pro backward classes tried to suppress the upper class agitation against the implementation of Mandal commission?' Baba said.

'But it's incorrect, isn't it? How can you reserve 50% of seats in government jobs basis some caste system?' Rohit jumped into the conversation.

'Well, I have a counterpoint to that,' Baba said.

'What's that?' Mandira asked.

'Right from the time when caste system in this country took shape there were primarily four castes Brahmin, Vaishya, Kshatriya and Sudra. The dharma of Brahmin was to uphold the belief of people in the almighty, in a manner he was the common man's conduit to God. The dharma of a Kshatriya was to protect and fight for the common man while a Vaishya was the custodian of economy and business. A Sudra belonged to the lowest of castes and was virtually shunned away from the lives of the upper three castes,' he paused to take a sip from his glass, 'now over the passage of time a number of castes sprung up within Sudras and some of them turned out into outcastes within outcastes. So, over hundreds and thousands of years these people have been denied a basic life, forget education, healthcare, a regular employment etc. etc etc.' Baba paused again.

'So?' Rohit asked looking a bit worked up.

'So, their simple point is that after screwing up their lives for so many centuries, it's high time that they be compensated by the society and some support is given to them so that they at-least develop some confidence to stand up and build a better life for themselves and their families,' he said.

'But that's not fair and the current generation should not be paying a price for this. How can you deny a fair chance to others on the basis of some ridiculous caste system?' Rohit asked hastily.

'That's exactly what the supporters of Mandal report are saying. How can you not give them a fair chance at-least now, to rise up on their feet after crushing them for centuries?' Baba asked.

'So, Sarvesh Singh do you realize that even you can also lose out to some lesser qualified and lesser intelligent bloke if this gets implemented,' Rohit said.

'I know and I am not supporting the implementation of Mandal commission *mere bhai*, I am just presenting a counterpoint,' Baba said.

'So, what do you support Sarvesh?' Mandira's dad asked.

'I am not against the implementation but I don't like the way it's being used to achieve ones own selfish ends by political parties. There is an issue and it needs to be resolved and in the end what should emerge is up-liftment of a particular caste and not anarchy within the society,' he said seriously.

'I agree and it's an impressive thought young man. I guess you guys should have a drink now,' her dad said tapping Baba's shoulder.

'Your friend is good *haan*,' Mandira whispered in Alok's ear as they picked up a glass each from the tray.

'I know,' he said.

The party was in its last-leg and it was close to twelve. There were about ten people left, the closest ones in Mandira's friend circle and all of them had formed a semicircle around Baba who had become the centre of attraction after the oratory brilliance that he had shown a while ago. They were discussing the sensitive issue of women's freedom in modern India after a series of topics ranging from increasing nudity in Indian films to the best kebab shop in Lucknow; Baba seemed to lead every topic with superior knowledge and confidence. He seemed to be thriving in the new found company. Mandira and Alok walked to the other side of the terrace and stood at its edge that was soaked under moonlight.

'So, what do you want to do in life Alok?' she asked.

'Not too sure, but I want to be connected with music in some manner. I don't want to lose the touch,' he said thoughtfully, his eyes searching through the darkness.

'And you?' he asked.

'I want to do my Masters in Business Administration from US and then tread the marketing line,' she said.

'Well, you seem to be quite clear in what you aspire to do,' he said.

'Yeah, I am. I have been working on this for past two years,' she said.

'But I don't know,' she said and paused.

'You are not your usual self Mandira, what's the matter?' Alok asked looking concerned.

'Nothing much,' she said.

'You can tell me if you want to,' Alok said and looked the other side.

'Yesterday when I had come to the University, Suvee had gone to IT college remember?' she asked. Alok nodded.

'She had gone there to meet one of her aunt who teaches History; who told her that this year they have been very tough in marking the answer sheets.'

'So?' he asked.

'So, I have done very badly in the ancient history paper. As it is I don't like the subject, the paper was so tough, and to top it if the marking is going to be tough as well, then…,' she sulked.

'If I fail or do poorly then it won't reflect well in my academic report and I am gunning for the top colleges in US Alok?' she brooded.

'Can that be so bad?' Alok asked.

'Yes; the top colleges are very particular about the candidate's academic record and they give it a substantial weightage. While you may do great in your GMAT's but if you have screwed up in your grad subjects then you may loose out as well,' she said teary eyed.

'Why didn't I prepare better, why didn't I?' she howled. Alok turned back and looked at the others, they seemed engrossed. He wrapped his arm around her shoulder and stroked her head.

'Don't worry; maybe it does not turn out the way you are thinking.'

'I know what I have written. I know,' she said.

'Who's your teacher?' Alok asked.

'Vishnu Sharma. Why?' she asked.

'Just like that, maybe we can do something,' he said. She wiped away the tears with her handkerchief.

'Anyways let's go, they would be feeling isolated. But thank you for listening to me, atleast I felt better,' she said.

'Don't even say,' he said and smiled with a heart that felt sadder because she was sad. She came close to him and hugged him tightly. Alok hesitated for a while but then wrapped her within his arms.

'I have found a good friend in you. You are nice,' she exclaimed.

'No man! You can't stretch your solo this long in the end! I have to let go of my chords earlier and Sandy needs to pick up the roll,' Chhotu said throwing his hands up in the air.

They had been rehearsing their act for over an hour now in the Commerce Block and Alok had already committed quite a few mistakes.

'Seems your heart is not in today Alok, what's the matter?' Sandy asked in a concerned voice resting his hands on the kit.

'No; I am Ok guys, let's go once again,' Alok said bringing his face closer to the mike.

'What Ok man? We haven't been able to proceed beyond three songs over last one hour,' Thoku said tightening his guitar strings.

'Ok. Let's go guys, one last time; and Alok full concentration,' Sandy said and struck the tom with drum stick. They raced through the song with a couple of minor glitches in between that were noticed by the band but they let it pass.

'No; man no. It's not right at all, the rhythm isn't good and there is no sense of timing here. Alok you delayed the end once again brother,' Sandy screamed.

'I am trying,' Alok said feebly.

'Your heart isn't here. Let's end this today right here and regroup tomorrow again. Alok you need to chill man, you did this song better without practice in the audi,' Sandy said as he got up.

'Yeah, I know, I guess I am stressed,' Alok said and switched off the mike.

'Stressed for what? Can we help?' Sandy asked.

'Nothing, I will handle it. I will see you guys tomorrow, same time,' he said.

'Yup,' Sandy said. The rest of the band had already started packing up.

Baba was sleeping when Alok knocked on the door of room number fifty five. He opened the door bleary eyed and crashed on the bed again.

'*Bhai*, feeling very sleepy. What time did we end yesterday?' he asked with his eyes shut.

'I think 1AM; didn't you sleep peacefully after that?' Alok asked.

'*Arrayy* this is not your house *bhai*, when I reached the hostel, guys from the neighboring room pulled me into their debate that went on till five,' he said.

'You could have slept by refusing them but your urge to talk never seems to subside. Don't you get tired?' Alok said flicking through a magazine.

'On the contrary, I feel rejuvenated,' he said as he got up.

'Remember your promise?' Alok asked.

'What?' Baba said sprinkling water from a glass onto his face in the courtyard outside the door.

'You had said that you will start writing once I start singing,' he said.

'I will Alok *bhai* someday for sure. But what brings you here early? Weren't you practicing till eight?' Baba asked.

'I need some help from you. We need to meet your *Gope Bhai* now,' he said.

'Gope. What help?' Baba asked looking surprised.

'I'll tell you on our way. Let's get going,' he said and threw a T-Shirt at Baba. They were out of Tilak Hostel in about five minutes on the road to LBS Hostel, where Gope stayed.

'So what is it? Can I know or will it be a surprise?' Baba asked.

'No Baba, I will tell you. But before that I want to tell you that you were the life of yesterday's get-together,' Alok said and smiled. Baba blushed.

'Never knew that you were a volcano waiting to explode. The chicks there were eating from your palms,' Alok chuckled and Baba almost went red in the face.

'Arrayy what Alok *Bhai; Kyon le rahe ho subah-subah (Why are you taking my case right in the morning)?* Now tell me what is this urgent need to meet Gope *Bhaiyya* suddenly?' he asked as he tried to match Alok's brisk steps.

'Hmm….situation *gambhir hai. Kya lagti hai vaise yeh ladki tumhari?'* a serious looking Gope asked. He sat on the wooden bed in his LBS Hostel room surrounded by ten odd cronies crowded inside the room.

'She is a friend Gope *bhai,*' Alok said .

'Oh…friend, *dost hai*? Nice *acchha hai,*' Gope said and looked at Kailash his perpetual sidekick.

'So, how do you want us to help?' he asked.

'*Bhaiyya,* her fear is that she would fail the ancient history subject or score very poorly and that would impact her chances for getting admissions in the University abroad,' Alok said.

'So?' Gope asked and inched forward with his hands clutching the smooth edges of the wooden bed.

'*Bhaiyya,* if you could help in someway then I would be grateful,' Alok said candidly.

Gope looked into Baba's eyes as if asking a question.

'*Bhaiyya*, she's a close friend of Alok *bhai*. It is the question of a student's career and everyone knows how much do you care for the students of Lucknow,' Baba said humoring him.

'Alok *Bhai* will be indebted to you if you can help out in some manner. I am sure he would leave no stone unturned in helping us in our election campaign. Isn't it *Bhai*?' Baba asked looking at Alok. Alok nodded in affirmation.

'*Arrayy bhai* Kailash now what to do? You know very well that I can't refuse the students of this city. Moreover, how can I refuse my favorite Baba,' Gope said.

'Who's the teacher?' he asked.

'Vishnu Sharma,' Alok said.

'Hmmm.. Vishnu Sharma....Vishnu Sharma...Sharma,' Gope scratched his head as he tried to place him.

'Arrayy *Bhaiyya,* he is the same one from Gorakhpur. Don't you remember meeting him at the convocation in Benares University two months back?' Kailash reminded him.

'Who? Oh yes *Panditji!* Wasn't he called *Panditji* by the entire teacher fraternity?' Gope said gleefully like a child who had just solved an arithmetic sum.

'Yes *Bhaiyya; eggjactly* the same teacher,' Kailsh said excitedly.

'I think we can get this done Baba, infact I am sure that this is possible,' Gope said looking at Alok.

'Thank you *Bhaiyya,* I knew that you would help us,' Baba said with gratitude flowing in his voice.

'Arrayy *Bhaiyya* is capable enough to do anything in this state. Don't you know that Baba?' Kailash said looking at Gope with reverence; like a devotee looking at his God.

'Thanks,' Alok said.

'It *eej* ok. *Arrayy* Kailash go to IT college and give that *Panditji* a call, tell him carefully what needs to be done,' Gope said. Kailash nodded like an Alsatian pet.

'*Acchha bhai* Baba and Alok, your work will be done and that friend of yours will also get good marks. But now that *elecsuns* are here we need your complete support in helping us achieve an unprecedented victory, *Theek Bhaiyya;* Ok?' Gope said and his eyes moved like a pendulum on to the faces of Baba and Alok.

'*Jee dada,*' Baba said.

'Yeah...umm sure *Bhaiyya,*' Alok muttered the words forcibly as something inside him made him wince in absolute pain. Yet he walked out of the Gope's room with a happy heart.

'What's on between you and Mandira?' Baba asked swirling whisky in his mouth. He sat on the chair, Harish was sprawled on the bed and Alok stood in front of the window staring into the darkness.

'What do you think?' he said after a while.

'I have no idea brother, you have hardly met her a few times and then you decide to help her in such a manner,' he added.

'Like what's so special? Anyone would do this for a friend,' Alok turned around and picked up his glass. He took a large sip.

'Maybe, but in bargain you have agreed to do something for Gope that you were completely against with,' Baba said.

'I think he loves her; and just that he is scared to admit it,' Harish laughed.

'What's wrong with you guys? I have had my share of love I guess,' Alok said.

'What shit Alok? Baba, just look at Alok, wouldn't any girl fall for him in the university today? A handsome, well mannered guy who happens to be a rockstar too; where else could one get such a combination?' Harish quipped.

'Yes that's true Alok *bhai*, I think Mandira has fallen for you and that too heavy duty. Why would any girl come to meet you all by herself and that too in the Lucknow University? Baba asked.

'And that too in a city like Lucknow? Don't we know how primitive this city is?' Baba slurred.

'I don't think so guys. She is just looking for a good friend here,' Alok pleaded as his heart tried to figure out an answer.

'Alok *bhai; Ek Ladka aur Ek ladki kabhi dost nahin ho sakte*,' Harish mimicked a famous bollywood dialogue from a recently released Hindi blockbuster.

'*Yeh to ek bahana hai, tadapti hui raton mein, dhadakte huye dilon ki pyas bujhane ka*,' Baba completed the dialogue and guffawed.

'You guys are drunk and completely filmi and what's all this *pyaas vyaas*?' Alok rebuked but then gave in to their banter. The room was roaring in laughter for a few minutes. By the time euphoria subsided they had tears in their eyes.

'So, don't you love her Alok *Bhai*?' Baba asked looking serious after a while.

Alok did not answer.

After a few minutes Harish got up and clumsily inserted his feet into the sandals.

'Let's go Alok, it's already 12. I have an early class tomorrow morning.'

The Spicy Bite restaurant near Hazratganj was buzzing with human activity at 3PM. Alok looked at his watch again and glanced through the glass door, no sign of Mandira as yet. He looked around at the adjoining tables and the hangout seemed to deliver completely on the promise that it was known for amongst the student fraternity. One helluva cheap and cosy place for couples looking out for a date. Now, who would mind that? You could sit at a table with two bottles of Cola for a couple of hours and no waiter would give you dirty looks. This made people come back to the restaurant time and again, while many amongst them frequented it daily. Alok looked at his watch again; he had been waiting for over forty minutes. He peeked at the door which suddenly burst open as she rushed in, smiling and looking thrilled. She looked around curiously and on spotting Alok her smile broadened as she hugged him. A few jaws dropped and whispers floated around but Mandira was undeterred. Alok by now was aware of her strange ways hence public display of emotions such as these did not seem to scandalize him any further.

'You look seriously happy. What's the matter with you?' he asked.

'Two great news,' she said. Alok gave her a quizzical look.

'Choose?' she raised her two fingers and laid them before Alok. He held one of them.

'I have been elected as the General Secretary of my College,' she exclaimed.

'That's great! And the next one?' Alok asked.

'I have scored a first division in the Ancient History paper Alok,' she said gleefully.

Alok merely smiled and nodded.

'I mean how can this be possible Alok?' she almost howled with joy.

'Don't you remember how sad I was the other day? And here I get a first class in a paper I thought I would surely flunk. God!' she gripped her forehead with excitement.

'I told you so. Sometimes we keep feeling miserable about the uncertainty in future and let go of our present,' Alok said.

'No Alok, do I look that kind of a person to you? I am serious man, I was damn scared about scoring poorly but this has turned out to be amazing,' she said.

'Anyways, now that it has turned out good let's enjoy the moment,' he said. She waggled her head.

'So, where's the party?' he asked.

'Tonight at my house, what say? I will call all my friends,' she said.

'No, not tonight, I have a show in the evening,' he said.

'So what man? I am coming for your show and then we can go home for the party, Ok?' Mandira bulldozed him into agreeing and Alok did not seem to mind it at all.

'How did you land up with so many women for my show?' Alok said getting out of Mandira's car in the portico of her bungalow.

'Didn't I tell you that I am the GSec now? And a leader is never seen in public without his followers,' she said and winked at him.

'Ramu *Bhaiyya* who all is already here?' she asked the house help.

'Around seven – eight people *didiji*,' he replied courteously and took the car keys from her hand.

'Haven't you turned into a full fledged student leader in a day? What happened to your US dreams?' Alok mocked.

'Power corrupts people, haven't you heard that?' she replied as they burst out into laughter.

'You should be thanking me for getting so many girls in your show. You have got so much of female attention today; that in your next show the guys would be queuing outside the auditorium, not so much for your music but for the chicks inside,' she said.

'I bet they would,' Alok said as they climbed the steps.

'Hey, hi man!' Rohit gave a Hi Five to Alok.

'What's up Alok? I thought you guys were superb today as well,' Suveesha said.

'Thanks ! Yeah, we had a great time,' Alok said.

'Aren't you having a drink?' Suveesha said picking up a glass of vodka and lime cordial.

'I already had a couple during the gig, I am not sure,' Alok hesitated.

'*Arrayy* have *na*! I am soooo happy today …*yaay*,' Mandira said and took a swig while handing out a glass of whisky to Alok.

'Yeah, I know. It's been a lucky day for you,' Alok said.

'Cheers to that,' she said and polished off the glass.

'Some live music now, Alok please sing na!' she pleaded. It had been over a couple of hours into the party and Mandira had been drinking like a fish.

'Mandira, I am tired. I had a show today and I just can't sing now,' Alok said.

'Please one song baby,' she slurred as she whispered in his ear. They were all sitting on mattresses neatly arranged on the terrace of her bungalow. It was close to twelve and her father was away to Delhi on an official trip, giving her the liberty to exercise full control over the time.

Alok shook his head and smiled, 'Ok.'

'Yaay, Rohit why don't you get the guitar from my room?' she said. Rohit obeyed her orders faithfully and the instrument landed in Alok's lap in a couple of minutes. Alok picked up the guitar and looked around at the small crowd of people sitting on the mattress and staring at him as he strummed the guitar.

'But underneath we had a fear of flying
Of getting old, a fear of slowly dying
We took the chance
Like we were dancing our last dance

I can still recall our last summer
I still see it all
In the tourist jam, round the Notre Dame
Our last summer
Walking hand in hand.'

Mandira had inched closer to Alok and rested her head on his shoulder by the time he finished the song. Everyone cheered when it ended and then they got up.

'We should be going now, it's already quite late,' Suveesha said looking at Rohit. He nodded. Alok kept the guitar on the side and whispered to Mandira, her eyes were closed and her face looked beautiful resting on his left shoulder. The gentle midnight breeze had forced a small tuft of hair to fall on her face that played gently with the moonlight, rising up and then falling back.

'I think, I should be leaving,' he said.

'Please don't go Alok. Stay,' she murmured in a voice that was laden with longing.

'See you Mandira, Alok please take care of her and drop her downstairs, I think she has had a bit too much,' Suveesha said and pressed Mandira's shoulder. Alok nodded.

'Bye,' Mandira slurred again and they left leaving the two of them alone.

They kept sitting in silence for a few minutes after her friends had left. Alok picked up the guitar and started playing around with the strings softly.

'I am so relieved Alok, I can't tell you. If I would have flunked this exam, I am not sure what would I have done?' she said leaning on him.

'I am aware Mandira. I know how passionate you are about doing MBA from States,' he said.

'But how were you so sure that I would do well?' she asked.

'I knew that nothing could go wrong with you,' he said.

'You are so sweet Alok. I am lucky to have you by my side,' she said and kissed him on the cheek. He felt a sudden rush of blood jetting through his body as her moist lips touched his cold skin. He looked at her as she opened her eyes slowly, a dash of naughtiness flashed through them.

'Are you drunk Mandira?' he asked.

'Drunk enough to be mischievous,' she said and wrapped her arm around his shoulder.

'What do you want?' he asked.

'What can you give?' she asked huskily.

'Mandira, are you sure about what you are doing? Do you love me?' he asked but she did not seem to listen, even to a word.

And then it happened, all of a sudden, unknowingly. Alok kissed her softly on the lips and she reciprocated passionately. He wrapped his arm around her neck and made her lie down on the mattress gently. She looked at him carrying the same glint of mischief on her face and pulled him close. The kisses grew in intensity and soon they were discovering each other physically, getting closer to the point of no return. She pulled up a blanket over them and beneath the covers the inhibition between them disappeared completely. As Alok experienced the touch of her skin; he felt a deep suppressed feeling of anxiety groping to emerge from within. He no more felt restrained but on the contrary his body and soul longed to be with her. It would have been quite a while when their tired bodies gave way for sleep to enter their senses.

'It's close to five. Oh shit!' Mandira said putting on her clothes.

'It is ok baby, come here M,' Alok said lovingly; while pulling her hand.

'No Alok. You should leave now, and what's this M business?' she said with mock anger.

'I like it. I will call you M from today,' Alok said getting up.

'Whatever,' she shrugged as she got up.

He got into his jeans and T-Shirt in a few seconds and turned back to see Mandira standing at the edge of her terrace.

'I love you,' he came and hugged Mandira from behind.

'Romeo, I think you gotta be going now,' she turned around and said.

'Ok M Ok. Are we meeting today?' he asked.

'Yup, hopefully and now goooo,' she scoffed.

'Ok. See you,' Alok said and left her house. There was a visible bounce in his steps and he felt much lighter than he ever had over last couple of years.

It was close to 12 when Alok's mother woke him up. He opened up his eyes to bright sunlight entering his room as he looked at his mother with 'why the hell did you disturb me' eyes.

'Your friend Sarvesh is here,' she said and left the room.

'Baba, at this hour in the morning?' he thought to himself and dragged his feet towards the living room.

'*Bhaiyya* has called for you,' Baba said as paced around the room. Alok stared at him with quizzical eyes.

'The campaigning starts from today and he wants you to canvass for him in all those classes that have a majority of girls,' he added.

'Why?' Alok asked.

'Because I told him so,' he said.

'What subjects?' Alok asked.

'Psychology, English, History, Geology, Botany, Sociology, Political Science…' Baba would have continued if he wouldn't have interrupted him.

'But that's virtually the entire university, isn't it?' Alok said irritatingly.

'It is, but now you can't do a thing, *Bhaiyya* helped you when you needed it the most,' Baba said. Alok sighed and shook his head.

'What if I say no?' he raised his eyebrows.

'You may want to try but I wouldn't advise you to do that,' Baba said candidly.

'And this is no Vinay, Alok *bhaiyya jee* he is Gajaraj Singh Gope,' he said stroking Alok's shoulder.

'It's not me Baba, I just can't bring myself into doing what my heart does not want me to,' Alok said in a pained voice.

'I know Alok *bhai* and that's why I had told you to be completely sure before you went asking for help from Gope. But now that you have, be ready to do all this and hope that he wins this time,' Baba said.

Alok looked submerged in his thoughts for a few moments before he looked up at Baba and smiled.

'*Koi Nahin*. No worries, lets go.'

Gope's entourage comprising of Alok and Baba entered the second year English Honors class in the afternoon. The last class had just ended and chatter filled the environment of the large auditorium. Gope entered the class with a pair of perpetually folded hands (*Alok believed that he slept and sat on the potty with hands that were folded perpetually*), closely hounded by Kailash and about twenty other supporters. Some of them looked old enough to pass off as fathers and uncles of students sitting in the class; who looked at them as if pirates from Somalia had invaded their private ship. Alok entered towards the end and the classroom filled with students seemed akin to him like an auditorium anticipating a rock show. In both the cases he was a performer, and today on this stage, it was his first performance. He felt a bit nervous and the skin behind his ear lobes warmed up. Gope fixed his piercing but small eyes on Alok and signaled him to start. Alok cut through the group and moved towards the front. He could sense that a few students among the group, mostly girls, recognized him and nudged their partners. A few of them started whispering into their neighbors ears. Alok cleared his throat and spoke.

'Friends, I am sure you would be surprised that why do we stand here in front of you with the student leader Gajaraj Singh Gope. Are you?' he paused. Some of the students nodded while others kept mum looking at them with a blank expression.

'The University today is not a good place; certainly from what we had wanted it to be when we took our first step inside the University Gate. Right from the maintenance of buildings to the standard of our canteens, from a secure atmosphere for girls to sports facilities for guys. Things seem to be in a mess. Mess anywhere breeds discomfort and drives discontent,' he paused.

'The University elections over the last few years have led to nothing. We elect fellow students; they become leaders and forget us. The Student Council building last year did not function for more than 24 days. 24 days out of 365; can you beat that?'

'We had more than 25 lac of rupees in the treasury lying with us; meant to be ploughed back for the benefit of the students. Do you guys even know where that money was spent?' he ran his gaze across the row of students.

'Only 1 lac was spent in buying some sports equipment while the balance 24 lacs went towards food and entertainment of the student council bearers who worked in the office for just 24 days,' he said.

'This works out to one lac of rupees each day among six candidates who were President, Vice President, General Secretary, Cultural Secretary, Science Secretary and Arts Secretary.'

'So, how much does that work out per elected candidate each day?' he asked a girl who took out her calculator to work out the answer.

'It would mean that each one of them spend about fifteen and a half thousand rupees over food and entertainment every day,' she looked amazed as she blurted out the answer excitedly. Alok did not react and took a measured pause.

'So, what's the per month salary you expect after graduating from here?' he asked a spectacled girl sitting in the first row. She looked intimidated at this sudden interruption but then opened her mouth slowly.

'About four thousand,' she murmured.

'So, let's get this one right, one guy spends a sum equivalent to your four months salary on food and personal expenses in one day. In one single day. Now how does this sound to your ears?' Alok said and looked at the changing facial expression of the students.

'Ridiculous,' said one.

'Disgusting,' another voice said.

'How can this be so blatant?' a third one roared in the auditorium.

It was a matter of few moments before the auditorium was buzzing with highly audible volatile chatter of students. Alok looked at Gope who was visibly alight with excitement. He glanced back at Alok with pride and nodded in admiration.

'Now, the big question is that who is at fault here? Is it the elected student leaders, the college authorities who do not demand accountability, or all of us in this auditorium?' he spoke loudly, modulating his voice as if in a theatre.

'Why us?' one thin girl with an aquiline nose spoke in her nasal voice.

'Because we are responsible for electing such guys and sending them to the student union office every year. It is we, who can't differentiate between good and bad and cast our vote basis hearsay or indifference. Don't you think so?' Alok asked.

'So, how is Gope different? We have all heard how closely he is associated with the state politics. We know where he gets all the money to fund his elections campaign from, and also about his muscle power,' the same girl replied. Alok listened to her patiently and then took a pause. Gope looked disturbed like a giant bull being needled by a stick.

'Am I a student leader?' he asked. The entire class shook their heads in negative.

'Do I have a political agenda?' they repeated the act again.

'Do I seem to have loads of money or muscle power?' he said smiling a bit. The entire class repeated their negative affirmation for the third time.

'So who am I?' he asked.

'A student,' someone said. He moved his gaze around and he could see heads confirming the statement.

'Like you?' he asked. They nodded again.

'Exactly. I am student and also a musician who has no agenda in supporting this gentleman standing here, unless he brings in some fresh changes in the way this university is being run by the council, and a whole range of student benefits along with it. Do you believe me now?' he asked.

A fresh round of murmurs started floating in the class and Alok could see partial agreement in the class.

'I know that Gope *Bhai* has got contacts within the state politics but that he has only to help students at all times. You tell me, what's the point in becoming a leader when one can't solve problems and issues of university students?' Alok asked vehemently. Some more amongst them looked convinced.

'I know he has got money and muscle power; but that's because of his lineage and family background. Tell me, if you are the son or daughter of a wealthy businessman, won't you come to college in a car; or wouldn't you have money in your wallet?' he added.

'*Bhaiyya jee lagta hai Alok Bhaiyya maidaan maar liye hain (I think Alok has won over them Bhaiyyajee),*' Kailash whispered in Gope's ear. Gope's smile grew bigger.

'So, friends for safety and knowledge, for student welfare and better avenues there's just one candidate to vote for, and he is none other than Gajaraj Singh Gope,' Alok said forcefully and pointed his finger towards the burly politician who folded his hands once again and bowed in front of the class. The students hesitated for a second but then the whole auditorium was filled with a thunderous applause.

'Alok *Bhai*, that was awesome, *chha gaye Bhaiyya*,' Baba said enfolding his arm around Alok as he came out of the auditorium. The troupe followed him.

'*Arrayy Bhaiyya Alok*?' Gope called him from behind. Baba and Alok stopped in their tracks.

'*Elecsun ka* starting superb *raha*, now the same model should happen in each and every class. Ok?' Gope asked looking elated. Alok confirmed his expectation through a gesture.

'Gaand Phate hai Sabki, Jab Aaye inko kope
Yeh hain Bhaiyya, yeh hain dadda
Gope , Gope, Gope, Gope.'
(Its time for everyone to get screwed once he loses his temper
He is our brother, He is our senior

Gope, Gope, Gope, Gope)

The entourage broke into rapture after a stupendous start to the election campaign of Gope.

'Fuck, I felt like a whore man, speaking all those lies for a favour,' Alok said to Baba as they walked behind the troupe.

'Let it be Alok, now that we have to do it, we better do it happily. But all said and done you were a revelation today,' Baba replied.

'*Sab aapse hee seekha hai Baba (I have learnt everything from you, Baba),*' Alok smiled at Baba. The charged slogan shouting followers of Gope were entering the Psychology department building where another well rehearsed but phony act was about to start in the next few minutes.

'Where the hell did you disappear after that evening? Haven't seen you for last few days?' Mandira said sipping her cold coffee. They were meeting at Ritz Restaurant in Mahanagar after about a week. The place was crowded as usual, being one of the favorite hangouts of old, young, families and dating couples who preferred to dig into north Indian delicacies or grab a bite of South Indian dosa or Punjabi chhole bathure.

'Don't ask, I was helping out a guy in University elections,' Alok said looking tired.

'Elections? You don't look that sort of a guy, why are you helping him?' she asked raising her eyebrows.

'They think that I can get them some female votes because of my new found popularity,' he said.

'Oh really? Yeah maybe, but why are you doing that? Is he your friend?' she asked. Alok shook his head and finished off the bottle of Coke in one breath.

'Can't help M, I have to,' he said looking at her.

'I missed you M,' he said as he held her hand.

'Why?' she asked.

'Don't you know?' he said. She swayed her head gently and pulled her hand back.

'You are really crazy, rock-star,' she smiled.

'I have got calls from four universities,' she beamed.

'Oh really, which ones are these?' he asked putting up a smile.

'Kelloggs, Columbia, Yale and Michigan,' she rushed through the names hurriedly.

'So which one are you going for?' he asked still maintaining that smile.

'Kelloggs because it's the best, yaaay,' she raised her fist in the air.

'When does the course start?' he asked hesitatingly.

'Three weeks from now, great na?' she chirped.

'Yeah,' he said as his mind went blank .

'What do you plan to do after grads?' she asked taking another coffee sip.

'Haven't given much of a thought, I guess something related with music?' he said.

'Is that good enough for a living?' she asked.

'Don't know; but good enough to keep me happy,' he said.

'Ok!' she said polishing off the last sip.

'As long as you are happy, Alok. Should we get going?' she asked.

'What about us?' he asked.

'What about it? We are friends and we will remain friends,' she said.

'I mean aren't we more than that. I love you M,' he said sounding pained.

'It's infatuation Alok, and nothing else. Is this a time to fall in love or have a relationship baby?' she asked.

'There is no time for love M. I think it just happens,' he said looking into her eyes.

'Yeah maybe, but not for me Alok and it's not good for you either at this point in time; now let's go,' she chided.

'I am not asking you to take a decision right now M. I mean you go and finish your studies, take your time,' he said and held her hand again.

'*Arrayy* no baba, this is not some love story where heroine goes away and the hero waits for her till eternity. Let's not complicate things further and remain great friends as we are. Aren't we?' she asked looking at him.

'Yeah,' he muttered trying hard to look and sound normal.

'And if you are still caught up in that night, I am sorry. I was high and it just ended in the way that it did,' she said.

'Yeah, maybe I am still there,' he said.

'But it's fine and it really is a great news that you are getting into Kellogg's,' he said as he got up.

They walked out of the restaurant in silence till she found a cycle rickshaw.

'When are we meeting next?' she asked.

'I will call you,' he said as he waved her good bye.

'We are late Alok *Bhai,* the counting would have already started,' Baba said as he increased his pace. Alok looked clouded in his thoughts as he walked while Harish looked attentive.

'What's the hurry?' Harish asked.

'For all these days we have been slogging our asses and now when the time of reckoning has arrived, you want us to stay in the background? *Kya baat karte ho Bhaiyya*?' Baba rebuked Harish as if he were a kid.

'Now let's walk fast. We have to be with *Bhaiyya* when the results are announced,' he said.

'Will Gope win?' Alok asked looking serious.

'I have sensed the pulse of the university and now after your canvassing and a strong support from girls, *Tiwari saale kee to lag gayi*,' he guffawed as they walked towards the Student Union building where the counting for the elections progressed to decide on the privileged ones who would walk into the the Student Council building, and then through the endearing gate of active state politics.

'Iski Maari, Uski Maari
Abki baari, Akhil Tiwari.'

'Gaand Phate hai Sabki, Jab Aaye inko kope
Yeh hain Bhaiyya, yeh hain dadda
Gope , Gope, Gope, Gope.'

They walked through the mob of supporters lined on either side of the narrow lane that led to the building of Lucknow University Student Council. The supporters of both the student leaders stood in groups on both the sides and mouthed the slogans of their student leader with visible excitement and chutzpah. With their fists lunging forward and aggressive expressions dancing on their faces, they longed for victory fiercely. Baba's eyes were searching through the crowd for Gope and his group of supporters, and soon he could sight them standing close to the Student Council building, leaning against the wall. Gope looked as comfortable resting there with his gang as if relaxing in the backyard of his domain.

'*Dadda*, what is the situation?' Baba asked looking concerned.

'Situasun ijj under control Baba Bhaiyya. No tensun, vensun . Dadda zaroor jeetenge aur yeh saala babua tiwari saala gooo chaatega (Gope Bhaiyya, will win for sure and this Akhil Tiwari will have to eat shit),' Kailash spoke vociferously. Gope smirked and others in the group copied his expression.

'Alok *Bhaiyya*, what do you think? Will we win?' Gope asked Alok who looked drained in his thought.

'Don't know, but I hope you do,' Alok shrugged.

'Hmmm...,' Gope murmured thoughtfully.

'Arrayy *dadda* Proctor Shukla has come out of the counting hall. I think he wants to give an update,' Kailash said and rushed a few steps ahead towards the podium of the Union building. The others turned their eyes towards a portly man in mid fifties standing on the porch with a hand held loudspeaker.

'Dear students, the counting is over for almost fifty percent of the votes. We have already counted about five thousand six hundred and eighty votes out of the total ten thousand and nine hundred of the total polled votes by the students,' he paused.

'The student leading on the Art Secretary seat is Rajeev Gupta,' he shouted.

A small crowd supporting him cheered under the banyan tree.

'On Science secretary seat it is Sudhanshu Singh who leads by a margin of nine hundred votes and on Cultural Secretary seat it is Prateek Dixit by a little over five hundred votes,' he spoke through the loudspeaker.

The supporters of the leading candidates raised feverish cries laden with excitement in the environment.

'Now, coming to the key seats of the elections,' he took a calculated pause again.

'Leading the General Secretary seat this year by a margin of one thousand and five hundred votes is Prashant Shukla and leading the Vice President seats by just two hundred votes is Jai Kumar,' he raced with the announcement. The crowd waited for the most anticipated announcement. Alok thought that there was no reason for him to be here.

'Lastly, on the President seat the student leading the elections this year till now by a margin of more than two thousand votes is....'

'Akhil Tiwari...,' a semi drunk voice from the crowd exploded.

'Gope,' someone else blurted out.

'It is Gajaraj Singh Gope, leading by three thousand votes,' the Proctor almost screamed into the loudspeaker.

Gope's supporters could not hold themselves any further and took to impromptu dancing within small scattered groups. Akhil Tiwari and his gang stood at a distance with morose faces, staring at the Gope gang angrily.

'*Arrayy abhi jeete nahin hain Bhaiyya. Thodi der tham toh jao (Bhaiyya hasn't won the election as yet. Why don't you wait for some more time?),'* Kailash pulled a supporter back by his shoulder.

'*Arrayy* Shukla Sir, which department votes are still pending to be counted?' someone amongst the Gope herd asked.

'Psychology, English, Statistics and Science,' he said casually as he walked back inside the hall.

'Hope we poll well across these departments,' Harish muttered.

'What *chutiatic* talk Harish *Bhai,* these departments have a majority of girl students. *Aur yahan toh Alok bhai ka jaadu chalega, hundred percent,'* Kailash guffawed and wrapped his arm around Alok's shoulder. Alok smiled wryly and looked away.

'Chalee Sawari, rahe pichhari
Gope ke peeche, akhil tiwari
(The Cart has moved and he is trailing
Gope is ahead while the loser is Akhil Tiwari)

The inebriated chants of the large mob that had accumulated in front of the Student Union's building were at its feverish pitch. The election results had been announced about an hour back and Gajaraj Singh Gope had won by a huge margin. The supporters who had gathered were showing no signs to retreat and were busy dancing wildly on the road joined by some local *dholwalllas* who had been arranged in advance.

'*Saale Akhilva ko toh dhool chata diye Bhaiyyajee (Bloody Akhil Tiwari has been left to bite the dust),'* Kailash said taking a large sip of whisky from the plastic glass.

'*Saala Kutte ka bacchha (Bloody son of a dog),'* he continued.

'Hmm... Kailash,' Gope said raising his finger. He looked pleased like a punch.

Kailash retreated into his shell immediately.

'Now, that we have won Kailash there is no point in keeping old grudges. We have to work towards student progress and move forward,' Gope said emphatically.

'Student progress, my foot,' Alok muttered standing at a distance from the newly elected president.

'*Arrayy* Alok Bhaiyya, *pleaje* come here, near us,' Gope said raising his voice.

'You helped us a lot in *elecsun* campaigning *bhaiyya* and now one last favor,' he smiled.

'You have to help us in thanking the students as well for our victory,' he continued.

'But how?' Alok moaned at the thought of one more favor to Gope.

'*Raak Sow*,' he said with gleaming eyes.

'What do you mean?' Alok asked.

'We will sponsor a rock show and invite the entire university. There won't be any entry ticket for this show. It will be free for the students of Lucknow University. A victory gift from their president Gajaraj Singh Gope,' he said beaming with pride and glanced at his bewildered followers as if he had announced a multi-crore incentive for Lucknow University Student Welfare Fund.

'A Rock Show sponsored by a student leader for winning elections? Sounds unusual?' Alok asked.

'*Arrayy* Bhaiyya, equally unusual was a *raak singer* campaigning for Gajaraj Singh Gope, wasn't it? But it did happen, didn't it?' he guffawed as he looked into Alok's eyes. The other cronies standing around him joined in the community laughter.

The Ganna Sansthan Auditorium was decked as if it was hosting a grand wedding today. The building was adorned with huge garlands of flowers hanging on the fascia of the building and was giving it a festival look. The pathway to the main building was lined with cutouts of Gope on both sides, draped with frills having bulbs that would light up at night. The rock show was about to start at 6PM but the free entry bait had made the students to start lining up at the auditorium an hour before.

Alok and the band had reached the venue an hour before and were busy setting up the equipment when Baba entered.

'Your girlfriend is here with the full gang,' he quipped.

'She isn't my girlfriend,' Alok said as he checked the mike.

'Whatever *bhaiyya*, but she was desperately looking for you and I didn't have your whereabouts,' he said.

'Hmmm…,' Alok nodded.

'Is the bass sounding ok?' Thoku asked strumming the guitar.

'Let me go at the back and tell you,' Alok jumped off the stage and hurried through the rows of empty seats, towards the back of the auditorium.

'Thoku! Let it come now!' he shouted.

'Check the keyboards as well, after you are through,' Bubul shouted. Alok nodded in agreement.

They did a thorough soundcheck for over fifteen minutes before Baba reappeared in the auditorium.

'We are starting entry in ten, you guys prepare accordingly,' he shouted from the exit gate.

'Let's get going from the stage now,' Alok glanced at the band members.

'Hey there,' Mandira spoke from behind. Alok turned around to see her climbing up the steps of the stage. She looked beautiful and wore a plain white t-shirt over khaki cargo pants. She had let her hair loose and that was adding to her sensuality.

'Hi M,' Alok muttered.

'I mean Mandira,' he added.

'You can call me anything dear, I was just kidding the other day. So, ready for the big show?' she said. Alok nodded.

'Just wanted to tell you that I would be leaving day after,' she said.

'Where to Mandira? Some relative' he asked.

'Off to US Alok, didn't I tell you?' she said.

Alok's heart sank and he forced his facial expressions to remain intact.

'But that was some time away, isn't it?' he spoke with difficulty.

'Yeah, the course will start in some time but I want to get a head-start. I want to reach a bit early and get acclimatized, I have some friends there,' she said.

'How the fuck can you do this M? I had so much to say to you. How can you leave like this?' is what he wanted to scream.

'Ok, what else can I say except wishing you luck,' is what he said.

'There's still a lot of time for that, don't worry. I have my whole gang here and hope we have a rocking time today,' she said smiling.

'You bet,' he said.

'Ok, then see you after the show. All the best,' she said and left in a jiffy without noticing the tear that had cornered within his eye.

'Let's go through our ritual Alok, everyone's waiting,' Sandeep called loudly from the left hand wing and broke Alok's stupor. He walked back slowly into the green room.

'Cheers and all the best for today's show. Why don't you pick up your glass as well?' Bubul said handing over the whisky glass to Alok.

'What happened? You look fucked,' Sandy said taking a sip.

'Nothing,' Alok said and sipped from his glass. He polished it off in two sips.

'Wow; that was fast. Now don't get drunk *haan?'* Sandy commented. Alok nodded and poured another one.

'At-least, till we get another vocalist who is as good as you. I don't think that we can get lucky everytime when we run out of a vocalist. Someone like you ain't walking in each time when there is no hope,' Chhotu said as the band broke into laughter.

They were into the performance for over an hour and the crowd was ecstatic, roaring with energy. Alok was in the middle of a medley with Chhotu and Bubul when he saw Gope standing in the wings with five-six of his supporters and signaling for his attention. Alok moved towards them.

'*Bhaiyya,* let us come for five minutes. We are in a hurry. We have to go and meet the Chief Minister,' Gope hushed.

'Come where?' Alok asked.

'On the stage, where else *bhaiyya*? We have to say Thank You to all the students here,' Gope said as if Alok was an imbecile.

'Here?' Alok asked in a surprised tone.

'Yes, right here and right now,' Gope said as their group walked on the stage not paying any obeisance to the band that had not ended the song yet. The unassuming band and the crowd were caught unaware and were perplexed to see the uninvited guests. Gope walked over to the mike and cleared his throat like a seasoned politician.

'Friends, I am glad that so many of you are here to see this *mujical sow* by Alok *Bhai* and his friends,' he glanced at the stunned faces of Alok's band members.

'This *sow* is a gift from us to you for believing in us and giving us full majority to be elected as the President of University. Thank You,' he added and fleetingly looked at the crowd who seemed to have just one question going through their minds, 'Why the fuck is this guy up here right now?'

A few cronies hanging around in the darkness couldn't stay quiet for long and the hall that was reverberating with 'Hotel California' a few moments back was filled with:

Hamara Neta Kaisa Ho
Gope Bhaiyya jaisa ho

Gope enjoyed the applause for a few moments before opening his mouth again, 'if you need our help anytime, remember that we are there for you twenty four seven. Ok?' he paused. It was show-time for his cronies again and the auditorium was filled with an overwhelming applause.

'Alok Bhai, you start your *sow* now. Thank you,' he said and waved at the crowd before leaving the stage and the auditorium.

'Should we start?' Alok asked Sandy.

'After this political espionage in the middle of a rock concert? No way man! Let's go for a five minute break,' Sandy replied.

'Let's finish this off man, roll your drums,' Alok pleaded. Sandy looked at Alok's face that looked tired and sad. He nodded in affirmation as they kicked off the act again.

'This one is the last number,' Alok said as Sandy rolled his stick on the cymbal.

'And this is for someone who is leaving a day after on a new journey. A journey of new experiences, a journey of new dreams and a journey of new happiness,' he paused. A few sighs and whistles jostled with the silence in the auditorium.

'Despite being sad and a bit shattered,' he kept his hand on his heart. A few in the audience giggled and Alok let out a fumbled laugh.

'I am happy to see you go and follow your dreams. So this one is for you M,' he said and a nervous excitement broke into the crowd as they searched all around for this mystery M.

It was a shocker for Mandira who was sitting with her friends in the penultimate row and all she did was let out a full blown 'Oh my God' with her hands covering her face. It was only a matter of seconds before the crowd identified who M was, and she became a cynosure of all eyes before Alok started singing the final song.

'All my bags are packed and I am ready to go
I'm standing here outside your door

I hate to wake you up to say goodbye...'

The song was somewhere in the middle when Alok paused and signaled the band to soften down the music, 'M, would you come on the stage and sing this song with me,' he said on the mike and looked in her direction.

Mandira could feel him standing next to her and looking into her eyes. She was in a daze when others in the group pushed her out of the row. She slowly climbed down the steps gazing at Alok who had his sight fixed on her. She walked almost in a trance towards the stage with a few thousand eyes fixed on her. Alok came towards her and hugged her before he walked with her towards the mike. He picked up the guitar as he took the mike again and before he started humming he nudged her through his eyes to join him. She looked at the crowd and felt nervousness gripping her body and her mouth going completely dry. Alok sensed her discomfort and wrapped his arm around her. She felt better, her breath came back and so did the rush of blood in her body. She could hear Alok now who was almost towards the end of the song. She knew the song and she wanted to sing it with him. And that she did, slowly and then all the way:

'Now the time has come to leave you
One more time let me kiss you
Close your eyes; I'll be on my way
Dream about the days to come
When I won't have to leave alone
About the times, I won't have to say..'

'You sing well M. If you weren't going, these guys would have seriously considered you as my replacement,' he winked as the music played in the background.

'So, should I go or not?' she asked.

'No,' he whispered.

'Bastard,' she said and caught up with the lyrics again.

'So kiss me and smile for me
Tell me that you'll wait for me
Hold me like you'll never let me go
Cause I'm leaving' on a jet plane

Don't know when I'll be back again
Oh babe, I hate to go..'

The music took over from there and all that Mandira remembered after the concert; was a maddening crowd, rhythm of the guitar, bright lights and Alok along with her singing together into the mike.

'Wow, that was really something! I never knew that being on stage in front of a crowd could give you that much of a high. My three vodka shots were a complete waste in front of that experience,' she said leaning against the wall of the green room.

It had been about an hour since the show got over and Alok was stuffing his backpack. He zipped it up and turned around.

'Hmmm…now that you have seen it, let's get going,' he said patting her shoulder.

'Have you seen Baba somewhere?' he asked as they walked in the corridor.

'Naah..,' she replied.

They saw Harish walking towards them from the opposite direction.

'Where is Baba?' Alok asked.

'Baba full-toss *ho gaya*,' he said mockingly.

'Meaning?' Alok asked.

'What will happen if you mix half a bottle of Whisky with Marijuana?' Harish asked.

'Obviously blackout, but where did he get *ganja* from?' Alok asked.

'Kailash, who else?' Harish replied.

'What's the plan?' Harish asked.

'Nothing, I am walking down to Mandira's house and then straight home. And you?' he asked.

'I am going to check on Baba in the hostel. He left this place a couple of hours back,' Harish said a bit sheepishly.

'Bastard, don't I know all about your concern and this checking business? All that you guys will do is drink more,' Alok said landing a small punch on his chest. Harish retreated smilingly.

'Aren't you coming?' he asked.

'No man, it's already 9PM and I am done for the day. You guys have fun,' he said. Harish made a face at him and then walked away briskly.

They came out of the auditorium and walked till the main gate in silence.

'Should I take a rickshaw?' she asked.

'I will walk with you. It's a twenty minute walk from here to your bungalow,' he looked at her.

'Hmmm…all right,' she nodded.

It was over nine and the Butler Palace road wore a deserted look. A few hawkers had laid down their carts on both sides of the road and were managing their sales of groundnuts and fruits through borrowed street light and small lanterns placed on their carts. The vehicle movement was restricted to cycle rickshaws and an occasional two or four wheeler.

'So when do you leave from here?' Alok asked.

'Day after. I have a flight at ten to Delhi,' Mandira said.

'Will you be staying in Delhi for a while?' he asked.

'A couple of days; because dad is there. And then I fly to the US,' she said.

A few minutes of silence ensued.

'You don't sound excited like the other day,' he said.

'Yeah, kind of. I will be gone from here in a couple of days, so far away,' she said.

'But you will return during holidays. Won't you?' he asked.

'I am not sure. Dad has told me that they would prefer to come over to the US with my grandmother instead of me coming back to India. It will be a good change for them,' she said.

Alok's heart pounded and he felt a layer of blackness enveloping his sight. He tried hard to focus, and most of all on breathing.

'Wouldn't you miss this place, your home M?' he asked hesitatingly.

'What's there to miss? I would be coming back to India after I am through with my degree anyways,' she said.

'Hey, I am sorry, if I made you believe that there was something serious between us,' she said and held his hand.

'You are a great guy Alok but I am just not ready for any commitment as of now. I have too many things to do and too many dreams to follow,' she added hastily.

'It's fine M. I am glad that you came into my life and made it so bloody good. Though short but then what the heck, aren't our lives short as well?' he shrugged.

'Good, I feel lighter man. I had been feeling kind of heavy for last few days that may be I have pushed you into thinking about something that doesn't exist. Kind of mislead you! You know what I mean?' she said looking a bit relaxed.

'You didn't M and you are a lovely girl,' he said.

They stood outside her big iron gate after fifteen minutes.

'So,' she said looking at him.

'So,' he said with a quivering voice that knew that finally the time had come.

'I am going day after tomorrow,' she said.

'I know,' he said.

'Will you miss me?' she asked.

'Can I hug you M?' he asked. The tears in his eyes were desperately holding on to their turf.

She hesitatingly opened up her arms and embraced his body. She could feel his heart pounding like an engine and his breath falling on the skin of her neck, racy and non-rhythmic as if he wanted to cry.

'I will always miss you M,' he muttered.

'Hmmm… I will as well,' she said separating her body from his.

'Will we stay in touch?' she asked. He kept quiet.

'You didn't answer my question?' she repeated.

'I don't know M,' he said.

'Bye M,' he said.

'Bye and Take Care Alok,' she said. He smiled and turned back to walk into the darknes. She kept looking at him till his form disappeared somewhere within the distance, just when she retreated back to enter her bungalow.

'Alok get up! Harish is here,' he heard his mother's voice and fervent knocking at the door.

It took him a few seconds to break his stupor and look at the watch. He wondered what had prompted Harish to come in so early. He unlocked the door and wallowed into the living room trying to get rid of the drowsiness. Harish was pacing in the room and his face looked un-kept and worried.

'Hi there…what on earth brings you here so early?' he said yawning.

Harish gave him a puzzled look and then suddenly as if he had found an answer held Alok's hand and pulled him out of the living room and then towards the main door of the house.

'What the fu...k,' Alok said and before he could realize they were standing in the portico of his house. Harish loosened his grip from Alok's hand.

'Alok, something bad happened last night. Real bad,' Harish said with trembling lips.

Alok could sense that something was really amiss.

'Baba …mmm Baba, Alok,' he said with a face that was going paler by the second.

'What happened to him? Is he unwell after drinking himself silly last night?' he asked.

'Baba…Alok… Pub 55,' Harish mumbled.

'What Harish? What?' Alok shook him by the shoulder.

'They burnt down Pub 55 Alok…mmm they burnt it up,' Harish nervously fumbled through the words.

'What are you saying man? Why are you incoherent? Who burnt down Baba's room? Who??' Alok went wild as he heard this.

'Vinay, Vinay…Mmm…it was Vinay and gang. Baba stabbed him in the stomach…he collapsed there. Oh my God!' Harish covered his eyes with his shaky hands and howled.

'What ? Baba stabbed Vinay ! Where? How?' Alok gripped a bitterly weeping Harish's shoulder and questioned. A million questions were racing thorough his mind and Harish was proving to be of little help in answering them.

'Last night Alok! It all happened last night,' Harish spoke in a choked voice.

'Where is Baba?' Alok asked.

'He left for Balrampur, late night, his hometown in Gonda district. Baba was scared Alok, for the first time I could see fear on Baba's face.'

'He told me not to let anyone know about his whereabouts except you. This is going to spiral into a huge police case,' he said.

'Hang on Harish! Don't start assuming trouble unless you are sure. Do you know what happened to Vinay?' he asked. Harish shook his head.

'Hmmm...So, what do we do now?' Alok asked. The question was directed more at himself rather than Harish who stared at him with a blank expression on his face.

'How far is Balrampur from here?' Alok asked.

'About four hours by bus,' he said.

'Hmmm..,' Alok said and thought for a minute.

'We have to go to Balrampur in Gonda. You stay right here and I will be back in ten,' he said and rushed back into the house without letting Harish to even open his mouth.

They were holed up in a State Roadways bus to Gonda exactly an hour later that they had boarded from Charbagh Bus Stand. Alok and Harish sat cramped on the last row with eight others who seemed accustomed to this discomfort. Harish was limping back to normalcy and occasionally took a sip from the Bisleri bottle that he carried.

'So, what really happened?' Alok asked after a long silence. Harish took a deep breath.

'I reached the hostel after meeting you last night and did not find Baba inside his room. The room wasn't locked, and thinking that Baba would be around, I went in and decided to wait for him,' he paused.

'Then?' Alok asked.

'I waited for sometime and when Baba did not come back, I pulled out a whisky bottle from the cupboard and poured myself a drink.'

'I must have had two drinks when I heard a flurry of foot-steps in the corridor and before I could reach the door, Vinay alongwith atleast twenty students barged inside the room ,' he said and his face started displaying contours of horror that it would have lived last night.

'He was hoping to find the three of us there and was obviously very dejected after the election defeat. To top it all, yesterday's public celebration of Gope's victory and the concert was the final nail in the coffin. Akhil Tewari had put the entire blame of his election loss on Vinay for not being manly enough to garner enough votes in the University. Vinay, obviously did not seem to handle this at all. He was drunk and had lost complete control over his tongue. At first he lashed out at me and then asked for yours and Baba's whereabouts. I frankly had no clue and that's exactly what I told him,' he said.

'Then?'

'After a while they got a bit unruly. Vinay manhandled me and slapped me a couple of times. I tried to resist, but I was no match against so many of them. It was here when Khanna stepped in,' he said.

'Was he there too? What did he do?'

'He provoked Vinay; saying that the main culprit behind them losing a lot of votes was you and that there was no point in hitting out at me. I knew that the main reason of Khanna's aggravation was you replacing him in the band and had nothing to do with Akhil Tiwari's loss. Vinay got carried away by Khanna's claim as he had an old issue to settle with you as well. They stayed there for a while waiting for Baba and kept dishing out the choicest of abuses to you and Baba,' he said.

'Then?' Alok asked.

'Then as they were leaving, one amongst the group mentioned that this room was the place where the three of us met everyday and planned Akhil Bhaiyya's defeat. This was the place where the plans of Gope's election campaign were drawn and put into shape. It was here that our friendship blossomed, hence to let this place remain would ensure that it would keep giving shelter to creeps like us,' he paused and then shut his eyes.

'This fucking insinuation entered that bastard's Vinay's head and despite my pleading he picked up that bottle of whisky and splashed it around the room, on clothes, bed sheets and books,' he said recounting the terror. Alok stared at him without batting an eyelid.

'And then he lit it up with a matchbox. I was too stunned to react as I saw flames around me grow bigger and bigger. I was transfixed at the same spot and would have perhaps ended up inside the room if one of the guys with Vinay wouldn't have pushed me out of the room.'

'They stood there for a few seconds and then started walking back. The flames and ensuing commotion made other students come out of their rooms but they were too shocked to react,' he said and by now tears had reappeared in his eyes again. He wiped them away with his hand and continued.

'They would have reached the stairs when Baba staggered on the floor; I guess he was still reeling under the overdose of alcohol and marijuana. As he saw Vinay and the group approaching the stairs, his room caught up in fire and a picture of me completely hysterical, it took him no time to gauge what was happening. I remember his face changing contours; from looking drunk it turned livid,' he paused.

'What did he do?' Alok asked.

'He pushed Vinay hard when he reached closer and he fell on the ground; while he kicked hard on the locked door of Room No.50. The lock broke open and he rushed inside. Vinay who had fallen on the ground was taken aback by this sudden aggression; he took a few seconds to react and get up with the help of his cronies.'

'Then,' Alok guided him to speak.

'Baba was out with a knife that had a solid thick blade and an expression that meant business. He gripped the knife tightly and moved closer to Vinay. Vinay's entire group including that Khanna backtracked looking at Baba's wild demeanor. Vinay wanted to mumble something but I guess Baba's reaction and the knife about a foot away from his chest numbed his throat and nothing came out. And then without uttering a word Baba thrust the weapon in his stomach, not once but twice.'

'Oh my God,' Alok said as he held his forehead.

'Vinay collapsed on the spot and then there was hullaboo all around. The entire bunch that had come like panthers on the prowl ran down from the stairs like pussies on the run.'

'Then?' Alok asked.

'I raced up to him and the first thing he asked me was, 'Where is Alok?'

Alok took a deep breath and looked outside the window. They had crossed Barabanki about half an hour back and the bus trudged through the bumpy road like a snail.

After a few moments of silence, Harish spoke again, 'I told him that you weren't there and I could see his stiff face loosening up a bit. He told me that he was sneaking out to his hometown, Balrampur in Gonda and would stay hidden there till all this crap died down. And then he took the stairs from the other side and disappeared before other's reached there to take Vinay to the hospital.'

'What happened to Vinay?' Alok asked.

'Good that the bastard did not die. But the police apparently has charged Baba under Section 307,' Harish said expressionlessly.

'That's serious. It's an attempt to murder,' Alok said.

'Baba has decent connections, I think he will manage somehow,' Harish replied.

'It's not about managing people, Harish. It's his future. If this case is slapped on him it would jeopardize his future,' Alok said getting all worked up.

'Hmm... but what can be done now? Baba as it was never turning into another Isaac Newton,' he replied plainly.

'Damn you man. Anyways who has testified in this?' Alok asked.

'Khanna,' he said.

'Anyone else?' Alok asked. Harish shook his head in negative.

The elderly woman in her mid fifties eyed the two boys suspiciously in the huge living room of Baba's patrimonial house in Balrampur.

'So, how do you know Sarvesh?' she enquired with her eyes ready to pop out of the archaic glass frame.

'Who??'Alok asked surprisingly. Harish nudged him and whispered in his ear.

'That's Baba,' he whispered, reminding him about Baba's original name given to him by his mother sitting in front of them.

'Oh, Sarvesh! Aunty we are his closest friends actually,' Alok fumbled.

'Hmmm...but what brings you here? He isn't here, should be in Lucknow now,' she said casually.

Alok thought that there was no further point in beating around the bush.

'Auntie, we are his closest friends. We know about everything that has happened in Lucknow. Please understand that we are here to help,' he said. The earnestness in his voice seemed to have created an immediate impact with the lady and she softened up.

'Guddu...,' she shouted.

A lanky fourteen year something Guddu emerged from the neighboring room almost immediately.

'Bhaiyya ke paas liye jao, unke dost hain (Please take them to your brother; they are his friends),' she muttered. The boy inspected them like a police inspector and then signaled them to follow him. They thanked Baba's mother and followed the boy quietly.

They passed through a few odd narrow lanes, lines of dirty shops and shit flooded drains before hitting a tapered road that had an agricultural landscape on both the sides. They would have walked a couple of kilometers before Harish asked:

'*Kitni door*?'

The boy gave him a 'Have you gone nuts?' look.

'*Phat gayi kya? Chale chalo abhi,'* he said looking cheesed off. A few minutes later they were walking towards a partially constructed and unpainted farm house looking structure, standing discreetly amongst jungle grass and wild weed.

The boy strode rapidly towards the door and knocked it three times. They could sense some movement inside and when the door opened, a tired looking Baba emerged from inside.

'*Arrayy,* Alok *Bhai,* what a surprise…*Bhaiyya* Harish?' Baba smiled as he hugged them.

'Come on in, though its not the best place to welcome guests,' Baba said as he led them inside.

It really wasn't. The place was dirty and an old mattress was splattered on one side of the room. A few books were kept next to the mattress and a half filled bottle of whisky was placed near the pillow. Patches of dust rested on the floor and Alok could spot atleast three cobwebs in the first glance.

'This place had never been used earlier, until today morning. We had started constructing this place ten years back but somehow the work never got finished. All the land that you can see around this farmhouse also belongs to us but has never been used for farming,' he said.

'Why?' Harish asked.

'Who will do it? Dad is busy with his practice and I have been away for studies. Who has time?' he said.

'*Bhaiyya hum chalein*?' the boy asked. Baba nodded.

'Care for a drink?' he asked picking up the whisky bottle after they had settled on the mattress.

'Now?? Its broad daylight man,' Harish panicked.

'So? Don't you get a high in the afternoon?' Baba guffawed pouring a drink.

'Vinay seems ok now. He is out of the ICU,' Baba said taking a huge swig.

'How do you know?' Alok asked.

'*Bhaiyya kay touch main hain hum (I am in touch with Gope)*,' he replied.

'Can't Gope help?' Alok asked.

'He could, if that Khanna wouldn't have testified before the police. We could have managed everything. But not now,' he said.

'No way?' Harish asked.

'Only if he retracts his statement,' Baba said as he poured another drink.

'But what was the need to stab him Baba?' Alok asked.

Baba looked out of the window and then deep into Alok's eyes. Alok could sense them going moist.

'All my memories of Lucknow are in Pub 55. Those happy moments, sad moments, crazy moments, drunken moments, victories, heartburns, plans, jokes, friends,' he said.

'You didn't mention studies even once,' Alok said with a straight face. Baba smiled to become somber again.

'So much of time the three of us have spent there. Can you forget that Alok *Bhai*?' he asked emotionally. Alok sighed.

'And that bastard took all of it away by just twitching two fingers. Just like this?' he gestured as if he was hurling a matchstick.

'Pub 55 was my home; and they torched it down. Burnt down my home; my memories,' Baba started sobbing. Alok patted his shoulder.

'Let it be Baba. What's done can't be reversed now,' Harish said.

'What now?' Alok asked.

'I will stay holed up here and at other places till this shit dies out,' he said.

'And then settle here and become a farmer,' he added.

'Why wouldn't you want to study further?' Harish asked.

'Who will let me? That chapter is finished now,' he said with a pained voice.

'What about us? I mean when do we meet next?' Alok asked.

'No idea,' Baba said and finished his drink.

It was about 3PM when they decided to leave.

'Thanks Alok *Bhai,* it was good to have you here. I feel much better. And by the way your *raak* show was fantastic the other day. *Ekdum lallan top. Saare saaman saale let gaye zameen par. Hum to behenchod tunn thehey tab (Your show was superb that day Alok Bhai and everyone especially the women toppled on the floor with its impact. I was fucking smashed with alcohol at that time),*' he chuckled while hugging Alok. It was with a lot of restraint that Alok could hold back his tears.

'Hmmm… I will see you soon Baba,' Alok muttered.

'Hopefully, Alok *Bhai.* It all depends on him,' Baba said pointing his finger upwards to the sky,

Alok sleepwalked to the bus stand oblivious of the buzzing environment and sank into the seat of the bus that took them back to Lucknow. It was an inebriated Baba transfixed into his memory after the first rock show, in Pub No. 55, humming what was perhaps his first English song recital ever. Baba in his own inimitable *desi* Eric Clapton meets Kishore Kumar style:

If you wanna get down, down on the ground cocaine…

It was close to seven when they got out of the bus at the Charbagh bus stand. Lucknow was preparing for the night and tired looking faces glanced through vehicles of different shapes and sizes, cyclerickshaws; and walked across pavements and busy roads.

'So, should we head back home now?' Harish asked tentatively.

'No. I am going to meet Khanna. Where do we find him?' Alok asked looking resolute.

'Khanna? Why on earth would you want to meet that bastard?' Harish was surprised.

'Where can I find him?' Alok pressed again. The steely resolve on his face made Harish give in without any further resistance.

'He stays in the Subhash Hostel. That's all I know,' Harish replied.

'Finding his room number shouldn't be an issue. Are you coming?' Alok started walking towards a rickshaw. Harish thought for a second and then nodded.

They were standing outside the partially shut wooden door of Room

No.16 at Subhash Hostel. The smell of cheap whisky and loud guffaws stemmed from the room and the small merriment inside indicated that there wasn't much remorse over one of their friends getting stabbed last night. Alok's face displayed signs of disgust momentarily before he pushed open the door. They looked visibly surprised to see uninvited guests and especially the two of them. Four of them were sitting on the bed while Khanna sat on the chair wearing an Iron Maiden T-Shirt and a towel underneath.

'Why have you come here?' he asked in an angry tone.

'I wanted to talk,' Alok replied. A scared Harish looked around suspiciously.

'Talk about what? Hasn't your bloody friend talked and done enough?' he raised his slurring voice.

'Vinay provoked him to do what he did. Don't you know that?' Alok said. The others in the room merely played the role of silent spectators to their verbal volley.

'I don't care about provocation. I just know that he tried to murder Vinay and now he will have to pay a heavy price for what he did,' Khanna said taking a sip.

'Can I talk to you in private outside?' Alok asked.

'Why? I have already given my statement to the police, so what's the need now?' he asked.

'A few minutes won't harm you,' Alok said. Khanna gazed at the expression sapped faces of others in the room and then went silent.

'Ok,' he got up and walked towards the door. Alok knew that a spineless opportunist like Khanna would definitely relent.

'Yes, now what?' Khanna said resting his back on the wooden railing of the corridor.

'Why are you doing this Khanna? What will you get by testifying for a bastard like Vinay?' Alok asked looking into his eyes.

'He is my friend and that Baba attempted to kill him. I will make sure that your friend goes behind the bars,' Khanna replied with a menacing smile dancing on his lips.

'But why it's got to be only you Khanna? There were others in that group as well?' Alok said. Khanna carried the smirk as he spoke.

'No one else wanted to testify. Fear. Akhil *bhaiyya* asked everyone but fear of Gope, the winning President of the University kept a check on their emotions,' Khanna said.

'Then why did you agree?' Alok asked.

'Because no one hated Baba more than me,' he said.

'What? But Baba hardly knew you. Why would you hate him so much?' Alok gasped and looked at Harish who stood next to him.

'Because he was your friend Alok. He was your strength. You were an outsider who took away my band just like that. I would have done anything to stop you but for Baba. I knew he had support from students and most of all Gope,' he paused, 'and that stopped me from taking any action against you.'

'You deprived me of that adulation, that sense of achievement and of that high. In a matter of days I turned into a nobody from a star in this university,' he added and stared into the darkness.

'You know what your problem is?' Alok asked. He had Khanna's attention.

'You want to be on stage because you love the adulation and the stardom bit while I wanted to be there because I love the music,' Alok said looking into his eyes. Khanna kept staring at him.

'You can get your rockstar status and the fans and the adulation back,' he said after a few seconds.

'How?' Khanna looked eager to know.

'You withdraw your statement from the police and I will give your earlier life back to you,' Alok said firmly.

'But...but,' Khanna stuttered.

'Don't think but act Khanna; and you will have to do that fast,' he said.

'But...how can I do that now? How can I do that? What will people say?' he stammered again.

'You want your life back Khanna or bother about what others are saying?' Alok was taking a command over the situation. Harish watched them with a startled look on his face.

'Ok ...but what about you? I mean you sing for the band as of now,' Khanna, the bastard wanted to be sure.

'I will leave the band, Khanna. Infact I will leave the city soon. I will hand over that stardom to you in a platter, but for that you have to retract your statement tomorrow morning,' Alok said measuring his words.

'Ok. I will do that tomorrow morning. But you have to keep your promise as well,' Khanna said after a few moments.

He smiled sheepishly, 'I know Megha and I promise that we will go for a long vacation very soon,' he said as they looked at their daughter racing ahead and jumping across rectangular red stone tiles.

'I hope that this vacation destination is not Agra again,' she said.

'No darling, I chose it this time because it's the closest from Delhi,' he said.

'Atleast, she had whale of a time,' Megha said looking at Sneha.

'After how many years have you come to Agra?' Ashu asked.

'Don't you remember? The last time we were here; was when dad had expired,' she said.

'Yeah, before your mother moved to Delhi to stay with your brother, right?' Ashu asked. She nodded.

'My parents had moved to Delhi much earlier, just after we passed out of school,' Ashu said.

'I am sure you would have visited these places often; Agra is a case study in historical monuments,' he smirked.

'Anyone who has stayed here would. There isn't a choice, didn't you?' she asked.

'Yes of course, and especially when a relative would land up, to kickstart a guided tour to Tajmahal, Fatehpur Sikri, Agra Fort and Sikandra to say the least. Remember?' he said.

'Exactly,' she said.

'When were you in Sikandra last?' he asked.

She paused and took a deep breath, 'It has been long. It seems as if it was a different era.'

'Will you wait here with Sneha for a while?' she asked softly.

'Sure, but where do you want to go?' he asked.

'I want to walk to that old well, do you see it?' she asked pointing towards her left.

'Yeah, I think so. But why do you want to go there?' he asked.

'There is something Ashu. It's personal,' she said.

He shook his head in disbelief as if he had realized, 'Oh! It must be some holy thing, some *mannat vannat*?' She did not say anything.

'Cool, we will wait for you here; just come back soon.'

The handkerchief that he had tied on the cylindrical rod above the old, barren and dried up well was still there. She had to stretch her arm beyond her natural self to be able to reach the blackened piece of intently, nodding his head intermittently. She looked beautiful in a milky white salwar kameez and her fresh after a shower wet hair thrown onto her shoulders casually. Alok walked towards her.

'Hey! What a pleasant surprise? You never told me that you were coming to the airport?' Mandira hugged him instinctively.

'Just thought I will see you off since there won't be anyone else to drop you,' he said.

'So sweet,' she said while she signaled the driver to carry the bags. They walked towards the gate.

'So?' Alok asked.

'I am happy. I am excited. I feel good,' she said.

'I am happy for you as well M,' he said.

'So, you don't want to remain in touch with me right?' she rolled her eyes.

'It's not that M,' he said.

'That's what you said a day before, didn't you?'

'You won't understand M. It will get complicated,' he said.

'Why?' she asked. He did not reply.

'Anyway, whatever suits you Alok. I will send you my address; you decide what you want to do with it. Ok?'

They had walked up to the departure gate and visitors weren't permitted inside beyond that point.

'So, it's time to go Alok. Thank you for being a wonderful friend. I can never forget you and hope that you never forget me either,' she said.

'I will never M. Till we meet again,' he said and let her walk away through the departure gate.

She walked into the gate when a sudden surge of sadness gripped her heart.

'He is going away Mandira. This is the last chance. You are losing him!' her inner voice shrieked. She shut her eyes to forcibly block the voice's entry and then turned back to look at him. He was standing there looking at her as if waiting for something. She firmly raised her left hand and signaled good bye. He reciprocated by slowly raising his hand and waving in her direction.

It was the last time that they saw each other.

PART 3: SHONALI

24th June, 2011: Bandra, Mumbai

The house key made a creaking sound in the hole before it laid open the third floor's, two bedroom apartment at Hill Road in Bandra. A dreary looking Shonali dropped her handbag on the floor and tossed her body on the couch. The flight from Goa was late by three hours that left her doubly exhausted after the late night revelry at The Taj Goa. She pressed her eyelids hard against her pupils, trying to get rid of the tiredness and then took a deep sigh. The mobile phone buzzed inside her handbag and she unwillingly took the damn thing out.

'Hi, Siddharth!'

'How was the trip?' the voice asked.

'Oh it was ok, just that the flight got delayed,' she said.

'Hmm…is that Gupta happy?' he asked, indifferent with Shonali's concern.

'Yeah…we spent a lot of time together. I think we will get the business,' she said.

'Hmmm…good,' he said sounding pleased.

'Let's talk about it when you are in the office tomorrow.'

'Umm…Ok,' Shonali said with her eyes shut.

'Yeah, and one more thing.'

'What?" Shonali asked.

'I am going to my Panvel farm house this weekend. Why don't you come with me?' his request seemed more like an order.

'This week? I was planning to go home to see my folks in Dehradun,' Shonali frowned opening up her eyes.

'Later. We are going to Panvel this weekend,' he asserted.

'Ok,' she gave in. He disconnected the call.

She shut her eyes again and relaxed her head against the large black seat of the leather couch. It had been a long time that she had seen her mother and sister in Dehradun. It had been over fourteen years when she took a train from Dehradun to Mumbai, the city was Bombay then. The city hasn't changed much from then, but she has. From being a twenty one year old Radio Jockey who had dreams in her eyes and passion in her heart to tread the expanse of the glittering entertainment industry, she was now the Client Relationship Head at Planet Entertainment Networks. Did she want this? Did she come here to become what she was? She played the question in her mind for a moment till the reply flashed. She read it word by word and with a heart that pounded.

Name: Shonali Pandey. Age: 35 years. Marital Status: Single. Profession: Corporate Slut.

The mobile phone lying on the table now buzzed again and her trance was broken. She could feel a slight tremble in her hands as she picked up the device.

'Hello,' she said.

'Madam, have you been away for the last couple of days? The boy would have visited your flat more than five times,' a shrill voice that seemed to be in a hurry screeched on the other side.

'Who is this?' Shonali asked, annoyed.

'Delta Courier Madam! You have a courier that we have been trying to deliver for last two days. Finally, we got the mobile number from your neighbors today. Anyways, when can we deliver this packet? Are you at home now?' she hurried again giving Shonali no time to react.

'Yeah, do it now within half an hour. I have to leave after that,' Shonali said.

'Ok Madam, you wait there *haan*...don't go. I am sending the boy right now. He should be there in maximum twenty,' she said and hung up.

Shonali heaved a sigh and felt satisfied with her little lie.

'So, twenty more minutes before that goddamn courier comes in, and then I can finally sleep,' she muttered and shut her eyes again.

Name: Shonali Pandey. Age: 35 years. Marital Status: Single. Profession: Corporate Slut.

She raced through it again and paused on the last two words. Corporate Slut.

The transformation within her had been gradual. She wanted all her dreams to come true in Mumbai and she had plenty of them. From becoming a VJ and a model to opening up an academy for wide eyed aspirants seeking an entry into the glam world, she had an arrayy of aspirations that she wanted to realize really fast. The rejections came one by one and soon Shonali realized that Mumbai was not going to give in so easily to her desires. She became desperate and started clawing back to anyone who promised to help pull off her dreams. All of them did, Rahul, Sandy, Arjun and finally Siddharth Mehra. They kept lying one after another and she kept believing them, making mistakes, taking wrong steps and falling down rapidly to a point of no return. The years went by and soon she was walking down her thirties with unaccomplished dreams and a long life ahead. She had to survive at any cost and by all means. She did not want to fade within the obscurity of Dehradun after living it up in the fast lanes of Mumbai. She did not want to return back to the old government one and a half bedroom flat of her mother after being used to plush condominiums of Mumbai. To live a life that she had become used to but could not afford; required sacrifices. She made them all. Siddharth Mehra used her but then gave her a life laden with material pleasures that she couldn't live without. Designer clothes, vacations abroad, a flat in up-market Bandra, a twenty lac vehicle to drive. Could a lower middle class Dehradun girl, get this entire benefit package if she wouldn't have compromised her moral values and belief? No, possibly not.

The company Planet Entertainment Networks took her job title rather seriously. The Client Relationship Head tag that she carried on her business card; meant stretching the relationship to any extent for extracting business out of potential clients. Were there takers? Many. Shonali realized quite early that perhaps the last thing that a man would want to do before getting into his grave; is have sex. Planet Entertainment Networks used Shonali to extend these relationships beyond board-rooms and client offices to hotel rooms, farm houses and exotic locations all across the globe. Did she like all this? She had no other choice, actually. The phone lying idly for last few minutes on the table buzzed again. It was Abhi, her colleague from the office.

'Hey Abhi!' she replied drowsily.

'Hi Shonali! Have you been travelling? Haven't seen you around,' he said.

'Yeah. I have been away on work,' she said dryly.

'Ummm…Ok. What are you doing tonight? I was thinking maybe we could go to your favorite place…Indigo?' hesitation was audible in his voice.

'Not today Abhi, I am dead tired. Infact I don't intend to enter even the washroom,' she said. Abhi laughed feebly.

'Oh! Well, then you must take rest. Any plans for the weekend? Are you free then?' he took a chance again.

'Oh Abhi…I am soooo sorry. I have a friend coming over this weekend. Perhaps next week sometime? Ok?' she said as if cajoling a child.

'Oh! Ok Shonali, no issues. We will catch up sometime next week.

You take care and let me know if you need anything,' he sounded dejected as he hung up.

Shonali tossed the phone back on the table, stretched her lethargic body once again and stared at the ceiling blankly.

'Oh damn Mehra, you ruined all my plans,' she muttered under her breath looking at the ceiling.

Abhijit Dixit was actually a nice guy. He had been married once but got divorced rather quickly, in about two years. Shonali always wondered what made Abhijt's ex-wife divorce him. He was kind of an ideal husband material that an Indian woman would always desire for. He possessed good looks, came from a decent family and had a stable professional career with good enough money in the bank.

'Some women are just crazy!' she muttered again.

Abhijit Dixit had feelings for Shonali. Everybody in the office knew this and frankly Abhi made no bones in hiding his fondness towards her. He was always hovering around Shonali, picking up the minutest of pretext to be with her. They had gone out together, for movies, parties, dinners and to pubs, but for Shonali it was normal, it was like going out with anyone else. She liked Abhi and that was it, just liked. Shonali never thought that she could have special feeling for anyone; forget Abhi.

It was the doorbell that broke her trance this time. A sweaty man wearing the off white Delta Courier uniform stood at her doorstep with a white envelope that had her name written on it. She signed on the delivery challan and then walked inside the house with the envelope in her hand. She tore open the seal of the envelope and tossed her body back onto the couch. It seemed like a letter inside which she started reading:

Dear Shona

'Shona! Well, very few people call me by that name...,' Shonali muttered and continued reading.

Dear Shona

Hope Mumbai is treating you very well. So have you finally learnt to pronounce Delhi as Delhi and not Dilli??

She read the line again, 'So have you finally learnt to pronounce Delhi as Delhi and not Dilli??' There was a deafening piercing sound in her ears as her heart pounded wildly. It was him. Only he had said this to her, not once but so many times in the studio. She started reading it again.

Dear Shona

Hope Mumbai is treating you very well. So have you finally learnt to pronounce Delhi as Delhi and not Dilli??

By now you would have realized that it's me who is writing to you after fourteen years. Long time; but it seems just like yesterday when I met you for the first time in that conference room. We had so much fun together; remember those Night outs at Fireball, hot paranthas at Safdarjang, the great time we had at our conference in Goa and so many of such memories.

I stay in this peaceful yet picturesque hill station called Mussoorie now. I teach music in this beautiful town. The reason of writing this letter to you is that I have something in my possession that belongs to you. It has been with me for last so many years but now I can't keep it with me anymore. I want you to come and take it from me before it's too late.

I will wait for you on 28th June at the Dehradun airport. Mussoorie is about two hours away from the airport and I would recommend that you be in Dehradun by 4PM so that we can get into the town by the evening. Take care and see you Shona.

Yours

Alok
House Number 403
Off Mall Road
Near Government School
Mussoorie.

Shonali read the letter twice, folded it neatly and kept it on the nearby coffee-table. The letter was like a tranquilizer that had numbed the engulfed tiredness in her body. She stared again at the white ceiling that lay above her and dived into the past, reliving the time gone by that appeared in front of her eyes frame after frame. Live and breathing.

August 1996: New Delhi, India

Shonali adjusted her peach colored dupatta neatly over her shoulders and glanced around the pastel walls of the conference room. She looked at her watch, it was close to noon and it had taken her about an hour to wade through the sweltering heat and bustling traffic of Delhi to reach the four storied building of the largest media house in the country, The Indian News. Shonali had put in about two months of aggressive follow-up on phone with the HR department of The Indian News, to be here for an interview today in the conference room of Smile FM, the newly launched radio arm of the media giant. As she walked from the lobby to the conference room, she realized that the general vibe at Smile FM was energetic, the atmosphere – cool and the average employee-young. While sitting there she could see young men with curious eyes throw glances at her through the glass facade, wondering who this attractive visitor was. Did she enjoy the attention? You bet! She loved every bit of it.

She would have waited for about thirty minutes when a male head with long flowing hair that touched his broad shoulders, popped inside the conference room through the door.

'Shonali?' he asked. The sudden entry of this guy unnerved her a bit and she got up from her chair with a jerk.

'Relax. Alok Mathur,' he stretched his hand out. Shonali responded mechanically and shook his hand. The touch was warm and comforting. They sat on the opposite sides of the conference table as he got engrossed in her bio-data. She looked at the table for a minute and then pulled her gaze up to look at Alok. He was unshaven and dressed in a plain white T-Shirt and blue denims. The casual attire and a lean body made him look masculine and attractive enough to get noticed by the opposite sex quite keenly. He went through her CV in detail and then placed it on the table.

'So Shonali, why Smile FM?' he asked.

'Just like your tagline; music that makes you smile, I want to work at a place where there is fun and happiness all around,' she responded with a rehearsed answer.

'Hmmm…so basically you are here for happiness and not for some serious work?' Alok asked.

'It's not that. If you are having fun at work, then work doesn't really look like one boring work. It becomes a part of your life,' she said.

'True. What are your strengths?' he asked.

'Hard work, Persistence and patience,' she said chewing her words.

'Not result orientation?' he asked.

'Result is an outcome. The ones that I mentioned are the means to that. I guess they are more relevant,' she said with a 'Miss India look' on her face. He looked pleased.

'Why radio Shonali?' he asked.

'Radio is the theatre of the mind. It makes millions of people across the length and breadth of the country to conjure images from what they can't see but just hear. Isn't that a huge feat by itself?' she asked. Alok who looked convinced with her answer could just shake his head in affirmation.

'It looks as if you have prepared well for this interview,' he said.

'No, not at all. It comes naturally to me because I love radio,' she lied cheekily. All she wanted at that time was the god damn job with Smile FM.

'I like you Shonali, but currently we don't have any opening for an RJ,' he said wanting to gauge her response.

Shonali's heart skipped a beat but she managed to retain her composure.

'But I would like you to take up the role of an assistant producer for the time being, and learn the ropes of radio. I think you can also hone up your radio jockeying skills meanwhile, through thorough practice and be completely ready when the right opportunity arrives,' he added.

'Damn! What the hell? I will have to wait, but so what, at least I will get an entry within Smile FM and then we shall see,' she played with the thought in her mind for a while.

'So?' Alok asked breaking the silence.

'No issues, boss. I don't mind being an Assistant Producer to start with, but you do have to consider me as soon as a RJ vacancy comes up,' she said.

'Done deal,' a smiling Alok said and got up.

'So, when can you join?' he asked.

'Today. Can I?' she asked enthusiastically and found Alok looking at her admiringly.

'Great. I like it. Welcome aboard and let me get you to meet up with the team,' he said and signaled her to follow him.

'Yes!' Shonali mumbled while pumping her fist up in the air and hastily followed Alok who had walked out of the conference room.

'Hey Babs,' Alok greeted the portly mid thirties spectacled man seated on his oversized leather chair.

The guy did not respond and kept staring at the computer screen while nibbling on the apple that he held in his palm.

'We have got someone good within the team today,' Alok said.

'Hmmm…who?' Babs a.k.a Basab Dutta or Alok's boss finally opened his jaw to mumble.

'Shonali Pandey, smart girl,' Alok said and sat on the chair facing him.

'Doing something important?' he asked.

'Yeah, a management report that needs to go to *Agarwaljee*,' Babs said taking his eyes away reluctantly from the naked breasts of a Russian model. Internet was new in India and Babs was one of the few privileged ones in the county to have an access to it. He put this exclusive privilege to use by visiting pornsites all through the day, unabashedly.

'Oh. Ok. Should we record the weekend countdown today for all three metros?' Alok asked drumming the table with his fingers.

'Forget that man. I have a much bigger issue at hand,' Babs said with his eyes popping out of the sockets.

'What?'

'That actor is going to be in our office at 4PM,' he said.

'Who?'

'*Arrayy* that Delhi guy. Sahil Khan, the new star in Bollywood these days,' Babs eyes were rummaging through the computer screen again.

Sahil Khan was the newest sensation in Bollywood with three back to back hits. The films titled *Dil Deewana, Koi Darr Nahin* and *Main Jaadugar* had given a respite to an otherwise sluggish industry and catapulted the local Delhi lad to the top bracket.

'Wow, that's great news; we will get some great content from him. Being a local he would have so many Delhi-centric stories to talk about that would connect with local listeners extremely well,' Alok looked excited. Babs looked completely cheesed off.

'Just look at you Alok! While you are excited about getting good content from the damn star; I am worried about saving my job,' Babs said irritatingly.

'Why, what's this thing about the job?' he asked.

'*Arrayy* these owners; they just don't understand anything. *Agarwaljee* thinks that this Sahil Khan is my long lost brother who would do anything for me,' he said.

'Can you imagine Alok, he wants Sahil Khan to wear Smile FM T-Shirt and cap and pose in front of the camera?' Babs added hastily.

'And then he wants to use these pictures in his newspaper to promote Smile FM, for free,' he said shaking his head in disbelief.

'That's a good idea,' Alok quipped.

'Good idea? My ass Alok,' Babs huffed.

'What do you think; Sahil will do it for free? These guys will not even fart for free; they would even take money from their parents for giving birth to stars like them,' he said.

'And our Mr. Agarwal expects that Basab Dutta is some fucking Superman who will get Sahil Khan to wear his brand and not charge a penny for it. He thinks that just because Indian News is one big media group they can push anyone to do anything. And who does that for them? Poor fucking me,' Babs said looking completely rattled.

'Hmmm...looks tricky, but not impossible. I have to give it to Mr. Agarwal for the idea. If we get free publicity from Sahil for Smile FM, it would really be a killer,' Alok said, excitedly.

'Fuck the idea Alok, all these Harvard returned young scions of industrialists have unreal dreams like these and they expect people like us to fulfill them. If we don't, we get screwed,' he said.

'Anyways, now that we have to do it, how do we pull this off?' Babs looked pained like a lost kid.

'There must be some way Babs, there has to be,' Alok said and got off the chair thoughtfully.

Babs carried the same aggrieved expression on his face till Alok left his cabin, and then dived back into his familiar world of nudity and porn.

'What's the dope on Sahil Khan?' Alok asked Shonali who was sitting at her work station. She had been through a round of introductions with the entire Smile FM programming team over last couple of hours and had also been assigned a designated place. She couldn't understand his question.

'Sahil Khan is going to be in the station today. Do you have a clue about his personal likings through magazines etc.?' he explained.

'Umm...he loves Delhi food, the traditional old stuff you know and....and he loves music, 70's rock'n' roll,' she said.

'How do you know all this?' Alok gave her a surprised look.

'Stardust Magazine...your ultimate guide to Bollywood,' she chirped. Alok looked lost in his thought for a few seconds.

'That was good ....infact great,' Alok smiled and walked away.

'Has the star arrived?' Murli said peeping inside the dimly lit studio. Alok sat behind the studio mike fiddling with the settings on the RJ console.

'Not yet? Where is Andy?' Alok asked.

'He is briefing your team. By the way we haven't yet received the outputs on the three briefs that we gave you yesterday,' he said.

'*Bacchhe kee jaan loge kya*? Boss I am virtually running the station without enough people. Anyways, we have found someone good today and we should hopefully turn around all your stuff by tomorrow,' Alok looked up. Murli smirked and then disappeared from the door.

A few minutes would have passed when a visibly excited Raj, the studio technician appeared at the studio door again.

'He's here,' he muttered like a nervous kid.

Alok removed the earphones from his head and walked out to meet Sahil Khan, the star.

The entire office was cramped like sardines in the conference room and stared at the larger than life Sahil Khan as if he were some species from outer space. Sahil looked comfortable with the limelight and sat there oblivious to the prying eyes, profusely puffing away from his pack of Marlboro Lights. Babs sat on the chair next to Sahil, who looked completely unfazed by the insipid chatter that the manager was trying to make with him. He responded to his mumblings by a little nod of his head or an occasional glance at him. Alok tried to squeeze inside the tightly packed conference hall but no one seemed to be in a mood to relent. He stood at the conference door and gestured at Babs who took a couple of minutes to notice him. Babs asked him to hold on and then went closer to Sahil and mumbled something in his ears. Sahil looked instantly relieved and got up with a jerk to wade through the crowded conference room in Alok's direction, with Babs in hot pursuit.

'Let's do the interview now. He's in a hurry,' Babs said as he came near Alok.

'Did you speak to him about wearing Smile FM merchandise?' Alok asked walking alongside Babs. Sahil walked ahead, accompanied by his manager and couple of his cronies' alongwith Raj the studio technician.

'Yeah, I did, but the bastard ignored me as if I was talking to a wall. He didn't even seem to listen,' Babs whispered in a concerned voice.

'Anyway, we will try once more, after he is through with the interview. Hope you are prepared?'

'Yeah,' Alok smiled and entered the studio behind Sahil Khan.

'Hi Sahil, I am Alok,' he said offering him a chair opposite the RJ console.

'Hey, hi! And what do you do Alok?' Sahil spoke in his heavily accentuated drawl.

'I am the Programming Head cum producer cum part time RJ at Smile FM,' Alok smirked as he settled on his seat.

'How do you juggle so many things?' he asked taking off his sunglasses.

'The way you juggle your shifts while doing so many films together,' Alok quipped.

'Yeah...that was smart man. Yeah, I do...yeah,' Sahil kind of introspected.

'So, what are you going to ask?' he said.

'Whatever you may want to say, Sahil!' Alok said checking the equalizer levels. He glanced towards the giant studio window and caught the glimpse of Shonali who was curiously peeking inside. He signaled her to come in and she nervously stepped inside.

'Sahil meet Shonali! She works with us,' he said. Sahil Khan gave her a fleeting look and a lop-sided smile. Shonali nervously sat on the couch placed next to the door.

'No, I mean do we go through a standard questionnaire?' Sahil asked again.

'There isn't any predetermined format Sahil. I thought we will make it much simpler and free-flowing. This will be your first interview in Delhi after a long time and I thought we would make it sound very personal and local,' he paused for a moment, 'I thought that we could talk about your journey from bylanes of Daryaganj to your plush bungalow in Bandra, about the rock 'n' roll of 70's, your friends in Delhi, your favorite food from Delhi and interesting anecdotes from your life here. I thought we would make it very Delhi-centric for people to relate to,' Alok said passionately.

'Sounds interesting but without a format, I hope we won't be all over the place.'

'Don't worry Sahil; we will edit everything that's not required after we record it. Ok?' Alok asked reassuringly.

It appeared as if his answer allayed the underlying fear in Sahil's mind and he calmed down. Babs who was entering the studio after a quick leak tried to wipe away his hands with a handkerchief. Alok signaled everyone to be quiet and gestured at Babs to sit on the couch. Like a smooth operator he then switched on the mike and raised the console levels to start the interview. After playing a collage of Sahil's hit movie songs, Alok introduced Sahil dramatically in the show announcing him as the hottest star of today and as tomorrow's superstar. He traced back the star's past to his modest background, his old school, teachers who loved him, friends who always stood by him, to his fondest memories of Delhi that never seemed to leave him. Sahil Khan was completely absorbed in the discussion and they were pacing towards the end of the interview quite well.

'Isn't your fetish for wearing leather pants an inspiration from someone?' Alok asked.

'Who?' Sahil looked surprised.

'Jim Morrison, the bad boy of rock'n'roll,' pat came the reply. Sahil shook his head in disbelief and then smiled.

'For the first time in my bollywood career has someone noticed this, yeah its true.'

'Your favorite place in Delhi?' Alok asked.

'Qutub Minar.'

'Because that's where you used to go with your parents?' Alok asked.

Sahil gave him a long hard stare and then his face softened. The toughened eyes that were used to scare the bad guys and make heroines go weak in the knees had become moist. He tried to speak but his throat gave away and choked. Alok passed him a bottle of water and he took a couple of sips before speaking again.

'Yeah, that is the only memory that I have of *Abbajaan*, all of us used to go there once a month, four of us, my *amma*, my *khala*, my *abba* and I. We used to cook *seekh kababs*, *gosht* and *biryani* in aluminum tiffins for lunch that my abba carried all the way from Daryaganj in the DTC bus to QutubMinar. I was like a freebird in the wide expansive gardens of *Qutub Minar* which was a welcome change, after playing in the narrow and rickety lanes of Daryaganj. I loved running on the wet grass of the lawns barefoot with my *khala*, carefree like a wild deer or a bird,' Sahil stopped and a small tear escaped out of his left eye that he wiped away and wore his dark RayBans again.

'I can give up anything for those times, those memories and for my *abba* who is no more in this *jahan* today; but always in our prayers,' he added softly.

'He would indeed be very proud to see where you have reached today in life Sahil *Bhai,* through your hard work, determination and humility,' Alok said.

'*Inshahallah*,' Sahil said.

'*Inshahallah* Sahilbhai. We at Smile FM and everyone from this city of Delhi wish you a great future and may you achieve greater success and love of people not just from India but the entire world,' Alok completed the last link and brought the fader down.

'One of my best interviews so far. In-fact not one of them, but indeed the best,' Sahil announced and got up.

'The pleasure is ours Sahil, you were just fantastic,' Babs spoke like a sycophant.

'No, it was all Alok's doing. It was really brilliant the way he conducted the entire interview.

'Man you belong to bigger places, you should be in Bombay,' Sahil looked around for affirmation. Babs squirmed in his seat while Shonali looked at both of them in awe.

'No, really I mean it,' Sahil looked at Alok and got up from the chair. Alok shook his head in denial as he got up from the RJ chair.

'Thanks *Sahilbhai*, this kind of an appreciation coming from a star like you really means a lot,' he said.

'Now, for some food?' he asked Sahil Khan as they came out of the studio. A score of anticipating eyes and starstruck fans from other departments had all lined up outside in a queue to have a *dekko* at the star.

'No *yaar* getting late,' Sahil said walking in the aisle that led them to the main office.

'Ok boss, I thought that some *burra kabab* and *tandoori raan* from Karim's might interest you?' Alok mentioned casually.

'You mean Karim from Jama Masjid?' Sahil asked attentively.

'Yeah, and there is some *mutton biryani* as well,' Alok said.

'That's my favorite place in Delhi and I have been dying to have authentic Karim's food for so long man,' he almost jumped with enthusiasm.

'Ok, why don't you have some then?' Alok said.

'Ofcourse I will man; everything else can wait. Let's go,' Sahil said excitedly like a schoolboy.

Babs looked at Alok agape as if he were a magician who had pulled off a rabbit from his hat.

'Mmm...this is heaven man. There can't be any thing better than authentic Mughlai cuisine from Karim,' Sahil said while devouring scrumptious portion of tandoori ran with *khamiri* bread.

'Yeah, these burra kebabs are also awesome,' Babs struggled to speak with his mouth full. Babs lead a simple life with two frugal passions that he followed religiously; eating good food and watching hard core porn.

All of them were completely exhausted by the time their sumptuous meal ended, especially Sahil who seemed to be in a different world.

'Awesome man! I could give my life for a meal from Karim's. Thanks Alok, I owe you one,' he said with his eyes closed.

'My pleasure Sahil; but if you can just do me a small favor,' Alok said.

'Anything man anything,' he replied with his eyes still shut.

'Can you pose for some pictures with Smile FM T-Shirts and caps?'

Sahil Khan's manager who was sitting at a distance but with his ear buds transfixed on their conversation; jumped at this sudden demand.

'Oh no, not at all! Sir does not endorse any product just like that, and that too without a fee,' he said. Sahil looked at Alok with helpless eyes.

'Sahil *bhai*, Agarwaljee will screw my happiness. Rest is up to you,' Alok said with a straight face.

'But Sahil sir cannot endorse any thing just like that? Didn't I tell you?' the manager stared angrily at Babs who had an "I have no fucking idea" look on his face.

'Let it be Rikkujee...*itne pyaar se bol rahe hain*. What is the big deal in posing for a few pictures?' he gave a gentle nod and smiled at Alok .

'After the food Alok that you fed me, I could have done anything for you man!' he added relishing Karim's culinary again. Alok did not want to let go of the moment and the opportunity. He glanced at Babs who seemed to be in the seventh heaven witnessing the sudden turn of events. In a matter of seconds Babs organized T-Shirts, caps and branded bandana's of Smile FM.

'All of them?' Sahil asked looking at the gear.

'Yeah...whatever you may want to wear,' Alok replied hesitatingly. Rikku squirmed with anger like a wounded animal. Sahil picked up the clothing pieces one by one and willingly shot for a couple of photographs with each of them.

'Can I go now?' he mocked by bending down in front of Alok with folded hands.

'Don't embarrass me *Sahilbhai*, well of course. Thanks a ton,' Alok said and accompanied Sahil to the door.

'Hope to see you in Delhi and at Smile FM soon,' Alok stopped at the reception and shook hands with the star.

'Yeah, but I hope you don't serve me that food again!' Sahil smiled.

'Why?' Alok asked.

'Because that visit will cost me a few lacs like it did this time,' he winked at a desperate looking Rikku and walked away. Alok couldn't help but chuckle as he looked at the emerging superstar of Bollywood taking giant strides down the staircase of the building.

'Yoohoo...,' Babs screamed and waved his fist up in the air as Sahil left and they walked back into the office.

'The food did the trick Babs or else it was a gone chance,' Alok said.

'*Agarwaljee* would be so happy to see the pictures,' Babs gushed.

'Happier, because this is coming to him for free,' Alok added.

'Whatever! My ass is saved for now,' Babs admitted nonchalantly.

'Yeah, seems so,' Alok quipped.

'But you were kickass man, first the interview and then this Karim food. Where did you pull this one up from?' Babs said looking admiringly at his savior.

'She gave me the lead,' Alok said.

'Who?' Babs asked entering his cabin.

'Shonali, the new girl who has joined us,' Alok said.

Babs displayed a momentary gesture of appreciation on his face before lunging back into his computer and the alluring world of erotica.

Suddenly he looked up, 'This calls for a party Alok,' he said as Alok stopped in his tracks.

'Where?'

'Let everybody know that we are going to Fireball, this Saturday,' he said.

Alok entered the disco through the spaced out and dimly lit jaws of Darth Vadar, the symbol of power and evil from the world famous Star Wars movie series. The walls on either side of the passage were lit in blue giving it a spaceship feel. As he approached the main hall his ears got pierced with thumping sounds of 'Ski…ba…bop…ba...dop…pop' the current hit in the party circuit and his eyes fiddled with the darkness around, trying to recognize a known face. The rectangular dance floor in the middle of the hall flickered with laser beams doused in sharp colours that gave an eclectic feel to the overall environment. The floor was fifty percent occupied with girls and guys, men and women who swayed away with the rhythm oblivious to the world. Alok stood at one corner of the floor and glanced around expecting to find a known face.

'Hi,' someone tapped on his shoulder.

'Hey, when did you arrive?' he turned around and smiled at Shonali.

'Don't ask! There was hardly any traffic today and it took me only an hour to reach here from Lajpat Nagar,' she said amplifying her pitch to beat the noise level in the disco.

'Did you locate anyone from the gang?' Alok asked.

'I think those guys over there are from the office but I don't know them,' she said pointing towards the other side.

'Yeah, that's our team, come,' Alok said and signaled Shonali to follow him.

'When did you guys arrive?' Alok gripped Andy by his shoulder.

'A few minutes back and where have you been?' he turned around to shake hands with him and then looked at Shonali quizzically.

'Oh, meet Shonali guys! She has recently joined our team and will be helping us with the breakfast show,' he said.

'Great! Welcome to Smile FM,' Andy said. Shonali smiled to shake his hand and then went on to greet everyone in the group.

'So, is Babs coming over?' Sandy asked as he sipped beer from his glass.

'Only if he gets time from surfing porn and hogging away to glory,' Murli guffawed.

They had moved to the upper deck that overlooked the dance floor and were all seated on a three piece couch, that flaunted hue of blue and purple neon flickering over their heads.

'Hey, what's the commotion over there?' Nandan said pointing towards the entrance.

'Looks like some VIP has dropped in,' Sandy said.

'Yeah, this *gaon* called Gurgaon is swamped with politicians and goons alongwith cattle lying on the road as if it was their living room,' Murli passed a snide one.

'No, I think these guys look familiar. Isn't that Sahil Khan?' Shonali squinted like Bat Woman.

'Yeah maybe, he was supposed to ground in Delhi for that new film,' Alok said casually looking in that direction.

'Yes of course! Who else would know that? He is your long lost friend now, afterall,' Murli took a jibe.

'Bull! He is no friend- *shriend* boss! It's just that he had mentioned it the other day when he was at our office,' Alok gave him a ridiculous look.

'Yeah, that's Sahil,' he added as he saw him along with a couple of others taking the staircase to the upper deck.

'Sir, would you mind getting us an autograph from the superstar in that case?' Murli chuckled lowering his head dramatically.

Sahil Khan stepped on the upper deck with a couple of nondescript and overweight men who had thick gold chains dangling around their necks; like garlands around the deities in temples. Sahil's manager Rikku followed them looking disgruntled.

'Are you out of your mind? Why would I get autographs from Sahil?' Alok said and turned around to find Sahil and his entourage standing at a short distance behind them and looking around for a place to sit. Within a few seconds they were joined by two uniformed men who seemed to belong to the management of Fireball. They looked visibly excited to see the star at their venue as they muttered something in Rikku's ears and pointed towards the vacant couch next to where Alok and gang were seated.

Sahil's eyes met Alok's and he had a familiar look on his face.

'Hey! I think I know you. What are you doing here?' Sahil said and shook Alok's hand.

'Our office party,' Alok said.

'I hope it's not an incentive for fleecing a poor star named Sahil Khan,' he guffawed.

'You bet! No it's not for that and we didn't fleece you,' Alok smiled.

'It was meant to be a joke man! Chill and see you later,' Sahil said and went ahead to sit amongst the pack of portly men who had already parked their backsides on the sofa.

Alok diverted his attention from Sahil and looked around to see Murli's gaze fixed on him.

'What?' he asked.

'That guy is besotted by you. Didn't I tell you that he is your best friend now? Don't forget us once you are there in Bollywood,' Murli said theatrically.

'What makes you think I wouldn't?' Alok quipped and took a sip from the glass.

'He likes you boss! Trust me!' Shonali spoke after a long time.

'Naaah,' Alok said unbelievably.

'Hey, just look at these chicks swarming your hot friend,' Murli muttered and forced everyone to divert their attention towards a dozen giggling girls who had lined up around Sahil for an autograph.

Rikku looked unusually ruffled as he gestured at the club bouncers to jump in, and take control of the small crowd clamoring for the star. Sahil looked relaxed as he signed the autographs with ease like a seasoned veteran.

'These secretaries have to show off in a public place!' Shonali scowled. Alok looked at her and reclined back on the comfortable leather couch with a smile on his lips.

'*Bhai teri waali to aatti nahin deekhe (Brother I don't think your girl looks eager enough to join us here),*' a sharp Haryanvi accent floated in the air and pierced their eardrums.

Alok turned his head towards the left to find four rustic looking men seated on the edge of the couch. Every piece of clothing on their body fiercely held on to the skin and screamed for loosening up a bit. The drunken look on their face heightened their peculiar presence and they clearly stood apart from the trendy yet classy gathering in Fireball.

'What the hell has she been doing there for such a long time?' the guy sitting in the middle slurred in Haryanvi. He looked like their leader and wore a tight black t-shirt that had a silver colored python printed on it, and each time the laser fell on his body, the python glowed as if it were ready to jump out. He had folded up the sleeves of his t-shirt to showcase his so called biceps that would perhaps match the size of the wrist of Sylvester Stallone.

'Brother, she is busy making conversation with that Sahil Khan while leaving you alone here. I told you that she is not the right girl for you,' the guy sitting next to the *Haryanvi boss* and wearing equally awful clothes said.

'What are these Rambo's doing here?' Murli laughed.

'I think his *Anarkali* has gone out to flirt with our hero there,' Alok said and looked at Sahil's table. The autograph hunters were dispersing away after collecting their prized booty from Sahil, except one who seemed reluctant to leave. She looked to be making forced conversations with the star despite an angry looking Rikku and the Fireball staff trying to dissuade her to return back. She on the other hand looked unfazed by their presence, had her eyes stuck on Sahil Khan and was in no mood to relent. After standing for a while she suddenly sat next to Sahil and started whispering something in his ear.

'No brother this is not good. Not good at all. Just see with your own eyes, how close is she getting with that bastard,' the *Haryanvi boss's* crony said angrily.

'You guys wait here, I will go and get that bitch back and also teach that bloody star a lesson,'the *Haryanvi boss* said and tried to get up from the couch; despite the other three holding his hands and pulling him back. He tried to resist them by twirling his body in different positions but soon his overweight stature coupled with an overdose of alcohol made him fall back on the couch with a thud; and threw all four of them out of gear.

'No brother not here. He is a star and if we do anything here it would be against the law. Let's teach him a lesson outside,' one of his cronies said.

'If he is a star them I am also a MP's son. The fortune of a star changes every Friday but an MP is there for five years, *hai na*?' he asked his gang. They meekly surrendered by nodding in affirmation.

'*Oye Pappu,* just give a call to *Surender bhaiyya* and ask him to send *Balli* and his gang here immediately. This bloody Sahil Khan will have it from me today,' the hero hissed as his crony flashed a cell phone and punched furiously on the digits.

'This is getting serious guys,' Andy said raising his eyebrows and finishing off the drink from his glass.

'These neo rich Haryanvis are a real menace these days,' Murli muttered and signaled for another drink.

'Till yesterday these guys were a bunch of impoverished lot, who were finding it tough to manage two square meals each day,' he added.

'But suddenly today, they sell a few acres of their grandfather's land to some builder and make some million bucks to drive their asses on expensive cars, drink foreign liquor with chicks like these in tow,' Andy glanced at the *Haryanvi boss's* girlfriend who was still busy flirting unabashedly with Sahil.

'And what makes a better cocktail than mixing this quick money with politics? 'Nandan said.

'Why are we forgetting hooliganism?' Murli added.

'Aren't we seeing all of this right here on the next table? But, what do we do now since this seems to be getting dirty,' Alok said.

'What can we do?' Murli asked emphatically as if he was being asked to dance naked.

'Come on guys? We need to do something! These Bombay people are novices as compared to these goons sitting out here. They wouldn't know a damn about the law of the land in this part of the world,' Alok spoke softly.

'What will happen if we don't do anything now?' Murli spoke. Alok replied with a flabbergasted look on his face, 'don't be surprised if a hundred guys land up here, ready to break up everything in sight.'

'That would be great story for the media, Sahil Khan bashed up by a drunken MP's son,' Murli chuckled.

'What an ass Murli?' Alok scowled.

'Just joking,' Murli raised his hands.

'So, how would you save your friend?' Andy asked. Alok gave him a hard look as he sipped from his glass.

'*Rikku jee,*' Alok whispered in the ear of the secretary who stood next to the star. Rikku turned around and the frown on his face worsened as he realized that the disrupter was Alok.

'Yes,' he said coarsely.

'Can you just step aside for a second? I have something very important to tell you.'

Rikku followed him to an aisle a few feet away, 'Now, I hope you have a good enough reason to pull me here.'

'Do you see that guy sitting there in that python t-shirt?' Alok asked.

'Yes. So?' Rikku said.

'He is the local MP's son,' Alok said.

'So?' Rikku said.

'And that girl sitting next to Sahil is his girlfriend,' Alok said.

'So?' Rikku was visibly getting irritated.

'He thinks that Sahil is flirting with her,' Alok said.

'So? What's unique about that? All girls flirt with Sahil,' Rikku's irritation was palpable.

'All can, but girlfriends of politician's sons can't,' Alok said.

'Why? What's so unusual about that? It happens with him in Bombay all the time?' Rikku's expressions were changing gears.

'Maybe, but this is Haryana boss, the rules are different here,' Alok said.

'What do you think can happen?' Rikku asked.

'He just called for a truckload of his goons I guess,' Alok said.

'I can also call the local police and we can take help from the club bouncers,' Rikku said hurriedly.

'*Rikkujee* please! There are about ten bouncers around and by the time police reaches here the damage would have happened,' Alok said firmly.

'And even if they reach here in time, trust me they would not want to intervene at all if the matter is related to a local MP. Local police, local MP. Do you get the connection?'

Rikku's face gave it away. He understood that the matter was serious and needed instant amendment.

'So, should I push the girl away? I mean immediately?' Rikku asked.

'The damage I guess is already done. I don't think it will help,' Alok said.

'Should we leave then?' Rikku asked looking helpless by now.

Rikku paused to add by himself, 'No, I don't think Sahil would do that, and more-so if he gets to know the entire story, I am absolutely certain that he wouldn't budge out of this place. He has too much of this Delhi aggressive blood flowing in his veins.'

'So?' Alok was asking questions now.

'Can you do something?' Rikku asked hesitatingly.

'I have a plan,' Alok reassured him.

'Boss, do you have a minute?'Alok asked the python T-Shirt clad guy who looked completely wasted.

'Hmmm?' he murmured

'Can you just come over here for a second?' Alok held his hand and urged him to get up.

The cronies stared at Alok suspiciously.

'I am a friend, don't worry,' Alok attempted to assuage their anxiety.

Their inebriated leader fumbled while getting up but managed to reach Alok.

'Do you see that man there?' he said pointing towards Sahil.

'Yeah, Sahil that bloody film star,' he slurred.

'I am going to *sccreww* him tonight,' he slurred again.

'But why do you say that?' Alok said.

'He has been flirting with my girlfriend for a while now. He has to pay for it tonight,' he said gnashing his teeth.

'Oh no brother, I think you are completely mistaken,' Alok said unbelievably.

'Why? Am I lying to you?' he said rolling his eyes.

'Because I have been sitting right there all this while, and all that he has been doing is just praising you,' Alok said.

'Me? Why?' the hero said.

'Your personality the chiseled face, just look at your biceps,' Alok said while pressing them.

'Did he really say that? Well I have to work out a lot to maintain this,' he said and tucked his tummy inside by a couple of inches.

'Oh yes obviously, I can imagine that. Infact Sahil really thinks that you have a chance in Bollywood,' Alok added.

'What are you saying? Did he also say that?' the hero showcased his panmasala stained teeth underneath a smile, after a long time.

'Well of course he did. And let me tell you that Sahil is one such guy who usually doesn't open his mouth unless he is hundred percent sure,' Alok said emphatically.

'Hmm…true,' the MP's son replied completely in awe by now.

'Do you want to say hi to him?' Alok asked.

'Umm…well ofcourse. But just a second, I am getting a call,' he said and pulled out the cell phone from his pocket.

'Yeah. Ok, so have you guys arrived? Where are you right now?' he asked. Alok could understand that his fellowmen had arrived with the sole mission of teaching the Bollywood star a good lesson; unaware about the recent change in events.

'No don't do that, don't come inside,' he said reacting to the guy on the other side who wanted to come in.

'*Balli*, no! I don't want to do anything here. I can handle it. Just listen to what I say and go back to the village,' he said forcibly. Alok smiled. The MP's son signaled one of his cronies on the couch to get up.

'That *Balli* is standing outside. I have told them to get back to the village. Why don't you move your ass, go outside and ensure that it happens,' he said.

'But *bhai* aren't we teaching that *behenchod* a lesson?' he said looking startled.

'Just do what I have told you. Not an inch more and nor an inch less,' he said in an authoritative tone. The crony gave him one look and disappeared within the crowd. The humbled and captivated expression returned on the face of the MP's heir.

'Sir, can we go now?' he said to a smiling Alok.

'Sahil Bhai, he is a big fan of yours. Just wants to say 'Hi' to you,' Alok screamed in his ears amidst the deafening sound. The fan or the *Haryanvi boss* stood behind Alok meekly looking at Sahil.

Sahil turned to glance at him and stretched his hand out. The MP's son clasped the star's hand within his.

'Thank you. Thank you,' was all that could breakfree from his excitement choked throat. Sahil looked at him and smiled.

'All the best,' he said. This interaction caught attention of the fan's girlfriend.

'*Bittu*?? What are you doing here?' she screamed as if an untouchable had entered a Hindu temple.

'Nothing *Sweety;* you sit. He is a good guy. You sit,' he said and retreated.

'Thanks for your help brother. Should I give you my contact details in case he needs to contact me?' the MP's son looking pleased like a punch said.

'Sure, give it to him,' Alok said as he picked up a paper napkin and pointed towards a nervous looking Rikku who handed him a ballpoint pen.

Bittu a.k.a MP's son wrote the details on the napkin carefully and then folded the paper neatly.

'Thank you, once again,' he said while handing over the paper to Rikku with trembling hands.

'That was close, man. It was really smart of you to get rid of them or else we could have been in a real soup,' Rikku said heaving a sigh of relief.

'Hmmm…and Sahil didn't get to know about this either,' Alok said looking in Bittu's direction who had faded into the darkness.

'Yeah. These Delhi guys can really get aggressive sometimes if you aren't careful, but how do you explain this to our man who himself is a *dilliwalla* at heart?' Rikku said glancing at Sahil.

'But thanks, nevertheless, for helping us,' Rikku said.

'It's not me *Rikkujee*, it's the city,' Alok said as Rikku looked at him curiously.

'*Sirjee, yeh Dilli hai hee Dilwalon kee,*' he quipped.

Babs was furiously munching on a thick *aloo parantha* and ogling at the curvy breasts of some Russian stripper on his desktop when Alok entered his room.

'Busy boss?' Alok asked before tossing the weekly programming report on his table.

'Yeah! Kind of! But tell me?' he removed his glare from the screen looking pained.

'What do you think of us Babs? Morons? Don't we know what kind of work keeps you busy all the time?' Alok muttered.

'What? Did you say something?' Babs devoured a juicy portion of the parantha.

'No! Well there is the weekly report for you to see,' Alok said pointing towards the bunch of papers.

'Ok, I will look at it once I am through with this,' Babs said looking at the report with miniscule interest.

'Oh yes, there is something more,' Babs spoke in a garbled voice emerging from a mouth working vigorously on the mashed potatoes.

'We are going to Goa,' he finally spoke clearly.

'That's great, the entire team?' Alok asked. Babs nodded.

'Occasion?'

'Shobha has called for the annual sales and programming review,' Babs said.

'Hmm...that isn't a very exciting occasion to be in, but nevertheless. Let me inform the team.

'When are we going by the way?' Alok asked.

'Thursday. HR department is making the travel and stay arrangements,' Babs said as he moved his gaze back on the fourteen inch computer screen.

'Yaay! I am so happy. It's going to be my first trip to Goa,' Shonali glowed with excitement.

'Mine as well. I think the team is going to have a great time,' Alok said sipping from the hot cup of tea. Andy looked at him and smiled.

'I am going to get fucked. Shobha will screw me in Goa this time.' Murli seemed stuck in a thought.

'This fourth *samosa* that you are gobbling, wouldn't ease your situation but is surely going to add a few more inches around your already forty inch waist,' Alok remarked.

'I am going to get raped and all you guys are doing here, is giving me *gyaan,'* Murli said in a pained voice.

'Don't think too much about it. Maybe she is in a good mood?' Andy said.

'Shobha Sarin and good mood? I think the lady has been PMS'ing forever,' Murli said.

'It seems as if they are sending you to Iraq and not Goa,' Alok got up to pay at the counter. The others followed.

'I wish it was Iraq without that woman. Trust me man, Iraq will be better than going in front of that woman without doing your sales numbers. Can I make an excuse?' Murli asked walking behind them.

'Yes, you can but only after tendering your resignation. It's a conference and not your weekend trip,' Andy chuckled as they walked ahead of a completely psyched Murli.

They exited through the crowded arrival lounge of the Dabolim Airport in Goa at 10.30 in the morning. It was the month of October in Goa where humidity in the air was slowly giving way to a pleasant weather. They were greeted at the entrance by a burly dark skinned Goan who held a branded placard of Hotel Fort Aguada in his hand that had 'Smile FM, Team Delhi' scribbled over it.

'Hi! We are from Smile FM,' Babs said munching on a packet of chips.

'Welcome to Goa, sir. The coach is just parked round the corner, so please assemble here with your luggage and I will go and get it here,' he said and quickly vanished from the sight.

'The weather is good. I wish we could head for the beach straightaway,' Alok said.

'Beach? Shobha wants us to be in the hotel conference room by 12,' Babs said.

'Are we going to the conference room directly?' he asked making sure.

'It's not a conference room my boy, it's the slaughterhouse,' Babs said coldly.

'The performance in Delhi has been very average this quarter. Isn't it Dilip?' Shobha asked the scared looking finance head.

The lifeless wrinkles on her face; and eyes devoid of any emotion indicated the brazenness in her character that had seeped in after staying alone for almost forty years. The forehead that remained perpetually excited gave way to a nicely rounded face that would have looked attractive somewhere down the line; but had eventually roughened to look worn out and angry. The clothes did hardly anything to lend a womanly credibility to her image. A half sleeved shirt worn with camel colored loose pants made her look like a tyrant general who was ready to fire at his own men at any time rather than the enemy in the battleground. Everybody hated her except for herself.

The poor accountant nodded or else his head would have got chopped off.

'Just twenty percent growth over last quarter Dilip?? I mean, are we running a company here or a charity?' she said as she looked at the hundred odd people who sat scattered in the conference hall.

Babs and Rajeev the Sales Head at Smile FM were sitting in the first row and looked nervous like hell.

'Rajeev, your team has not been able to deliver on the projections that were promised in this quarter. Do you have an explanation?' she asked as her eyes pierced through the mortal flesh on Rajeev's body.

'Umm...well maam some of the clients did not launch their products as per schedule while some have delayed the marketing campaigns; and that has primarily been the reason for this shortfall,' he said sheepishly.

'So, what do I do?' she said coldly.

Rajeev didn't know how to react hence he glanced around nervously.

'So, what do I do Rajeev?' she raised her voice.

'Madam, we could have been proactive in scoping for new clients I guess,' Rajeev said.

'So why didn't it happen?' she asked.

Alok could see tiny beads of sweat lining up on his forehead; ready to dash on his face.

'So why didn't it happen Rajeev?' Shobha screamed at the top of her voice instigating Rajeev to stand up from his chair with a jerk. The guy was ready to break into tears at any moment.

'She reminds me of Gupta,' Alok whispered. He sat in the fifth row with Shonali sitting next to him dumbfounded, trying to acclimatize herself with the horror movie that was just getting unleashed before them.

'Who's Gupta?' she asked focused on Shobha's histrionics.

'He used to be my Maths teacher in school,' Alok replied. She heard Alok and turned her face around to give him a surprised look.

'Does she always behave like this?' she whispered.

'Don't you remember what Murli said the other day?' Alok replied. She shook her head in the negative.

'She is forever PMS'ing.'

'Maam...some guys failed badly on deliveries. I guess we are all responsible for this,' Rajeev muttered.

'Ok...I would like to know from you that who are these distinguished people who failed miserably this quarter?' Shobha said clasping her hands together and looking eager to butcher those select few.

Alok glanced at Murli who sat in the corner of the third row paralyzed with fear and anxiety.

'A few of them madam...Ajay, Gurdeep and Murli missed their numbers, but I am sure they would make up for them in this quarter,' Rajeev said making a last ditch attempt to save his teammates.

'Can I see them at-least? Can these guys put their hands up?' Shobha said firmly. Alok could see hands rising up slowly within the room, and that the last one belonged to Murli.

'This quarter is surely going to turn out good for sales numbers,' Alok could hear himself aloud. A lot of heads turned around to see the owner of the voice who had the audacity to disturb the protocol of the room.

'Well, who's that? Oh! Alok! And why do you say that?' Shobha diverted her attention.

'Because we have so many specials, festivals and then Christmas and New Year round the corner that would give numerous opportunities to advertisers,' he said.

'I am sure we should be able to make up for all our backlogs in this quarter,' he added.

The festival thought perhaps tickled Shobha. She looked at Dilip and he for once showed optimism on his face.

'Well, actually Madam in the October to December quarter last year; we grew by forty five percent plus,' he said looking at his sheets.

'And we have already done eighty percent of our months targets in just ten days,' Rajeev added looking invigorated. Shobha softened up a bit but her natural instinct couldn't just allow her to stay quiet.

'But we can't let go of the past failures? Can we?' she asked the crowd.

'No, we can't madam but we shouldn't dwell in the past either. If we do, how would we move forward? Especially in an industry as nascent as radio where everyday is a learning experience and can bring unexpected results,' Alok said.

'What matters today, is how can we win now and tomorrow rather than thinking why did we lose yesterday?' Alok said. The conference room went completely silent and an unknown anticipation of things to come reflected on everyone's face.

'But there are always learnings to take from our past mistakes,' Shobha said sternly.

'Yes madam I agree, but only learnings.'

'Why are you ganging up with Sales, Alok? They are a different department,' Shobha asked.

'Yes, but we are one team madam,' Alok replied after a brief pause.

Shobha kept looking at him for a couple of moments, immersed deep within her thoughts and then her lips moved, 'Let's hit the pool guys.'

'Cheers,' Murli said raising his third glass of whisky.

It was their third and last night at Goa and what a trip had it turned out to be. After their brief encounter with nervousness in the conference room on the first day, the rest of the trip had been a joyride. They were completely spared from meetings, business plans and anything that was remotely official. It had been two days of complete bliss and freedom; from Calangute Beach to Tony's garage and from Panjim to Miramar; they explored everything with Shobha in tow. As Murli had joked in a state of drunkenness on the first day:

'Shobha doesn't PMS daily now! Courtesy our man here,' he had guffawed pointing towards Alok.

'Cheers guys,' Rajeev and Babs raised their glasses for a toast.

'I don't see our man around, because of whom this trip has turned out to be what it is,' Rajeev said sipping from his glass.

'There he comes,' Babs said looking towards the doorway of the open air restaurant that over-looked a slightly unruly sea. Alok walked into the restaurant with Shonali.

'Hey there,' he said to the mélange of the group that stood near the large open aired windows.

'Hi dude, where have you been?' Murli asked.

'Nowhere, just went for a walk along the beach,' he said.

'I have been observing that your business of *walk shalk* with her has been kind of growing for last couple of days,' Murli pulled Alok closer to him and muttered in his ears.

'What shit Murli? You really think from your ass,' Alok said.

'Anyways, so what's the plan guys, because tonight is the night,' Babs said relishing a jumbo prawn.

'Plan? Tonight we drink and we sing but nobody gets to sleep,' Murli said.

'No sleep? Don't you recall what Shobha said? Our flight is at nine and we have to be at the reception by 6 AM because the bus leaves the hotel at 6.15,' Babs said.

'So?' Rajeev asked.

'So, the bus waits for no one mister. If you get late, either you fly to the airport or you miss the flight. Simple!' Babs said shoving shredded lamb in his mouth.

'Ok guys, can we just stay in the present instead of thinking too much about tomorrow? So, we drink now, right?' Alok asked picking up a whisky glass. Shonali picked up a bloody Mary.

'Yeah,' Murli said.

'Cheers to Goa then,' he said and took a large swig.

'Where's Shobha?' Alok asked.

'She has gone back to her room,' Rajeev said.

'Great. Then the night is still young,' Alok said to a smiling Shonali.

'I can still recall our last summer
I still see it all

In the tourist jam, round the Notre Dame
Our last summer
Walking hand in hand..'

Nandan's eyes were shut as he sang while strumming his guitar. It was way past twelve and most of the guys from the team had staggered back to their rooms unable to hold on to their drunken slumber. A few of them had gathered on the couch in front of the swimming pool loosening themselves up to alcohol, to the gentle breeze that sashayed on their beings after touching the gushing waves of the sea and ultimately to the soothing sound of the music.

Alok seemed to be deeply engrossed in Nandan's song and had a forlorn look on his face.

'Why do you look so pained?' Shonali came closer to him and whispered. He shook his head and his expressions changed.

'Don't lie,' she whispered again.

'I was remembering one such get together in the past,' he said.

'Was it good?' she asked.

'Yeah,' he said as Nandan finished singing.

'Can I try?' Alok asked.

'Sure. Can you play?' Nandan asked handing over his guitar.

'Yeah, I think so.'

'*Arrayy* he used to play for a band and all, don't you remember?' Murli spoke with a peculiar slur in his voice.

Shonali curled up her feet under the body, 'I am impressed.'

'Don't listen to them, they are liars,' he said as he strummed the guitar with perfect ease.

'Before you slip into unconsciousness
I'd like to have another kiss
Another flashing chance at bliss
Another kiss, another kiss.
The days are bright and filled with pain
Enclose me in your gentle rain
The time you ran was too insane
We'll meet again, we'll meet again..'

It took him hardly a few minutes before music started flowing in his veins and once it did, the result was intoxicating, sucking everyone around, into it. No one dared to move, not even for alcohol. The other peculiar thing about music is that it transcends time, and lets your mind wander through it and takes you back to places where you had treaded once. It was her house, it was her party and there were old friends. Suveesha, Rohit, Harish, Baba and her. M was there in front of him.

'That was awesome, Alok. No one knew that you were so good,' he woke up to celebrated applause.

'You should have tried your luck with music man! What are you doing at Smile FM?' Babs said.

'I am feeling sober now. All that alcohol has disappeared from my body. I have to drink more,' Murli poured another drink.

'Nooo…we can't let you go away with one. You are my muse for the night,' Shonali screamed.

'No I can't. This one was enough. Nandan come on; we want more from you,' Alok nudged him.

'Noooo…..Noooo. We want more,' Shonali who seemed a bit high reiterated her demands.

Alok forced the guitar in Nandan's hands and pleaded him to carry on.

'That isn't fair boss, you must sing more,' Shonali said leaning on his shoulder.

'I think you guys can carry on, I will go for a small walk,' Alok said getting up.

'Why, what happened?' Sandy said.

'Not feeling too good,' Alok said excusing himself.

'Okay, we are waiting for you here. Come back soon,' Andy said as Nandan started with an old Kishore Kumar melody.

Alok walked towards the stairway at the rear exit of the hotel that led to the majestic rampart that overlooked the Arabian Sea. He walked towards the old structure erected by the Portuguese in the sixteenth century as a guard against the Dutch and the Marathas. It was a full moon night and that made it easier for him to take the narrow line of steps that led him on the top of the parapet. Alok stared at the vast expanse of the rough sea that lay in front of him, the waves rising high in the air making a warlike sound and then colliding against the old yet thick walls of the structure, falling back and armoring yet again for a war with the thick concrete. The view of the sea was stunning as Alok stood there alone, soaking his being in the beauty of the night.

'This is such an amazing view, isn't it?' Shonali tapped him from behind.

'Hey, when did you come?' Alok turned around.

'I followed you,' she said looking at the sea.

'So, did you enjoy your first conference in Smile FM?' Alok asked.

'Yes very much. But I think the fun is all courtesy you, as Shobha had different plans,' she said.

'Naah. But I am glad that you enjoyed.'

'Yeah, I did. After a really long time,' she said.

'You had said that you are from Dehradun,' he said. She shook her head.

'Who all do you have in your family?' he asked.

'My mother, and a sister who is two years younger than me, she said.

'Dad?'

'They got separated when I was in class three,' she said.

'Hmm,' he replied.

'Do you have a girlfriend?' she asked. He shook his head in the negative. She looked surprised.

'Have you ever been in love?' she asked.

'Yes, twice.'

'What happened then?' she asked.

'That's the sad part because nothing really happened,' he seemed to be hiding pain beneath the smile that he flashed at her.

'What makes you happy?' she asked.

'To be able to do what I want to do,' he said.

'That's it?' she asked. He nodded.

'And you?'

'Success and lots of it,' she chuckled.

'That's it?' he asked. She gave him a surprised look.

'When will I become a full time RJ, Alok?' she asked.

'Hopefully soon Shonali, just keep going,' he said.

'Wow that sounds good! You have made me happy now,' she said and held his hand.

'You know what boss?' she said and came closer to him. Alok looked at her.

'You are very different,' she said and moved her face closer to his, expecting.

Shonali looked so beautiful under the moon-light; her warm eyes, the flawless smooth skin that covered her face and tapered down under her neck to run smoothly all over, the alluring fragrance oozing out of her body trapped Alok for a few seconds before he forcibly detangled himself.

'Let's go Shonali. They would be waiting for us,' he said. She did not look pleased at all and after glancing at the wild 'n' furious sea for the last time, followed him to the hotel.

Alok was woken up by a continuous thumping on the hotel door. He staggered towards the door and unlocked the latch.

'We are fucked,' a distraught looking Murli screamed.

'They have left us behind. The bus is already gone,' Andy matched Murli's decibel and looked equally screwed. Shonali stood behind them completely puzzled, holding her handbag.

'What's the time?' Alok asked.

'It's almost 7AM,' Sandy said.

'Fuck! Just go to the reception and call for a cab immediately. I am getting there in a minute,' Alok said and raced inside the room.

'Is the cab there?' Alok ran towards them with his bag thrown across the shoulders.

'Yes it is, but I don't think we have a chance,' Sandy said.

'Let's get in first,' he said getting onto the front seat alongside the driver, while the remaining three squeezed themselves at the back.

'How much time will it take to the airport?' he asked the cabbie.

'About one and a half hours sir,' he replied.

'Our flight is gone man! We are fucked,' Murli muttered.

'We want to reach there in one hour,' Alok said.

'Not possible sir!' he replied.

'What's the fare to the airport?' he said.

'500 bucks sir!' the cabbie replied.

'I will give you two thousand if you get us there in one hour,' he said.

The cabbie gave him a curious look before stepping on the accelerator, 'Ok! I will try sir.'

'2000!! That's four times the fare! Are you crazy?' Murli yelled in

Hindi or the cabbie would have understood.

'Money and Praise are two biggest motivational tools Murli; and simple praise wouldn't have worked here,' Alok said taking off his backpack.

'And anyways, paying additional fifteen hundred bucks and taking a shot was a better deal than paying twenty grand from our pockets for the airtickets. Isn't it?' Alok turned behind and winked at Murli.

The cabbie tried hard and he really gave it all. The speedometer of the cab was put to severe test during that sixty minute drive and so was cabby's general knowledge about the roads in Goa. He drove as if there was no tomorrow, overtaking, jumping redlights, flying over potholes, honking endlessly, yet landed his cab at the airport in sixty minutes flat. Alok was paying the cab driver when the Smile FM coach entered through the gates of the airport. Shobha was the first one to get off the coach and her face changed colors as she saw them standing near the departure gates.

'So, how did you guys manage to reach earlier than us? Did you fly?' she asked.

'Yes we did madam, we surely did,' Alok said looking at his cab mates.

'Thanks man! You really saved our ass today,' Alok said gratefully. The cabby simply smiled and drove away.

'Now that we are safe, time to get into the '*Susegaad*' mode,' Alok said walking into the gate with the handbag swinging by his side

'What's *Susegaad* mode?' Shonali had a serious look on her face.

'Time to relax and enjoy, it's the Goan way,' he said as everybody smiled.

Three Times Loser.... # 200

'So, how many months have you spent in Smile FM Shonali?' Alok asked as he entered the studio. Shonali had her headphones on, and looked engrossed into something. She removed them as she saw Alok's lips moving.

'Did you say something?' she said.

'Yeah, how many months have you spent at Smile FM?

'Over three months,' she said.

'You have been a quick learner then,' he smiled.

It was true. Shonali had been picking up the ropes pretty fast. She had been dabbling with everything, right from managing the music to working on the console, helping RJ's with their daily prep sheets to picking up interesting topics of the day for daily content.

'And you have been a good boss. Infact you have been instrumental in making me learn so much in such a short span of time,' she smiled.

'Your butter won't help, I don't like eating it,' he said.

'No, I am serious,' she said.

'Anyways, I have good news for you. Do you want to know?' Alok teased her.

'Of course! Please tell me, please?' she pleaded.

'You are going to be on air; two weeks from now,' he said casually.

Shonali couldn't believe what was just said and went numb for a few minutes.

'Are you serious?' she asked as if she had just seen a ghost.

'Do you think I am joking?' Alok asked.

She stared at Alok with a blank expression on her face before walking up to him and hugging him tightly.

'Wow! That's awesome boss. I have been dreaming to become a full time RJ for so long,' she exclaimed still hanging on to him.

'What is going to be my timeband?' she asked.

'Breakfast,' he said.

'What? Breakfast?' she couldn't believe her ears and looked up. Alok moved out of her cuddle and settled on the chair.

'Yeah, that's right. The breakfast jock Shalini is moving to Dubai hence we have decided to give you that prime band,' Alok said.

'This is a dream come true and I am going to need all your support to be ready for this challenge,' she said.

'That's always there Shonali, but more than me it's going be your self belief and preparation that will make you a good breakfast RJ.'

Alok got up after a few moments, 'Then let's get going for next two weeks, and don't worry we will spend a couple of hours everyday in the evening towards your training.'

'Absolutely. And thanks for all your help,' she said.

'Anytime,' he smiled and walked towards the door.

'Did Babs agree to this?' she asked.

'It wasn't easy,' he said as he pulled the handle of the door.

'How did you manage then?' she asked.

'I bought him a double egg 'n' double mutton Nizam's kathi roll; after which he couldn't say no,' he said with a straight face and walked out of the studio leaving Shonali splitting her sides with laughter.

Alok was busy charting out specials for the week on his PC when the telephone on his desk rang. He picked up the phone with his eyes glued on the computer screen.

'Sir, Shonali madam on the line,' the receptionist said and put the phone on hold. Alok looked at his watch, it was 3PM and there had been no news of Shonali since morning.

'Hello,' her voice sounded peculiarly low.

'Hi Shonali! Where have you been since morning? There is so much to do *ya* and your launch is just about four days away. We have so much ground to cover,' Alok said in a concerned tone. There was unwarranted silence from the other side.

'Hello Shonali! Are you there? Why aren't you speaking?' Alok asked.

'I am sorry Alok, I am stuck in something and I don't think I will be able to come in today,' she let out a sob.

'Hey what happened to you? Are you ok?' he sounded concerned.

'Yeah! I am fine Alok. I will manage,' she said.

'No, you are not. Tell me what's the matter and then maybe I can help,' he pushed her.

'I am looking for a place to stay Alok and right now I don't have any,' she said.

'Why? What happened to your current house?' he asked.

'My landlord had been pestering me for a month to look for another pad, but I just didn't have the time to find one. So finally he is here today; and hell bent on not letting me stay here beyond the day,' she sobbed.

'How the hell can he do that? Don't you have a rental agreement with him?' he asked.

'It's some hundred square feet room in Kotla Mubarakpur Alok, and not some fancy apartment in Jorbagh,' she said.

'Hmmm...don't you have any relative around?'

'None. If I had I wouldn't be this bothered.'

'Friends?'

'I am new to the city and the only people that I know are the office guys,' she said in a choked voice.

'Do you want to stay in my apartment? It's in Noida and I think we can manage space for you,' Alok said instantly.

'No boss, how can I do that? I mean that wouldn't look good,' she said sounding surprised.

'It's not an alien concept in Delhi Shonali, and many single men and women friends do that. I have a two bedroom flat that I share with a friend of mine and you can stay there for a short while till the time you may find a new accommodation,' he said.

'But your friend? I mean will he agree?

'You leave that to me,' he comforted her.

'But will it look right?' she asked.

'I would think about it if I had an option in hand,' Alok said.

'Yeah, you are right I guess. Where do I have to come?' she asked.

'It's already 3PM. I think you wait where you are right now, and I will pick you up from there around 5PM. How much luggage do you have?'

'Not much, a couple of suitcases and a mattress,' she said.

'Cool, that means we will need to hire an auto and you can come with me on the bike,' he said.

'Your address?' he added.

'You will have to wade through a maze of narrow lanes to reach there. I think it will be better if I see you at South Ex market,' she said.

'Fine, I will see you around five there,' he spoke in a reassuring tone.

'Ok, thanks Alok,' she sounded relieved.

They entered his two bedroom apartment in Sector 21, Jalvayu Towers around 7PM. The city of Delhi had entered the month of November when early mornings and evening carried a tinge of the winter chill, forcing the inhabitants to pack themselves up in warm clothes. Alok switched on the tubelight of the living room and flung his leather jacket on the sofa.

'So that's our pad and unfortunately it's in a bit of a mess. Your notice of coming here was too short otherwise I would have cleaned it up a bit,' Alok smiled.

'It's much better than where I was putting up anyways,' she said.

'Let me show you around, come,' he touched her hand.

'This is my room and you can stay here for tonight,' he said. She glanced around the room that had hardly any furniture except a mattress that lay in one corner and some books by the bedside. The walls were painted in the light shade of pink and a wooden cupboard was placed in the left hand corner of the room.

'There is a lot of space in there, and you may use it if you want to,' he said pointing towards the cupboard.

They walked to the other side of the living room and Alok pushed the door latch to enter another bedroom.

'That's Vishal's room,' he said. Shonali peeked inside and then walked to the main hall.

'What does your friend do? Is he from a similar sector?' she asked.

'Naah...has his own business, he is a clearing agent,' he said.

'Oh! Ok!' she muttered.

'You may want to freshen up and then we can decide what to do next,' Alok said pointing towards the bathroom.

He knocked before entering his room and found her putting her clothes inside one of the empty racks in the cupboard.

'I hope it is ok?' she asked hesitatingly.

'Of course,' he said.

'What's that?' he pointed towards a framed picture that she had placed on the window sill near the mattress.

'It's my dearest possession in this world. This is my family in front of our house in Dehradun,' she said while picking up the picture that had her mother, sister and herself striking a natural family pose.

'Looks nice,' he said.

'So, where would you like to stay?' Vishal popped a salted peanut into his mouth and took a sip of rum from his glass.

'Anywhere in South Delhi,' Shonali replied.

'Do you know a broker there?' she added.

'Yeah, that's the advantage of self employment, you come across all kinds of people,' he smiled. Vishal was the lanky flat-mate of Alok who was inching towards thirties. He belonged to the family of prosperous businessmen hailing from Western Uttar Pradesh, and had taken fancy to currency right from his cradle. Alok strummed his guitar sitting next to Shonali was oblivious to their conversation.

'Great. I am sure you would give me quick leads, so that you can push me out of your pad as soon as possible,' she said and took a swig from her beer bottle.

Vishal was taken aback by her instant reaction, 'No *ya*...you can stay here for as long as you desire.'

'I was kidding,' she smiled and leaned back against the wall. She looked at Alok who seemed engrossed in his guitar and suddenly felt a surge of relief within her heart that had grown alarmingly anxious a few hours back.

'What are you up to?' she asked caringly.

'I just can't get this rhythm right. I think I am out of practice,' he sat there fiddling with the strings.

'What about dinner Alok? She is having dinner with us for the very first time and she deserves better than our normal course of bread and eggs or maggi,' Vishal said.

'Don't worry man! I have ordered for Chinese from Uncle's cabin, the guy should be arriving any minute with the food,' he said.

'Do you want to entertain us?' she asked Alok.

'No boss; no music as of now. All I need is good food,' Alok smiled as he put the guitar back into its case.

'Nice black guitar. Is it old?' Shonali asked.

Alok paused before polishing of the remaining glass, 'Not mine. It belongs to a friend and not quite old.'

'Do you want to have another beer?' Vishal looked at Shonali

'No thanks, I am done.'

'I want to eat something,' Alok said and the door bell rang.

'Food,' he exclaimed while getting up.

'I would have been so screwed up if you were not there to help today,' Shonali said. They stood in the narrow balcony of Alok's fifth floor apartment in Noida.

'It's started getting cold in Delhi,' Alok said staring at the lights emanating from the small sector twenty one market.

'You didn't even hear what I just said. That's mean,' Shonali complained.

'I did. Don't worry there a few places in Delhi where you could have found roof above your head, if not here in my apartment,' Alok said.

'Where is that?' she looked at him curiously.

'New Delhi Railway station,' he said with absolute seriousness.

It took her a few moments to react as she punched him lightly on the shoulder, 'That was so god damn mean Alok.'

'You asked for it Shonali. I mean what's so great about that? I would have done that for any other friend of mine,' Alok said.

'Anyway, I guess we should sleep now. It's almost one in the morning,' he said turning around.

'Hmmm,' Shonali followed him

'I am sleeping with Vishal, and you can take my room,' he said.

'We can go to the office together in the morning. See you at eight then,' he said.

'Sure,' she said while putting the latch on to the bedroom door.

'So, tomorrow is the day,' Alok said as he turned his face away from the monitor.

'Yeah, and I am as nervous as if appearing for an exam,' Shonali said rubbing her palms.

'Are you jittery?' he said.

'That's a pretty soft word to determine my present state.'

'Don't be! I think you have prepared well enough over last few days,' he said looking into her eyes.

'I hope that I don't get tongue tied during the show tomorrow,' she said.

'Just remember the basic rules for becoming an exceptional radio jockey,' he said.

'Let me recount them to you for the last time,' she said mocking him. He smiled and reclined back into his chair.

'You need to be as natural as possible and not at all pretentious.'

'Yes,' he said.

'The voice should be oozing warmth and affection for your listener,' she said.

'Remember that Smile FM is not an educative, informative medium like a newspaper.'

'Good,' he said.

'But a responsible entertainment medium for the society,' she stressed on the word responsible.

He smiled and gestured her to carry on.

'The content used by a radio jockey should be of common interest and ideally revolve around sports, bollywood and music because these are the passion points on which India thrives.'

'Very Good.'

'Never pick up controversies around politics, religion, police and judiciary to hold your listeners attention because they may fireball back at you,' she paused.

'Am I forgetting anything?' she looked at Alok quizzically.

'Caste, Shonali, Indian castes. We never talk about a particular community or make vague references about them.'

Then he smiled and got up from the chair to wrap his arm around her shoulders, 'I think we are ready to rock 'n' roll.'

They reached the office together on Alok's bike at six in the morning. The anxiety of her first show had robbed her of the night's sleep and she could hardly catch a few winks early morning. There were butterflies creating havoc in her stomach when she entered the studio, adjusted the mike close to her face and put the earphones over her head.

'Last minute jitters?' Alok said as he entered the studio. Shonali nodded sheepishly.

'Don't worry; a bit of nervousness brings out the best in you,' he said.

'How do you know?' she asked.

'I have been on your side as well, I mean on the stage, so I know,' he said offhandedly.

'When do you start?' he asked pointing towards the daily log running on the screen.

'Four minutes. The song ends in two minutes followed by some ninety seconds of ads, and then I go live after the show promo,' she spoke as she looked at her show prep sheet for the millionth time.

'Cool, just be yourself and you will do well,' he said and turned back.

'Aren't you staying? Where are you going?' she yelled.

'Not on the first day Shonali. You have to play by yourself. It's all yours now,' he smiled and showed her the thumbs up sign before walking out. Shonali's face displayed signs of displeasure before she gathered her composure and focused on the job at hand. She took a deep breath and then counted in her heart. One, two, three….

'Good Morning Dilliiiiiii on Smile 108 FM….here's your new host from today who will take you on a ride that you would never want to miss. It's your own *dilliwali, saadi kudi Shonali,'* Shonali's thumping heart slowed down as she mouthed her first few lines on the microphone. Suddenly, she felt her adrenalin levels picking up and confidence creeping within her skin. Her eyes surfaced through the prep sheet and she smartly mixed up Sachin's century yesterday in Australia with rising prices of the petrol. Shonali's first link lasted for a minute before fading into the first chartbuster from the super-hit *Raja Hindustani.* She heaved a sigh of relief and looked up through the studio glass. Alok stood there with a satisfied smile on his face.

Alok looked at her with swelling affection like a painter would look at his superlative creation with contentment after completing it. She looked up and their eyes met which made him smile. He turned around and humming the same song that currently played on Smile FM, he walked back to his desk and switched on the radio that lay on one side of his table. He scrolled through the daily log on his computer. Shonali had perfectly placed the songs for the day; they were all in sync with the mood of a radio listener in the morning. It was a veritable mix of peppy and melodious chartbusters, enough to lighten up the morning of an average Delhiite. The song had ended and Shonali's second link filled up the room through the radio. There was a vast improvement over the first link, the nervousness was fading away giving way to confidence. The girl was picking it up fast.

It was close to 9.30 AM when Babs tapped his shoulders and smilingly shook his hand, 'This girl is doing a great job Alok. I have been hearing to her right from the start.'

'I know Babs. She is improving by the minute.'

'This has been a solid discovery boss; and it's actually turned out better for us that Shalini had to move to Dubai,' Babs winked.

'Yeah, I know. Shonali needs to keep working hard like this,' Alok said.

'And you would be surprised to know what else happened in the morning?' Babs exclaimed. Alok feigned ignorance.

'Mr. Agarwal called me on my mobile phone in the morning,' he said and took out his Siemens handset.

Alok gave it a cursory look, 'For what?'

'*Arrayy,* he had been listening to her while traveling to the airport in his car and he loved her show. He called me up to congratulate on this wonderful discovery. Do you know for how many minutes did he speak to me on the mobile phone? Twelve minutes!' Babs said sounding excited like a kid in the zoo for the first time.

'Wow, twelve minutes? That's really a lot,' Alok maintained a straight face.

'Four hundred bucks on a phone Alok, isn't that really steep?' he added.

'But not to worry Alok, this is company paid,' Babs said and raised the booty that had just been launched to revolutionize the way mankind communicated.

'We must cut a cake or something for this girl. She is a real find,' Babs said looking around for someone who could help him fulfill his wish.

'It's too early Babs, this is her first day. Let her spend some time and become consistent,' Alok intervened between his desires.

'No, she will feel motivated,' Babs tried to ignore him.

'Is this about her show Babs or Mr.Agarwal calling on your mobile phone and congratulating you?' Alok said candidly.

'Both,' Babs had a stupid grin on his face.

'What a day it was…Yaay!' Shonali raised the vodka glass in air.

'Yeah, and it turned out great for you,' Alok said.

'We could have gone out for dinner with everyone, only if you had relented,' Alok said taking a sip.

'I was so tired Alok, haven't slept the entire night,' she said.

'It's so nice and peaceful today. Isn't it?' she asked.

'And cold as well,' he said wearing his jacket.

'It's the happiness inside that is making you see things in a different light,' he said.

'Yeah, I guess so. It was really sweet of Babs to organize that cake today after my first show. Wasn't it?' she asked.

'Yeah, Babs is a sweetheart,' he hid the real reason behind his boss's generousness.

'Everyone was congratulating me Alok, everyone. I think I can make it big,' she said with stars in her eyes.

'Why did you keep saying *Dilli* and not Delhi during the entire show? It was sounding so odd!' he mocked.

'You are so mean Alok,' she made a face. They didn't talk for a while.

'You were good Shonali, but we still need to put in a lot of effort everyday till the time there is a definite consistency in your presentation,' Alok said.

'I know Alok but I rocked today, didn't I?' she said cutely.

'Ofcourse you did, who's arguing that?' he said.

'Can you pass me that bottle? I want to pour myself another one,' she stretched out her hand for the bottle.

'Are you sure? I think you have already had quite a few,' Alok said while passing her the bottle.

'Don't worry boss, I wont do anything, I am fine,' she said naughtily. Alok looked into her eyes and smiled.

'Do you want to go out for dinner? Vishal is also away on a business trip,' he said.

'Nooo, who wants to go out? Maggi is good if we want to eat,' she said.

'Actually I wanted us to be together today,' she said.

'Why?'

'Because everything that I have been able to achieve in this city within this short span of time is largely because of you,' she said.

'I may have helped Shonali, nothing beyond that. There's no need to get emotional and all after drinks. Ok?' he summoned mock anger on his face.

'Ok, Ok, Ok. But one last time, thank you,' she said and got up.

'Will you give me a hug?' she pleaded.

'What's that for? Ok,' Alok resisted but then got up to hug her tightly.

She didn't let him go out of her embrace, 'Let's go out in the balcony.'

They walked out together holding each other and soaked themselves under the gentle presence of moonlight.

'I want to achieve a lot Alok,' she said looking at the blue moon.

'And what's that?' Alok said feeling her close to his body.

'I want to do television after radio, as that will be really big in the future. Then I want to go to Bombay,' she said.

'Bombay? What for?' Alok said thoughtfully. He thought of Mandira strangely at that moment.

She leaned against his shoulders, 'because that's the hub of entertainment. If you are not in Bombay you have just scratched the surface of the world of media and entertainment. Don't you want to be there?'

'You seem to know a lot about this world. As far as I am concerned I am happy doing what I am doing currently. I haven't thought much about the future,' Alok said.

'I like you. You are so simple, so uncomplicated,' she said and looked up to him. Alok could not break away from her smoldering eyes. It seemed to him as if time stood still and the earth stopped rotating at that very moment. Shonali stood up on her toes and breathed closer on his face for a moment before he felt the soft touch of her skin on his lips. He didn't react for a few moments but as her lips ran on top of his, the inhibition was cut loose and he kissed her deeply not once but many a times.

'Let's go inside,' she said with hungry eyes that wanted to explore more.

'Are you sure you want to do this Shonali?' he mumbled.

'Yes, absolutely, I really want to,' she said; literally pulling him inside the living room.

'Is it right Shonali? Is it real?' Alok muttered as she kissed him on the neck and the world started disappearing before his eyes.

'You are special Alok, very special,' she said as she undressed herself and pushed him on the mattress gently. Shonali's words were ringing in his ears as he looked at her naked body towering over his in its mesmerizing beauty. He touched her face and slid his palm around her neck to pull her close and kiss her softly. As their bare skin started getting acclimatized with each other, it cried for closer proximity, uninhibited and vital. They made love till the time the bodies could cope up with their unbridled passion, after which they were engulfed by exhaustion and sleep.

Alok woke up to the third beep of the morning alarm on his pager. The mattress was in a mess and so was the state of the room, unfinished snacks on the plates, half empty glasses and clothes strewn around. He smiled at himself and looked lovingly on the other side, Shonali wasn't there. He got up and stretched his body and walked towards his room when he heard the sound of the shower.

He picked up his clothes from the cupboard and knocked on the door while going to the other bathroom, 'Good morning Shona. We only have thirty minutes before we leave.'

'Good Morning. That's it?' Shonali yelled from inside.

'Yeah! Do you want to be late on the second day of your show?' he shouted.

Shonali made a face under the shower and yelled out, 'Ok.'

'Hey, when do you want to leave?' Shonali asked Alok who was working on the weekly programming calendar.

He glanced at his watch, 'It's not even four Shona? Are you done?'

'Yeah, I am. Let's go, please,' she pleaded.

'Are you done with tomorrows prep sheet?' he asked.

'Not completely, will work on it at night,' she hurried her reply.

'You won't get time Shona, why don't you finish it?' he asked.

'You know what? Babs came up to me and congratulated me on the good job that I am doing. He was telling me that Mr. Agarwal, the MD of Smile FM has also liked my show,' she said excitedly.

'I know Shona but what about the prep sheet?' he asked again.

'I will do it *ya*, let's go for now at-least,' she said throwing her hands up.

He smiled and then relented, 'just half an hour more and then we'll leave.'

They exited the lift on the ground floor and walked towards the main entrance door.

'I have never left the office so early. I had work to finish,' he said.

'Are you complaining?' she asked. He shook his head. A bunch of sales guys walked towards them from the opposite direction. Alok waved at them and they responded back.

'Hey Shonali! Hi! Your show is sounding fabulous. One of my clients talked about it today,' the tall good looking guy amongst the bunch said.

Shonali's face lit up immediately, 'Thanks.'

'Did you see those reactions, it's happening,' she said and pumped up her fist.

'Hmmm...,'Alok said as he pulled out his bike from the stand.

'What's this place called?' she asked looking around.

'Aunt's kitchen, the food here is awesome,' Alok said.

'Isn't this place a bit dingy?' she asked.

'No, I don't think so. It's small but pretty clean,' he said looking surprised at her comment.

'Hmm..,' she said and went quiet.

'It's close to ten,' she looked at her watch.

'When are you planning to complete your prep sheet Shona?' Alok signaled for the waiter.

'Why are you stuck with that stupid prep sheet Alok? Didn't I tell you that I will finish it off?' she muttered annoyingly.

'Ok…Shona let's order food,' he said.

They were halfway through their dinner and Alok was busy narrating her some anecdotes about Babs and Shobha when she stopped him midway.

'Shhhh…listen to this,' she muttered.

'What?' Alok gestured.

She pointed towards the table behind them where four college boys were seated.

'Yeah, that prank played by that new RJ was awesome; the way she tricked that doctor by posing as a patient was hilarious,' the scrawny guy said.

'The breakfast show on Smile FM has really improved ever since the new girl joined. What's her name?' the one sitting next to him asked.

'See; they are talking about me,' Shonali hushed.

'She calls herself Shonali, try catching her on Smile FM tomorrow in the morning,' he said as they got up.

'It's catching on; and people like me. Isn't it great Alok?' she said with twinkle in her eyes.

'It's great Shona but please don't get carried away with all this. This is the time to harness your strength, work hard towards becoming an excellent RJ,' Alok said biting on to the piece of chicken.

'Ok *baba* no more lectures. Can I eat now? Please?' she said not looking too happy. Alok touched her cheek with affection and smiled.

'I am feeling so sleepy now,' she said after getting down from his bike in the parking of Jalvayu towers. Alok wanted to remind her about the prep sheet again but he kept his mouth shut.

They were walking towards the elevator when they came across a group of three pretty looking young girls having an animated conversation. Suddenly one of them looked up in their direction and smiled;

'Aren't you Shonali?' she said.

Shonali nodded, 'Do I know you?'

'No, you don't. I am Vidya and they are Shalini and Neha,' she smiled and introduced her friends.

'I had seen you around a couple of days back and it was then when the building watchman told us that you are a radio jockey with Smile FM,' she said.

'We heard your show today and it was really good,' Neha her friend jumped in.

'Oh! I never knew that news travels this fast,' Shonali smiled and looked at Alok.

'Good news does,' Alok quipped as they all smiled.

'All three of us fly with Club Airways,' Vidya added.

'You mean you guys are airhostesses! Well that's a cool job,' Shonali said.

'Yeah, you get to explore a lot of things on the job,' Shalini said with a naughty smile flirting over her lips.

'What do you mean by that?' Shonali asked.

'Not so soon. You will need to meet us often for that,' Shalini guffawed.

'Yeah, why don't we catch up whenever you have time? We guys are back these days by five because all of us are operating on early morning flights for this month at-least,' Vidya said.

'And we stay right there in your next wing, fourth floor,' Neha said.

'I will for sure. As it is I hardly have friends around,' Shonali said.

'Do that and we will have some great fun together,' Neha said.

'See you then, bye!' Vidya said as they walked away.

'Looked like a friendly bunch of guys,' Shonali yawned.

Alok picked up his pair of cycling shorts from the room and was about to leave when Shonali held him by his wrist.

'Where are you going?' she asked.

'To sleep, in the next room,' he replied.

She switched the lights off and whispered, 'Can't you stay here with me tonight?'

'This is not working right, Shona!' Alok turned his face towards Shonali who was pulling her hair back.

She took out the skin lotion from her bag and turned its lid around. The sticky white lotion poured out slowly into her hands.

'What's not working?' she asked casually, while applying it on her face.

'It's just been over a month since you have gone on air and you have already started getting on the show without a proper prep sheet,' he said; looking at her moving hands on her face.

'Don't get worked up Alok, I was prepared,' she said.

'Don't try to fool me atleast!' Alok sounded disturbed.

'You went on and on around that pollution thing in Delhi for four links because you had nothing else to talk about,' he said.

'So? Isn't pollution the biggest issue in Delhi as of now,' she said applying the cream on her hands.

'But no one wants to listen about pollution for one, fucking, hour Shona. It's important, all right talk about it in one link and then it's over. Listeners want entertainment at the start of the day and not some *gyaan* that goes on and on,' he said getting worked up.

'But listeners like my show and that's the feedback that I have been getting from the time that I have been on air. It's not you and me Alok ultimately it's the listener,' she said, still sounding casual.

Alok looked at her intently, 'How many of such listeners have given you this feedback Shona? Ten, twenty or thirty max? The horizon of Smile FM is way beyond that, it stretches out in millions.'

She answered brazenly, 'So?'

'So, Shona you cannot decide how good or bad you are basis a feedback from thirty people.' he paused calming his tone.

'By that logic Alok, you are that one single listener as well who is claiming that my show isn't good,' she said raising her eyebrows.

'I am not for once saying that Shona. I am just saying that you need to stick to the basics so that you become better everyday. I don't want this initial excitement and some adulation to cloud your mind from working hard enough,' he said measuring his words.

'Do you think I am not working hard?' she looked in his eyes.

'I just think that you need to work harder,' he said.

'I really don't agree with you when everybody including your boss thinks that I am pretty good,' she said with a smirk.

'Fine, Shona. The argument ends, if you don't want to believe what ideally you should,' he said and turned around to face the computer again.

'Can we leave at 3PM today?' she asked after working on the next day's prep for an hour.

'Are you done with tomorrow's prep?' he asked.

'Why are you stuck on this prep thing boss?' she said exasperatedly.

'Because I have a god damn department to take care of Shona and that includes everything; including your shows and your performance,' he said maintaining his composure.

'I will take care of my performance Alok, you need to relax and trust me,' she said while zipping up her hand bag.

'No, I can't leave early everyday, I have work. Why don't you wait till six?' he asked.

'No I can't. I want to take rest for a while because there's a get-together at night,' she said.

'Where are we going?' he asked informally.

'Vidya had called. They have an airline party in their apartment tonight, and she has invited me for that. Umm... you can come if you want though,' she said not sounding comfortable enough.

'No Shonali; you carry on. I have a lot of work to finish today. Would you like to have dinner at home?' he asked.

'No, I guess there would be some dinner there and I might be late. So, see you then,' she picked up her bag and walked away.

Alok kept looking at her taking rapid steps towards the exit and disappearing behind the frosted glass door.

It was almost ten when Alok entered his dark fifth floor Noida apartment. The cold winter of North India had invaded Delhi city, and he felt better being inside the warm confines of his apartment than facing the dry chill on his motorbike. He kept the Studds helmet on the table alongwith the key and chucked his jacket on one of the chairs. He stretched his arms and looked around to decide the next thing to do. There was none. He had dinner outside and Shonali was not at home, so at present there were just a couple of options, watch the portable idiot-box or play the guitar. He chose the latter and picked up his guitar to settle on the armchair.

Alok's tryst with music went on for quite some time and that he realized when he looked at his watch.

'Fuck, it's ten past twelve, where is Shonali?' he muttered to himself.

He walked towards the arrayy of windows that lay on the other side of his living room and served the architectural purpose of cross ventilation adequately. The line of windows also peeked openly at the flats in the other wing. He glanced at them trying to recollect Vidya's flat number that she gave the other day. The lights in most of the apartments had been switched off, an indication of people retiring to their beds rather early in winters. He looked towards his left when the bright lights and excitement traveling out of an apartment in the form of laughter, music and muffled voices, grabbed his attention.

'Yeah, fourth floor. That's what Vidya had said,' he recollected their chat and concentrated on that apartment hoping to catch a glimpse of Shonali somewhere.

He moved his gaze around, there was loud music playing, about twenty odd people on the floor swaying away to music, a couple of scattered groups holding beer cans and glasses filled with liquor, and an odd couple in the balcony trying for closer physical proximity.

'This looks like a rocking house party,' he thought to himself and continued his search for Shonali.

'Yeah, that's Shalini and next to her is Vidya,' he said zeroing in on two girls who were rather skimpily dressed for a house party.

'It must be the airline code,' he thought and smiled to himself.

'Yeah, that's Shonali,' he muttered cheerfully on finding her at last. It was her pink top that she had bought from GK- 1 market last Sunday, acting as the vital clue. She danced in a group alongside Vidya, Shalini and a couple of good looking guys and seemed to be enjoying it to the hilt.

Alok kept looking at her fondly for a few moments when suddenly the music stopped and there was a pause.

'I think they are changing the music CD,' Alok muttered. One of the guys from her group, with long hair, who danced with them leaned forward and whispered something in her ear that made her chuckle.

'Poor girl's been having a tough time over last few days, I am glad she's enjoying,' he whispered again. The music returned and they started dancing again.

Alok stretched his body to yawn and walked towards his bedroom.

He was woken up by creaking sound of the entrance door followed by the clicking of her stiletto heels at around three in the morning. By the time he could get up, Shonali had entered the room already. She did not even bother to change her clothes but slid into the quilt and hugged him tightly.

'How was the party?' he said softly.

'Very good,' she mumbled. Shonali's voice reeked of alcohol.

'Did you have too much to drink? Do you want to eat something?' he asked.

'Hmm...Wine! No I don't want to eat,' she slurred.

'How will you do the show tomorrow?' he asked.

'Stop it Alok, let me sleep. I will do something,' she said sounding irritated.

In a few minutes Shonali was gone. Alok couldn't sleep after that and it was only towards the morning that he shut his eyes again.

Akash Verma # 219

Alok opened his eyes lazily to the sound of the buzzing pager kept next to him. He looked around and then at his watch. It was close to ten and he lied alone on the mattress. He picked up the pager that had three messages from Babs. He found this a bit odd as Babs hardly messaged him and that too early in the morning. All three of them had a similar text, 'Please call back immediately. Very Urgent: Babs.' He got up from the mattress and sauntered out of the bedroom into the living room. There was absolute silence in the house with Shonali having left for her show in the morning. He reflected on the urgency in Babs's message and walked up to the nearest STD booth in the community market.

'Where on this earth have you been Alok?' the anxiety loomed large in his voice.

'Nowhere Babs, I wasn't feeling too well hence decided to take it a bit easy in the morning,' he said.

'Hell has broken loose Alok,' he said excitedly.

'What?' Alok asked.

'Your morning RJ has made some nasty remark against a Union Minister,' he almost screamed.

'You mean Shonali?' Alok couldn't clearly comprehend what Babs said.

'Of course Alok, she has gone and said something crazy about Minister Ram Prasad Verma who belongs to the minority committee. Guess who is after Smile FM now? Everyone Alok everybody, police, judiciary, the minority committee itself that upholds the interests of these castes, millions of people residing all over north India who belong to this particular caste and the minister himself. The office has already received some hundred odd calls in the last one hour and this seems to be growing like wild fire,' the excitement in his voice was rising inorganically.

Alok's mind went blank as it struggled against the possible repercussions.

'He is a Union Minister, isn't he?' Alok asked blankly.

'Of course he is, and this girl says that because of ministers like him who take kickbacks worth crores of rupees, infrastructure in this country is fucked up,' he howled.

Alok swiped off the sweat from his forehead that had surfaced braving a chilly winter, 'But there are very strong evidences against the minister and the Supreme Court is investigating it.'

'Yes, the court is investigating Alok. The matter is still subjudice, and this girl has gone and announced on prime time radio that he has taken money and because of people like him this country is in a shitpit,' Babs howled.

'Maybe it dies a natural death Babs, let's be patient.' Alok said numbly.

'This is fire Alok, the only way it will go is up,' Babs mellowed down suddenly.

'I am reaching office in next half an hour Babs,' Alok said as he put the receiver down.

Shonali was getting out of Babs's cabin when Alok bumped into her. She looked visibly distressed, eyes puffed up, a pale looking face and watery eyes ready to give up any moment.

'Hi,' Alok mumbled. She didn't reply but just walked away. Alok entered the cabin where Babs sat with a red face and morbid expressions.

'She has screwed us man,' he said as he pressed his two temples with his fingers.

'And where the hell were you Alok? Didn't you know what she was going to speak in the show today?' Babs lashed out.

'I mean... I did Babs, but I guess this was something at the last moment. RJ's just write the key topics that they would be picking up in the show for the day, it's not the entire script,' Alok said measuring his words. Babs seemed to cool down when his mobile phone rang. He looked at it curiously and then his face went white once he read the caller's name.

'It's Mr. Agarwal, I think he knows what has happened,' he said as he picked it up nervously and got up.

The next ten minutes on the phone looked like sheer torture for poor Babs. He paced around the room furiously and his replies were only limited to yes Sir, no Sir, right Sir, sorry Sir, I will do that Sir and I will take action Sir. Alok felt hopeless sitting there, looking at Babs whose pants were being taken away inch by inch by Mr. Agarwal and the situation he knew would only worsen, from there on. He thought of Shonali who would be distressed like hell on being through such a catastrophe at a time where her career was at the threshold of taking off, and he cursed himself for not being there with her on the show in the morning. Maybe he would have been able to stop her from being so irresponsible and careless in front of millions of people. Maybe she would have prepared well for the show despite being drunk and sleeping for just a couple of hours. Maybe she could have prepared a good enough prepsheet that had enough topics. Maybe this disaster could have been prevented. Maybe all this would not have happened and he wouldn't be feeling like shit as he did sitting on that chair. Maybe!

'He was livid,' Babs was almost shivering after the ten minute phone call.

'He has told us to run an apology on air immediately. He had received a call from the minister's office and the minister spoke to him personally and admonished him for being so irresponsible,' he added.

'Some heads are going to roll Alok; and first one will be mine,' he kept speaking blankly.

'It's not your thing Babs, relax. Let's do now, what needs to be done,' Alok said. Babs looked at him and nodded impassively.

Raghu the administration manager entered the cabin abruptly, 'Sir, we are getting calls on all our landline numbers from people across north India representing this particular caste. They are asking for written explanations.'

'Tell them that we are coming out with it shortly,' he said and looked at Babs who looked as if he was about to cry any moment.

'I will get the apology organized and put on air immediately. I am also getting one drafted for our newspaper for tomorrow's edition in both English and Hindi,' he said and got up.

'That girl goes off air from tomorrow. She doesn't get to do the show,' Babs said assertively and looked up.

Shonali sat with her head down on the workstation.

'Hi,' Alok tapped her shoulder. She looked up and then plummeted back into the same posture.

'Not feeling well?' he asked her as he dialed for studio and instructed the promo-production guy to record an apology in another RJ's voice.

'Babs blasted me today,' she raised her head up. The eyes were red and her face was all swollen up.

'He is in a bad state, his ass is jacked big time,' Alok said as he typed the apology script on the computer.

'Is it that bad?' she asked.

'Very. It's a disaster,' he said.

'But I don't think that I said something very wrong. I mean see today's headlines, the entire world knows that he is pocketing the money, all the newspapers and television channels are tracking this case so closely,' she said throwing her hands up.

'Shonali, they are reporting on the case and not passing a verdict,' he said with his eyes glued on the screen.

'So what wrong did I say Alok? I just said that he has pinched people's money and that's the reason why we don't have enough to take care of the country's other pending needs such as infrastructure, poverty, education,' she said.

'How can we decide that he is guilty Shonali? We are a goddamn entertainment station and not a newspaper. The courts are still investigating the allegations; while we go out and tell the world that here's the culprit because of whom you are not getting what you were supposed to. Don't you remember the golden rules for an RJ that we went through so many times Shona; no caste, no religion, no politics and no judiciary? Didn't you remember them when you were on air and spoke so frivolously for god's sake?' Alok spoke in a helpless tone.

'So, you guys have decided that I am guilty?' she asked.

'It's not me Shonali , it's about those hundreds of calls that the office is getting, from people representing this particular community saying that they have been specifically targeted, from committees that uphold basic rights of people belonging to this community, from the minister himself and god knows who all will be calling us up now,' he said desperately.

'So? It doesn't mean that I have done something wrong,' she said stubbornly.

'I am not for once saying that your comments are right or wrong. I am just saying that you carelessly forgot that such half-baked and frivolous comments can have implications that are humungous not just for you but the organization,' he almost howled.

'What do you mean Alok? I wasn't careless,' she said raising her voice.

'Did you plan to talk about this yesterday or didn't you just pick it up right from the morning newspapers, because you couldn't think of anything else to say within your show?'

Shonali's seemed to be in quandary, 'No…no I was prepared.'

'Show me those twelve links written down for your three hour show Shonali. Show me your prep sheet?' Alok asked. She went blank and did not react as moments passed.

'Just let it be Shonali, we are all in it now. Let's try and resurrect what we can,' he said while getting up. He stood there for a few minutes trying to regain his lost composure.

'You don't worry, just stay calm. Relax,' he assured her.

'I can apologize tomorrow during my show,' she murmured.

'You are not doing the show from tomorrow. Atleast for the time being; till this dies down,' he pressed her shoulder.

'Why?' she asked in desperate tone.

'Because the government may shut the station if you come on air again, or atleast till the time this controversy is alive,' he said.

'Will this take a long time?' she asked.

'Looks like,' he said.

'Will I lose my job?' she asked.

He wrapped his arm around her and said, 'No you won't. Trust me. I am there with you Shona.'

The mayhem did not settle down for the entire day and by the time Alok wrapped up his work it was close to ten. Shonali had not called for the entire day even once. He walked towards Babs's cabin and found him in a pensive mood. It was quite unusual for someone like Babs to be in the office till so late, engrossed in his thoughts and not in internet porn.

'How do things look Babs?' he asked settling on the chair.

'They look bad as of now. There have been various demonstrations in the north by people from the minister's community; largely peaceful but then a few of them turned violent and police had to intervene and use force. There have been a few arrests in Lucknow and Gorakhpur while some people at different places have been hospitalized as well, after being injured during clashes with the police,' Babs sighed.

'That's bad,' Alok said.

'Mr. Agarwal has been calling up all through the day. He has received some information from a close aide in the Information and Broadcasting ministry,' he said grimly.

'What is that?' he asked.

'In a couple of days, I&B ministry might issue an order to ban Smile FM. For how many days they do it, depends,' he said.

'How can they do that? That would mean a huge revenue loss for the channel. What about the commitment from clients and agencies?' Alok raised his eyebrows.

He turned his face towards the ceiling and sighed, 'The ministry is not concerned about our revenue loss Alok. They want the channel to pay a penalty for screwing up law and order within the country; and this order from them proclaims to the world that they have taken some real action.'

Babs's reply was convincing enough, 'Is the news certain?' Alok asked.

'Looks like, unless Mr. Agarwal can really pull up some strings,' he said.

'How long will this continue Babs? What do you think?' Alok asked concernedly.

'God knows Alok. I think it will take some time. All I have done today is give away interviews and sound bytes to media apologizing for the whole god damn thing,' he said and looked up again.

'Hmmm... the apology is running on air and I have also drafted one out and sent it to group publications,' he said.

'Ok. Well we can only curb the extent of damage now and not salvage the situation,' Babs said.

'Mr. Agarwal is very upset Alok. I fear a drastic action from the management,' Babs confessed candidly.

Alok got up from the chair to look at him, 'I know Babs and I am sure.'

'Did she have her dinner before sleeping?' Alok asked Vishal who was busy watching an old Sanjay Dutt flick on their portable black and white television.

'I don't think so. She sat here to watch TV for some time and then went back to the room,' he said without moving his gaze.

Alok got up and knocked on the bedroom door. She opened the door after he had knocked it thrice.

'Yeah,' she said drowsily.

'All well Shona? Can I pick up my clothes?' he asked. She nodded and moved aside to let him enter. He carefully scouted for his clothes in the darkness and walked back to the door where she waited.

'Good Night,' he said.

It had been seven days since the controversy had erupted and shaken the very foundations of Smile FM. Things were coming back to normalcy with media frenzy diminishing by the day and backward community agitation fizzling out due to an out of court settlement between the minister and Mr. Agarwal. As Babs aptly gave words to such an alignment; Media and politics are strangers by the day and lovers by the night.

Alok had retuned home early, to rest for a while before visiting a doctor. He had practically been feeling unwell for the last few days. Shonali had been on leave for last four days as she was finding it tough to be sitting idle in the office for the entire day. She said, it was virtually choking her. She had applied for leave and Babs was more than happy to sanction it; for it would keep trouble out of the way for a few days at least. He pulled his body lethargically to the elevator and rang the bell of his apartment. Alok had to wait for about five minutes before she opened the door. Shonali was wearing a nightgown and looked a bit startled as if she wasn't expecting him so early.

'Hi,' he said and walked in. A strong stench of beer and cigarettes greeted him. He didn't say anything but kept his bag on the table and lied down on the mattress.

'How was your day Shona? Was anybody here?' he asked.

Shonali was artificially spontaneous, '*Arrayy,* no one... Vidya and Neha were here for a while. They had a weekly off today, that's why.'

'Looks like you guys had fun,' he smiled and looked at her.

Shonali's face squeezed a tinge of red, 'Just a couple of beers.'

'And cigarettes,' he added and smiled again.

'*Arrayy* that Neha smokes sometimes, it wasn't us,' she said.

'Don't bother Shona, I am not complaining. Why don't you come here and sit next to me?' he asked.

It looked as if she hesitated to accept the proposal at first but then got up to sit next to him. It was strange that why he felt as if he was sitting next to a stranger. He kissed her on the forehead and wrapped his arm around her shoulders.

'How did you manage to finish off your work so early today?' she asked.

'I wasn't feeling too well,' he said.

'Hmm...what is new in the office?' she asked plainly.

'Nothing much, except that it is subsiding by the day and things should be okay within next few weeks,' he said.

'Can I get back on air then?' she asked.

Alok took a long pause, 'Looks unlikely Shona after all this. I would suggest that you get back to being a producer for next few months and hopefully during this time this controversy would die down completely. Then we can look at launching you as an RJ with a different name.'

'Why would I change my name?' she asked.

'A lot of RJ's have different on-air names. There's nothing wrong with that, don't film stars have it too?' he asked.

'Maybe they do, but I wouldn't like to change my name and also I wouldn't like to go back to a desk job in the interim after being an RJ. There isn't any fun in it,' she said firmly.

'I know, but there isn't any option before us as of now. Even if you would quit and go to any other radio station in this country, no one would touch you because of this controversy,' he explained.

'What's the point Shona? Can't we just accept the situation for a while instead of experimenting with unknown territories?'Alok added.

'I just can't do this producers role anymore Alok, it will kill the artist inside me. I am fine if I don't get something that I like here in Delhi. I am ready to go anywhere looking for it,' she said.

'Where would you go Shona?' he felt hurt by her sudden admission.

'Wherever,' she said.

'Will you leave me?' he asked. She went quiet and did not respond. Alok didn't want to push her further.

'I think I will sleep for a while,' he said.

'Yeah, ok. I would be going out to Vidya's house in the evening. It's Shalini's birthday today and they are celebrating,' she mentioned casually while getting up.

He got up feeling hungry and weak post ten at night. There was absolute silence in the house indicating that Shonali had been long gone. He kept lying still for few minutes, disturbed with the conversation that had ensued between them a few hours earlier.

'It's been tough for her over last few days. She was right there; at the cusp of becoming a celebrated RJ and now sinking at the bottom of the heap would be so painful for her. Poor Shona, her disturbed state is making her mind wander in different directions,' he thought sympathetically.

'With no one around and an unstable family backup, who wouldn't want to succeed as soon as possible? Isn't that natural?' he thought further.

He strained himself to get up and staggered towards the refrigerator. He pulled out a bottle of water and picked up a couple of raw eggs that he intended to mix up with Maggi. He sipped from the bottle and glanced through the window at Vidya's pad on the fourth floor. The scene was similar, men and women happy with alcohol, dance and smoke in the air. This time he could locate Shonali quiet clearly, she looked unrestrained dancing to the beats of music; she wasn't with a group but dancing alone with some guy. They seemed to be quite close and on observing closely he realized that it was the same good looking guy with long hair. He kept the eggs back into the refrigerator and moved away from the window. The hunger seemed to wear away with every passing moment and weakness was gripping his body. He switched on the television and flicked through various channels mindlessly before settling on an English music channel. The door bell rang and he got up excitedly, hoping that Shona would have returned.

'Hey Alok! Have you had your dinner?' a beaming Vishal said.

'No, not yet,' Alok said forcing a smile on his face.

'Want to go out?' he asked.

Alok shook his head, 'Not feeling good Vishal, there is bread and eggs at home.'

'Cool, let me make that for you as well. The day has been good for me as we have got a huge order from France,' Vishal said as he whistled aloud.

'Fantastic,' Alok mumbled.

'So, here's eggs and Maggi for you,' Vishal emerged from the kitchen with two plates in hand.

'Thanks man but I will eat in a while. Why don't you just leave it in the kitchen?' Alok said.

He stopped in his tracks and then raised his eyebrows, 'Ok, cool. As you say.'

'Where's Shonali today?' he asked sucking out a noodle from the fork.

'She's gone out,' he said with his eyes stuck on the television.

'She's going out a lot these days. *Dilli kee hawa lag gayee hai,*' he quipped. Alok didn't react and this made him cut short his jibe.

It was an hour after Vishal had slept, when Alok struggled to get up. He felt very weak as he walked towards the window. The decibel of the music on the fourth floor had reduced considerably and the genre had changed to romance; bringing some couples very close as they held each other while they danced. A few of them were lounging on the couches that laid on one side of the room, drawn in an animated conversation. Alok rummaged through them trying to look for Shonali. He scanned carefully through the room trying to locate her in that beautiful purple dress but all attempts went futile.

'Where would she go at this time? Is everything all right? Should I go and check at Vidya's place?' the questions zipped through his mind. He was turning back when his eyes caught a glimpse of purple in the balcony towards the left hand corner of their fourth floor apartment. It was dark outside, but scattered light that fell on the balcony through windows was enough for his eyes to narrow down on the balcony and realize that the girl in the beautiful purple dress was Shona, it was her. Alok's vision blurred and he felt excruciating pain enter his being through his ribs and slowly gripping his entire body. She had her back towards him and she was there with the same guy whom she danced closely with, a while back. They kissed passionately.

Alok could barely manage to stand and tottered to reach the mattress. He felt helpless as his body engulfed in pain, anxiety and weakness slid inch by inch into a quagmire and lost consciousness in a short while.

He felt as if somebody shook him gently as he opened his eyes to the bright sunshine that fell inside through the windows of his apartment.

'Are you fine?' Vishal asked. Alok could see another man sitting at the corner of the mattress along with him who seemed like a doctor. Shonali stood behind them with an expressionless face that hid more than it showed.

'Yeah, I am fine. What had happened?' he asked.

'No idea. It's just that I tried to wake you up in the morning and you did not respond; so I called Doctor Shah,' he said.

'Is this happening to you for the first time?' the doctor asked.

'It has happened a few times earlier doc,' Alok said feeling completely sapped out of energy.

'These kinds of blackouts are not good at your age. I would recommend you to undergo all tests that I am writing on this prescription. You can't take this lightly at all,' he said while scribbling on his pad. Alok nodded and smiled at Shonali.

'When did you get back?' he said gently.

'Late last night, but if you were unwell you could have called for me,' she said.

'I will be fine in a day. Not to worry,' he said.

'Alok, you need to undergo these tests today. Do not delay,' the doctor looked into his eyes while handing Vishal the prescription.

Vishal took the prescription and led the doctor to the door.

'What's the plan? Are you coming to the office?' he asked getting up sluggishly.

'No, I don't think so. I plan to go to Dehradun for a few days,' she said.

'Is it something urgent?' he asked. She shook her head.

'You need to take care of yourself man and do get these tests done today. I hope there isn't anything serious. Dr. Shah has recommended atleast a couple of day's complete rest for you,' Vishal said handing over the prescription to Alok.

'Thanks for your help. I will get these tests done today,' Alok said.

'Anytime,' Vishal said and left for work.

'Who's that guy you are hanging out with?' Alok asked as he rested his back against the wall.

'Who?'she asked.

'The same guy whom you have been hanging out with.'

Shonali stared at his face which said that he knew.

'Oh Rahul! He is just a friend,' she said casually sitting on the chair.

'Is he just a friend?' he asked. She nodded.

'Yeah, he is not a part of the airline crowd. He works for a television company in Bombay. He has been helping me out with some leads,' she said.

'Who am I Shona?' he asked.

'You are a friend, Alok. A close friend,' she said.

There was a long pause between them.

'I saw you guys together last night,' he said.

'Were you keeping a tab on me?' she asked. He shook his head.

'Why didn't you tell me that you don't love me?' he asked.

'I never told you that I love you,' she replied.

'If all that was not love then tell me what love is?' he cried. She didn't reply as minutes passed in between. He got up to walk towards her and pulled her up by the shoulders.

'You think about it Shonali when you are in Dehradun, you think about it hard enough. I will wait for your answer once you come back,' he said gently.

The pager lying on the mattress buzzed and he walked back to pick it up.

'Please come to the office soon. Very Important- Babs.'

'I need to go to the office. When are you leaving?' he asked.

'My bus is at three in the afternoon from ISBT,' she said with an emotionless face.

'Do give it a hard thought. Shona.' he said as he rushed into his room to change.

Babs was talking on his mobile phone when he entered his cabin. He gestured at Alok to take a seat. Alok could make out that he was talking to Mr. Agarwal and updating him about the current status of the controversy. Babs looked relaxed and that was an indication of things getting back to normalcy.

He finished the call and took a hard look at Alok, 'All well?'

'No Babs, I guess health is slipping up,' he said.

'Hmmm..,' he said and took a deep breath before taking a long pause.

'It seems that Mr. Agarwal had to lobby big time for preventing that order to come out,' he said.

'Is it confirmed that we are safe?' Alok asked.

Babs scratched his head, 'Looks like, that's what he just said.'

'That's good,' Alok let out a sigh of relief.

Babs cleared his throat once, 'Alok the top management and Mr. Agarwal have taken this issue very seriously.'

'They would for sure and there are reasons for it,' Alok said and stared at the growing nervousness on Babs face.

He cleared his throat again, 'Alok, he wants to set up an example to the world outside and within the company, so that such negligence is never repeated.'

'We have taken action Babs; by pulling out the RJ from the show,' he said.

'That's not enough with Mr. Agarwal. He wants her to resign,' Babs said measuring his words.

'But why would one do that Babs? She is insignificant in the whole scheme of things. What will we prove to the world by making her resign?' Alok argued excitedly.

Babs threw his hands up in the air, 'Well, it does not matter Alok. He wants the responsible person to resign. He is not going to settle for less.'

'I can go and talk to him Babs if that is the case,' Alok said.

'He is not listening Alok, don't you think I have reasoned with him enough?' Babs pleaded.

'We'll screw her career Babs. She is not getting a job elsewhere, atleast an anchor's job if we do this,' Alok said.

'It's better than us getting screwed. At least,' Babs said.

'We have decided between Mr. Agarwal and myself that someone has to own it up and should resign,' Babs said. There was silence in the room for a while.

'I will resign in that case.' Alok's words cut through the silence.

'What? Are you crazy Alok?' Babs got up from the chair.

'At the end of it Shonali was my responsibility Babs, and if she fucked up, it was because I didn't have enough systems in place to prevent her,' Alok said.

'Perhaps, I took it lightly, and did not pay much attention to the prep-sheets that she was doing,' he added engrossed in his thoughts.

'Do you even know what you are speaking? Nobody will hire you in this industry if you go out in the market,' Babs said.

'It doesn't matter Babs. I myself was not going to spend my life in this industry,' he said.

'Why would you want to do this for her? You are doing well in your career; you should get ahead Alok and not get caught up with these silly calls of the heart,' Babs reasoned.

'You won't understand Babs but if it's between me and Shonali, I am ready to put down my papers,' he said. Babs went quiet and pondered over it for long before opening his mouth.

'Someone has to go Alok, this decision can't be reversed now,' he said sincerely.

'In that case it would better be me, Babs,' Alok said and got up from his chair to leave his cabin.

Alok was typing his resignation when her phonecall arrived on his desk.

'Alok,' she said.

'Hi Shonali,' he said.

'I want to meet you before I leave. I have to tell you something,' she sounded depressed.

'Ok Shonali. Where do you want to meet up?' he asked while giving a print command to his resignation letter.

'Can we meet at ISBT? My bus is at three from there,' she asked.

'Yeah, fine Shona. See you at ISBT,' he said as he put the receiver down.

Alok reached ISBT bus station fifteen minutes before the scheduled departure time of the bus. He inquired about the bus from the main ticket-booking window. The bespectacled betel chewing man pointed towards the parking bays on the right and mumbled something from his red froth filled mouth that sounded like five. The buses were lined up neatly like aircrafts on chutes ready to take off any moment. The platform bustled with people of all ages and sex eager to embark on a journey and that showed in the excitement they revealed as they stood there, waiting or boarding their destination carriers. Alok reached the designated bay number five where an air-conditioned coach marked New Delhi- Dehradun- New Delhi waited patiently for its quota of passengers. Alok looked around for Shonali and saw her at the STD booth engrossed in a call. He walked towards the booth and knocked on its glass door to draw her attention. She turned around and signaled him to wait.

'When did you reach?' he asked as she finished her call and came out.

'Some time back. How is everything in office?' she asked as they walked towards the bus.

'Things are springing back to normalcy Shona. I think by the time you are back from your trip; things should be fine,' he said.

'I am not coming back Alok,' she stopped in her tracks.

'What do you mean? Why?' he held her by the shoulder and asked.

'There is nothing left for me here Alok. I am going to Bombay,' she said measuring each word and not looking into his eyes.

'Bombay? Just like that? What will you do there Shona?'

'Rahul has agreed to help me get an entry within the television industry; it's booming as of now,' she said.

'Rahul has said and you have agreed Shonali? You have a job here, a readymade career and you are going to do some unknown television shit,' he cried.

'I know Rahul enough to trust him. I know he will help,' she said.

Alok didn't have much to say after those words nearly numbed him.

'I could have helped you Shonali, and I don't think that what you are doing is right,' he mumbled.

A steak of anger ran on her face, 'You didn't Alok. You couldn't do anything when I was thrown out of the morning show.'

He wanted to tell her that giving up his own job that he did an hour back; was perhaps the maximum that he could do to help her. But he didn't, and allowed silence to do the talking. The bus honked; signaling that it wanted to leave.

'I have collected my entire luggage from your house and I am taking it away to Dehradun,' she said.

'Everything?' he mumbled with disbelief. She nodded her head as she looked to be in a thought.

'But anyways Alok; you were a great help and I can never forget you for that,' she said.

She walked ahead, 'And thank you for making me believe in myself Alok.'

'Let's meet whenever you are in Bombay or I will definitely call you in case I am in Delhi,' she said. Alok knew; that what she said would never come true.

'Wait,' he said and hugged her, 'Take care Shonali.'

'I will. Bye Alok,' she said and as she climbed up the steps of the bus. She turned around to smile at him; and he smiled back

It was the last time that they saw each other.

PART 4: ALOK

26th June, 2011: Gurgaon, India

The door creaked at twelve in the night as Ashu sneaked quietly inside his Beverly Plaza apartment; with the duplicate key dangling in his hand. He unloaded his bag and the files that he carried, on the table next to the entrance and loosened his tie to look at the watch again He heaved a sigh of fatigue and helplessness, some of the luxuries of being a successful criminal lawyer. The guilt of not being able to give any time to Megha and Sneha over last two months surfaced again as he quietly entered the bedroom. Megha was lying on the bed with her left arm covering her head, her usual sleeping posture. He carefully pulled out his night clothes that lay neatly on one side of the cupboard; and thanked Megha in his heart for that, as he entered the washroom. A few minutes later he emerged again and like a guilty criminal sneaked quietly inside the sheet to keep his palm over her shoulder. She switched the table lamp on.

He was surprised to see the light fill up the room suddenly, 'I thought you had gone off to sleep.'

'How was your day?' Megha asked.

'It seems as if the courts have decided to hear only my cases for last two months. It has been crazy Megha, with court cases everyday, client meetings and then preparing for all these cases. I think my team will stage a demonstration any day,' he said stroking his forehead with his fingers.

'And I know Megha, that I haven't been able to give you and Sneha any time over last two months. Even the weekends are going away in these heavy duty preparations,' he added.

'Two months Ashu? This has been going on since the time we got married. When have you been able to find this time?' Megha asked.

'This time one hundred percent Megha, in two weeks we are going for a vacation for sure. Where do you want to go? Thailand? KL? Or no, let's go to Bali this time,' he said trying to make up.

'I am not complaining Ashu, you get over with your work first and then we will decide. Secondly, we also have to consider Sneha's school schedule; we just can't upset it with unplanned vacations,' she said.

'Yeah, you are right; we will plan this out but we are definitely going this time,' he said and pulled her by the other shoulder to turn her around and face him.

'Hmmm...I am going to Dehradun day after,' she said looking at his face closely.

'Why so suddenly baby; some relatives or friends?' he asked massaging her head.

'I am going to meet Alok,' she said and felt his hand stopping dead in its tracks. The expression on his face also went into a pause mode. He did not speak for a few minutes.

'Why do you want to see him after so many years Megha? What's left now? You know I have never liked this relationship,' he said as he pulled his hand away.

Megha caressed his shoulder, 'Have I ever hid anything from you about me and Alok? You know about this thing from school, don't you?' He nodded.

'Have I ever complained about anything over last fifteen years of our marriage?' He kept quiet.

'But you were not happy about it when you got married?' he said.

'But I accepted you Ashu and that was one big thing,' she said.

'You have to trust me Ashu that if I am going to meet him after all these years, there has to be a good enough reason. He wants to meet me just once; and it sounded as if he really wants to,' she said.

'I will not disappoint him this one last time,' she sounded as if she had already made up her mind.

Ashu could not battle her resolve, 'When do you go?'

'28th June. I have booked myself on the 2PM Kingfisher flight,' she said.

'I could have dropped you off to the airport if I didn't have to be in the court,' he said.

'Don't bother, I will manage. I have sounded off the maid and she will take care of Sneha full time, but if you can, please try and be home early for these couple of days,' she said.

'I will,' Ashu whispered.

A weak smile played on her lips as she switched off the table lamp.

28th June, 2011: New Delhi, India

'Good work, Mandira!' Mark exclaimed as she presented the P&L statement of the new product range on the final slide of her one hundred and twenty six slide presentation.

'Yes Mark; incremental ten percent growth due to the new juice flavors range and the business breaks even from year two,' Arvind her immediate boss smiled expanding his boss's statement and furthering his belief.

'We need good managers like you to boost the Uni-Cola business in India,' Mark spoke in his Oxford English and with a face growing redder with the anticipation of future growth.

Mandira pulled out the laptop chord from the socket, 'Yeah Mark, we need some great execution now, as the strategy looks pretty good.'

'Yeah, certainly it does. I am going to soundoff all the sales heads in our quarterly review tomorrow. Should we do that Arvind?' he said and looked at his deputy. Mandira winked at Srini who had sat through the entire presentation praying to his choicest of deities for it to go off well, or else his upcoming appraisal would have born the penalty. He smiled back showing off his full set of thirty two to his loosened up boss.

'Yeah sure Mark; I am asking Mandira to be there as well so that she may take them through this launch strategy in complete detail,' Arvind said and looked at a cagey Mandira.

'Yeah, sounds good,' Mark commented.

'I am sorry Arvind and Mark, that won't be possible. I am off for a couple of days,' she said.

'Can't you postpone Mandira? This can be a great opportunity to build a strong case for the new launch internally,' Arvind tried to bargain.

'I am sorry boss, this is very urgent. Srini can fill up for me tomorrow,' she said and looked at Srini who made a face after being draped up as a scapegoat once again.

Arvind had no other option but to let out a routed sigh that said: Ok, whatever, as we can't do a shit.

'And what about the Executive Committee dinner? No one misses that lady!' Mark spoke playfully almost flirtingly.

'Dinners can wait Mark, this thing can't,' she said smilingly and turned around towards Arvind, 'I need to rush boss; I have a flight at two.'

Arvind nodded in pure submission.

She looked at Srini and smiled, 'Take care when I am gone dude.'

By the time this dude could react, Mandira had vanished out of the conference room leaving the three men looking at each other.

28th June, 2011: Mumbai, India

Shonali was woken up by the ring of her mobile phone. It was about four in the morning when she had slept and this phone call at eleven did nothing better than to irritate her completely.

'Yeah,' she murmured angrily without even looking at the caller's name on the screen.

'What time are we leaving?' the caller was familiar.

'Siddharth! Hi! What?' she asked half asleep.

'Didn't I tell you about going to Panvel, Shonali? Why are you confused?' Siddharth said sounding irritated.

'And I told you that I had to go somewhere. Didn't I?' she said having woken up completely.

'Listen Shonali, I don't have much time and patience. What time do we leave?' his voice became coarser.

'I had told you Siddharth, it's tough. I have to be in Mussoorie,' she almost screamed.

'You had said Dehradun the other day, what's all this?' he sounded confused.

'Mussoorie is Dehradun. Dehradun is Mussoorie Siddharth,' she said.

'Okay! I got it Shonali. They are damn close. Can't you go there next weekend?' he said looking for a ray of hope.

'No Siddharth. I have to. It's critical,' she said while looking at his letter that lay on one side of her bed.

'Hmmm…so what do I do this weekend?' Siddharth the bastard asked sounding all worked up.

'Why don't you take your wife there for a change?' she chuckled.

There was silence on the other end and she could hear him clearing his throat.

'What a bitch, Shonali? I will see you next week. Ok?' he asked; perhaps with a face that had gone beetroot red.

'I hope so honey. I hope so,' she said as she hung up on him. She looked at her watch, it was eleven fifteen. She had only ninety minutes to reach the airport for her flight at one thirty. She pulled herself up lazily and walked towards the washroom.

28th June, 2011:4 PM, Mussoorie, India

The Jolly Grant Airport in Dehradun wore a deserted look for most of the day because of only a limited number of private airlines operating daily to- and- fro flights from there. The situation would take a complete U turn although, before the arrival and departure of an aircraft. The staff at the airport would have a flurry of activities to attend to; a fleet of taxis and private cars would line themselves up at the departure, out of nowhere; hotel attendants from nearby hill stations would wait anxiously at the departure gate holding placards that had fancy names written on them. To sum it up; the airport would come alive like a filmset waiting for the camera to roll.

Mandira walked towards the arrival with one piece of hand baggage that she had carried for a day's or maximum a two-day trip. She glanced around through her silver rimmed Oakley's and realized that her looks coupled with the smart black formals that she wore, could gather ample attention and admiration from people around in the airport. As she emerged from the doorway the circumspection became intense, because now the prying eyes no more belonged only to the co-passengers: but to the taxi drivers, car drivers and locals who seemed bereft of such travelers visiting their sleepy town often. It felt as if she were in a zoo, locked up in a cage, with onlookers piercing her with their eyes. She looked around hurriedly hoping to find Alok. But how would she recognize him after so many years? He could have got a huge paunch, become older, could be sporting a moustache or a beard and worse gone completely bald. Someone tapped her on the shoulder and she turned around in anticipation to find a guy with salt 'n' pepper beard, steel rimmed glasses and curly hair that were thinning in the centre. He wasn't Alok.

'Hi Mandira,' he said with a glint in his eyes.

It instantly reminded her of someone. She looked at him carefully beneath his beard and the years gone by.

He smiled as if trying to help her, 'You know me Mandira. Sarvesh, Sarvesh Singh.'

She couldn't, as she fought with her memory again.

'Baba, you would remember me by this name,' he said.

'Of course, I do Baba. How can I forget? You have changed a lot,' she said as she hugged him reassuringly.

'You haven't and you look just the same,' he said.

'How can you say that? I must have changed as well. Gone older,' she said casually.

'No, you haven't. Look,' he said and stretched out his hand that carried a picture of hers. It was the same picture that she had. Alok and her on stage inseparable, together.

She looked embarrassed as if someone had sneaked into their privacy, 'How… how do you have this?' she fumbled.

'Alok gave it to me, in case I fail to recognize you,' he said plainly. For a moment she did not like Baba carrying their picture.

'Where is Alok? Is he around?' she asked, curiously looking around.

'No he isn't,' he said.

'Is he busy somewhere?' she asked sounding a bit irritated.

It seemed odd to her that someone who was so eager to meet up after such a long time wouldn't be there to receive her.

She spoke trying to drive the fickle thought away, 'Should we get going? I believe Mussoorie is some ninety minute drive from here.'

Baba was busy staring at the stream of passengers emerging from the arrival gate and glancing intermittently at some papers that he carried in his hand.

'Are we waiting for someone?' Mandira asked impatiently.

'Yes. Just give me a few minutes and we will leave. I do not want to miss them as I haven't seen them before,' he said scanning the passengers carefully.

He looked as if he had already focused on someone who was right behind her.

'Excuse me madam, do you happen to be Megha?' he yelled.

Megha looked towards her left and saw a portly bearded man who appeared to be in his early forties calling out at her.

'Yes, do I know you?' she asked looking surprised.

Mandira turned around to look at the woman whom Baba had called out at. She appeared to her like a perfect bride who had just leapt out of the matrimonial advertisements appearing across various websites; and looked like an apt choice for any progressive Indian male wanting to get married. She was tall, fair, had hair falling on to her shoulders that heightened her beauty, as they seemed to be left open deliberately. She was wearing an ethnic yet chic *Salwar Kameez* picked up from one of the fancy designer stores in Hauz Khas and she carried herself with a poise that only a very small percentage of women could boast of, besides Mandira herself.

Baba walked ahead leaving Mandira behind, 'No you don't, Megha. I am Sarvesh Singh, Alok's friend.'

'Oh....so you are Alok's friend. I have never heard about you Sarvesh,' she smiled.

'How could you Megha? I was his friend in Lucknow, at the University. He couldn't have told you,' he said as a matter of fact.

Megha was stunned for a few seconds, 'How would he know that we never met or talked after he left Agra? Has he been talking to people?'

Baba ignored her thought and added causally, 'You can call me Baba. Everyone calls me by that name,' he smiled graciously.

'Where is Alok?' she asked gathering herself.

'He isn't here. He is in Mussoorie,' Baba replied. Megha didn't appear pleased with the answer and that reflected in the form of a cynical smile.

'Is she family?' Mandira hushed in Baba's ears.

'No, I am his friend. Alok's friend from school,' Megha said and moved forward to shake hands with this lady who seemed to have straightaway jumped out of some five-star conference room business meeting.

'Megha,' she said.

'Mandira,' she said.

As they exchanged pleasantries, Baba's eyes were still transfixed at the arrival gate.

'Baba, can we please leave now?' Mandira asked in a desperate tone, 'This suit is killing me.'

'Just a few minutes more Mandira, the Mumbai flight has just landed. We need to take one more guest with us,' Baba said.

'Who's this one now?' Megha asked.

'I hope Alok is not getting married and we are not called to some surprise wedding party?' Mandira said, frustrated. Megha bounced off a hard glare at her.

Baba smiled thoughtfully at her remark, 'No, he is definitely not getting married Mandira.We are just waiting for one more friend of his.'

'Oh...No...,' Mandira scoffed at him, 'How many friends does he have and why are all of them arriving at the same god damn time Baba?'

She looked at him as if trying to decode a mystery, 'I hope this isn't one silly gag Baba?'

Baba didn't reply and kept staring at the arrival gate. He seemed to be narrowing down on a group that walked out from the right side of the gate.

'I think that should be Shonali,' he said as he walked towards her; continuously looking at the stack of papers in his hand.

'Isn't she dressed a bit boldly for a town like this?' Mandira said while they cautiously inspected the girl with whom Baba was trying to strike a conversation with.

Shonali wore a pair of blue cotton shorts and a sleeveless white T-Shirt. She wore a loose acrylic maroon scarf around her neck and with a black pair of slippers and a tote-bag dangling across her shoulder; she didn't appear to belong to that place at all. She looked Bohemian. They saw her shaking hands with Baba and then both Shonali and Baba walked towards them.

'Hi, I am Shonali!' she beamed at them.

'I am Megha.'

'Hi there, I am Mandira! And if we are through with picking up everyone Baba, can we get on to Mussoorie now?' Mandira pleaded mockingly with folded hands. Baba smiled as he gave a gentle nod and they walked to the airport parking lot.

'Isn't it funny that both of us board the plane from the same airport, sit in the same plane, come here for the same purpose and yet don't know each other till we meet here?' Mandira exclaimed while looking at Megha and getting into the white Toyota Innova in the parking lot.

'Do you mind taking the back seat Megha? I tend to get nausea if I am not at the window,' Mandira said.

'Bloody Liar,' Megha muttered as she squeezed herself between the two bucket seats on the second row and slipped on to the third. Shonali had already parked herself comfortably on the left side by entering through the other door. A morose looking Baba sat in the first row along with the driver, a twenty something lad from the hills.

'How did you recognize us without a placard, we haven't even met up earlier?' Shonali asked taking off her tote- bag.

'Here,' Baba said and handed them two pictures from the stack of papers that he carried.

Megha stretched her head out from the third row to take a look; the picture was taken at the annual day celebration of St. Thomas, it was Vanita and Vandana her friends along with her in the centre and Alok.

'Oh my God! Where did you find this one?' she said snatching the picture while staring at it.

'And this one, even I don't have it,' Shonali said rolling her index finger between her teeth and looking at their group photograph from Goa, where they had gone for the Smile FM conference.

Baba turned towards them and gently took the photographs back, 'He gave them to me for helping me to recognize you.'

Baba glanced at them once and then looked at the road ahead. The car went quiet for a while.

'Why do you look so serious man? Baba you used to be such a lively guy in college; where's all that fire gone?' Mandira punched him lightly on the shoulder.

'So, you guys know each other from college?' Shonali asked.

'Of course, we do. We used to hang out a lot together, Alok, Baba, Suveesha, myself and there used to be one more guy whose name I seem to forget,' she said while trying to remember.

'Harish,' Baba reminded her.

'Yeah, Harish, that's right. Do you remember Alok's concerts Baba?' she asked.

'How can I forget them?' he replied.

'He used to sing for a full time band in college, didn't he? We had heard about it in our Smile FM days, but never knew that it was that serious,' Shonali said.

'Yeah, he did and the concerts rocked, didn't they?' she asked. Baba nodded.

'He had taken off to music from the school days. I could see it happening from the last annual day celebration in school,' Megha said looking out of the window.

'Hmmm…I wish he could continue it and make a good career out of music. What did you say Shonali? Was he with Smile FM?' Mandira asked.

'It's the number one radio station nationally now, and a company like mine, UniCola, spends a bomb on it annually,' she added.

'I don't think he is working there currently, otherwise why he would be a music teacher in Mussoorie? I don't know why he left everything and moved out to come here,' Shonali said with a perplexed look on her face.

'You said that you guys were colleagues in Smile FM?' Megha asked. Shonali nodded.

'So, was he still there when you moved to Mumbai?' she prodded again.

'Yes.' Shonali said.

'Why did you leave Smile FM?' Mandira asked.

'It's a long fucking story. Let's keep it for some other day,' Shonali said shaking her head as she lit up a cigarette.

'Were you two in touch after that?' Megha asked circumspectly.

'Never,' Shonali said as she exhaled the first puff.

Mandira turned behind to look at Megha, 'So, how do you know Alok? Did you go to the same school?' Megha shook her head.

'Were you guys' family friends?' she asked again.

'We went to the same coaching class,' Megha said and felt an odd pressure around the centre of her heart. She could visualize them engrossed in their question and answer session on the notepad discreetly; as Gupta carried on with his Mathematics.

'I hope not a school fling,' Mandira chuckled.

'No, not a school fling,' Megha replied coarsely, clearly unhappy with her vocabulary.

'Just kidding,' Mandira raised her hands.

'Did you go to the same college as Alok?' Shonali asked blowing a puff.

'No, I went to a different one. We had similar tastes and that made us hang out a lot together.'

'Like boyfriend and girlfriend?' Shonali said instantaneously.

Mandira turned a shade of red, 'We were close but nothing like that because I always wanted to go to US for my management degree,' she spoke hurriedly.

'What do you mean by close? It's either a yes or a no,' Shonali said and her words could barely be heard by Mandira whose thoughts meandered wildly through all the time they spent; from unbridled fun at his rock concerts to their transparent discussions in Spicy Bite and finally on the terrace of her house where they had made love for the first time.

'So is it a yes or a no?' Shonali's words hit her ear drums again.

'Umm...I don't know,' Mandira muttered and looked askance.

'I am sure that since he has specially called you here, you guys are more than just colleagues,' Megha broke the silence after a few minutes and looked at Shonali.

'We were close. Pretty close,' Shonali said and shut her eyes.

'He was a very close friend; infact the only friend that I have had in my life,' she shut her eyes again, 'If only I would've listened when he wanted me to.'

Megha did not probe further, 'You said that you belonged to Dehradun, didn't you?'

'Yeah! I am going to stay with my family for the next few days after I meet up with Alok. I thought that this could be a good chance to spend some time with them after eight long years. Alok's letter came just in time,' she said while rubbing her eyes. Mandira noticed that she wiped out some tears that had welled up as well.

'Did you receive a letter from him too?' Megha asked.

'He wrote to me as well,' Mandira turned around and looked at Shonali, 'Did he call you?'

'No, he didn't. I received a letter from him, as I just said. Why would he write to us and call everyone here on the same day?' Shonali said as she looked at Mandira.

'God knows? Let's ask him only when we meet,' Shonali said and reclined on her seat.

The vehicle made its way through the road that meandered through the hilly terrains to enter into the bustle of the town called Mussoorie.

'Are we there, finally?' Mandira asked half asleep.

'Yes we are! How beautiful do the mountains look?' Shonali said clapping her hands and gazing at the line of mountains that circled the town, in awe like a child.

'Where are we going?' Megha asked in her weary voice.

'Are we meeting Alok now?' they asked in unison.

'We can meet him later,' Baba said as the vehicle stopped at Hotel Park Plaza.

'Why can't we meet him now?' Megha argued.

'Yes, I would rather meet him before and then check into the hotel once and for all,' Mandira said looking unwilling to get out.

'I need to visit my family after meeting him. Can we see him now, please?' Shonali asked putting all her womanly charm in her voice.

'After half an hour, the visiting hour is between seven and eight,' he turned back, 'You can freshen up meanwhile.'

'Visiting hours? What's happening here' Megha almost screamed. The other two were taking time to comprehend what he spoke.

'He is dying guys. Alok is dying,' Baba could barely mumble.

Even a heartbeat didn't move for the next few seconds.

'What has happened to him?' Megha asked as tears grappled furiously with the fair skin on her face.

'He has Cancer. It's the final stage,' he muttered and shook his head like an atheist in a temple would.

'Can't anything be done now? I mean is there a chance?' Shonali muttered. Baba let out deep sigh that gave away the answer.

'When did it happen?' a choked Megha asked.

'It was detected about eight years back,' Baba muttered.

'I will pick you up in half an hour. We need to be there by seven. He doesn't have much time,' Baba spoke again with an honest urgency that made them get out of the vehicle. He drove away leaving them alone and speechless at the porch of the hotel.

They waited in front of the private ward at St. Mary's Hospital in Mussoorie. None of them had checked into their rooms but waited at the reception eagerly for Baba to return and take them to the hospital where he was. Baba walked towards them after speaking to the doctor who had emerged from inside of the room.

'The doctor has advised that we must take turns to meet him,' he said.

'I can't go now, it's better that one of you goes inside,' Megha said while succumbing on the wooden bench outside the ward. Shonali walked towards the ward with measured steps leaving Mandira behind. She pushed the door gently and entered the ward making the least amount of sound.

Before she could acclimatize herself with the new surroundings, a familiar voice leapt into her ears, 'Hey Shona! Hope you reached here comfortably.'

Shonali wanted to reply but her parched up throat couldn't let a word out as she saw him lying over a white mattress. He looked fine; would have lost a few kilos but never looked like someone who was about to die any moment. The long curls had gone giving way to creased hair that appeared very thin on the forehead. But then people do loose hair at a very young age. The face looked dry and fatigued like that of a traveler towards the fag end of a journey. But then it could have been one of the many journeys, and not the ultimate one. How could someone like him who had an answer to every question; a solution to every problem; and a balm for every bruise die? How can someone like him be lying on that mattress alone and waited to die any moment?

She looked at him with helplessness as her eyes gave way to tears instead of her throat giving way to the words.

'You can drink water from that bottle Shona,' he understood as he pointed his shaking finger towards a bottle lying on a table near the window. Shonali almost raced to the bottle and gulped the liquid inside, as if she had been thirsty for hours. She walked towards him and sat on the stool kept next to the bed. She looked at him; the smile had not changed, it was still as infectious as before.

'How have you been Alok?' she asked.

'Pretty good; so far. Nothing to complain about Shona,' he spoke gradually.

'And you?' he asked.

'Don't you see, still single and free,' she said and smiled weakly.

'Hmmm…happy?' he asked.

'I don't know,' she shrugged.

'How did this happen?' she asked.

'I wish I had a clue,' he smiled.

'Why did you call me here? I always thought that you would hate me for what I did to you,' she said.

'I never did.'

'Why?'

'Because I don't know how to hate in the first place,' he said as he smiled again.

'Why did you come here out of all places?' she asked.

He shut his eyes and she thought that he was tiring up.

'I wanted to teach music and the college needed me here,' he said, 'I was happy here.'

'I wish I could do something like this now. I am so tired with my life,' she exclaimed.

'Stop running. Shona.'

'What?'

'Stop running from yourself, from what your heart says,' he said calmly, 'and you will be happy.'

'Is it?' she asked as if in a daze.

'Just try once; and if that doesn't happen, the party is on me,' he chuckled and then began to cough. Shonali got up to pick up the water bottle. He gestured her to stop while he collected his breath.

'I am unsure about the venue if I lose though; because it could either be heaven or hell,' he said as they smiled.

He held her by the hand and smirked, 'Make this promise to a dying man that you would listen to your heart once and if you don't, then you agree to go to hell.'

'I promise you,' she murmured.

'You had forgotten this in my apartment many years ago. I had kept it to give it back to you one day,' Alok said as he picked up a framed photograph kept on the side rack, 'It's your most treasured possession in the world.'

'Oh my god Alok, I have been looking for it all these years,' her face lit up as she hugged him looking at the photo. It was her family picture; her sister, mother and she in-front of their house, in their garden, overlooking the hills. They sat in silence looking at each other.

'You should be leaving now, I only have an hour,' he murmured.

'Can I come again sometime?' she asked.

'I don't think it will be required Shona,' he said compellingly. Shonali couldn't fully grasp what he had said. She walked slowly towards the door and paused for a few moments. She turned around and looked at him as he lay motionless with his eyes shut.

'Bye, Shona,' he said with his eyes still shut.

'Hey there! How have you been rockstar?'Mandira forced a chirpy demeanor as she entered the huge private ward of the hundred year old hospital. The walls had been freshly painted and the room smelt of a typical medicinal concoction. She looked at his bed whose size paled in comparison with the magnitude of the room.

'Hey M, it's been a long time! You look just the same,' he said and spread out his arms to hug her. She wiped off the tears as she embraced his withered body and sat on the stool.

'You look good as well,' she mumbled.

'You don't need to lie M. The locks are gone and so have the looks,' he muttered smilingly.

'But you look tired,' she said.

'I am about to die for heavens sake M, I can afford to look tired atleast,' he said pretending to be irritated.

'I am sorry, but let's just keep this dying thing aside,' she said as her burning eyes yearned for throwing up additional tears.

'How was US?'

'It was good. I missed you sometimes.'

'You could have written to me,' he said and she could see his eyes gathering moisture.

'I didn't have your address.'

'M, you are such a bitch,' he smiled.

'How's your dad? Where is he these days?' he muttered.

'He is settled in Lucknow, in Gomtinagar,' she said and looked at him.

'I heard about your divorce, it made me sad,' he let out a sigh.

'It was good that it ended soon,' she said as a matter of fact.

'So, whom do you stay with?' he asked.

'Alone,' she replied.

'Happy?'

'It's a relative term Alok. Who has the time to look out for happiness? The work and the pressure kill you by the end of the day,' she said.

'You don't need to look out for happiness M, you need to look within,' he said calmly.

'Look within? How can I find happiness within me?' she asked.

'There's happiness within you that you need to give away and whatever you give away M, would double up and come back to you,' he said.

'It surely isn't as simple as it sounds,' she said tentatively.

He gently held her hand, 'It is M and it's very simple. Let's say you have a happiness bank within you; you take a portion of it and give it away to someone; but what you receive back from the environment, is your principal plus interest. And most of the time this interest in itself would be bigger than your principal.'

'I understand it,' she nodded after a pause.

'Then I want you to promise a dying man that you will follow this once, and if your happiness doesn't double up, then let this dying man go to hell,' he guffawed and the room resonated with his laughter.

'I promise Alok,' she said clutching his palm tightly and feeling lighter.

'You wanted to give me something. Right?' she reminded him

'Yeah, how can I forget? Can you open that please? It's lying inside,' he pointed his finger towards the steel cupboard.

She couldn't move for a few seconds as she laid open the doors of the cupboard.

'That's my guitar which my dad gifted me. Did you steal it?' she said fondly holding her black guitar.

'No, I borrowed it,' he smiled.

'Will you sing something M? It's been a long time' he asked.

'As long as you play the guitar,' she said.

'I will try with whatever strength is left in my frail body,' he said, while struggling to hold the guitar with his hands. Mandira adjusted the upper portion of the hospital bed so that he could recline on it. He strummed the guitar and she hesitatingly started till they hit the melody and relived the old times; with a song on the lip and tears in her eyes; Mandira sang with him perhaps for the last time:

'Now the time has come to leave you
One more time let me kiss you
Close your eyes, I'll be on my way
Dream about the days to come
When I won't have to leave alone
About the times, I won't have to say..'

Singing made him breathless soon; which was followed by incessant coughing. Mandira took away the guitar immediately and helped him lie down on his head. He came back to normalcy after a while.

'The heart wants; but the body can't. That's the irony M,' he said.

'It's quarter to eight and I am tiring up. I think you should leave M,' he said looking at the clock on the white wall.

She got up wearily to clutch his hand; he looked at her with a twinkle in his eyes.

'When do I see you next?'

'I don't think ever. M.' he said as she walked away weeping uncontrollably out of the door.

'Where were you Megha?' he murmured when she entered the room.

'I was here only, just outside,' she said while sitting down on the stool next to him.

'You have put on some weight but that's ok, considering that it has been a while when we met last. It's been such a long time.'

'Do you even remember how I looked?' she asked with a face overflowing with tears.

'There hasn't been a day in my life when I haven't thought about you,' he mumbled. It seemed that he was tiring up by the minute as he spoke with difficulty.

'Liar,' she said.

'No, I am serious,' he said.

'Then why didn't you come back Alok? Why didn't you stay?' she howled.

'Don't fight like a wife Megha and give me a break because it's me who's dying here,' he said flashing a weak smile.

'I am not fighting and if you are not feeling well then I can come back in the morning,' she said.

'Morning? I wish I had time like that.'

'Shut up Alok,' she said.

'I am not afraid of death Megha. It's an end to begin again,' he mumbled, 'Death is just like sleep that prepares us for the next day vigor, death is a state in which one rests and replenishes for the next life, a new life.'

'I am looking for that new life Megha and I see myself inching towards it,' he said with composure reflecting on his face.

'I feel very tired now. Can you open that cupboard and get that brown envelope kept inside?'

She handed him the brown envelope. He sunk his wrist inside to pull out a notepad that he handed her.

'Does it look familiar?' he asked as she fumbled with it and sobbed inconsolably while reading what was written inside:

Why?
I don't even know you well. How can you hold my hand?
But anyways, thank you.
I will not always be around when you get one of those heart attacks.
Why is Gupta so rude?
That's because we are the only people he can be rude with.
Why?
He is a henpecked husband, atleast that's what everyone says and he is so scared of the school princi.
But what does he achieve by pulling us down? That's not learning I would say, that's plain ridicule.
Ridicule is the tribute paid to the genius by the mediocre, always remember.
Wow, that's a great line. Who said that?
Me.
Liar.

'It's our notebook,' she could barely speak. He gestured if she carried a pen with her. She took out one from her leather bag and handed it over to him.

This was your notepad remember: He scribbled on the same notepad.

Yes, I thought that I had misplaced it: She wrote with the same pen on it.

No, you didn't. I had kept it with me: He wrote.

Megha, will you promise one thing to this dying man: He wrote.

Please?: He wrote.

What?: She wrote and made a face.

Try to forget Megha: He wrote.

Forget what?: She wrote.

Everything. That you have left behind: He wrote.

Why?: She wrote.

Because only then can you find happiness: He wrote.

It's tough Alok: She wrote.

But that's the only way: He wrote.

Could you forget?: She wrote.

I tried to: He wrote.

Then: She wrote.

I was unlucky. I couldn't succeed: He wrote.

So?: She wrote.

You are not unlucky like me. Forget your past to accept the present: He wrote.

I love you Alok, how can I forget that: She wrote.

I love you too Megha. I am just asking you to accept the present: He wrote.

And that you can accept only when you forget the past. Don't live in it: He wrote.

What about us?: She wrote as tears welled up in her eyes again.

It was beautiful whatever it was and till it lasted. Forget it now because soon I will cease to exist: He wrote.

But it's not the end Megha. I will wait for you when I will start my next inning: He wrote as the pen slipped out of his finger and he shut his eyes.

'Alok?' she shook his body gently and he opened his eyes. She picked up the pen again.

Do you promise?: She wrote as the tears blurred her sight and she could hardly see anything.

I promise: He wrote.

Then I promise to forget: She wrote

'I think it's time to say goodbye,' he was almost incoherent.

'So soon?' she said as if she never wanted to leave.

'I need to get up early in the morning,' he said.

He looked at her intently; perhaps for the very last time, 'You have a good life Megha and see you soon,' and then he shut his eyes.

He felt as if he were passing through a long dark tunnel; a tunnel that seemed to be unending and he was falling in it smoothly like a feather would, in a large vacuum container. He got separated from the body in a while as he looked at his own falling body plunging into the darkness, smoothly. Then suddenly the images started to appear. They flashed in front of his eyes like frozen moments scooped out from his life that gradually faded one after the other; Megha and him scribbling on the notepad in Gupta's class, Happy driving his car en-route to Delhi, his mother waving out to him as he raced his bike to school, Megha pacing behind his train on the station, him drunk and singing with Baba and friends in Pub 55, Mandira and him on stage as they sang inebriated, waving out to Mandira at the airport, hugging Shonali in the apartment and finally Megha looking at him with tears running like crazy all over her face as she left the ward. As this ended, a ray of light that seemed to be growing every passing moment started enveloping him, expecting no welcome as it dissolved into his being… unassumingly, silently, joyously and rewardingly. He embraced it with open arms smiling; devoid of any anxiety; and at that moment he left his body.

Present Day

'Hi, Srini! How did the meeting with the sales heads go?' Mandira loomed over the miserable Brand Manager's workstation out of nowhere and scared the shit out of him.

He was tongue tied for a few moments before he could open his mouth, 'Umm…it went off fine Mandira, I guess they were pretty excited about the range of new products that we are launching,' he said anxiously.

'Good! And how did the marketing presentation go? I mean your presentation?' she asked.

'It went off fine as well; I had worked overnight to incorporate Arvind and Mark's feedback,' he said.

'Did you get any feedback about my presentation from Arvind by any chance?' he added hesitatingly.

'Yeah, can you come to my room please?' she said plainly and turned around.

'Fuck! How could this woman forget about not whipping me for the two days that she was away?' Srini cursed and staggered towards her cabin.

'When did you get back?' he said while entering her cabin and hoping that his inane conversation could make her forget about the whip.

'Yesterday evening,' she said as she opened her drawer to pull out a wrapped box.

'Is this my termination letter wrapped in a box? Has the company made revisions in its employee termination policy?' he thought while accepting it.

'Open it,' her words seemed more like a command.

Srini hesitated; as terror and agony danced with their bottoms stuck together on his face, 'I can do that later,' he mumbled but then relented by her piercing gaze.

He un-wrapped the box and looked completely knocked out as he saw what lay inside, 'A Tissot watch? Is this for me?' he looked at Mandira as the whole thing seemed quite unreal; like straight out of a bollywood movie.

She smiled as she got up and stretched out her hand towards him, 'That's for all the hard work that you put in dude, it's a very small token of appreciation from me.'

'Thank you Mandira. It means a lot to me,' he said with a grateful face that had thank you written all over it, and eyes that could shed tears anytime.

A spontaneous smile played on her lips when she saw him showing off the present from his boss to other colleagues through her transparent glass cabin, as she picked up her mobile phone.

'Papa,' she muttered.

'Oh…Mandira beta, how have you been my child?' he asked concernedly.

'I am fine Papa, how are you?' she asked.

'I am doing fine considering my old age; Ramu takes good care of me,' he replied.

'Papa, I think it's time that you give yourself a break after having lived alone for almost the whole of your life. It's time that you retire,' she said.

The old man guffawed after a few moments of pause, 'Ha ha…and what do you want me to do after I retire?'

'Stay with me Papa, I have also asked the principal of Scindia to release Ankit after his last term gets over this month,' she spoke with sincerity.

'Why?' he asked.

'So that he can stay here, with me,' she said.

'Did they agree?' he asked.

'Not easily, but I coaxed them into it. Ankit's final term was getting over anyways,' she said.

'Mandira,' he took a pause, '*Beta*, I am proud of you. This is perhaps the wisest decision that you have made in your life.'

'You can help me take the second one Papa,' she said.

'But, Mandira it's been fifteen years since I retired, it will get difficult for you to adjust,' he said earnestly.

'Papa, we have hardly stayed together from the time that I have been born because of your regular transfers, my college in US and everything. I don't intend to be a loner like you as I grow old,' she said.

'Ok Mandira,' he paused, 'When do you want me to come?' he asked. She thought that the old man smiled on the other side.

'As soon as possible Papa,' she said happily, 'Bye Papa. See You.'

'Bye,' he said and hung up.

She threw up her fist in the air as she saw Alok smiling through the sun rays that seeped into her glass cabin on the sixth floor; and brighten up her life after a real long time.

'Let's say you have a happiness bank within you; you take a portion of it and give it away to someone; but what you receive back from the environment, is your principal plus interest. And most of the time this interest in itself would be bigger than your principal.'

Shonali sipped from her glass of white wine while sitting on the open courtyard of Salt Water Café in Bandra. It was her third straight date with Abhi in the current week and this was kind of abnormal. She looked up and found him staring at her intently.

'What?' she asked.

'Nothing,' he shook his head and smiled.

'How are things at work?' she asked.

'Couldn't be better Shonali, we have over achieved out targets and I believe we will get a three hundred percent bonus,' he said.

'Wow, that's great Abhi, what are your plans for the future?' she asked.

'Can I tell you a little secret?' he said cutely.

'I have a great offer at hand and I think I will pick that up once our bonus is disbursed,' he said as he winked.

'What's that?' she asked.

'I am sure you would have heard of Channel Entertainment?' he asked.

'Who hasn't heard of them?' she took a sip, 'America's largest media conglomerate, presence in sixty countries, turnover going into countless zeros.'

'Yes, exactly, and they want me to head their South East Asia business,' he said and winked again.

'That's great Abhi,' Shonali felt genuinely happy for him.

'But the job isn't based here, I will have to move to Hongkong,' he said with a tinge of remorse hanging on his face.

It was strange that she felt sorrow instantaneously which she had to hide or else it would have jumped out on her face, 'That's great in fact, isn't it?' she asked as she picked up the glass of wine to hide her face behind it.

Abhi leaned forward and held her hand, 'You know about my feelings for you Shonali; and also that it's not short term. I am not looking at a fling but a relationship here,' he said with utmost seriousness.

Shonali looked into his eyes that were loaded with sincere love, 'What do you want Abhi?'

'Let's get married Shonali, and start our lives afresh from Hongkong. It's a great place to be in,' he said.

'Can you give me a day to think Abhi?' Shonali heard herself speaking.

'Sure,' he replied.

'Will Mehra let you go easily?' she asked.

'Who? Siddharth Mehra?' he asked. Shonali nodded.

'I will manage him Shonali. He is a bastard anyways; and he won't mind it beyond a point. Guys like him are thick skinned,' he said and guffawed.

It was close to midnight when he dropped Shonali at her hill road apartment.

'Do you want to come up?' she asked him perhaps for the first time.

'Only after I hear your answer tomorrow,' he said as he smiled, 'Just kidding.'

'I will call you,' she smiled and turned around.

'Can I call you Shona? It's much cuter,' Abhi yelled from behind.

She stopped dead in her tracks as her heart raced like a wild horse. It took her a few moments to gather her bearings before she turned back.

'Yes, you can, Abhi.'

He smirked and then drove away in his Honda Civic.

She was unlatching her apartment door when her phone beeped. It was Mehra. She took the call rather unwillingly.

'Where have you been over the last few weeks?' he asked.

'I have been in the office all this while, didn't we meet there?' she asked cynically.

It seemed as if Mehra wasn't expecting this reply, 'Yeah, we did but

I didn't mean meeting in the office, I meant otherwise,' he replied.

'So?' she asked.

'Our trip to Panvel has long been pending. Let's do this the coming weekend for sure. Ok honey?' his question as always sounded more like a command.

Shonali could feel sudden rage surge within her heart and for once she let it go,' No, we are not going Mehra. Neither this weekend or any other,' she said.

'Are you sure Shonali? ' he tried to reconfirm what his ears had just heard.

'Zip up your pants Mehra. The honeymoon is over,' she said coldly.

Mehra went speechless for a while and then fumbled, 'Shh...Shh... Shonali, I hope you understand the implications.'

'Forget it Mehra. We will meet in the office,' she disconnected the call.

She dialed Abhi's number immediately after that. He picked up the phone in the second beep and sounded surprised.

'Abhi, are you driving?' she asked hesitatingly.

'Yeah Shona, I have just reached SV road,' he said.

'Then I am cutting this really short,' she said.

'Let's get married,' she said and paused.

'*Yaay*,' Abhi yelled into the ears of a tongue tied Shonali.

She lay on her bed feeling light like a feather with her eyes staring at the ceiling above. As sleep descended into her eyes she saw his face flash on to the ceiling; a face that smiled at her with affection.

She opened her eyes and then switched off the table lamp kept on her bedside, 'Tonight is going to be a good night,' she said.

'Stop running from yourself, from what your heart says,' he said calmly, 'and you will be happy.'

'It was a day well spent,' Ashu said as they exited the main tomb and stepped on the red stone laden pathway at Sikandra in Agra.

'You have managed well Ashu, trading this weekend getaway with a trip abroad,' Megha commented.

She added cynically, 'And the weekend trip happens in a place where I have spent half of my life. Wow?'

He smiled sheepishly, 'I know Megha and I promise that we will go for a long vacation very soon,' he said as they looked at their daughter racing ahead and jumping across rectangular red stone tiles.

'I hope that this vacation destination is not Agra again,' she said.

'No darling, I chose it this time because it's the closest from Delhi,' he said.

'Atleast, she had whale of a time,' Megha said looking at Sneha.

'After how many years have you come to Agra?' Ashu asked.

'Don't you remember? The last time we were here; was when dad had expired,' she said.

'Yeah, before your mother moved to Delhi to stay with your brother, right?' Ashu asked. She nodded her head.

'My parents had moved to Delhi much earlier, just after we passed out of school,' Ashu said.

'I am sure you would have visited these places often; Agra is a case study in historical monuments,' he smirked.

'Anyone who has stayed here would. There isn't a choice, didn't you?' she asked.

'Yes of course, and especially when a relative would land up, to kickstart a guided tour to Tajmahal, Fatehpur Sikri, Agra Fort and Sikandra to say the least. Remember?' he said.

'Exactly,' she said.

'When were you in Sikandra last?' he asked.

She paused and took a deep breath, 'It has been long. It seems as if it was a different era.'

'Will you wait here with Sneha for a while?' she asked softly.

'Sure, but where do you want to go?' he asked.

'I want to walk to that old well, do you see it?' she asked pointing towards her left.

'Yeah, I think so. But why do you want to go there?' he asked.

'There is something Ashu. It's personal,' she said.

He shook his head in disbelief as if he had realized, 'Oh! It must be some holy thing, some *mannat vannat*?' She did not say anything.

'Cool, we will wait for you here; just come back soon.'

The handkerchief that he had tied on the cylindrical rod above the old, barren and dried up well was still there. She had to stretch her arm beyond her natural self to be able to reach the blackened piece of cloth that fluttered with the wind. She untied the piece of cloth and brought it down from the iron rod. The lipstick on the handkerchief, could not weather twenty one years that had passed in between and had vanished totally, leaving behind just the cloth, enveloped in black color. The wind had started to blow with force and it seemed as if a storm was on the anvil. She placed the piece of cloth gently in between her palms and looked at it fondly as she caressed it. The force of the wind was growing gradually, making it hard for her to stay there in the open. She looked at it for one last time before releasing it in the air hesitatingly. The piece of cloth danced around her in the air for a while as if rejoicing on its new found freedom; after being imprisoned on that cylindrical rod for so long. Then it started rising up in the air, growing its distance with her gradually. She kept staring at it till it turned into a tiny speck and then completely vanished in the oblivion. As Megha turned around, she saw him through the dust and a storm that wailed; she saw him standing near the well and smiling.

She looked at him as she smirked, 'Do keep your promise, Alok,' and then she walked back to her waiting family.

Forget your past to accept the present and only then can you find happiness.

EPILOGUE

Baba shut the manuscript and kept it aside on the table. He looked at the bird shaped clock on the wall and then gazed at them sprawled on the sofa and on the mattress in his living room.

'It's almost six in the morning,' he paused, 'And I am no more used to night outs any more.'

He stared at their faces that had turned dry after a long sleepless night and then at their barren eyes that looked like an arid river which once overflowed joyously with abundant water in it's banks. It seemed as if those eyes couldn't shed tears anymore.

'When did you write this book?' Megha asked.

Baba cleared his throat, 'I stayed with him for over two months in Mussoorie and it took me a lot of effort in persuading him to open up.'

'The last chapter though is completely fictional; a writer's imagination if you may call it,' he added.

'It's very real, pretty close,' Mandira muttered.

'Yeah, mine as well,' Shonali said.

'I never knew that he had resigned from the job when he came to meet me at the bus stand. He never told me,' Shonali said.

'And I never knew that he got my marks pushed up; so that I may go to the US,' Mandira mumbled.

'How can Ashu stoop so low like that?' Megha spoke disgustedly.

Baba looked at them, 'Forget the past to accept your present and only then can you find happiness. Remember?'

Megha was about to say something when she paused, 'Yeah. It seems that you are right.'

'All that he gave away for the years that he lived, was just love and happiness and yet the same love deluded him for his entire life,' Mandira said.

'I guess that is what they call; the irony of life,' Baba said.

'Why did he call all of us to Mussoorie? Was it to give back what he had?' Shonali asked.

Mandira sighed, 'Yes, but not my guitar, your photograph or Megha's notebook.' Shonali looked at her intently.

'It was to give us back, what was missing in our lives. Happiness,' Mandira said.

'All three of us sitting here bask under the joy that he infused in our lives,' Megha said.

'Not just the three of you, include me as well,' Baba said.

Shonali nodded, 'Yeah.'

Mandira removed the cushion behind her back, 'When did you turn into a writer Baba?'

Baba got up and walked to his writing desk and looked at the only picture-frame that sat on it. It was a picture of him and Alok taken in his room; Pub No. 55, saying cheers and holding whisky glasses in their hands, 'He always said, Baba you speak so well; why don't you write? So, I wrote, finally. I am glad that I did.'

'When do you go to Hongkong?' he asked Shonali.

'Three months later, after we get married in February. Mom and sister are coming for it,' she said. Baba smiled.

'I am glad that all of you could come here for a day, to hear this manuscript,' Baba said.

'I couldn't have missed it for my life,' Mandira said.

Baba looked aside, 'What should we call this book? What should the title be?' he asked. The room drowned in silence for a while.

Megha mumbled through the pervasive stillness, 'Three times loser.'

'Loser?' Shonali retorted, 'How can he be a loser?'

Megha spoke with an expressionless face, 'I guess that's what the irony of life is.'

Time took a pause in that room.

'Yes. Three times loser, it is,' Baba said as he walked towards the window and pulled open the curtains.

They basked under the warm rays of the morning sunlight as it filled all the dark and cold corners of that room; to turn them alive.